The Legacy

The Legacy

Yrsa Sigurdardóttir

Translated from the Icelandic by Victoria Cribb

MINOTAUR BOOKS

A THOMAS DUNNE BOOK
NEW YORK

A THOMAS DUNNE BOOK FOR MINOTAUR BOOKS.
An imprint of St. Martin's Press.

THE LEGACY. Copyright © 2014 by Yrsa Sigurdardóttir. English translation copyright © 2015 by Victoria Cribb. All rights reserved. Printed in the United States of America. For information, address St. Martin's Press, 175 Fifth Avenue, New York, N.Y. 10010.

www.thomasdunnebooks.com
www.minotaurbooks.com

The Library of Congress has cataloged the hardcover edition as follows:

Names: Yrsa Sigurdardóttir, author. | Cribb, Victoria, translator.
Title: The legacy : a thriller / Yrsa Sigurdardóttir ; translated from the Icelandic by Victoria Cribb.
Other titles: DNA. English
Description: First U.S. edition. | New York : Minotaur Books, 2018.
Identifiers: LCCN 2017041608 | ISBN 9781250136268 (hardcover) | ISBN 9781250136275 (ebook)
Subjects: LCSH: Women psychologists—Fiction. | Police—Iceland—Fiction. | Murder—Investigation—Iceland—Fiction.
Classification: LCC PT7513.Y77 D5313 2018 | DDC 839/.6935—dc23
LC record available at https://lccn.loc.gov/2017041608

ISBN 978-1-250-30838-2 (trade paperback)

Our books may be purchased in bulk for promotional, educational, or business use. Please contact your local bookseller or the Macmillan Corporate and Premium Sales Department at 1-800-221-7945, extension 5442, or by email at MacmillanSpecialMarkets@macmillan.com.

First published in Iceland under the title DNA by Veröld Publishing

Previously published in Great Britain by Hodder & Stoughton, an Hachette UK company

First Minotaur Books Paperback Edition: January 2019

D 10 9 8 7 6 5 4 3

This book is dedicated to Palli

I am indebted to the following people for their help with information for this book: Bragi Gudbrandsson on the Child Protection Agency and Children's House, Thorleikur Jóhannesson on the world of radio amateurs and communications, and Hallgrímur Gunnar Sigurdsson on radio communications and their monitoring. I owe them all my sincere thanks. Any mistakes are entirely my own.

Yrsa Sigurdardóttir

Pronunciation guide for character names

(Nicknames in brackets)

Huldar – Hool-dar
Freyja – Fray-a
Karl – Kahdl
Elísa – El-eesa
Margrét – Mar-gryet
Sigvaldi – Sik-valdi
Ástrós – Owst-rohss
Ríkhardur – Reek-harth-oor
Erla – Edla
Egill – Ay-idl
Börkur – Berr-koor
Haraldur (Halli) – Hahr-ald-oor (Hal-lee)
Arnar – Ahd-nar
Stefán (Stebbi) – Stef-own (Steb-bee)
Bárdur – Bowr-thoor
Silja – Sil-ya
Karlotta – Kahr-lotta
Védís – Vyeh-dees

1987

Prologue

They sat on the bench as if arranged in order of size; the girl, who was the youngest, at one end, her two brothers next to her. One, three and four years old. Their thin legs dangled from the hard seat, but unlike normal children they didn't swing them or wriggle about, and their new shoes hung motionless over the shiny linoleum. There was no curiosity, boredom or impatience in their faces. All three stared at the blank white wall in front of them as if watching a *Tom and Jerry* cartoon. Viewed through the glass, the scene resembled a photograph – a study of three children on a bench.

They had been sitting there for nearly half an hour. Soon they would be allowed to get up but none of the adults watching them were particularly keen to reach that point. The recent upheaval in the children's lives would seem insignificant compared to what lay ahead. Once they walked out of here nothing would ever be the same again. This time the change would probably be for the better but it had potential drawbacks, which might in the end outweigh the benefits. That was the dilemma confronting the group gathered around the table.

'I'm afraid so. We've considered all the other options but this is what the experts recommend. The children need to be settled in permanent homes as soon as possible. The older they are, the smaller their chances of being adopted. Just look at how much harder it's been to find a home for the boys than the girl. Prospective parents are well aware that the younger children are, the more successfully they adapt to a new life. In two years the girl will be as old as the younger brother is now, and then we'll be facing the same problem with her.' The man took a deep breath and brandished a sheaf of papers to lend weight to his words. These were reports and psychiatric assessments by the experts who had examined the children. The others nodded, their faces sombre; all, that is, except the youngest woman there, who had been the most vocal in her opposition to the proposal. She had the least experience of child-protection cases and still harboured a spark of hope that repeated disillusionment had long since extinguished in the rest of them.

'Shouldn't we hang on a little longer? You never know, we might still manage to find a couple prepared to take on all three.' She glanced over at the children, who were sitting on the bench as if turned to stone. Her arms were clamped tight across her chest as if she were trying to prevent her kindly instincts and innate optimism from draining away. She could vividly recall the way the siblings had looked when their case first came to the attention of the authorities: their dirty, tangled dark hair, filthy clothes and emaciated bodies. Their eyes bright in their grimy faces; their cheeks streaked with tears. The young woman turned back to the other social workers, her expression full of sadness. 'There has to be a chance.'

'I've just been over this.' The man with the reports sounded exasperated. He checked his watch for the third time; he'd promised to take his children to the cinema. 'We've got couples fighting over the little girl, but very few are interested in the boys. We should be grateful to have found this solution; it would be futile to go on hunting for some hypothetical perfect couple. All prospective adopters come to us and we've been through the list with a fine-tooth comb. In the circumstances this is by far the most satisfactory outcome.'

There wasn't much that could be said to this and they nodded gravely, all except the young woman. Her eyes radiated desperation. 'But they seem so close. I'm worried being separated could damage them for life.'

This time the reports were shaken so vigorously that the resulting draught lifted the hair of those present. 'Two different psychiatrists have stated in no uncertain terms that it would be in the best interests of the younger two to be parted. The boy has assumed the role of protector for his little sister. He's smothering her with all the love and care he's missed out on himself, even though he's only a small child. He won't leave her alone; he's tormented with stress and anxiety on her account. The boy's only three years old, for God's sake.' The man paused for breath. 'It's not a question of having to read between the lines – the reports are explicit. Being separated would be best for both of them. His relationship with her isn't healthy. In fact, both boys have been worse affected than their sister. They're older, after all.'

There was a movement on the bench. The younger boy had shifted nearer to his sister. He put his arm round her shoulders and pulled her close. You would have thought he'd heard them through the glass.

'I for one don't think we can afford to cast doubt on their professional opinion.' The woman who said this had also intimated that her time was limited. She spoke quickly, impatiently tapping her foot. 'They're the experts. We can't begin to imagine what the children's lives have been like. For what it's worth, *I* think we should hurry up and get it over with. It would be naive to go on searching for a fairy-tale solution. It doesn't exist.'

'But what'll happen when they're older and realise that breaking them up was avoidable?' The oldest member of the team now weighed in. 'Most of us here are familiar with what happens when people are filled with bitterness against the system. It can take over their lives.' He was fast approaching retirement and hoped against hope that this would be the last difficult case to land on his desk. Surely that wasn't too much to ask? His hair had long since turned white, he was on medication for his blood pressure and his face was deeply scored with lines.

'The adoptive parents will keep their background secret. It would be in all their interests, especially the younger two. It shouldn't be too difficult either, since they're unlikely to remember anything. The girl's barely one. I suppose there's a risk the eldest boy might retain some memories, but we can't be sure. And even if he does, they'll be muddled and fade over time. I mean, how much do you remember from when you were four?'

'Plenty.' It seemed the young woman was alone in retaining such early memories. The others could recall only vague, dreamlike fragments. But even she couldn't remember anything from when she was one. The little girl, who was so much in demand, would come out of it best and not only because she was adorable. The boys had been harder hit by the events of the last couple of years and were already displaying the signs: the younger by his excessive love and solicitude for his sister; the elder by his indifference towards the world. The brief report from the police officers who had gone to the scene in response to the mother's phone call had been so shocking that none of those present wished to recall the details.

It would be a mercy if time obliterated all trace of the events from the children's minds.

Sadly, though, the young woman doubted this would happen. The trauma would have been too great. 'My memories are generally associated with bad experiences, like when I shut my finger in the door of the bakery, aged three, or saw my friend hit by a car when I was five. But those are nothing compared to what these kids have been through. I'm worried the boys will be able to remember. Their sister too, though that's unlikely.'

'What about their relationship, has that been established?' The woman who was strapped for time changed the subject before they could digress any further into childhood reminiscences. 'Surely there's a limit to how much effort we need to make trying to keep them together when they're probably not even full siblings?'

At this point the man with the reports finally went up in the estimation of the emotional young woman. 'In my view the question of their paternity is irrelevant. They're siblings as far as they're concerned, though whether that's only through their mother is anyone's guess. The younger two have no known father. But the older boy's different. In the opinion of the doctor who examined them, the younger boy and girl are probably full siblings and the eldest is only their half-brother. Though admittedly that's based on the statement of the man alleged to be the elder boy's father; he swears blind he had no further sexual relations with the mother after their son was born – after she was forced to move back in with her father.'

The man made a face and swallowed before continuing. 'But it would require a DNA test to establish the children's relationship and there's no time or money for that. And, quite frankly, nobody wants to know the results. It's preferable for all concerned to assume they have "normal" fathers. All three, not just the eldest.'

Nobody spoke. They were all familiar with the story. About the children and their mother. About their grandfather and the unspeakable crime he was suspected of committing against his daughter. Now the fate of three little children with scars on their souls was in their hands. What were they to do?

'What about the father, this Thorgeir?' The younger woman broke the silence. 'Isn't there any chance he'll have a change of heart?'

'We've tried everything. He neither can nor will take on his son, let alone all three of them. He's had no contact with the boy and isn't even certain he's the father. According to him, he agreed to give the boy his name because he'd had a brief fling with the mother, but he was never sure she hadn't been sleeping around. If we put pressure on him to take responsibility for his son he'll demand a paternity test. That'll delay things and whatever the outcome, I don't see him as a particularly desirable option. If he turns out not to be the father, there's no point even discussing his adopting the boy. And if he is, he doesn't want him. Would that be a happy situation for his son? I very much doubt it.' The men present exchanged glances, showing more sympathy for the alleged father's decision than the women, who kept their eyes lowered.

'It's the best solution.' This time, instead of brandishing the reports, the man tapped them with his fingers. 'Unfortunately, we don't have a time machine to tell us how well they'll turn out. All we've got to go on is the opinion of the experts. The prospective parents have all been vetted and received first-class references. I suggest we finalise things. The children's records will be altered in the system and in time their horrendous background will be consigned to oblivion. It's best they never find out their history, and being split up will help them forget. The sooner they start a new life, the better for everyone. Are we all agreed?'

The young woman opened her mouth but thought better of it. The others murmured their assent as if to suppress any further objections from her side. Turning her head, she looked through the glass at the three children on the bench. The little girl was trying in vain to break free of her brother but he only clutched her tighter, seeming almost to hurt her. Perhaps the experts were right after all. Turning back to the group, she nodded despondently.

With that it was decided.

The group split up to take care of the formalities. The young woman lingered in the corridor, so she was the sole witness when the children embarked on their new lives. They didn't give up their old one without a fight. The younger boy, especially, took it badly. He wept and screamed as he watched his sister disappear down the corridor in the arms of a paediatrician. The little girl gazed at him over the doctor's shoulder, waving bye-bye, her face blank. Then all hell broke loose. A man in a white coat had to restrain the little boy by force. When he realised he was overpowered, his screams dissolved into sobs.

The young woman couldn't tear her eyes from the scene. Given that she was partly responsible, she felt she should have the guts to face up to the consequences. The elder boy made a marginally less harrowing sight. But although he didn't struggle or cry, the terror in his eyes said it all. The children had probably never been parted before.

The young woman didn't shed any tears as she stood and watched the two little boys disappear the same way as their sister. When finally she made a move, she saw no sign of the children anywhere in the hospital corridors. They weren't in the foyer or in the half-empty car park outside.

Their new life had swallowed them up without a trace.

2015

2015

Chapter 1

Thursday

It takes Elísa a moment or two to work out where she is. She's lying on her side, the duvet tangled between her legs, the pillow creased under her cheek. It's dark in the room but through the gap in the curtains a star winks at her from the vastness of space. On the other side of the bed the duvet is smooth and flat, the pillow undented. The silence is alien too; for all the times it has kept her lying irritably awake she misses the sound of snoring. And she misses the warmth that radiates from her permanently superheated husband, which requires her to sleep with one leg sticking out from under the covers.

Out of habit she's adopted that position now, and she's cold.

As she pulls the duvet over her again she can feel the goose-flesh on her legs. It reminds her of when Sigvaldi was on night shifts, only this time she's not expecting him home in the morning, yawning, hollow-eyed, smelling of the hospital. He won't be back from the conference for a week. When he kissed her goodbye at the central bus station yesterday he had been more impatient than her to get their farewells over with. If she knows him he'll come back reeking of new aftershave from duty-free and she'll have to sleep with her nose in her elbow until she gets used to the smell.

Although she misses him a little, the feeling is mingled with pleasure at the thought of a few days to herself. The prospect of evenings in sole command of the TV remote control; of not having to give in to the superior claims of football matches. Evenings when she can make do with flatbread and cheese for supper and not have to listen to his stomach rumbling for the rest of the night.

But a week's holiday from her husband has its downsides too; she'll be alone in charge of their three children, alone to cope with all that entails: waking them, getting them out of bed, dropping them off and picking them up, helping with their homework, keeping them entertained, monitoring their computer use, feeding them, bathing them, brushing their teeth, putting them to bed. Twice a week Margrét has to be taken to ballet and Stefán and Bárdur to karate, and she has to sit through their classes. This is one of her least rewarding tasks, as it forces her to face the fact that her offspring display neither talent for nor enjoyment of these hobbies, although they don't come cheap. As far as she can tell her kids are bored, never in time with the rest, forever caught out facing the wrong way, gaping in red-cheeked astonishment at the others who always do everything right. Or perhaps it's the other way round: perhaps her kids are the only ones getting it right.

She waits for her drowsiness to recede, aware of the radioactive green glow of the alarm clock on the bedside table. She normally begins the day by hating it, but doesn't experience the usual longing to fling it across the room as the luminous numbers show that she's got several more hours to sleep. Her tired brain refuses to calculate exactly how many. A more important question is niggling at her: why has she woken up?

To avoid the fluorescent glare of the clock, Elísa turns

over, only to choke back a scream when she makes out a dark figure standing by the bed. But it's only Margrét, her firstborn, the daughter who has always been a little out of step with other children, never really happy. So that's what woke her.

'Margrét, sweetie, why aren't you asleep?' she asks huskily, peering searchingly into her daughter's eyes. They appear black in the gloom. The mass of curly hair that frames her pale face is standing on end.

The child clambers over the smooth duvet to Elísa's side. Bending down she whispers, her hot breath tickling her mother's ear and smelling faintly of toothpaste. 'There's a man in the house.'

Elísa sits up, her heart beating faster, though she knows there's nothing wrong. 'You were dreaming, darling. Remember what we talked about? The things you dream about aren't real. Dreams and reality are two different worlds.'

Ever since she was small, Margrét has suffered from nightmares. Her two brothers conk out the moment their heads hit the pillow, like their father, and don't stir until morning. But the night seldom brings their sister this kind of peace. It's rare that Elísa and her husband aren't jolted awake by the girl's piercing screams. The doctors said she would grow out of it, but that was two years ago and there has been little sign of improvement.

The girl's wild locks swing to and fro as she shakes her head. 'I wasn't asleep. I was awake.' She's still whispering and raises her finger to her lips as a sign that her mother should keep her voice down. 'I went for a wee-wee and saw him. He's in the sitting room.'

'We all get muddled sometimes. I know I do—' Elísa breaks

off mid-sentence. 'Shh . . .' This is more for her own benefit. There's no sound from the hallway; she must have imagined it. The door is ajar and she strains her eyes towards it but can't see anything except darkness. Of course. Who'd be out there, anyway? Their possessions are nothing special and their badly painted house is unlikely to tempt burglars, though their home is one of the few in the street that doesn't have all its windows marked with stickers advertising a security system.

Margrét bends down to her mother's ear again. 'I'm not muddled. There's a man in the house. I saw him from the hall.' The girl's low voice sounds wide awake, betraying no hint of sleepiness or confusion.

Elísa switches on the bedside light and gropes for her mobile phone. Could her alarm clock have stopped? It's had to put up with all kinds of rough treatment over the years and she's lost count of the times it's ended up on the floor. It's probably not worth putting Margrét back to bed; probably time to start the morning chores, pour out three bowls of buttermilk, shovel over some brown sugar, and hope she'll be given a chance to rinse the shampoo out of her hair while they're eating. But the phone's not on the bedside table or on the floor, though she could have sworn she'd brought it in with her last night before turning off the lights. She wanted it to hand in case Sigvaldi rang in the early hours to let her know he'd arrived safely.

'What time is it, Margrét?' The girl has never wanted to be called Magga.

'I don't know.' Margrét peers out into the dark hallway. Then, turning back, she whispers: 'Who comes round in the middle of the night? It can't be a nice man.'

'No. It can't be anyone at all.' Elísa can hear how unconvincing she sounds. What if the child's right and someone *has* broken in? She gets out of bed. Her toes curl up as they encounter the icy floor. All she's got on is one of Sigvaldi's T-shirts and her bare legs prickle with gooseflesh again. 'Stay here. I'm going to check on things. When I come back, we won't have to worry any more and we can go back to sleep. Agreed?'

Margrét nods. She pulls her mother's duvet up to her eyes. From under it she mutters: 'Be careful. He's not a nice man.'

The words echo in Elísa's ears as she goes out into the hallway, making an effort to appear unconcerned, confident that there's no intruder. But Margrét has sown a seed of doubt in her mind. Oh, why couldn't this have happened last night when Sigvaldi was home? Would that have been too much to ask? Elísa hugs herself against the cold, but it doesn't help. When she turns on the light, the brightness hurts her eyes.

The door of the boys' room emits a faint creak as she looks in to check that they're sleeping peacefully. They're lying in their bunks, eyes closed, mouths open. She pulls the door quietly to behind her.

There's no one in the bathroom. In Margrét's room her gaze is met by a row of dolls and teddy bears lined up on a shelf. Their eyes seem to follow her as she hastily closes the door again. She wonders if this arrangement might explain Margrét's nightmares. Personally if she woke up in the night she wouldn't want to be confronted by those rigid stares. In the gloom there seems to be an air of malevolence behind their cuddliness. It might be worth moving them to see if that would help Margrét sleep any better. She'll do it after work this evening.

There's nobody in the bedroom hallway or in the rooms opening off it; no sign of any mysterious intruder. But what was she expecting? Footprints? A cigarette butt on the floor? A broken flower pot in one corner? By the time she approaches the sitting room and kitchen she is feeling much calmer. The illumination from the streetlights is enough to convince her that it must have been another of Margrét's fantasies. The dark always sends one's imagination into overdrive. Now she can see that there's no one in the sitting room, just the empty popcorn bowl in front of the television and swathes of Lego round the coffee table. Everything is exactly as it was when she went to bed. How silly to get in such a flap.

The smile that curls her lips disappears abruptly from her face. The sliding door dividing the dining area from the kitchen has been pulled shut.

But it's never shut.

Slowly, warily, Elísa tiptoes towards it. Her bare soles stick to the cold parquet, her fear rising with every step. She presses her ear to the white door. At first there is silence, then she recoils violently at the sound of chairs being scraped back in the kitchen.

What is she to do? Her immediate instinct is to sprint back to bed and pull the covers over her head. Whoever is in there is bound to come out soon. Elísa couldn't care less about their belongings. The burglar can take anything he likes, just so long as he goes away again. But what the hell is he doing in the kitchen? It sounds as if he's sitting at the table, and for a moment she wonders if Margrét or one of the boys could have slipped past without her noticing. But no, that's impossible.

To her horror, she hears the intruder getting up. All she can think of is to press her ear to the door again. A drawer is opened and closed, then another and another, until she hears a rattle of cutlery. Or knives. Then the silence is broken by the sound of the little sliding door to the larder opening. What kind of burglar would be interested in tinned food and packets of cereal? In a broom, dustpan and cloths, bucket and vacuum cleaner? Instead of being reassured by this development, Elísa's terror intensifies. People who behave irrationally are far more dangerous than those who abide by conventional rules. Backing away from the door she retreats noiselessly across the sitting room. Her phone must be on the coffee table. Or in the bathroom. They decided to give up the landline two years ago and for the first time she misses it. Glancing into the entrance hall, she considers running outside, screaming for help and praying she'll manage to rouse the neighbours in time. But that would mean leaving the children behind. With a man who may have armed himself with a kitchen knife. She takes a single step towards the front door, then stops; she can't abandon the children. Instead she turns and heads for the bedroom hallway. She's almost there when she hears the sliding door to the kitchen opening. Instantly she dashes into the hallway, pulls the door closed behind her and switches off the light. She doesn't dare to pause and check if the man is coming after her.

Frantically, feeling as if her head's going to explode with the strain, Elísa tries to work out what to do. How is she to get away? Her bedroom door won't lock; most of the keys were missing when they moved in and they've never seen any reason to replace them. The bathroom locks but barricading herself in there would be as bad as fleeing the house: the children would be left unprotected. She darts into the bathroom anyway in search of her phone, flinging aside towels and pulling out drawers with shaking hands. But it's futile, the bloody thing's not there. Tears well up in her eyes as she surveys the mess. When's she supposed to tidy this lot up? As if she didn't have enough on her plate already.

She returns to the hallway, aware that she's losing her grip. All she can think about is the time she's wasted searching for the phone when she should have been trying to get the children out of here. Though she's not sure how she could have done so, and it's too late now anyway. She can't bite back a scream when she sees the door at the end beginning to open. But her cry is neither loud nor piercing, more like the thin sound a rabbit might emit *in extremis*. She can't bear to see the intruder, so she dashes into her bedroom and closes the door behind her. She hears the man's footsteps, then a clatter, as though he's dragging something behind him. But what? Her heart is hammering.

'Margrét?'

Her daughter is nowhere to be seen.

'Margrét?'

Her voice cracks, which does nothing to boost her courage. She simply cannot decide which to hunt for first, the phone or Margrét. Before she can make up her mind the door behind her opens and the man comes in. He pauses and the clatter sounds louder, as if he's jerking something over the threshold. She can't look round; her body is paralysed. She feels an overwhelming urge to close her eyes. Though the rattling noise is familiar Elísa can't for the life of her remember what it is. Her brain is rapidly shutting down all its vital nerve centres, the ones she has most need of right now.

Rigid with fear, Elísa hears her name whispered behind her. The whisper is muffled, as if the man has a scarf over his mouth. She doesn't think she recognises his voice, but what do people sound like when they whisper? Quite different from normal, surely? Margrét didn't sound like herself when she whispered to her earlier. But the warm, sweet breath that tickled Elísa's ear then is a million miles from the hoarse rasp that fills her with blind terror now.

Who is he? What does he want? He must know her, or her name anyway. Did he see it in the kitchen? On an envelope, or the postcard on the fridge from her friend Gunna?

Elísa feels a strong, apparently gloved, hand seize her neck, then something sharp sticking into her back. A knife. 'Please,' she whispers. She leaves the rest unsaid: please don't hurt me. Please don't rape me. Please don't kill me. Please, please, please don't hurt my children. The point of the knife is withdrawn, he releases his grip on her neck and before she knows what's happening he's blindfolding her. Her panic increases when she realises that he's using strong, thick adhesive tape, winding it round and round her head. As in the bathroom earlier, logic deserts her and her fears for her own and her children's safety momentarily recede before the worry about how she is to get the tape off again. It's stuck on so tightly that it's bound to rip out her eyebrows and lashes when she tries to remove it. Her tears well up with nowhere to go, dissolving the glue, which stings her eyes.

'Please, please. I won't tell anyone. You can take what you like. Anything. Take everything.'

'Thanks but no thanks,' she hears him whisper behind her.

Elísa's knees buckle. 'Please. Take it all!' The tape is wound round her head yet again and she jerks as he cuts it. He runs his hand roughly over the back of her neck to stick down the loose end. Then she is spun round and flung down on the bed. The mattress yields as the man sits down beside her and she ducks her head instinctively as he strokes her hair. Suddenly his gentle caress changes, he grabs a fistful of hair and wrenches her head towards him.

He whispers again, a little louder this time. She doesn't recognise his muffled voice.

'I'm going to tell you something. A little story. A tragic tale. I advise you to listen carefully.'

Elísa nods. He tightens his grip on her hair so it hurts. Why does he want to tell her a story? Why doesn't he demand to know her PIN number or where she keeps the valuables? She would tell him anything. He can have all her cards and access to the bank accounts. He can have the silver she inherited from her grandparents. The few pieces of jewellery she has acquired during her lifetime. Anything. So long as he spares her and the children. Nothing else matters.

Through her sobs she manages to ask if he's going to hurt the children. She misses his reply and this only increases her anguish. Then he relapses into silence. The promised story doesn't come and they sit there together without speaking, Elísa blindfolded, her heart pounding fit to burst. She hears and feels the man stand up, and experiences a flicker of hope that he might be about to leave; go no further. She daren't entertain this hope. She needs to stay alert; perhaps he's going to attack her from behind. She hears clattering again and thinks she detects a clunk like something being plugged in over by the door. Mentally she runs through all the electric appliances in the house that could inflict damage: the drill she gave Sigvaldi for Christmas, the hand whisk, the hedge clippers, her curling tongs, the iron, the sandwich toaster, the kettle. Which would be the worst? Which would be the least frightening? Elísa is breathing so fast and shallowly she thinks she's going to faint. Then she remembers that most of these horrible gadgets have too short a lead to reach the bed, which reassures her slightly. But the feeling doesn't last long.

Hearing the man approach the bed again she loses control and makes a last-ditch attempt to escape, an attempt she knows is doomed to failure. He can see; she can't. He's bigger and stronger. Even so, she flings herself across the bed in an effort to reach the floor on the other side. She hears an angry exclamation and feels the man's weight land on top of her as she lies on her stomach, half on, half off the bed. One arm is bent underneath her; the other is hanging down to the floor, her hand groping under the bed. The man delivers a heavy blow to her back. Her spine judders and she is momentarily winded. He straddles her, pinning her down, and she hears him tearing more tape off the roll. Vainly she fumbles on the floor for a weapon. Her fingers crawl spiderlike under the bed. An unexpected but familiar obstacle gives her a moment's pause. She gropes at the warm, soft entity and suddenly twigs. Elísa just has time to raise her finger to her lips and mouth 'Shh' before her arms are jerked roughly upwards and her wrists are taped together behind her back.

The man drags her up and shakes her until her brain feels loose inside her head. Everything is black and she's afraid that this is no longer due to the tape; that her eyes have stopped working and her ears are going the same way. The small sounds that accompany the man's violence seem to fade, then grow louder again when he hauls her close and starts to pour out the promised – threatened – story.

When he has finished, he stands up, rolls her over on to

her back and jams a knee on her chest to prevent any further attempts at escape. Then he picks up the roll of tape and winds it tightly round her ears and nose. Round and round. She can hear the roaring in her ears but the desperate snuffling in her nose is far more worrying. And painful. The pressure on her chest lifts. Through the tape she hears a faint noise and finally it dawns on her what it was that the man dragged into the bedroom. Of all things, she hadn't been afraid of that. When he grabs her again she realises how foolishly optimistic she had been.

Chapter 2

Helgi was running late. He had slept badly, repeatedly disturbed by odd noises that had ceased when he sat up. Once he had finally dropped off he thought he would never be able to surface again. He had hit the snooze button on his phone four times, but when he tried it a fifth, his mobile refused to stop its shrilling.

He was supposed to be chairing a meeting at work; perhaps not the most significant of his career but pretty important nonetheless. He worked for a security company. The government purchasing department had recently invited bids for the installation of a security system at a large retirement home, and the purpose of the meeting was to put the finishing touches on their tender by the midday deadline. Yesterday evening he had read over the text, and the papers he was carrying now were covered in his scribbled comments.

There was a fierce gust of wind as Helgi turned in the doorway to call goodbye to his wife. Védís wasn't due in until ten today; she taught Danish and the school probably didn't think it reasonable to expect sixth-formers to grapple with grammar at the crack of dawn on a Friday. The door slammed before she could answer, and anyway Helgi didn't have time to wait for her to shuffle out in her slippers to kiss him goodbye. He clutched the bundle of papers to him as he dashed to the car, and breathed easier once he was inside, the documents safely deposited on the passenger seat. If the traffic was no worse than usual, he should just make it.

The engine emitted its friendly purr and he relaxed as the wheels began to turn. He was going to get away with it. But no sooner had he left his drive than he had to slam on the brakes: Stefán and Bárdur, the little boys from next door, were standing in the middle of the road. Leaning forwards, Helgi noticed that they were barefoot and wearing their pyjamas. The temperature was freezing and there was a vicious wind. What were their parents thinking? The boys stood there apparently at a loss, huddled together, staring at him help-lessly. This must be some kind of bad joke. He couldn't be this unlucky. Not today. He glanced over at his neighbours' house in the faint hope of seeing Sigvaldi or Elísa come running out, but the front door was closed and there was no sign of life. Their cars were parked in the drive, so they must be home. Perhaps they'd had a bad night too and overslept.

Helgi considered easing the car carefully around the chil-dren and continuing on his way. He could ring Védís afterwards and ask her to check what was going on; claim he thought he'd spotted the boys in the rear-view mirror but wasn't sure. Suddenly the younger boy began to howl. Hell. He couldn't drive away from a weeping kid. Could he? The meeting mattered more than he cared to admit. Business had been going through a bad patch recently and it was clear there would be redundancies if they couldn't attract new, more promising clients. If he messed up this bid, it was obvious who would be first for the chop.

Swinging the wheel to the right, he drove off as slowly as

he could. As he eased the car past the brothers they stood and gaped. The younger boy was so incredulous he paused in his howling. They were still young enough to be under the illusion that all grown-ups were good. Except the bad guys, of course, but then the bad guys didn't look ordinary like their neighbour. They had a lot to learn.

Once Helgi was safely past the boys he put his foot down and simultaneously rang his wife.

The police officer obviously wasn't having the best of days. He kept sighing heavily, though he was no longer young and must have witnessed his share of grim sights over the years. The broken veins that spread in a thick band from his nose across his cheeks made it appear as if he was blushing. He and his partner had been first on the scene after the notification had come in from a woman saying she was stuck with her neighbours' children and needed help restoring them to their parents. It had sounded like a job for no more than a couple of officers. There was every reason to believe the parents had overslept and the little wretches had locked themselves out. But this had turned out to be far from the truth, as the officer was attempting to explain to the detectives. His partner, a rookie in his first month on the force, had been sent back to the station. The garden path still stank of his vomit.

'The woman in question escorted the boys round to the property and proceeded to ring the bell several times and knock on the door. She could hear the bell inside but assumed the ringing was too weak to rouse their parents. She was sure they must be asleep because their vehicles were parked outside.' The policeman rested his hands on his heavy hips and shook his head. 'Sadly that wasn't the case. The boys knew nothing; they said they'd woken up to find themselves locked in their room. When they realised no one was going to open the door, they climbed out of the window.'

'Go on.' The detective, Huldar, stood as far away from the older officer as he could in the narrow hall, without making it too obvious. The gusts of hot air created by the man's constant huffing and sighing gave the impression that he had breakfasted on garlic and little else. Huldar would have opened a window were it not necessary to seal off the scene. It wouldn't help much anyway: the younger officer had disgraced himself just outside.

Through the glass Huldar watched his partner and closest colleague Ríkhardur repeatedly raising a hand to his nose as if he wanted to pinch it shut but knew it was against the unwritten rules. He was wise to resist the temptation; his detractors on the force didn't need any more ammunition against him. Huldar watched him pick his way painstakingly along the withered hedge, prodding with a pole in search of evidence, and wondered yet again why the man had ever joined the police.

Ríkhardur belonged in some government ministry, not halfway under a bush at a crime scene. His elegant suit and overlong coat were completely out of place. He could just about get away with his sartorial style at the station, but only just. The same applied to the immaculate haircut that was never permitted to grow out, and his perfectly manicured hands. Of course a certain standard of neatness was encouraged at the station – they were not permitted to dye their hair or beards bright orange, for example – but Ríkhardur went a step further than required. The fault of his upbringing, no doubt. Both his parents were judges and he had completed all but the final year of a law degree when he underwent a change of heart and enrolled at the police training college instead. He explained that he had needed a break but had every intention of finishing his legal studies eventually. That seemed unlikely to happen any time soon. Ríkhardur showed no signs of quitting, despite the endless sidelong glances he had to endure and the hard time he had coping with all the ugliness that went with the job.

In circumstances like the present he invariably opted to perform the tasks that would take him furthest away from any gruesome sights, which was why he was now busy combing the garden, inadequately dressed for the cold. Huldar wouldn't be surprised to see him pull out a wet-wipe any moment to clean off the dirt.

Lately, though, Ríkhardur's standards had been slipping. This morning, for instance, he had come to work with a tiny scrap of loo paper on his neck. Huldar couldn't help raising his eyebrows, though he wouldn't have turned a hair if anyone else had cut himself shaving.

The mess in Ríkhardur's private life was evidently taking its toll. His wife had left him, shortly after suffering her third miscarriage, and their perfect marriage was in ruins. A blow like that would affect anyone, of course. Perhaps Ríkhardur had reached the end of his tether and cracks would begin to appear in the flawless surface. But that was unlikely. He had weathered a number of storms in his personal life without breaking down and this would probably be no different. Three times he had proudly announced to his colleagues that he was going to be a father; three times he had subsequently whispered to Huldar that his wife had lost the baby. On two of the occasions Huldar had felt sorry for him. The third time he had experienced pure relief.

Huldar watched Ríkhardur pause to clean some leaves from his shoes with the pole. A picture of Ríkhardur's equally perfect ex-wife sprang unbidden to Huldar's mind and he flushed slightly as he turned back to the uniformed officer with the foul breath.

'After speaking to the woman next door, we went round to the property and attempted to rouse the occupants. No one answered the bell and we were unable to hear any sounds from inside. While Dóri waited by the door, I made a circuit of the property, looking in the windows where the curtains were open. I didn't observe anything untoward – or any people either. The curtains were drawn in the couple's bedroom, so I couldn't rule out the possibility that they were sound asleep inside. But I began to have my doubts when banging on the glass had no effect. I could see where the boys had climbed out of their room. Their window was still open but there was no way Dóri or I could squeeze inside.'

'I see.' Huldar didn't look up from his notebook. 'What then?'

The older man frowned, trying to be sure that he had the sequence of events right. 'We rang the two mobile phones registered at this address as there doesn't appear to be a landline. One was listed as belonging to Elísa Bjarnadóttir and the other to her husband, Sigvaldi Freysteinsson. Neither answered. Sigvaldi's went straight to voicemail but Elísa's just kept ringing. I tried phoning again but couldn't hear any ringtone through the bedroom window. At this point I became concerned, because you would usually expect people to be in the same place as their phones, wouldn't you?' Huldar didn't dignify this with a reply, so the man went on: 'My main thought was that one of the cars must have broken down and that either the husband or the wife had gone to work by taxi and the other had stayed behind and overslept. All I could think of was that the battery must have run out in the phone of whoever was at home, so their alarm hadn't gone off. Either that or something must have happened to him or her and maybe to the phone too. Slipped over in the shower with the phone in their hand, that sort of thing.'

'I see.' Huldar was lying: who would take their phone into the shower? And why didn't the woman's voicemail kick in if her phone had run out of juice or was broken?

'The neighbour had mentioned a daughter who should be in the house as well, so I began to think maybe she'd gone in the taxi too – to school.' The girl wasn't in the house; her bed was empty and although they had called her name repeatedly, they had received no reply. When a call to her school confirmed that she had not gone in that morning, a search was ordered. Some of the officers called to the scene were now combing the neighbourhood in case she had wandered off like her brothers. They could only hope that this would prove to be the case. Huldar didn't like to think of the alternatives.

The policeman resumed his account. 'The more we banged on the doors and windows, the more likely it seemed to me that whoever was inside must be unconscious. I was increasingly inclined to believe that the girl and one of the parents had gone off somewhere and that something had happened to the parent left at home. It was hard to credit that anyone could sleep through the racket we were making. It just didn't seem possible.'

'Was that when you decided to force an entry?'

'Yes. I made the decision to act. By that point I suspected that one of the parents must be lying unconscious inside, or worse. I'd even begun to suspect suicide. But not this.'

The man heaved another sigh, emitting a blast of garlic that caused Huldar to lean backwards. He was tempted to offer the man some of the nicotine gum he carried everywhere these days in a bid to quit smoking. 'No. No one could have anticipated this.' He couldn't be bothered to reprimand the officer for failing to ring the couple's workplaces before leaping to conclusions. One call to the National Hospital would have established that the husband was abroad at a conference. Then the search for the little girl could have started sooner.

'I returned to the neighbour's house while Dóri was waiting for the locksmith. The woman seemed more curious than worried – she kept grilling me. I managed to fob her off and didn't mention what I was afraid of because the little boys were in the kitchen having their breakfast.' He described how the boys had stared at him with big eyes over their cereal bowls and how bewildered they had looked later when they were driven away in a police car. He could cheerfully have punched the woman when she fuelled the boys' fears by pursuing them out to the car, demanding to know what was going on. In the end they had managed to shoo her back indoors. Now she was glued to the sitting-room window. No doubt the sight of Ríkhardur would confuse her since no one would take him for a policeman.

'After the locksmith had finished, I tried calling out again before entering but received no answer. I knocked on the door to the hallway as it was closed, like the door to the couple's bedroom.'

'Were you wearing gloves?'

The colour deepened in the man's cheeks. 'No.' In his defence, at least he didn't try to make excuses.

'I'm assuming we have your fingerprints on record? And your partner Dóri's too?'

'Yes. Well, mine, at any rate. I can't answer for Dóri. They should have been taken when he joined the force.'

'Right.' Huldar looked up from his notebook. 'What did you two do after you'd opened the door and seen what was inside? Did you touch anything?'

The man shook his head. 'No. Dóri put his hand over his mouth and ran out. I went over to the woman to check if she was still alive, though I was fairly certain she couldn't be. While I was doing that I rang the station to notify them.'

'Did you check her pulse?'

'Yes.'

'Where?'

'On her neck. I couldn't find one. She felt cold to the touch too, so I assumed she was dead. It wasn't really possible to come to any other conclusion. I didn't need to check her pulse but I did it out of habit. Just in case.'

'Did you touch her anywhere else?'

The man reddened again, the flush spreading down into his collar. 'Yes.'

'You'd better go in and show the pathologist exactly what you did. He'll be checking the body for fingerprints.' Huldar snapped his notebook shut. 'Come with me.'

They entered the master bedroom together. The smell that hit them in the doorway was so bad that Huldar almost missed the garlic.

Elísa was lying across the double bed. Her head was wound

33

like a mummy in duct tape which obscured her eyes, nose and mouth. Only the upper part of her forehead was visible and the hair sticking up wildly above it. Most disturbing of all, though, was what had happened to her mouth. The metal tube of the vacuum cleaner had been forced down her throat and secured with more tape. The hose snaked down to the vacuum cleaner itself on the floor by the bed. No wonder the rookie officer had gagged and fled.

It was all too plain that the woman's end had been far from easy. In the circumstances it was a mercy that so little of her face could be seen. The grimace of agony concealed by the wide strips of shiny silver tape must be truly horrifying.

The pathologist was bending over the woman. He had just arrived and hadn't yet put on the outfit he usually wore on such occasions. His assistant was standing in one corner, screwing a lens into a camera.

The pathologist shook his head. 'This doesn't look good.'

'No.' Huldar had nothing to add. He moved further inside to reveal the police officer behind him in the doorway. 'This guy was first on the scene. His prints'll be all over the victim's neck. Would you like him to show you where he touched her?'

'No. Not now. I don't want anyone else in here while we're conducting the preliminary examination. It'll have to wait. You'd better go back into the passage yourself.'

Huldar obeyed with alacrity, cursing himself for his thoughtlessness. He was no better than the old beat cop, though at least his breath wasn't as rank. While the pathologist was pulling on his protective suit, his assistant began photographing Elísa from all angles. The flash dazzled them until their eyes grew used to it. Once he had finished with the victim, the photographer turned his attention to the rest of the room, including the walls and floor. He disappeared from view as he bent down to take pictures under the bed, only to leap to his feet, white as a sheet. 'Shit!' He gesticulated downwards. 'There's a child under there.'

Forgetting the pathologist's orders, Huldar charged into the room. He tore aside the white valance and peered under the bed. A small girl in a nightie was lying huddled in a ball underneath, eyes shut tight, chin buried in her chest, hands clamped over her ears. To Huldar's intense relief the thin body moved. This must be Elísa's and Sigvaldi's daughter; the girl they were currently scouring the neighbourhood for. They hadn't searched the room yet for fear of compromising the crime-scene investigation. It simply hadn't occurred to anyone that the child might not emerge from hiding when her name was called and it became evident that the police had arrived.

Before Huldar could open his mouth, another member of the team called from the hall. 'We've found something in the kitchen that you need to see.'

He couldn't imagine that anything could be more important than the child under the bed. The kitchen would have to wait.

Chapter 3

A housefly was bashing against the little window high up by the basement ceiling. Its strength was waning, the buzzing and knocking on the glass were growing gradually more sporadic, its struggle was almost over. Goodness knows what the fly was so desperate to reach outside that it was worth sacrificing its life for. The garden lay under a blanket of snow, bordered by skeletal bushes. The fly wouldn't stand a chance out there. At least it was warm here in the basement. Yet it persisted, caring nothing for the corpses of other flies littering the dusty windowsill after failed attempts to escape the same way. Perhaps it was time to give the sill a clean. Karl decided to wait until this fly joined its fallen comrades or he would only have to repeat the exercise, and picking up a duster wasn't really his thing.

He was finding it hard to adjust to the quiet. Before, he wouldn't even have noticed the buzzing. Raising his eyes, he studied the yellowing ceiling tiles. No sounds filtered through them from the floor above. How often had he longed for this? To be able to sit in complete silence and concentrate on listening without constant disturbances from upstairs. Without having to put on the battered headphones that always made his ears ache. Now, apart from the fly, there was nothing to disturb him; his wish had been granted. But strangely this didn't bring him the anticipated pleasure. No celebratory fireworks went off in his head; no smile of satisfaction rose to his lips. It shouldn't really have come as a surprise since his dreams had a habit of falling flat on the rare occasions when they came true. But the anticlimax was unusually intense this time, as he had been craving silence for so long.

Ever since he'd caught the amateur radio bug in his teens he had been driven spare by the constant low-level intrusions. To begin with he had set up a simple CB radio set designed for general users to communicate on a 27 megahertz band, but his flimsy bedroom door had proved hopeless at insulating him from the everyday noises outside. It was about as much use as a sheet hanging over the doorway. His mother had refused to let him use noise-cancelling headphones, so he didn't even have the choice of putting up with the interruptions or enjoying peace and quiet at the price of sore ears. She had got it into her head that it was dangerous for him to be unaware of background noises. She used to lecture him on the risks of house fires and all manner of other potential hazards to which he would be oblivious if he couldn't hear what was going on in the house. She was particularly eloquent on the possibility of a burglar murdering her in cold blood while Karl failed to register her screams. Needless to say, none of these doom-laden predictions had come true, apart from a break-in in the middle of November. All the thief had got for his pains was half a bottle of brandy and some small change from the bowl on the chest in the hall. And since neither Karl nor his mother was home at the time, there had been no chance to test whether the intruder would have been seized by a killing frenzy mid-burglary.

After his elder brother moved out, Karl had taken over the basement. By then his original interest in CB radio had developed into a serious amateur radio hobby, with the consequence that his equipment had proliferated and took up a good deal more space than the original little set he had acquired as a teenager. He had learnt Morse code and passed the exam for an entry-level licence that permitted him to transmit in Morse on a limited, low-power frequency. In due course he had taken the exam for the long-desired full licence, which allowed him to use voice transmissions and operate on higher-power frequencies. His small bedroom was crammed to bursting with equipment, books and files related to his hobby, so Arnar's departure was a heaven-sent opportunity to move his gear down to the basement. Until he left home, Arnar had had the place to himself so he could study in peace. The new arrangement was a significant improvement, but the racket from upstairs still drove Karl up the wall. It was amazing how much noise one person could generate. Arnar, morose and taciturn, his nose perpetually buried in his school books, had never been any trouble, but their mother was a different story. She seemed incapable of staying still and was constantly bustling from room to room, fetching or tidying. If she stayed put for any length of time it was only because she was on the phone, and that did nothing to reduce the noise level.

The sounds that accompanied her presence had been as mundane as the rest of her existence: the creaking of floorboards; the clatter of crockery in the kitchen sink as she washed up by hand instead of using the dishwasher that she insisted on saving for special occasions. Snatches of ancient, forgettable Icelandic pop songs. The metallic clicking of needles busy knitting clothes that nobody wanted. Endless enquiries from the top of the stairs about whether he'd like a snack or a drink. That had been particularly annoying as he was over twenty, for Christ's sake, and hardly likely to starve. Or die of thirst. Though there was no denying that he hadn't had a square meal in the three months and more since he finished the leftovers from the funeral reception. If he went on like this he would have to invest in a smaller belt. He had started using the innermost hole some time ago but his trousers were loose at the waist again and dragged on the ground like those of the teenage boys who spent their evenings hanging around the neighbourhood's little nucleus of shops. For the first time in his life he was inadvertently trendy.

The buzzing ceased and all he could hear was his own breathing. If he listened hard enough he'd be able to hear his heart beating. Again he was surprised at how little pleasure the long-desired peace had brought him. He actually missed the noise associated with his mother. Perhaps it was his conscience nagging at him since her death had been rather sudden. She had been three months short of her seventieth birthday, which she had been intending to celebrate with a coffee party that she had spent ages planning, without much enthusiasm from Karl. If he had known what was going to happen he could at least have faked an interest in the cake recipes that she was forever cutting out of the papers and asking his opinion about. In hindsight, he should have realised something was wrong. She'd been under the weather for a while, though not in a way to ring any alarm bells. Then suddenly one day she could barely stand, and only then did she go and see a doctor. He sent her for tests and she came home with the news that a malignant cancer had taken up residence in her body. She had tried to put a good face on things but in the end she was admitted to hospital.

Karl was just beginning to grasp the severity of the situation when she passed away one night during Advent, alone in a bleak hospital ward. Had the cancer not been in such a hurry, Karl would have had more warning and could have treated her better. Visited her more often and taken her more chocolates and flowers. Looking back, the pathetic bunch he had grabbed from the local supermarket for one of his last visits was a disgrace. Even he wouldn't have wanted that before his eyes as he lay dying.

Mind you, Karl hadn't behaved any worse than Arnar, who hadn't even bothered to come home to Iceland to be at their mother's deathbed. Karl had had to do everything: sort out the affairs she was so insistent should be taken care of, return all kinds of crap she'd borrowed, post her farewell letters and procure an overview of her finances so she could figure out the details of her estate. All of which he had performed with bad grace. He had traipsed to the post office with one letter after the other, knocked on countless doors and handed the occupants a variety of Tupperware, books and DVDs. From the astonished looks he received, Karl suspected his mother of using this as a means of breaking the news to friends and relatives that she was at death's door. That way she didn't have to do it herself. Oh no, that was Karl's job. And of course it greatly increased the risk of receiving return visits, or so he had thought at the time, which made him even more resentful about being lumbered with the task. Now, though, he wished he had been more generous when fulfilling her last requests.

He would be feeling better now, no question, if he'd let his own desires take a back seat during those few weeks; if he'd run her errands and sat at her bedside the rest of the time.

Because in spite of all her messages, visitors had been few and far between.

To be honest, though, he doubted he would have behaved much better even with more warning. What could he have said? What words were adequate to explain to someone that you loved her really, in spite of years of behaviour that indicated the opposite? Wouldn't she have stared at him sceptically from her sickbed, remembering all the times he had been ashamed of her and refused to be seen with her?

Until he was six it had never dawned on him that his family circumstances were any different from other people's; it didn't occur to him that his mother was unusually old or that there was no father in the picture. The realisation had hit him like an icy wave. It began with an innocent question – was that his grandmother? – followed by an embarrassed giggle when he answered no, it was his mother. This quickly developed into teasing; infinite variations on the theme that his mother was really his grandmother and that he had no father. The children's words caused a deep wound that was constantly being reopened and never really healed. The odd part was that the other kids didn't realise how much this hurt him. It never occurred to them that he didn't find it as funny as they did, or so it seemed to Karl.

Strange how a single incident could blight your life, force it on to a course from which it would never deviate. The mocking of the other kids on his first day at school had set the tone for his future relations with them. He was never popular. His fellow pupils were indifferent to him. He was never bullied, though, remaining under the mean kids' radar throughout his time at school, and for that he was grateful. Arnar, who had experienced much the same eight years earlier, had no advice for his little brother. Or at least no interest in sharing any with Karl. Besides, their situations were different: Arnar had never skulked around but walked tall, like the one in a position of power, however hollow this illusion. His attitude must have been provoking but the other kids left him alone, though few wanted to be his friend in any case. Karl suspected they had already sensed what it took him several years to discover – that Arnar wasn't like other people, so it was best to leave him alone. The arrangement suited both brothers: Arnar had a very limited need for human contact, and Karl found him boring company.

The move to sixth-form college and a new environment did little to alter Karl's existence; he continued to plough his lonely furrow. He made few acquaintances and rarely took part in social events. The fear of being left out was usually enough to keep him at home. Unfortunately, he didn't make proper use of the resulting free time; he passed his final exams with a decent enough grade but his average was nowhere near the heights achieved by Arnar. After that he wasted a year; instead of going on the trip to Asia with his classmates, he stayed at home twiddling his thumbs, pretending to be busy contemplating his future. Eventually, no longer able to justify his idleness to his mother, he enrolled in a chemistry degree at the university and embarked on his higher education, still in the role of class outsider. He had never left home, never had a girlfriend and still had very few friends. Most of the people he associated with fell somewhere on the spectrum between acquaintance and complete stranger. There were two exceptions, though: Halli and Börkur. They weren't what he would have wanted in an ideal world, but beggars couldn't be choosers.

For the most part, he satisfied his need for human contact through his radio. This type of interaction worked for him, though the uninitiated would probably regard it as remote and impersonal. You spoke and you received an answer. And when Karl wasn't in the mood to talk, he could listen instead, or transmit in Morse.

A welcome crackling from the transceiver caught his attention. Karl put on his headphones and rested his fingers gently on the fine-tuner. As he did so, he surveyed the wall above his desk. It was papered in framed QSL-cards that he had collected over the years. They were proof of his contacts with other radio amateurs in far-flung parts of the world that he would never visit in person. Only the cards he was most proud of were given this place of honour; the rest he kept in a drawer. It was a long time since he had bothered to request confirmation via QSL-card since by now he had made contact with operators in most countries and it was rare that he came across a transmission from a new region. The last time he had actively sought the cards was during a competition to form as many connections as possible within a given time limit. That had been a year and a half ago. Although these competitions were still held, he could no longer be bothered to take part in them.

He didn't like to admit to himself that this was because he never won. Never came close. Even when he took part in team competitions he seemed to act as a jinx – a jinx that the other radio hams couldn't fail to notice. Like in dodgeball games at school, he soon ended up being the last person to be picked for a team. The rejection hurt, like it had at school, but he didn't betray the fact. He didn't know why, since all his pride achieved was to make the others feel less guilty about ditching him. Going off in a huff would probably have been a better policy, but it was too late now.

Karl bent towards the microphone. 'Charlie Quebec Delta X-ray, this is Tango Foxtrot Three Kilo Papa standing by.' The code CQDX signalled that he wanted to make contact with amateur radio operators abroad, while TF3KP was his call-sign: TF for Iceland, 3 for the Reykjavík area and KP – Karl Pétursson. Not that he had any real claim to this patronymic: Pétur had been his maternal grandfather. He was adopted and had never known the names of his real parents. Apparently their story had not been a happy one, and his mother took the view that there was no call to rake up the past. If she was to be believed, they were both dead, so there was no point trying to trace them. It had quickly become apparent to him as a child that questions about his biological parents were unwelcome and achieved nothing. So Karl had stopped asking; ceased to give them any thought. It was a different story with Arnar, who never stopped asking questions. He was adopted too, and although the brothers had the same patronymic they were no more related than two strangers who happened to sit next to each other on the bus. Different in appearance; different in their habits. 'Tango Foxtrot Three Kilo Papa. Standing by.'

He listened but there was no reply. Perhaps he had just caught the tail end of a transmission. He tried again, anyway. 'Tango Foxtrot Three Kilo Papa. Standing by.' Nothing.

He remembered his old ambition to collect a card from every state in the US. Maybe he should revive the idea? It wouldn't take long as he had already picked up quite a few. Now that he was alone he had nothing to do outside his classes except pursue his hobby. But he couldn't decide if he could be bothered. Any more than he could decide whether or not to attend the amateur radio club meeting that was due to start in forty minutes. He would have to make up his mind soon. Probably best to skip it and get down to some studying instead. He was falling behind; the vague interest he'd had in chemistry when he enrolled was fast disappearing. His desk at the other end of the basement was gathering dust and the poster of the periodic table on the wall above it was peeling off at one corner.

Perhaps his interest would rematerialise if he knuckled down. The club meeting wasn't important. He had nothing special to say and doubted the others had either. Membership was dropping off every year and almost the only hams left were old men who didn't share his interest in making contact with foreign amateurs. They mostly operated on channels in the 14 and 21 to 28 megahertz frequency range, while Karl preferred to listen to amateurs transmitting in Morse or used three and a half megahertz. Perhaps it was an age thing. There weren't many hams transmitting on 28, and those who did tended to be too philosophical for his taste. The old blokes were also more interested than Karl in hardware and building sets; very few shared his enthusiasm for more recherché pursuits, such as listening to numbers stations. In fact, since Börkur and Halli stopped coming along to club meetings, he was the only one left who was into that.

Karl unplugged the headphones from the transceiver and plugged them into the old Collins shortwave receiver instead. Then he carefully scanned the low-frequency spectrum until he reached a numbers station he knew of, in the hope of catching a transmission. He could make no more sense of the broadcasts than anyone else, yet he found them utterly compelling. They consisted of long strings of numbers and letters read out by synthesised female or sometimes children's voices, or sequences in Morse code, static and interference, and even folk melodies. The broadcasts would have had limited appeal were it not for the mystery of their origins and purpose. No one knew for certain what they meant or who operated on the high-frequency shortwave bands between 3 and 30 megahertz, which used waves reflected off the ionosphere, thus achieving a far wider dispersal than conventional radio broadcasts. The most popular theory was that the transmissions were coded messages from government intelligence services to their agents in the field, though some may have been communications between drugs networks and the smugglers they employed. Phone calls could be tapped, letters and e-mails could be read and traced, but it was impossible to track the recipients of a radio broadcast.

Therein lay the fascination. The number sequences recited by those coldly dispassionate yet innocent-sounding voices might be orders for executions or attacks. Like the other hobbyists drawn to them, Karl dreamt of successfully cracking one of the codes used by the stations, though cleverer people than him had been forced to admit defeat. Even Arnar had given up, after finally condescending to take notice of Karl's hobby. He had pored over the number groups for hours, pencil in hand, only to throw it down and declare angrily that it was a load of bloody gibberish. But Karl knew better. It was code: code that was impossible to crack without the key. But that didn't stop people from wrestling with the problem.

He was in luck. The stations usually broadcast on the hour or half-hour, and it was now just gone half past seven. He stumbled upon a familiar transmission from a station popularly known as 'the Russian Man'. A harsh male voice recited a string of numbers in Russian, repeating them over and over, embellished with static interference. '*A-deen, a-deen, pyat, syem, pyat, null, null.*' Most of the stations followed a set template: the broadcast began with a characteristic prelude that could be a specific word like 'Ready? Ready?', '*Achtung!*' or '*¡Atención!*'; a melody, or a series of letters or numbers. This was an identifier and in some cases probably also indicated the intended recipient. Usually this opening routine was repeated several times before the body of the message itself was transmitted. This consisted of sequences of numbers or letters, often preceded by an announcement about how many number groups there would be, also repeated several times. After this came the sign-off, which was individual to each station, though more often than not it simply consisted of the words 'end' or 'end of message' in the relevant language. There were also cases where the end of a broadcast was marked by music or a series of zeros.

This was how the Russian Man ended, for example. Karl listened to him signing off: '*Null, null, null, null.*' Silence and crackling. '*Null, null, null, null.*' Silence again, then finally: '*Null, null, null, null.*' The broadcast went off air.

Karl quickly searched for another station and this time encountered one he didn't recall having heard before. He pricked up his ears when he realised that the language sounded Nordic. After adjusting the fine-tuner, he was able to hear the speech quite clearly, which only intensified his astonishment: '. . . nine, two, zero, five, six, nine.' The number group was repeated and this time he caught the whole thing. 'One, seven, zero, three, nine, two, zero, five, six, nine.' The voice was female and, as usual, machine-generated. 'One, seven, zero, three, nine, two, zero, five, six, nine.' The voice fell silent. Karl leant back in his chair, ran his fingers wonderingly over his forehead, then clasped his hands over his head. 'One, seven, zero, three, nine, two, zero, five, six, nine.' Dropping his hands he reached for the notepad and pen, which he always kept close by. As he was about to write the numbers down the voice began to recite another group: 'Two, four, one, two, seven, nine, seven, three, one, nine.'

The pen wouldn't work at first and Karl had to be careful not to break the tip in his frantic haste to scribble the numbers down. Then suddenly the ink began to flow. 'Two, four, one, two, seven, nine, seven, three, one, nine.' He read over the numbers on the page as they were repeated, trying to detect an accent, but the synthetic voice didn't sound foreign. Could some Icelandic organisation, either illegal or government-operated, have set up a numbers station? It didn't seem possible. It must be a foreign station using Icelandic to confuse people. But the broadcast was clear, too clear to come from far away. Karl listened to the sequence, mystified. Surely it couldn't originate in Iceland? Even if someone in this country did feel the need to pass on secret messages, he would have bet his bottom dollar that the internet would be the chosen method of communication. Shortwave was too passé for his fellow Icelanders.

As if to hammer home its point, the voice began to read the original number group again: 'One, seven, zero, three, nine, two, zero, five, six, nine.' Karl copied it down and stared at the result: *1703920569*. He read the sequence over again as it was repeated. 'One, seven, zero, three, nine, two, zero, five, six, nine.' All the numbers were right. It must be an absurd coincidence. Or some kind of joke aimed at him.

It was his ID number.

Karl examined the other series: 2412797319. That could be an ID number too. He tapped it into a search engine on his phone and 122 results came up, none of which were Icelandic. He tried adding a hyphen in the appropriate place after the first six digits and searched again. Bingo. The owner of the ID number turned out to be a woman whose name – Elísa Bjarnadóttir – he didn't recognise. He tried searching for images of her but that didn't help. Her face was no more familiar than her name. Karl put down his phone. The whole thing was bizarre and uncanny. The broadcast of the message had finished and the soulless voice signed off with the words: 'Goodbye, more later.' This was followed by a melody played on a musical box. Then silence. He took off his headphones.

There was a feeble buzzing from the fly in the window. Karl turned towards the sound, wondering if he should let the poor creature out and grant it its longed-for freedom. It would of course perish in the freezing conditions outside but at least it would die happy. But he forgot the fly when he heard the faint sound of a voice from the headphones. The broadcast from the mysterious station was starting up again. Karl replaced his headphones and heard: 'Hello. Hello. Hello.' After this the same number groups were repeated. It was clear that he would not make it to the club meeting after all. This was a pity seeing as he finally had something to report. But perhaps it would be better to keep this to himself for the time being. Especially if it turned out to be a prank aimed at him.

While Karl sat listening intently, the fly threw itself at the glass one last time, then fell down dead.

Chapter 4

Saturday

Margrét seemed to have no idea that she was being watched. She was sitting on a small sofa that barely had room to accommodate her and the huge cuddly animal propped at her side. She hadn't touched the toy. Her green eyes roved restlessly around the sparsely furnished room in search of something to fix on, sliding away from the gaze of Silja, the young woman in the chair next to her, who was trying to keep up a flow of conversation with simple questions. Silja smiled at Margrét and took care not to glance unnaturally often at the large mirror on the wall facing the sofa. The girl's eyes, on the other hand, kept returning to stare at her own reflection, completely unaware of the people watching her on the other side. She hadn't said a word, restricting her responses to a nod or shake of her head as appropriate. This didn't matter as Silja's questions hadn't yet touched on any important issues. She had to win the child's trust first, and anyway they were still waiting for the police representative to show up.

'This is a disgrace. Where's the bloody cop?' The girl's paternal grandfather had brought her to the interview. Although he must have been on the right side of sixty, his curly hair was so white it was almost translucent. He had turned up unshaven, his badly crumpled shirt collar sticking

50

up on one side. In other circumstances Freyja would have been surprised he didn't feel the collar chafing against his jaw, but it was normal for people to arrive at the centre in a distressed state. No one took any notice; they had seen worse. He had more urgent matters on his mind than shirt collars or shaving: his daughter-in-law had been murdered, his son was still abroad, and he and his wife found themselves looking after their three grandchildren with no idea how to cope with their grief and trauma. Saliva sprayed from his mouth as he spoke, the fine drops spattering the polished surface of the table. They gleamed there briefly before evaporating. The others affected not to see. 'Are you going to subject her to endless bloody questions about her school and friends? Can't you see how she's feeling? What the hell does that stuff matter? Aren't there more important things to discuss?'

The people sitting round the table all turned as one to Konráð Bjarnason from the State Prosecutor's office. By common consent they seemed to regard it as his job to answer the man. From Freyja's limited experience of Konráð this did not bode well. He was the type who put on a Teflon suit each morning in the hope that no responsibility would stick to him during the day. He lowered his gaze and dusted some imaginary fluff from the garish tie that was completely out of keeping with the sombre atmosphere. When it became clear that no answer would be forthcoming, all eyes turned to Freyja instead. She could hardly play the same silent game and wait for their attention to move on to somebody else. If everyone passed the buck they'd be here all day. She wondered how best to handle the grandfather. There was little point pleading the excuse that the case had come up without warning and she hadn't had a chance to make the necessary preparations. It was true, though; she hadn't even been given the name of the man in charge of the investigation, let alone had an opportunity to speak to him before the meeting. The Police Commissioner's office had simply told her to assemble the team and to expect a little girl for interview; someone from the police would provide the necessary questions. But the officer in question hadn't turned up.

Freyja cleared her throat, squared her shoulders and adopted a carefully neutral expression. She could feel her hastily secured ponytail slipping down her neck. She'd had no more time to get ready than Margrét's grandfather; when the phone call came from the police she'd been sitting in her dressing gown at the kitchen table, enjoying her first coffee of the weekend, her eyes still full of sleep. The time she could have used to tidy herself up had been spent instead on assembling the team: the psychologist Silja who was to interview the girl, a representative from the Child Protection Agency, a doctor and a nurse. The last two were not regular employees of the Children's House but were brought in as required. Freyja had summoned them in case, on top of everything else, the little girl had suffered some form of abuse at the hands of the murderer. It was better to be prepared for every eventuality; a man who could brutally murder a young woman in her own bed was capable of anything. The precaution had proved unnecessary, however, as it turned out that the girl had already undergone a medical examination. But since the women had arrived by the time this was established, and the cost of their call-out had already been incurred, Freyja had decided to keep them there, to be on the safe side.

There was a lot riding on their successful handling of the case as it wasn't every day that the police requested the help of the Children's House in a criminal investigation. Although they were always brought in when sexual abuse was suspected, they had little experience of eliciting disclosures from children who had been exposed to other types of crime.

It had been hinted to Freyja that this unusual course had been taken because the girl had flatly refused to set foot in the police station and had been equally unwilling to answer the detectives' questions at her grandparents' house. The centre was a last resort and it was imperative that they do a good job, since it was unlikely that they would be given another opportunity to show what they were capable of. If this went wrong, it would be Freyja's fault and she could expect a reprimand from the Child Protection Agency. The Children's House was her baby and as director she was responsible for the day-to-day running of the centre as well as for the individual cases referred to them. She had only been doing the job for four months and today's interview was probably the most important since she'd taken over, if you could single one out in this way. After all, every case involved the possibility that the life of an innocent child had been wrecked. It was a cause for celebration whenever all suspicion of a crime could be dismissed, an outcome that fortunately wasn't uncommon, though sadly wouldn't apply in today's case.

The social worker from the child protection services raised his eyebrows. Freyja got the message; she was taking too long to answer. Little Margrét was fidgeting on the sofa, her eyes trained on the door of the interview room. From her grandfather's expression it was plain that his patience was running out. Who could blame him? Freyja forced a smile.

'I realise that the psychologist's conversation with Margrét might seem pointless, but the questions aren't as random as they sound. Silja's an expert in the forensic interviewing technique specially designed for children like your granddaughter. It's essential for her to establish a rapport with Margrét before she moves on to more important questions.'

The man shook his head, then said in a more subdued voice: 'Well, I only hope you lot know what you're doing. She's been through enough trauma.'

'You need have no worries on that score.' Freyja noticed out of the corner of her eye that Silja was tapping her ear as if the earpiece concealed there was on the blink. It was hardly surprising; she was expecting to be fed questions but none were coming through. Freyja switched on the microphone. 'The policeman hasn't arrived yet, Silja. Keep talking if you think that's OK. Otherwise we'll have to take a break or postpone the interview.' The woman on the other side of the glass gave a discreet thumbs-up. Over the intercom they heard her ask yet another question, this time about pets.

'Have you got a dog, Margrét? Or a hamster, maybe?'

The girl shook her head, her red locks swaying. A strand of hair caught in the corner of her mouth and she pushed it away with ivory fingers. Her skin was so pale she looked as if she'd never seen the sun.

Her grandfather was watching her intently. He looked as dazed as he had when Freyja first saw him and Margrét walking hand in hand up the drive. The Children's House was located in a residential house with only two parking spaces and by the time they arrived, both had been taken. He had been forced to park further down the street and they had trudged here through the freshly fallen snow. Walking was clearly an effort and the little girl had balked every now and then and stood staring at the house in bewilderment. Each time, her grandfather had bent down to encourage her. Now, though, he heaved a sigh and seemed to regret that he hadn't given in to her wish to turn back. 'The kids had a cat that died. It was run over. At the time we thought it was the worst heartbreak the poor little things would have to suffer.'

Freyja reached for the microphone again. 'Silja, avoid talking about pets. Her cat was hit by a car.' Again the woman gave a discreet sign that she had received the message. Changing the subject, she asked instead if Margrét owned a toboggan and had been sledging recently. Freyja glanced at the wall clock and decided to give it ten more minutes. If the policeman hadn't arrived by then, they would call it a day. They couldn't subject the little girl to much more of this. There was too much at stake. The first meeting with a child was usually crucial, but she would have to come back. Again and again. A whole host of people would want to hear her statement – the police, the judge, the lawyer defending the person eventually charged with the crime, and the prosecutor as well. It would be a miracle if they managed to extract all the information they wanted from her in one go, to everyone's satisfaction.

The screen of Freyja's phone flashed on the table in front of her. It was the letting agent who was trying to find her a flat. She longed to answer; there was stiff competition for the few properties that came up for rent and the place was bound to have been snapped up by the time she rang back. But there was no way she could take the call now. She would have to make do with her brother's dump for a while yet. It took some getting used to after the flat she had until recently shared with her partner, but then her ex was a well-paid financial consultant, while her brother was an inmate of Litla-Hraun Prison. Unfortunately, since she had owned no share in her ex's luxury pad, she had left the relationship as skint as she'd entered it. It was only thanks to her brother's situation that she wasn't out on the street. He had just under a year left of his sentence, and the way things were going it would take her that long to find a place to rent. The alternative was to fall for some guy and move in with him. But given her success rate during the months she'd been single, there was quite frankly more chance of the President of Iceland driving over to the prison and granting her repeat-offender brother a pardon.

Freyja had done her best to meet a new man, dutifully going out on the town with her girlfriends and constantly checking out the talent on and off the dance floor. She was blessed with good looks, and knew how to tart herself up when necessary, so it shouldn't have been a major challenge. She had seen a couple of men she liked the look of, both extremely attractive and apparently after the same thing as her. On each occasion she had struck up a conversation and downed a few drinks with the guy before dragging him home with her. The first had broken down in tears when she sat beside him on her brother's battered old sofa in the hope that he would finally make a move. He had confided that he was gay but didn't dare come out as he was a masseur and feared he would lose all his male clients. Sighing, Freyja had encouraged him to do the right thing. She hadn't a clue if he'd followed her advice as she hadn't encountered him again.

Things had gone better on the second occasion – to begin with, at least. The man, a carpenter called Jónas, had recently moved to Reykjavík from Egilsstadir in the east of the country. Luckily, he had proved to be straight, and although they had been a little self-conscious with one another while upright, once horizontal they had fitted together like a well-oiled machine.

But she woke up the next day to find that the man had done a runner and she hadn't heard from him since. The really galling part was that she'd gone to sleep contented, feeling fairly confident that she'd met a man who was at least worth giving a chance. Plainly the feeling hadn't been reciprocated.

The clock on the wall showed that half the extra time was up. Margrét's voice came over the intercom, clear but sad. For once the girl had taken the initiative in the conversation: 'Why's that big mirror there?' All those sitting round the conference table turned to face the glass. The girl was staring back, as if straight at them. Silja looked in their direction as well. She was sitting closer to the mirror, so the little girl couldn't see the face she made for Freyja's benefit. They had been caught out, as sometimes happened, and in such cases their policy was to tell the truth. It wasn't fair to demand honesty from the children while lying to them in return. The two-way mirror was a recent innovation; previously interviews had been watched on a TV screen. Freyja had proposed the change soon after she took over, after watching several interviews by the old method. The screen tended to increase the viewers' detachment from the subject, evoking involuntary associations with a TV programme. The verdict was that the new arrangement helped people to connect better with what was happening, simply by virtue of seeing the child and interviewer full size.

Silja turned back to Margrét. Her voice was as composed as before but her smile had faded. 'It's a sort of magic mirror. The other side's like a window, so people can watch without having to squash in here with us. Clever, don't you think?'

Margrét shook her head. She chewed her lower lip, frowning. 'Is there somebody there now?' she asked, fear and anger mingling in her voice.

'Yes.' Silja twirled her pen as if she were walking ahead of a brass band with the world's tiniest baton. Freyja had begun to recognise the characteristic signs of tension.

'Who?'

'Your grandfather, for example.'

Margrét dropped her eyes. 'I don't want to talk to you any more. I want to go home.' She looked up suddenly. 'To Granny and Grandpa's. Not to my house.'

'But we've only just started chatting. Shouldn't we stay a little bit longer? Then you won't have to come back. Not for a while, anyway.'

The girl's eyes narrowed. 'I don't want to be here. I want to go home with Grandpa.'

Freyja switched on the microphone again. 'Wrap it up, Silja. The cop still hasn't arrived and it sounds as if things are going downhill. We'll just have to reconvene when she's in a better frame of mind.' It wasn't unusual in difficult cases to have to cut short the first interview. Sometimes the child wasn't in a receptive mood, or the psychologist failed to establish a rapport. In either case the team generally judged it wiser to take things slowly, call it off and try again another day.

Konráð from the State Prosecutor's office coughed. 'I suggest we keep going. The man'll be here any minute and it's absolutely vital we talk to the girl as soon as possible. May I remind you that a murder has been committed and she's the only witness?'

'Her name's Margrét.' The nurse's voice came out sounding unusually gruff. She'd been attending call-outs at the Children's House ever since it had been set up seventeen years earlier, during which time she'd had to witness such appalling tragedies that Freyja was worried it was beginning to get to her.

She rarely smiled and had a short fuse when annoyed. Like now. 'You could at least get that right.'

'And you could at least appreciate that we're under no obligation to question the girl here. The judge who recommended it only suggested we try this solution. But it looks to me as if we should stick to our original plan and interview her down at the station.' Konrád's face had turned crimson, clashing with his garish tie.

Jóhann from the child protection services gave Freyja a discreet kick under the table. She didn't need him to spell it out; she was perfectly aware that they were making a mess of things. As a representative of the government agency, he was in a sense her superior. She tried to de-escalate the tension by keeping her voice level. 'Let's just stay calm. We all know how important Margrét's disclosure is. Please don't forget that we're experts in this area and know when it's right to suspend an interview with a child. May I also remind you that it's not our fault how things have turned out. Where's the police officer who was supposed to supply the questions? We know next to nothing about the case. We were simply told to turn up here at ten o'clock, which we did, like Margrét and her grandfather. It's your man who's let everyone down, Konrád, not us.' Freyja hoped he wouldn't start grumbling that he was from the State Prosecutor's office and had no authority over the police. As far as she was concerned they amounted to the same thing.

Konrád took out his phone, his hectic colour fading a little, and hurriedly selected a number. He waited impatiently for an answer, then bawled out the person unlucky enough to pick up. In doing so he broke one of the few rules that had been laid down at the beginning of the interview. The glass was not completely soundproof, so it was always impressed on the observers that they should speak quietly when there was a child on the other side. A loud noise near the microphone could also fluster the interviewer, or even damage her ear.

'Keep your voice down.' Freyja waved furiously at Konrád, who turned away and continued his tirade.

Freyja noticed Margrét glance up at the mirror. Silja did too, with a grimace. She was understandably annoyed as it was her job to keep Margrét calm. She threw up her hands and Freyja thought she could read her lips: 'What's going on?'

A faint sound of weeping began to cut through Konrád's ranting. It increased in volume until the room was echoing with a loud sobbing. Even Konrád shut up, lowered his phone and stared at the girl who was on her feet now, her thin body trembling.

Before Silja had a chance to comfort her, the girl's lips began to form words and the intercom conveyed the half-whispered question: 'Is the black man there? Is he behind the mirror?' Margrét cowered, averting her eyes from the glass.

'No, Margrét. It's only people who want the best for you. Who's the black man?' Warily, Silja placed her hands on the little girl's shoulders and tried to steer her gently back to the sofa. She resisted.

'He hurt my mummy.' The pain in the small voice cut the listeners to the quick.

'Did you see this man, Margrét?'

'Yes. He was black.'

Silja shot a glance at the mirror. Freyja bent to the microphone and urged her to continue. Silja gave an almost imperceptible nod. Then she spoke again, her tone calm and composed: 'Now I need you to think carefully, Margrét. Was he black because it was dark in the room or because he was a black man?'

'What do you mean?'

'Was his skin dark?'

'Yes.'

Silja licked her lips and continued cautiously: 'Did you see his hands?'

Margrét shook her head. She sniffed and rubbed her cheeks clumsily to dry her tears. 'His head. I saw his head.'

'Did you see his face, Margrét?'

'No. Not his face. Just the back of his black head. He had a very big head.' Margrét turned her back to the mirror. 'I want my grandpa. I'm not saying any more. I don't want to talk about it any more. Ever.'

Silja tried to talk her round but couldn't coax another word out of her. The interview was over, just when it had appeared to be taking a turn for the better. All in all, it had been a dismal failure, the exact opposite of what the team had been aiming for. Silja sat down with a sigh.

At that moment the policeman finally put in an appearance. He turned bright red when he saw Freyja. Her mouth dropped open, and she momentarily forgot the collapsing situation. It was none other than Jónas the carpenter from Egilsstadir. Their eyes met; hers stormy, his stunned. Then he looked away and addressed the others: 'I'm Huldar, from the Police Commissioner's office. Sorry I'm so late. Something came up.'

Chapter 5

As a policeman, Huldar was used to all kinds of receptions. He was seldom a welcome guest; people usually only spoke to him when forced to, eyeing him all the while as though he smelt funny. It was clear from their expressions that most of those he dealt with blamed their predicament on him – and possibly on whichever police officer happened to be standing at his side. Not that he cared; since joining the force he hadn't given a damn what people thought. The spitting, the abuse, the dirty looks, he remained untouched by it all. As the only boy and youngest child, he'd been forced to develop a thick skin – his five elder sisters had seen to that. Though even their treatment had never quite plumbed the depths of your average citizen when he'd downed a few drinks.

So he had been disconcerted to find himself blushing when he entered the little meeting room. There were six people gathered there, the sexes equally represented, split down the middle by the smartly polished table. His apology was met with a silent stare but that wasn't what brought the blood rushing to his cheeks. He cursed himself for not having had the forethought to check who would be there. Freyja's name would have set off alarm bells and given him time to prepare. He could have phoned her beforehand, asked her to forget their previous encounter for as long as it took to interview the child. Instead, he was doomed either to suffer her black looks or to discuss their private affairs in front of the others. Well, that was out of the question. He debated asking her to step outside with him for a moment but thought better of it. Her expression, from what he could see out of the corner of his eye, suggested she was unlikely to cooperate.

'What the hell do you mean by turning up so late?' barked a man in a suit that appeared to have shrunk in the wash. The snug fit was probably in fashion; young men strutted out of law firms and banks dressed like that. And the tie, too – so dazzling it was almost fluorescent. Achingly trendy. Like the man's hair, which was too styled for the casual effect he was no doubt aiming at. Between the garish tie and sleek coiffure was one of those nondescript faces that were impossible to recall afterwards; the sort of face criminals dream of possessing. Neither ugly nor handsome, neither coarse- nor fine-featured. No distinguishing marks, no scars or freckles. Only eyes, nose and mouth, all neatly set in the appropriate places. It took Huldar a moment to figure out that he'd seen the guy before. He had a feeling his name was Konrád. A prosecutor. So it was unfortunate their relationship should have got off on such a bad footing.

Still, Huldar was glad the man had shouted at him; it gave him an excuse not to have to speak to Freyja. He knew why the prosecutor had raised his voice; few methods were as effective as threats and reprimands. Recently the senior officers in CID had attended a management course on how to offer praise and incentives, but their subsequent attempts to employ this technique had merely proved how ineffectual it was. Personally he couldn't imagine praise galvanising him the way a good bollocking did. But unfortunately this trendy lawyer was unlikely to respond well to being bawled out in return, and the others certainly wouldn't appreciate it. It was time for the kid-glove approach.

'Like I said, something came up.' Huldar refrained from explaining that his useless boss, Egill, had been unable until the last minute to make up his mind who to send. Huldar hadn't for a moment expected it to be him; he was used to being overlooked when positions of responsibility were doled out. They were usually assigned to older, more experienced men, as long as they weren't so old that they were on their way out. As a result he had given up hope of ascending the ranks. He wasn't like his colleagues; he had a different mindset and didn't offer unquestioning obedience, which meant he had few supporters among the top brass. So while his colleagues were speculating over who was likely to lead the investigation, he had been quietly sipping his coffee, not dreaming that he could be in with a chance. He wasn't the only one taken aback by his boss's belated announcement that he had just been promoted.

The silence around the table was broken by an older man. His hair and clothes looked dishevelled, his big hands rested on the table with fingers clasped as though in prayer. 'I've had enough of this. Margrét and I are leaving.'

Huldar guessed this was the girl's grandfather, who had been given temporary custody until her father could take over. The father had returned from America that morning, been met at the airport by the police and taken straight to the station for questioning. As far as Huldar knew, the interview was still going on. If only Egill had got his act together sooner, Huldar could have directed it himself. Now he would have to make do with the transcript.

Through the glass, Huldar saw that the little girl Margrét

was crying and a young, dark-haired woman in a yellow dress was trying to comfort her. The quiet sobbing was relayed over the intercom in the middle of the table, together with the woman's soothing words. Having witnessed the scene at the girl's house, he wasn't surprised she was crying. He'd gathered that a judge had recommended the girl should be interviewed at the Children's House after it proved impossible to persuade her to set foot in the police station.

Faced with her inconsolable grief, Huldar felt profoundly relieved by the arrangement. He couldn't picture himself in the role of the woman who was now drying Margrét's tears. Especially not in the spartan interview room at the station. It seemed he wasn't the only one affected by the sobbing, because Freyja suddenly reached over and switched off the intercom.

A strained silence ensued and the group's attention shifted from Huldar to Margrét and the woman in the yellow dress, as though they were watching a huge flat-screen TV with the volume turned down.

No one said a word but they were probably all thinking the same thing. What had the girl seen or heard? It was still unclear how long she had been under the bed and how she had come to be there in the first place. But since it seemed unlikely she had hidden there after the murder had taken place, the logical conclusion was that she must be in possession of crucial information about the night's events. Her brothers, who had been found wandering around outside the house, hadn't been aware of anything, so there was nothing to be gained from them. Their interviews had already been satisfactorily completed. The boys' statements were consistent and in spite of their youth they had been able to give coherent accounts of what had happened. They had woken up in the morning to find their bedroom door locked, and after banging and shouting in vain, they had climbed out of the window. The woman next door had spotted them in the street. She claimed she had slept like a log that night but her husband said he'd been woken a couple of times by a noise he couldn't identify. Huldar and his colleagues thought Elísa had probably managed to scream more than once while the murderer was preparing her slow, grisly demise. Only a few metres separated the master bedrooms of the two houses, so her cries could conceivably have carried in through the neighbours' open window. The police had interviewed the other neighbours but none had noticed any comings or goings in the night or anything else out of the ordinary.

All the indications were that Margrét was the only witness. It had proved impossible to lure her out from under the bed and in the end Huldar had resorted to dragging her out by force. He had managed, with some difficulty, to carry her out of the room without letting her see her mother's body or the ghastly thing that had been done to her head. They hadn't been able to get a word out of the girl at the time. She had refused to look at him and kept straining her head away, covering her ears and screwing her eyes shut. After Huldar had made several unsuccessful attempts to question her, the pathologist had intervened, ordered him to stop, and phoned for an ambulance. He had been extremely concerned about the girl's mental state. After the children had been examined at the hospital, social services had placed them with their paternal grandparents until their father came home. No one said as much but everyone involved in the investigation knew it would be best to complete Margrét's interview before father and daughter were reunited. The man was more likely to create difficulties than the grandparents. He was bound to be in shock and might also have something to hide. In the majority of cases where women were murdered in their own homes, a husband or lover was responsible. They had not yet been able to verify that he had left the country before his wife was killed, though all the evidence suggested that he had. Even so, that wouldn't necessarily clear him. If their marriage had been on the rocks, for example, it wasn't out of the question that he could have hired somebody else to do the job.

All of which reminded Huldar how urgent it was to complete the girl's interview. Yet it seemed to have broken down irretrievably. The child's grandfather was on his feet and judging from his expression he would not take kindly to a request for more time. Before Huldar could even broach the subject, the older man spoke again: 'This is an absolute disgrace. I'm not sitting through a moment more of this farce. How do I get in there?' He was watching his granddaughter as though prepared to break the glass to reach her.

'I'll take you.' A woman Huldar didn't recognise showed him to the door. Her face was grim, though the smile lines round her eyes and bracketing her mouth hinted that this harshness didn't come naturally to her. She bestowed such a glare on Huldar as she walked past that he half expected to be jabbed by an elbow. From the badge on her breast, she appeared to be a nurse.

'What the hell do we do now?' The prosecutor Konrád was torn between exasperation and despair.

'Did you get any information out of her?' Huldar affected to be cool and unruffled. He had long ago learnt the trick of not letting other people's agitation disconcert him. His five sisters had made sure of that. It was how he had emerged victorious from the majority of their quarrels. As an adult he had tried to apply the technique to his private life, but it had backfired badly in the few serious relationships he'd had. For some reason the method that worked so well on other occasions proved disastrous in quarrels with girlfriends. Before he knew what was happening the situation would have been turned on its head; suddenly he was in the wrong, and he invariably ended up saying something he regretted. Little by little the relationships would fall apart, however hard he tried to undo the damage. He suspected that the conversation he would sooner or later be forced to have with Freyja would end the same way. If she spoke to him at all, that is. His decision to abandon the search for a permanent relationship and concentrate on one-night stands instead had cost him dear. First there was all the crap he had gone through with Ríkhardur's wife Karlotta, and now this. Still, coming unexpectedly face to face with Freyja was nothing compared to the nightmare that had followed his and Karlotta's brief interlude last autumn. A shudder ran down his spine at the thought.

'Of course we didn't manage to ask her anything. You were supposed to supply the questions.' Freyja sounded just like his ex-girlfriends at their most pissed off.

Deciding, in the light of experience, that it was better to ignore this, Huldar addressed the prosecutor instead. 'You must be as well informed about the case as I am, Konrád, if not better. Couldn't you have started the ball rolling while you were waiting for me?' He avoided Freyja's eye as he talked. Her withering look threw him; his sisters could have learnt a lot from her. He was assailed by a sudden craving for nicotine gum. 'You could have asked some simple, obvious questions without me. The whole thing's recorded, isn't it? I could have listened to the answers afterwards.'

At this point a woman, who Huldar recognised as a doctor associated with the Children's House, decided to weigh in. He had heard her testifying in sexual abuse trials and her mechanical delivery had seemed appropriate in the courtroom, but now she sounded rather more heated. 'Or *you* could have had the courtesy to turn up on time.'

'Yes, granted.' Huldar didn't bother to explain. It would do no good to say he'd come as fast as he could. He'd rather take the blame than try to shift it on to someone else.

'The only thing we could get out of her before she retreated into her shell was that the murderer is probably black.' Konrád shook his head. 'Though I wouldn't put any faith in that. There was no chance to question her further.'

'Black?' Huldar made an effort to hide his relief for fear of being misunderstood. It had nothing to do with race; only that if the girl was right, it shouldn't be difficult to track down the killer. There weren't many black people in Iceland, and those who did live there must be the peace-loving type as Huldar couldn't off the top of his head remember a single violent incident involving a black person. Though it was bound to happen sooner or later.

'And he's got a very big head, don't forget that.' Freyja addressed this to Konrád, as if Huldar wasn't present.

'Big head?' Huldar frowned. 'Is there a recording of this?'

The others were looking at Freyja, so she was forced to answer, though her reluctance was obvious. 'Yes,' she snapped. 'You can have it later.' The others seemed a little taken aback by her tone.

Konrád broke the awkward silence that followed. 'It's hardly worth your while listening to the recording. It was totally unsatisfactory.' He sighed heavily. 'Anyway, we need to decide the next move. How are we to proceed?' His eyes dropped to his phone as if seeking the answer there. 'We could always take her to the station, whether she likes it or not, and finish it off there. We really can't postpone any longer.'

'No. Agreed.' Out of the corner of his eye Huldar saw Freyja stalk out of the room. A moment later she reappeared on the other side of the glass where she started talking to the young woman in the yellow dress. Margrét had gone, presumably with her grandfather.

'That would be extremely inadvisable.' The doctor now sounded like the automaton familiar from the courtroom. 'The girl's seriously traumatised and you risk compromising her evidence if you handle her in a clumsy, ignorant manner. How often do we have to remind you people?' She showed with a forceful gesture of her hand that she was referring to Konrád and Huldar as representatives of the State Prosecutor and police. 'Children of that age are extremely suggestible; they have an overwhelming tendency to say what they think people want to hear. If you want to confuse her and implant a false impression in her head, then by all means carry on. And good luck when the defence lawyer – if you ever apprehend the culprit – makes mincemeat of her testimony in court. If I've understood correctly, it's not as if you have any other witnesses.'

'That has yet to be established.' Huldar spoke against his own conviction. Naturally they would interview the husband and friends of the dead woman, her closest colleagues and so on, but it was practically a foregone conclusion that these people would know nothing about what had happened that night. The interviews would merely serve to round out their picture of the victim and, with luck, provide pointers about anyone who could conceivably have resorted to such an appallingly brutal act.

Huldar caught himself staring at Freyja through the glass. Easy on the eye though she was, it wasn't her appearance that drew his attention but the fact that from their body language she and the woman in the yellow dress appeared to be discussing something important. The woman who had been talking to Margrét was holding a hand to her breast and seemed upset. Perhaps it wasn't surprising – her role was to prevent the child from becoming distressed. He glanced quickly away when Freyja turned and seemed to be looking straight into his eyes. Then he remembered the mirror. He returned his attention to the doctor. 'But, in spite of that, I agree with you that we should stick to the present arrangement if possible. When do you think we can have another go?'

The doctor shrugged. 'They'd know better than me.' She gestured at the glass. Freyja and the woman in the yellow dress were leaving the interview room. 'Though I assume we won't make any further attempt today.'

'I'm sorry but that's out of the question.' Huldar shook his head. 'We need to speak to her without delay. And that means today. We urgently need answers, even if only to a few basic questions.'

Behind him he heard a cough. When he looked round, Freyja was there. It was uncomfortable having to meet her gaze. He realised that she was as stunning as he remembered, and the faint, familiar scent of her conjured up memories that were inappropriate, to say the least, given the situation. Pulling himself together, he pushed the thoughts away.

'Right at the end, Margrét told Silja something you'll want to know.'

Huldar interrupted before Freyja could continue. 'What was it? Could she give a better description than just his skin colour?'

'If I can finish?' Freyja's colour had risen. He seemed to have sunk even lower in her estimation. 'Margrét told Silja that the black man was going to kill again. Another woman.'

Suddenly Huldar no longer cared what Freyja thought of him.

Chapter 6

Elísa Bjarnadóttir lay naked on the stainless steel dissection table in the National Hospital pathology department, as if patiently waiting for the post-mortem to be over. But her rigid attitude – slim arms at her sides, legs straight – was one no living person would adopt. Her long, dark hair hung from the table, still wet from the wash they had given her body after they had completed the external examination and the nightmarish task of prising the duct tape off her head. Countless strips of tape were now hanging on a drying frame in the corner. It was hoped that some of the murderer's hairs would be found clinging to them. Naturally, the innermost layer was covered in Elísa's own hair, although they had exercised the greatest possible care when removing it. The strips would also be checked for fingerprints, in case the murderer had touched the tape with bare hands. The forensic technicians certainly had their work cut out. They were unlikely to discover any prints, though, given that none had been found on the body apart from those belonging to the policeman who was first on the scene. The presumption was that the murderer had been wearing gloves since it must have been necessary to manhandle the woman quite a bit.

From the thirteen bruises he had found, the pathologist concluded that the killer had attacked Elísa violently and that she had fought back. She must have done. It was unthinkable that she would have surrendered to her horrific fate without a struggle. The white flesh of her arms was covered in marks left by hard fingers, and the pathologist deduced from the large, round contusion on her chest that her assailant had leant the full weight of his knee on her. The front teeth in her upper and lower jaws had been smashed, apparently by the brutal act of forcing the metal tube of the vacuum cleaner down her throat. The pathologist assumed they would find the broken crowns in her stomach. Her nose was grotesquely squashed to one side, and this, along with the welts left across her face by the tape, which had not faded when she was washed, provided further visual evidence of her ordeal. In the corner of the lab, beside the drying frame, a silver vacuum cleaner sat waiting to be taken away for further analysis. Recalling the circumstances in which he had first seen it, Huldar felt an impulse to avert his eyes. The sight of the woman was even worse, yet it wasn't easy to look away either.

The occasional drip fell from her shining, wet hair and a small puddle had collected on the tiled floor underneath.

'It's not every day you're faced with something like this.' The pathologist shook his head. 'I saw some grim stuff during my training in Scotland, but since coming home I've had nothing like this land on my table.'

'Any vacuum-cleaner killings there?' Huldar hoped his voice wouldn't betray him. He'd seen a fair amount in his job, including dead bodies and people smashed up in accidents and fights. Two images in particular rose to mind: one of an ear torn off a man when his car had turned over, which Huldar had found lying on a bed of moss; the other of a body in the aftermath of a house-fire, which had fused to the melted linoleum. But these and countless other unpleasant incidents had felt different somehow; not nearly as upsetting. He'd never before had to poke around inside a corpse or watch as a pathologist probed every orifice in search of specimens that might shed light on the identity of her killer.

Up to now Huldar had managed to avoid post-mortems; others had dealt with that side of things in the few murder investigations he had worked on. And just as his bosses had shielded him when he was a rank-and-file officer, so he couldn't delegate the task to a subordinate now that he was in charge of his first major inquiry. He would have to tough it out. If word got around that he couldn't hack it, he'd be head of the investigation in name only. His team would spend more time bitching about his lack of balls than obeying orders – not that they would cope any better. He'd command as little respect as Ríkhardur. It wasn't a case of becoming desensitised to the horror but of putting on a brave face, faking indifference, even though his insides were turning over at the sight and smell.

'I don't just mean in Scotland. Have you ever heard or read about anything like this?'

The pathologist shook his head. 'No, not that I remember. I've read about some pretty unorthodox murder weapons, like high-heels and even a corkscrew, but never a vacuum cleaner.'

'No. It's not exactly the first thing that springs to mind if you want to kill somebody.' Huldar glanced briefly at Elísa's battered, waxen face, then away again. 'I'm asking myself, why go to all that trouble? It would have been much simpler to use a knife.' A large kitchen knife had been found at the foot of the bed, along with three rolls of duct tape; only the cardboard centres had been left of two, but there were still several metres' worth of silver tape on the third. It had been used to blindfold Elísa and block off her eyes, ears and nose, presumably to ensure that the vacuum cleaner could do its job without drawing in any more air. A preliminary examination indicated that the knife had been used to cut the tape. No blood had been found on the blade or anywhere else at the scene.

'Yes, you'd have thought so. The M.O.'s so outlandish that in your shoes I'd concentrate my energies on that. Is the murderer trying to make the history books? Does he have a phobia about blood or prefer to kill by some method that doesn't involve piercing the flesh? Or could it be symbolic in some way? That's plausible. Otherwise it's hard to imagine why he would come up with such a bizarre method.'

'What if he's a psycho?' The thought had struck Huldar the instant he laid eyes on the scene in the victim's bedroom. He hadn't had the time or imagination to come up with any alternative explanations.

'A psycho?' The pathologist appeared surprised by the question. 'I assume you're referring to a psychotic. You'd better be careful if you're going to pursue that angle. The mentally ill are rarely violent. In fact, they're much more likely to be victims than perpetrators. And if they do act violently, it's usually against themselves. No, I don't think you're looking for someone who's mentally ill. He's almost certainly got a serious personality disorder, but the evidence doesn't point to the sort of hallucinations or delusions associated with psychosis.'

'No. Maybe not.' Huldar wasn't prepared to abandon the insanity theory entirely, though he was willing to put it to one side while considering the method and the murderer's apparent squeamishness about blood or piercing and cutting flesh. Unfortunately, though, this was unlikely to provide them with a lead, since there was no national database of people's phobias. Then again, the angle might come in useful once they had a suspect in their sights. If they ever reached that point.

While the pathologist was preparing the next stage, Huldar inspected the small, transparent plastic bags and glass jars on the trolley beside the table. If no evidence was obtained from the adhesive tape, it was still possible that these biological specimens might help identify the culprit. Some of the jars had already been removed, since the assistant had taken advantage of the hiatus to pass them on for analysis.

As a rule, Icelandic murderers confessed as soon as they were caught, so cases were rarely won or lost on the strength of forensic evidence, though occasionally it had to be produced in court to bring stubborn individuals to their senses. In practice, most saw the light once the evidence was stacked up against them, and even seemed relieved at the chance to unburden themselves. Before you knew it they were busy trying to convince themselves and others that it was all an accident; they were fundamentally decent people and the whole thing had been an unfortunate mistake. It was amazing how keen most were to ingratiate themselves with the police in an attempt to make them understand their side of the story. As if it mattered. It wasn't the police's job to pass judgement, merely to establish the facts. Huldar wondered if Elísa's murderer would react the same way once he was standing before him. How would he justify what he had done? Or would he belong to the tiny minority who never confessed?

A clear, viscous fluid oozed from the corner of Elísa's mouth like a teardrop that had gone astray. Huldar raised his eyes to the pathologist, only to see that he had picked up an electric saw. His stomach turned over.

The doctor examined the tool as if debating its suitability. Then, apparently satisfied, he placed it on a tray with the other instruments. Each looked more sinister than the last. You could tell they weren't designed with a living patient in mind: Huldar would have run a mile if he saw a doctor approaching him with one of those.

'Who do you suspect? The husband?'

'Too soon to tell. He's only just got back to the country. They questioned him this morning but I haven't had a chance to read the transcript yet. I had to dash straight here from the Children's House. But I had a word with one of the guys who interviewed him and it sounds unlikely he was involved. According to them he's distraught. And we've got confirmation that he was abroad when the murder was committed. He was at a conference with another Icelander who travelled over with him, so he can't have gone anywhere near the actual killing. Though maybe he's a good actor – paid someone else to do his dirty work. The only information we've managed to extract from the little girl so far is that the killer was black.'

'Black? That should make your life easier.' The pathologist's expression grew serious again. 'What sort of state's she in?'

'Shit.' There was no other word to describe Margrét's condition. Huldar steered the conversation back to the murder, uncomfortable about discussing the girl in the presence of her mother's corpse. 'It's not clear yet if she meant the man was wearing black trousers and shoes, or if she was referring to his skin colour. She probably got a glimpse of his feet and legs from under the bed, though she claims she saw his head too, presumably before she crawled into hiding. She described it as unusually big.'

'Big?'

'That's what she said. But what would a child regard as a big head? I don't know.' Huldar lowered his eyes to avoid having to watch as the pathologist prepared to resume work. The little he had seen so far had been gruesome enough. He half hoped the assistant had got lost in the hospital's labyrinthine corridors so the second part of the post-mortem would have to be postponed. He was desperate for nicotine but couldn't stomach the idea of putting anything in his mouth. Certainly not gum. Even if a lit cigarette was placed between his lips he wasn't sure he could face smoking it. The less he inhaled in here, the better.

'Don't ask me. Can't you get an artist to sit down with her?'

'Sure. All in good time. She's refusing to see anyone at the moment, so we've given her a bit of breathing space. We'll test the water again later this afternoon or this evening. We urgently need to get this straight. I can't send my people out hunting for a dark-skinned suspect when she could have been referring to his clothes.' Huldar suddenly remembered what he had wanted to ask the pathologist. 'Elísa's husband is a doctor here at the hospital.'

The pathologist raised his eyebrows. 'Oh? Who is he?'

'Sigvaldi Freysteinsson. He's a gynaecologist.'

'Never heard of him. Is he the same age as his wife?'

'Yes.'

'Then I'm unlikely to have come across him. They're a different generation. I'm so old I hardly know any of the younger doctors.' The pathologist snapped on a pair of latex gloves. 'Leaving aside her husband, I'd be willing to bet she knew her killer. It's rare for a complete stranger to attack a victim with the sole purpose of torturing them. And you can't call this anything else. Though her death can't have taken long, her ordeal must have been indescribable. You saw her teeth – it would have required an act of incredible brutality to shove the tube down her throat. And the air was sucked out of her lungs with such force that they collapsed, probably resulting in burst eardrums and a number of other internal injuries that we'll discover when we open her up. It won't be pretty, I can promise you that. No, Iceland's too small to contain an individual sick enough to do that to a victim picked at random. He'd have been identified and taken out of circulation long ago, before something like this happened.'

'We can't be sure of that.'

'Maybe not, but fortunately torture's uncommon here in the West, at least as an end in itself. In the rare instances when it's used it's generally associated with extreme sexual abuse. You do occasionally hear of examples among the criminal underworld in big cities abroad, but our home-grown thugs have stopped short of it up to now. Sure, they administer beatings but as far as I know their method of torture usually consists of intimidation. No one's died or incurred permanent physical damage from being tortured in Iceland. If they had, I'd have heard about it. It doesn't matter how tough you are, if you're tortured, you'll take yourself to hospital as fast as you can. The incident would show up in the system.'

'Yes, I suppose you're right. What kind of sick bastard would be capable of this?'

'That's the million-dollar question. However much they might want to torture someone to death, few people would be capable of it. Most of us have inhibitions that prevent us from overstepping the conventional moral boundaries. Which brings us back to the fact that no sharp weapons were used and the act itself merely consisted of pressing a switch.' The pathologist turned his head to Huldar. 'Of course I can't be certain, but given that there's no evidence of rape, I would assume that the person who did this felt an overpowering loathing for the woman. There's no sign that the attack was sexually motivated – unless semen turns up at the scene. It's not unknown for perverts to masturbate over the victim instead of committing rape. But none was discovered while I was there, and I think it's unlikely we'd have missed it.'

'None was found during the second examination of the house either.'

'Was she involved in anything shady? Should I be prepared to find traces of illegal substances in her bloodstream?'

'No. Not that we're aware. So far, the little we've dug up on her suggests she was squeaky clean. She worked for the tax office, looked after her family and did the usual outdoorsy stuff in her free time. Her life looks so blameless that I'd be astonished if we uncovered anything dodgy – and even more so if she was tortured to reveal information of some kind. It would have to have been one hell of a secret or you'd assume she'd have been falling over herself to confess when threatened with a hideous fate like that.' His eyes strayed inadvertently to her disfigured face. The blue lips were parted to reveal a glimpse of broken front teeth. Overwhelmed by nausea, he dropped his gaze. 'I doubt there's any point trying to get our heads round what motivated him. Nothing could justify what he did.'

'Are you positive it was a man? In the absence of semen you could potentially be looking at a woman.'

Huldar thought. He was no more confident about that than about any other aspect of the case as the investigation had only just got off the ground. 'No. Not necessarily. But I'm inclined to think it was a man, and that would fit with the girl's testimony as well. A woman would have had more difficulty pinning Elísa down while she wound the tape round her head and arms. She must have put up a hell of a fight.'

'Indeed. As her injuries suggest.' Both men contemplated the bruises on the body. 'Of course there are plenty of strong women out there, but Elísa seems to have been in good physical shape, so her attacker would have had to be unusually tough. Unless she acted in a frenzy. Madness can lend people strength.'

'Some frenzy. How long do you think it would have taken?' Huldar had seen people go berserk, both sober and under the influence of drugs or drink. That sort of outburst seldom lasted long, though there were always exceptions.

'Hard to say. I'd estimate that the attack lasted around twenty to thirty minutes, but I doubt the post-mortem or any further tests will be able to give us a more precise answer. We can probably establish the actual time of death with more accuracy, but that's all.'

Huldar nodded. It was about what he'd guessed. The man must have been in a hurry to finish. He wouldn't have wanted to be in the house any longer than strictly necessary. 'Have you any idea about a possible motive?' The question was a delaying tactic. Huldar needed a little more time to prepare himself mentally and physically before the pathologist embarked on the internal examination. The assistant had reappeared in the doorway, which presumably meant the next stage was about to begin.

'No idea. I'm glad to say that's your problem, not mine. The post-mortem's unlikely to provide an explanation. That's not how it works. But for what it's worth, my immediate guess would be that she'd exposed someone through her job at the tax office. I'd look into that angle, anyway. People can become completely unhinged at the thought of losing money. Especially if they stand to lose everything.' The man scratched his chin, his glove leaving a powdery white mark. 'There's one thing I forgot to ask. What was in the envelope? Did that shed any light on the matter?'

During the preliminary investigation of the crime scene they had found an envelope on the fridge. Unlike the rest of the memos and pictures fixed there with decorative magnets, it was stuck on by one corner, using the same silver tape as had been wrapped around Elísa's head and arms. No fingerprints had been found on the envelope, which turned out to contain a message formed of letters and numbers cut out of newspapers, like a kidnap note in a movie.

'We don't understand the message, if it is a message. All it said was: "So tell me", followed by a colon, then a long string of numbers that don't make any sense. We've got people working on it but they haven't got very far yet.' That was an understatement: they hadn't got anywhere at all. 'I made a photocopy in case you wanted it for your records.'

The pathologist pushed his glasses a little further down his nose and studied the series of numbers: *53, 16 · 53, 90–1 · 4, 43–6, 65–5, 68 · 43–6, 8 · 106–16, 53, 23, 63–92 · 90, 89–6, 7 · 43–6, 8 · 75, 58, 53, 23, 63–92.*

'What on earth is it supposed to mean?'

'It's anybody's guess at this stage. It didn't ring any bells with the husband and we still haven't come up with any ideas. The guys who've been studying it think it's a code that could prove impossible to crack. They believe the numbers represent letters and the dots probably mark word breaks, but the dashes are a mystery. And we have no idea if it's in Icelandic. We'll continue to work on it, but it may well be the product of a deranged mind, which only makes sense to the person who wrote it.'

'Well, that's possible.' The pathologist sounded unconvinced. 'But don't forget what I said before about psychotics. It would have required considerable effort to construct this note; to cut out the numbers, arrange them in the right order and glue them to the paper. I myself wouldn't go to that sort of trouble unless it served a purpose. You get the impression he has an agenda. In fact, it looks like a personal message. Don't you agree?' He put down the photocopy and spread a piece of plastic over it to prevent it from being splashed when he got to work with the saw and forceps.

Huldar tried to distract himself from what was about to happen by concentrating hard on the conversation. 'Yes, maybe.' The more he had racked his brains over the words and the series of numbers that followed them, the less sense they had made. Why use a code in the first place? Who was the intended recipient and what could the message mean? It could hardly be for Elísa since the murderer had killed her before she had a chance to open the envelope. So, logically it must have been intended for the police or for her husband Sigvaldi, though he claimed to be completely in the dark about what it could mean. Perhaps they would discover something in Sigvaldi's past, though he swore he had no enemies.

Huldar half hoped they would uncover some terrible crime he'd committed, which would enable the inquiry to get off the ground. They needed a lead if the investigation wasn't going to be stuck forever. If the post-mortem didn't throw up anything new, it was hard to see how they were to proceed. He glanced at Elísa's maimed body and swallowed. Any minute now he would see what she looked like inside. A wave of dizziness hit him and the colour drained from his face.

The pathologist held out a pot that he had taken from his assistant. 'Rub some of this under your nose. I can tell you're not feeling too good, but believe you me, the next bit's the really tough part. The smell will be pretty overpowering but the cream helps. It doesn't entirely block it out but it'll make it more bearable.' Smiling, he put on the mask that had been hanging round his neck. 'If you need to vomit, make sure you don't get any on the body. It's been known and I never want to have to go through that again. Remember to pull down the mask first as well. I don't want to have to witness that again either.'

Huldar nodded and took the pot. The gelatinous cream reeked so strongly of mint or menthol that it made his eyes sting. He had used it before; bad smells went with the territory. He donned the mask, which helped a little but did nothing to diminish his dread. Watching the pathologist prising open every orifice in her body had almost unmanned him. The rest hadn't been quite as bad, but he'd felt ill the whole time the doctor was probing the dead woman. The worst part was when he examined her face. Although Huldar knew better he had kept expecting to see twitches of pain round Elísa's eyes and mouth; goodness knows what he would start imagining when he saw the pathologist wielding the saw.

'Ready?'

Huldar read doubt in the pathologist's eyes. He nodded with little conviction, and the doctor shrugged.

'You don't have to be present unless you really want to. Your predecessors set up this arrangement. They thought it was a good idea. I can't say I see any point in it except to provide us with a bit of company.' He nodded at his assistant who grinned and snapped on a mask. 'Perhaps it'll make you doubly determined to catch the culprit.'

'Perhaps.' There might be something in what the man said. Huldar already felt a burning desire to see the killer behind bars and that desire was definitely stronger now than when he had arrived. It would violate his sense of justice if the person responsible for this atrocity got away scot-free. It was unthinkable.

The pathologist's gloved hand hovered over the tray of shiny instruments. He seemed unable to decide which should have the honour of starting the job. Huldar watched, trying to predict which one he'd pick. But before he could reach a conclusion, the pathologist turned and looked him in the eye for a moment before saying: 'Doesn't it strike you as a bit odd that you were assigned this case?'

Huldar was riled by the implicit doubt in his abilities, not least because it was precisely what he himself had been wondering. 'What are you implying?'

'Oh, you know. This is one of the most brutal murders ever to come our way. I'd never have dreamt of asking one of the juniors in my department to perform the post-mortem. Is it possible that you've been chosen for other reasons than your competence? As far as I know, CID has plenty of detectives more experienced than you.'

'I'm not the right person to answer that.' In fact, he could have given a more honest explanation, which was that all the most senior detectives had seriously blotted their copybooks. CID had been having major image problems in the wake of an inquiry into past misconduct, an inquiry that had been launched when it emerged that a special prosecutor, appointed to preside over the investigation into criminal activity related to the banking collapse, had committed gross breaches of the law when collecting evidence. As the majority of the prosecutor's team had previously served in the police, the decision had been taken to check whether this reflected endemic malpractice in the force. This had opened up a whole can of worms. The list of violations turned out to be a long one: phone-tapping; house and office searches undertaken without a warrant; paperwork fixed after the event; evidence going astray; attempts to suborn witnesses; the use of psychological – and physical – violence. The media storm had lasted for weeks, and the names of all the high-ranking detectives had been dragged through the mud. There had been no firings or demotions, however, and Huldar doubted it would come to that. The most galling part was that the majority of police officers performed their roles with integrity, but as long as the bad apples escaped sanctions, it cast a shadow over the rest. Regrettably, though, it seemed that nothing was going to change; the detectives in question were determined to ride out the storm. Over the years the occasional officer had been exposed for even worse offences without being held to account, and clearly this had set a precedent. The upshot of it all was that those implicated were keen to keep their heads below the parapet until the furore had died down. Whoever led this inquiry would have to hold press conferences and the last thing any of them wanted was to remind the public that they were still holding on to their positions. So the job had fallen to Huldar. He had a clean record at work, even if he wasn't quite so angelic in his private life.

'Don't take it personally. I just wanted to warn you. If you were assigned this case for the reasons I suspect, and I think you suspect them too, you can be sure your colleagues won't want to see you succeed on your own merit. Although they desperately want this case solved they would probably prefer you to trip up along the way. So watch your back. I mean that kindly. If you cock up this investigation, you may not get another break. Certainly not any time soon and most likely never.'

Huldar was silent. The reek of menthol was suffocating and he snatched a gulp of fresh air under the mask. The pathologist's eyes crinkled in an invisible smile, then he clapped his hands together as a sign that it was time to start work. He selected a scalpel and aimed it over Elísa's abdomen. Huldar took up position beside him and closed his eyes as the man cut a long incision down the woman's sternum.

Chapter 7

Sunday

The newsreader sounded grave, almost sad. Ástrós Einarsdóttir usually liked the woman. When she was reporting something cheerful, like a festival in town or the opening of a new road, there was no disguising her pleasure. Occasionally she overdid it slightly, sounding as though she had some personal stake in the affair, as if she were in charge of the festivities herself or had been waiting impatiently for a new stretch of road to some benighted spot. But she adopted a more sombre tone when she had serious news to impart and slowed her delivery to ensure that every word would get across.

Like now.

In this case the slow delivery might also have been intended to spin out the announcement since the report itself was brief and uninformative in the extreme: a woman had died in Reykjavík on Thursday night and the police were not ruling out murder. They were refusing to release any further details at this stage. Given that there seemed to be nothing more to say, she wondered why they had reported the incident at all. Why should people be so desperate to know about a possible murder? Couldn't they wait until the facts had been established? Personally, Ástrós felt she had gained nothing by hearing the news.

She stood up to turn down the volume before the sports news, which hurt her ears as badly as the screech of chalk on a blackboard, a sound she had never got used to in all her years of teaching. She had welcomed the advent of board markers and never minded when someone forgot to replace the lid and the ink dried up. Anything was better than the grating noise, dry skin and dust associated with chalk. She switched off the radio and immediately felt better. This was the only positive change to have come about as a result of her husband's death nearly two years ago. He used to sit glued to the radio while what seemed like every last match result in the world was read out, always with the volume turned up full blast. The arrival of the internet and the ability to check the results in peace and quiet had made no difference. No, he insisted on listening to the scores the old way.

But she missed the cosy companionship, the love and warmth, so badly that she would gladly have had a radio broadcasting twenty-four-hour sports news grafted to her ear if only it could have brought him back.

Ástrós's phone bleeped from the kitchen where it was lying beside the remains of her lunch. She'd prepared the food in a desultory manner, with no sense of anticipation. Since she'd stopped working it had ceased to make any difference if it was a weekday or a weekend. In the past, she would have taken the time to lay the table nicely, leaving a place for the newspapers beside her plate. She would have perused them as she ate, then had a nice cup of coffee. But now there was an endless list of unhealthy foods that the doctor had banned her from eating, which included butter, salt and fat; in other words almost everything that made food worthwhile. As a result there was no point taking trouble over her meals: cottage cheese with cucumber and spelt bread was never going to be particularly exciting, no matter what she did to dress it up.

The screen of her phone glowed blue and she picked it up curiously. These days few people contacted her on a Sunday. Or any other day, for that matter. And it was even more unusual for her to receive a text. Neither her sister nor her friends used this method of communication. They were as long-sighted as her and had difficulty finding the right buttons to press. She felt a certain smug satisfaction at being the only one who had worked out how to switch off the predictive texting function that was forever trying to pre-empt what she wanted to say.

Ástrós opened the message. It must be some mistake. Was it possible that autocorrect would suggest numbers too? *39, 8, 92 · 5, 3–53, 8, 8, 66 · 83, 43, 1.* It didn't resemble any sequence she could call to mind; no phone, credit card or lottery number. The sender was anonymous. Perhaps it was some sort of computer virus. Hers was a smartphone, after all.

Rather than waste any more time wondering, she decided to call the phone company. After a long wait she was put through to a young man who spoke very fast. She explained what had happened and answered his questions, but he seemed unable to grasp that she had all her marbles. She kept having to repeat herself and answer irrelevant questions. The phone bleeped again in the middle of their conversation, which confused her, especially since the young man claimed not to have heard anything. Finally, deciding this was futile, she rang off, still none the wiser about whether her phone had a virus. From what she had understood, she could submit a special request – on a working day – to have the message traced, though it had sounded from the way the young man phrased it as if the process wasn't that simple. Anyway, she didn't really care who had sent it, she just wanted to know if her phone needed to be scanned for viruses.

The bleep had heralded a second text consisting of another string of numbers, no less incomprehensible: *39, 8, 92 · 75 · 10, X, 65–5*. This couldn't be a good sign. Whatever that boy had said, the bloody phone probably had a virus. She considered ringing the telecom company again but couldn't face it.

The phone bleeped a third time. Another message from the same unknown sender: *66–39, 8 · 90, 63–92 · 42–8, 85, 108*. Ástrós hurriedly closed the message in case the virus spread. Then, to test that her phone was still working properly, she rang a friend. Their conversation had no sooner begun than she regretted her haste. The phone seemed to be working fine but now she was condemned to listen to her friend's description of the cruise she and her husband were planning. Ástrós couldn't suppress a twinge of envy, even though the couple weren't going for another eight months. In the end she managed to cut the conversation short in the middle of a solemn account of how much extra it would cost to book a cabin with a balcony, by lying that there was someone at the door. Ástrós reminded herself not to call this friend again for a while, at least not until she had got over the worst of her excitement.

The screen went dark after Ástrós had hung up and her phone seemed perfectly normal. Nevertheless, she picked it up and put it on silent. Tomorrow she'd take it to the shop and ask the people there to have a look at it. They would be able to find out what was wrong and sort it out if it did have a virus. She had nothing better to do, after all.

Yet again she regretted having stopped teaching. She had taken advantage of the rules on early retirement for public-sector workers, but a month after she resigned her post she had lost her husband to a heart attack. Once she had recovered from the initial shock and grief, she had taken herself down to the sixth-form college to which she had devoted most of her career to offer her services again. But by then the school had employed a young man in her place and she was no longer required to teach pupils the mysteries of biology.

The memory was still painful enough to bring a flush to her cheeks as she stood staring at her phone. At the time she had stammered that she had of course known about the new teacher but had simply wanted to offer herself as substitute; to cover for the young man when he was ill, for example, or they needed an examiner. Unfortunately, though, Ástrós had spoken with characteristic directness when she asked for her old job back and there had been no chance her words could be misconstrued. Since then she had avoided her old workplace. She couldn't face running into the head of HR or any of her old colleagues, aware the story must have got back to them.

Now that the radio was off and she was no longer talking on the phone the flat was uncomfortably quiet. She could even hear the people downstairs. Relations with her neighbours hadn't been particularly friendly since she was widowed. It had all started just before her husband died, when they couldn't agree on a colour to paint the building. Ástrós, who naturally hadn't been at her best after her bereavement, had insisted on the shade that she and her husband had both wanted, though in reality she didn't have a strong opinion. In the thick of grieving she had thought of the battle as a way of serving her husband's memory. With the passing of time, she had come to realise how foolish this was, but by then it was too late to undo the damage. Relations between the floors were beyond salvaging.

The dispute over the paint colour eventually died down, but it wasn't long before they fell out again. The couple downstairs claimed she wasn't doing her share of maintaining the garden and communal areas. However hard she tried, they always looked disapproving. She had attempted to discuss the matter with them and find a compromise – she would look after the garden and keep the dustbin store clean if they would touch up the paintwork, change the light-bulbs and keep the pavement clear of snow. The cost of tradesmen would be equally split. But that had really put the cat among the pigeons. The wife had snapped that they had drawn the short straw – summer, when the garden needed tending, only lasted three months a year, and the bin store didn't require much effort either. Whereas shovelling snow, changing light-bulbs and decorating involved far more work. Ástrós tried to point out that there was only one shared light-fitting and that she could take care of that if it mattered that much. But she couldn't shovel snow.

Eventually, since the couple seemed disinclined to cooperate, she had suggested paying someone else to take care of it all. That was when relations really deteriorated. The frustrating part was that when her husband was alive they had put much more effort into all the maintenance, snow-clearing and gardening than the people downstairs. But the neighbours had a short memory. How shabbily people could behave. The bloody man had dared to fling in her face at the height of their quarrel that he and his wife had always taken much better care of the communal areas and that they weren't going to stand for it any longer. He spoke with such conviction that Ástrós's certainty wavered. But only for a moment. Of course she and Geiri had done far more.

The memory made her want to stamp on the floor in the hope of annoying the couple, but she checked the impulse. Not because she thought it was a bad idea but because the phone on the table had suddenly lit up. Ástrós couldn't resist taking a quick peek. Yet another message, again from an unknown sender. She assumed they must all be from the same person, or it would be too much of a coincidence. To her relief the text consisted of letters this time, conveying the brief message: *Not long till my visit – excited?*

Whose visit? She wasn't expecting anyone. Was she? She couldn't remember issuing any invitations. Going into the hall, she peered in the mirror and saw that she would need to smarten herself up a bit if she was to receive guests. What a pity it didn't say when this mysterious visitor would arrive. *Not long till my visit.* That could mean anything, depending on where the sender was at the time. In the countryside? Abroad? In the next street?

Ástrós hurried into the bathroom and jumped in the shower after a brief debate with herself about whether she had time. She didn't want to answer the door in her dressing gown, hair wrapped in a towel and face bare of make-up, but she decided to go ahead anyway, and beat her own speed record. As she stood in front of the misted-up mirror, wiping away the steam, she felt depressed by her lonely fate. The way she was behaving you would have thought she hadn't seen another soul for days or even weeks. Well, this strange visitor who omitted to give their name could simply wait outside until she was ready.

She was confronted in the mirror by the alien face that had slowly but surely replaced her own in recent years. It looked like the face of a much older woman, with wrinkles round the eyes and mouth, deep creases across the forehead and pronounced pouches under the eyes. Who the hell are you? Who invited you to my party?

Picking up her foundation, Ástrós set to work concealing the worst signs of ageing. She went about it methodically, with no sense of urgency. What she did feel was an ominous foreboding that the visit would not bring her much joy. Where had that thought sprung from? The green light on her curling tongs lit up. She studied her face with some satisfaction, then put aside the make-up and began to do her hair, strand by strand. The hot smell of singeing helped her to relax. However pleasant or otherwise the visit turned out to be, at least she would look halfway decent.

Chapter 8

From the outside, the house looked no different from countless others built in the sixties and seventies. Plain concrete, single-storey, around 180 square metres, with a simple, sloping roof. The layout inside was no doubt designed to meet the requirements of another age: a master bedroom, separate dining room, poky kitchen and several tiny children's rooms with wardrobes to match, reflecting the limited choice of clothing available to kids in those days. A house of the type that, as a little girl, Freyja used to dream of living in when she grew up, together with a vaguely imagined husband and two beautiful children, one girl, one boy. And a cat and a fish-tank too. The complete opposite of her current existence.

Tubs containing the shrivelled remains of last summer's flowers flanked the gate, but these were the only reminders of mortality. The house stood innocently on its plot, as if nothing had happened there. If she hadn't known better she would have assumed that life was carrying on as normal inside; there was no cordon of yellow police tape – not even, as she would have expected, stretched across the front door. Freyja found herself wondering if the architect who had designed the house with a happy, nuclear family in mind would have changed anything had he known the fate that awaited the future occupant. Would he have drawn the windows larger to facilitate Elísa's escape, put in bars, installed huge security fences around the garden? Or given the house a more forbidding façade to warn the family off buying it? She studied the building through the dirty window of her car but came to no conclusion. She had parked outside in the road, for fear of spoiling any evidence that might still await discovery on the concrete drive, but given that the parking area wasn't cordoned off and there was a police car there already, her caution was probably unnecessary. Still, she didn't want to risk a reprimand for the sake of saving herself a few extra steps.

She had switched off the ignition but was still holding the key, reluctant to face the cold outside, though it wasn't that much warmer in her brother's clapped-out wreck of a car. The heater had given up the ghost on the way there and the windows had ice on the insides. The interior stank of old cigarette butts from the ashtray that she hadn't got round to cleaning out, and the colder it got, the worse the smell became. It wasn't helped by the sickly odour emanating from the cardboard Christmas tree dangling from the wonky rear-view mirror. The taste of this morning's fried eggs lingered in Freyja's mouth, clashing unpleasantly with the fragrance of artificial pine. She took a hefty swig of Coke to ward off incipient nausea. The half-frozen drink rattled in the can but slid down her throat smoothly enough. She felt a little better, and better still when she stepped outside and breathed in the fresh, wintry air.

God, it was cold. She wasn't dressed for visiting murder scenes or hanging about outdoors. When she received the call she had been on her way to meet her girlfriends for lunch in town and her clothes had been chosen to strike the right balance; not too scruffy, not too smart. Though she had probably erred towards the latter.

She fumbled with the zip of her jacket, impeded by her gloves, but finally managed to pull it up to her neck. Then she took a better look at the house. She could have sworn there was an ominous atmosphere, that the grey winter light had a gloomier, chillier quality here than it did over the neighbouring properties. But she was just being fanciful. Shrugging off her unease, she put the car keys in her jacket pocket and concentrated on breathing calmly. Thin clouds accompanied her breath, and the impacted snow on the pavement creaked underfoot. Apart from that a deathly hush reigned. The dense silence belonged to winter; it would be unthinkable in summer. There were no birds singing in the bare trees and nothing moved in the stillness. Freyja could have been alone in the world when suddenly she heard the slam of a door nearby, followed by rapid footsteps. Someone about to miss a bus, perhaps? Glancing round, Freyja saw that it was a woman. She was halfway to the house when the woman caught up with her.

'Hello. Excuse me.'

Freyja stopped and turned. The woman hadn't had time to wrap up properly before running outside. She stood there, teeth chattering, in a thin raincoat designed for a warmer season. Her hair was scraped back in an untidy ponytail, and only one of her eyes was made up, which gave her an oddly lopsided appearance.

'Excuse me, I'm Védís. I live next door. It was me who found the boys.'

Freyja looked over at her house, which was identical to Elísa's and Sigvaldi's, and saw the outline of a figure in the window. The husband, presumably. He moved away when he saw Freyja watching him. She returned her attention to the woman, who had started speaking again:

'We . . . I – the rest of us who live in the street, I mean – are very upset.'

Freyja was silent, unsure how to respond, which made the woman even more awkward. Freyja almost felt sorry for her; no doubt it had seemed like a good idea to dash outside in the hope of hearing news, but like many rash decisions it didn't seem so clever in practice.

'I was just hoping you could tell me how Sigvaldi and the kids are doing. We couldn't help noticing that you lot were round here yesterday and the day before, but no one will tell us anything. They asked me a ton of questions but wouldn't answer any of mine. Then I heard about a suspected murder on the lunchtime news and nearly had a heart attack. Is it the same case?'

'I'm afraid I can't help you. I'm not with the police.'

'Oh?' The woman frowned. 'Who are you with then?'

Freyja answered levelly: 'I'm a civil servant.' She didn't want to mention the Child Protection Agency or Children's House. It would only give the street more to gossip about, and it could lead to misunderstandings. When people heard mention of social services, their thoughts immediately went to unfit parents, while everyone knew that the Children's House was involved with sexual abuse cases. The police were bound to release more details soon and that would give the woman the information she desired. 'I'm afraid I'm not at liberty to comment on my reason for being here.'

The woman made a face as if Freyja were deliberately trying to exclude her.

'Well, we know something's happened.' All it needed was the addition of a petulant 'so there'. Instead the woman continued: 'We saw the ambulance arrive. And leave.' She opened her mouth, then closed it again. There was no mistaking it when a dead person was carried out to an ambulance; the sick or injured did not have their faces covered. 'It's driving us crazy not knowing what's happened. They're more than just next-door neighbours, you know. Elísa was quite a good friend of mine.' The woman appeared to be in her early thirties, the same age as Elísa, so this could well have been true. Freyja noticed that she referred to Elísa in the past tense. The woman shivered with cold, or perhaps it was a shudder. 'Who was it on the stretcher?'

'I'm sorry, I'm not allowed to comment. I'm sure more information will be made available soon.' Freyja kept her expression neutral, so the woman wouldn't be able to read her face.

Momentarily distracted, the woman glanced at something behind Freyja, then looked back at her. 'I've half a mind to complain about the way we've been treated. Me especially.' She was speaking quickly now, apparently guessing that their conversation was about to be cut short. How prescient of her.

'Well, I can't stop you.'

The anger that had briefly distorted the woman's features now gave way to resignation. 'Of course I won't really. I just thought it would be a basic courtesy to fill me in on what's happening. It's not like I'm a stranger or have nothing to do with it. I live next door and it was me who found the boys. So I'm involved, sort of. At least as a witness; I was given a real grilling by the police. Isn't there a duty to keep witnesses informed about the cases they're involved in?'

'I'm afraid it doesn't work like that.' Freyja hoped the woman would go away before she froze to the pavement. 'I'm sure they'll have another word with you once things have quietened down a bit. But I'm not part of the investigation team so I can't help you. Sorry.'

Freyja turned on her heel, putting an end to the conversation. Behind her she heard retreating footsteps. Now she could see what had attracted the woman's attention: Huldar was standing at the front door, subjecting her to a hostile glare. This morning's eggs suddenly repeated on her. It hadn't occurred to her he would be there in person. There were plenty of other officers who could have come instead, and she had assumed he would avoid her like the plague after their awkward reunion at the Children's House. Perhaps he was even odder than she'd thought. Freyja raised her chin and returned his disapproving stare with one of her own.

As she drew near she glimpsed a hand-painted plaque over his shoulder, announcing the names of the family. The decorative flowers in the corners had weathered away until only the odd petal remained but the black lettering was intact, and Elísa's name was uncomfortably conspicuous in the second row. That aside, there was little to see in the porch, only two brightly coloured sledges leaning against the wall, one stacked inside the other, and a brand-new snow shovel propped up in one corner, which was unlikely to be required any time soon. Digging out the drive would hardly be a priority in the immediate future.

'Hello.' Freyja did not extend her hand. She didn't want to touch the man, and anyway it would seem ludicrously formal in the circumstances.

'Hello.' Huldar sounded cross. He must be tired, judging

by the dark shadows under his eyes, the stubble and crumpled clothes. He appeared not to have changed since yesterday's fiasco at the Children's House. But as he stepped aside to let her enter, she realised his bad mood wasn't only due to lack of sleep.

'When I offered to meet you here I didn't expect you to start acting as police spokesman to the neighbours, or I'd never have agreed to it. We're more than capable of dealing with public relations ourselves.'

Freyja retorted indignantly: 'All I said to the woman was that I couldn't comment.'

Huldar was wrong-footed. 'Oh.' He coughed. 'Sorry. That couple have been lying in wait for us ever since we first arrived. They're both eaten up with curiosity.' He smiled sheepishly. 'I've had to tear a strip off so many of my own people for getting sucked into conversation with them that I automatically slipped into the same mode.'

'It doesn't matter.' But it did matter. Freyja couldn't stand criticism, especially not from him, and when she didn't even deserve it. She had come here to fetch clothes and other essentials for the three children. Since none of their relatives, not even their father, was permitted to enter the house, Freyja had agreed to help out, although it would make her late for lunch with her friends. As far as she was concerned she was doing the police a favour, so she had expected a rather different reception. 'Don't worry about it.'

She took care not to bump into a coat stand laden with jackets, woolly hats and scarves, most of them in bright, childish colours. The floor of the hall was littered with footwear as though the children had kicked off their shoes any old how when they came in. Freyja glanced around for a place to leave her own shoes. This was all new to her; she'd never visited a crime scene before and had no idea of the protocol. 'Should I take my shoes off?'

'No, not unless you want to. But I don't advise it. The floor's not exactly clean after our lot have been tramping in and out.' He stared, fascinated, at her shoes. It was probably a ploy to avoid meeting her eye. His obvious discomfort restored her self-confidence and filled her with satisfaction. He deserved to suffer.

Eventually, tired of looking at the top of his head, Freyja coughed. 'Hadn't we better get this over with? People are waiting. Where should I begin?' This wasn't strictly true; no one was waiting with bated breath for these clothes.

'What? Oh, yes.' Huldar raised his head so suddenly that Freyja was afraid he'd crick his neck. He opened the door to the living area and she followed him, trying not to picture their night together. Feeling herself turning pink, she thanked God he couldn't see. Bloody man.

She focused on the house. It didn't seem to have been altered inside as so many had nowadays. The ceiling was clad in dark yellow panels that had no doubt originally been much lighter. The ceiling-lights were also from a bygone age: large, domed spotlights, set into the panelling. It was obvious from the texture of the walls that the wallpaper had been painted over. If it dated from the time the house was built it was a pity it had been covered up: bold patterns were back in fashion.

Huldar turned and opened his mouth but Freyja deliberately interrupted before he could speak, asking the first thing that entered her head. 'Were they well off?'

The furnishings gave the impression that Elísa and her husband had been comfortably provided for, though nothing looked expensive. There was a crumpled blanket on the sofa in front of the TV, a large picture book, a child's sock and a remote control. The other sock lay among the Cheerios spilt all over the coffee table, along with a folded newspaper, a bowl containing some crumbs of popcorn and a half-empty glass of water. Lego bricks were strewn over the floor. Freyja suspected that Elísa would have taken five minutes to tidy up if she'd known what was coming. It was all too clear that she had been caught on the hop. Perhaps that was why Freyja liked to have everything tidy around her: she wouldn't want strangers entering her home if it was a mess. It occurred to her that she had better not die while she was living in her brother's flat. She still hadn't found the willpower to give the place a real blitz, though she'd cleaned the living room enough to be able to receive guests without embarrassment.

'They were doing OK, I believe. Their bank statements indicate that they usually paid off their bills every month, though they didn't have any big savings. The murder is very unlikely to have been about money.' Huldar looked back over his shoulder as he entered the bedroom hallway, apparently relieved to find a neutral subject to talk about. 'The woman doesn't appear to have had life insurance, which pretty much rules out murder for her inheritance. The husband would hardly have resorted to killing her for her share of the house. It's mortgaged to the hilt anyway.' He stopped at the first door. The floor in front of it was covered in a fine powder that could also be seen on the doorknob.

'Did you find any fingerprints?'

'I don't know yet, but probably not. Most things in here are covered in the family's prints, and all the indications are that the man was wearing gloves. At least, the most recent prints on the children's bedroom door-handles were theirs or Elísa's. If the murderer had had bare hands, we'd have found an extra set of prints. He locked the boys in their room. Luckily, because it spared them the horror of finding their mother's body.' Huldar suppressed a yawn. 'The door to Margrét's room was locked too but, as you know, she wasn't inside. There were some stuffed toys under the duvet, which may have misled the murderer if he peered in before locking it. In the dark it would have looked as if a child was lying there.' His eyes met Freyja's, their whites covered in a network of red veins. 'Would you lock your children in at night?'

'I haven't got any children.'

He seemed pleased by her answer. 'No, neither have I.' He smiled. 'As far as I know.'

Freyja didn't return his smile. Was he trying to come across as some kind of stud? 'Well, I know I don't have any. I couldn't have failed to notice.'

'No. Of course not.' He didn't seem to register her sarcasm. Too tired, probably. 'But if you did have kids, would you lock them in at night? What if there was a fire?'

'No, I don't suppose I would.'

'Exactly. So it's highly unlikely Elísa did, and her husband agrees. They weren't in the habit of doing that.'

The doors were original, like the rest of the fittings. Freyja stared, puzzled, at the keyhole. 'How did the boys get out if it was locked from the outside? Did they have a key?'

'No, apparently the older boy crawled out of the window and persuaded the younger one to follow him.'

'Where's the key now?'

'At the station. We only found one. It was in the boys' door. The same key works for all the internal doors. The rest have probably been lost. Sigvaldi says he can't remember how many there were as they hardly ever used them. So it's possible that the murderer took one or two with him. Though I can't imagine why.'

'How did he get in?'

'Either the outside door was unlocked or he had a key, because there are no signs of a break-in.' He opened a bedroom door. 'Here you are. You can touch anything. We've been over it repeatedly.'

The contents of the room were covered in more of the same fine powder. It was like being the first to enter a tomb that had been closed for centuries; a tomb that also served as a playroom. The place was a shambles of toys and children's clothes, but Freyja noticed that some of the garments were still folded. She assumed the chaos had been caused by the police. The room couldn't have looked like this before. Seeing the empty wardrobe with its door hanging open, she guessed that the neatly folded clothes had been piled on the shelves inside before the police swept them out on to the floor.

'Am I supposed to pull clothes out of this heap?'

'I suppose so.' Huldar leant against the door jamb, watching her as she turned in a circle, hunting for the least dusty garments. She regretted having worn such tight trousers; a long, full skirt would have been more suitable. The idea that he might think she'd dressed like this to impress him was intolerable. Feeling self-conscious under his gaze, she wished she could ask him to leave the room. But before she could summon up the nerve, she'd lost her chance.

'There are some clothes in the laundry room as well but they're not much better. And they're dirty too.' He smiled, the weariness leaving his face for a moment.

'Right.' Freyja shook the fingerprint powder off two pairs of trousers and shirts, leaning backwards to avoid the resulting cloud of dust. She rooted around in the mess again until she had extracted some underpants and socks, then left it at that. She could always come back another time. 'This'll do. Next room, please.'

Huldar escorted her down the hallway to Margrét's room. The trail of chaos left by the police was no less obvious here but as the room was a little larger the mess didn't seem as overwhelming. The clothes were different too: there were girly dresses among the jeans, and the T-shirts were mostly decorated with cats or other cute animals. No dinosaurs or crocodiles here. Freyja got straight down to work; the dust had begun to irritate her nose and eyes and she longed to be out of here. Once she had tracked down the girl's school bag and some clothes, all that remained was to collect the toothbrushes and some scrunchies that had been especially requested.

Huldar cleared his throat. 'By the way, my name *is* Jónas. Huldar Jónas. It wasn't a total lie. And I was born and raised in Egilsstadir.'

Freyja stiffened where she was stooping over a pile of clothes. She had been hoping to find the girl's school things underneath. Straightening up again, she smiled mockingly at Huldar. 'Good for you. Don't tell me you're a carpenter on the side as well?'

Huldar looked stung. 'No. But the rest was true. More or less.'

Freyja turned back to the pile. 'You know what, I really couldn't give a toss. And I'd be grateful if you didn't refer to the incident again.' She was glad he couldn't see her hot cheeks. If only one could delete unwanted memories like old

computer files. 'I'd rather forget about it. It wasn't that memorable, anyway, which makes it easier. I hope you feel the same.'

'I just wanted to apologise and explain.'

'Thanks but no thanks. No need for apologies.' With an
effort she stopped her voice from giving her away. The truth
was that she was still smarting from the stupid affair; it had
been like a scene from a bad movie. Waking up and reaching
out an arm only to encounter a cold, empty bed where her
lover should have been. No aroma of coffee from the kitchen,
no sizzling of bacon. No note. Nothing. The most humiliating
awakening she had ever experienced. Usually the men she
invited to share her bed were in no hurry to knot the sheets
together and escape out of the window. She supposed it was
some comfort that he'd made do with the stairs.

'The thing is, whenever I tell women what I do for a living—'

'Yeah, right. My heart bleeds for you.' Freyja picked up a
piece of paper that had been concealed under a stripy jumper.
It was a drawing, signed 'Margrét' in one corner. She examined it, turning it round. 'What's this?'

'Looks like a drawing by the girl.' Huldar seemed relieved
at the change of subject. 'Never mind that sort of thing.
We've taken away everything of significance. The room's full
of the girl's drawings. The kitchen too.'

Glancing around, Freyja spotted more pieces of paper. Some
showed conventional scenes of the sun setting behind two
pointy-peaked mountains but it wasn't long before she found
another like the one she was holding. 'This is no normal
child's drawing. Nor's this.'

'Normal? What's a normal drawing?' Huldar took the paper
from her. 'It's just a house and a man. I can't see anything
strange about that.'

'Part of my job is to analyse children's pictures. This is no normal drawing. You should take them both with you.' Freyja rose to her feet. 'I advise you to collect them all up and have them analysed. We can help, if you like.'

Huldar examined the picture sceptically. Freyja went over to stand next to him. 'This is her house. The house we're standing in. You must be able to see that.'

'Sure.'

'And this person here,' Freyja pointed to the black figure who was depicted far too large in relation to the house. 'Do you see the way he's standing, apparently staring at the house? His arms are sticking out as if he's about to start a fight. The black colour implies that he's a bad man. There's every chance she drew something she'd actually witnessed. Perhaps the murderer had been stalking the family, scoping out the territory, or whatever it is that murderers do. She may well have sensed there was something wrong, though she didn't mention it to her parents. Children have a tendency to repress things, but they can emerge in their drawings. Not always but often. If she saw a man hanging around the house, she might be able to provide a more detailed description of him.'

Huldar raised his eyes from the sheet of paper. 'You're telling me.' His face hardened. 'I want her brought in for interview today. You have one hour to arrange it.' He took the other drawing from her. 'Starting now.'

Clearly, Freyja wasn't going to have time to search for scrunchies, let alone make it to lunch with her girlfriends.

Chapter 9

The shortwave receiver stood in its place on the table, tuned in to the Icelandic numbers station. Despite frequent cracklings and static over the amplifier, the broadcast still hadn't come on air. Karl was growing restless, picturing the glances his friends must be exchanging behind his back. 'I can't understand it.' He had been repeating this for the last hour but however often he told himself to shut up, he couldn't stop blurting it out at regular intervals. 'Perhaps it'll begin at seven.' It was still ten to.

Halli yawned behind him. 'Or not.'

Karl made a face and took a deep breath. This was a total disaster. Why did nothing ever go right for him? What were the odds that things would go wrong for a person every single time? Remote, surely? He'd have to be one of the luckiest men alive for the next few decades if he was to achieve the average. Not once could he remember things going right for him, yet again and again he fell into the trap of assuming that they would. It never occurred to him to have a back-up plan. If only he'd had the sense to move the TV down to the basement they could have watched a film or played computer games if the broadcast was delayed. What a loser he was. But when he mentally pictured the TV in the sitting room he realised he would never have done it. Although it wasn't an old CRT set, the flat-screen was almost as clunky, and hardly any bigger than a computer monitor. His mum had gone for the cheapest model, as always. The most expensive stuff in the house was the radio gear he had saved up for himself.

There was no chance of moving the radio receiver upstairs either because Karl wouldn't dream of letting his friends loose in those embarrassingly naff surroundings. The furnishings weren't even the kind that would come back into fashion if you waited long enough. He had herded Halli and Börkur straight down to the basement after letting them hang up their coats in the hall. Above their heads, Che Guevara stared into space looking a little surprised, a relic of his mother's ill-defined left-wing politics that had mainly consisted of sneering whenever the subject of America came up. Karl was relieved the faded poster hadn't fallen off the wall while his friends were bumbling around underneath it – the cheap frame was coming apart at two corners. He couldn't give a damn what happened to the picture but would rather his friends didn't notice it.

Why on earth hadn't he removed the poster, and others like it? Laziness – sheer laziness. If he didn't like something about the house, it was up to him to change it. To be fair, he had invited an antiques dealer to give him a quote for the contents, but after walking round with a pen and notebook, the man had declined to bid, on the grounds that none of it was worth anything. Apart from Karl's radio equipment, that is, in which the guy had shown an uncomfortable degree of interest considering it wasn't for sale.

Karl could really have used the money. His mother had spent every last króna paying off the mortgage before she died, so he was stuck with the existing contents until he could save up for new ones. He was on a study loan and would be in trouble this spring if he didn't knuckle down and pass his exams. Though the chances of that happening were now so slim that he was beginning to think of selling the house and buying somewhere smaller; a flat that he could furnish to his own taste, with a bit left over to liven up his dreary existence.

He just hadn't got round to it.

Every time he thought about moving he remembered the trouble he'd had acquiring permission to mount the giant radio antenna on the house. He guessed it would be even more of a hassle to erect one on the roof of a block of flats. Besides, half the house belonged to Arnar, and Karl's share might not even cover the cost of a small flat. At least he was living here for free. For the moment, anyway. There was no knowing how long his brother would put up with that state of affairs. Probably the only reason he hadn't yet insisted on dividing up the legacy was that he was too busy; it could hardly have been from any fraternal feeling. They had never been close and since Arnar had moved to America their relationship had been dying a natural death. Even when Arnar was still living at home it had mainly involved nodding to each other over the breakfast table, or asking about some item that had been mislaid. At Christmas and on birthdays they had dutifully thanked each other for the presents their mother had bought on their behalf, and that was pretty much it. When he was younger Karl had tried to penetrate his brother's shell but had given up in the end. It was futile.

Perhaps Arnar would simply forget about Karl, the house and what remained of their modest inheritance. Although there had been a slight improvement in their relationship after Arnar had grown up, it was perfectly possible that he would never contact Karl again. He was content with his new wife and his career, and seemed likely to settle on the other side of the pond for good. Their phone calls had become more frequent while their mother was ill, but after she died they had soon petered out again. Arnar had blamed the time difference, which reminded Karl of the way their mother used to blame the age difference for the brothers' lack of closeness when they were boys. Time difference, age difference. There would always be some source of difference between them.

Karl glared at the Collins shortwave receiver, as if he could force a sound out of it by willpower. At that even the crackling ceased. He could feel himself growing hot and wanted to howl with impotent rage, but made an effort to breathe calmly and this seemed to work. The situation was out of his control, so there was no point giving in to disappointment. Yet he couldn't help feeling aggrieved and frustrated. Instead of impressing his friends with the weird Icelandic numbers station, he was boring them to death.

Eventually, he turned round in his chair. Halli was sound asleep on the ugly little sofa, head lolling back, his shiny black hair touching the wall. Karl gloated at the thought of the stiff neck he would have when he woke up. Serve him right. The least he could do was have the courtesy to stay awake. No doubt the two beers he had downed were partly to blame. Or the dope they'd smoked. Halli emitted a grunting snore and for a moment it looked as if he was about to wake with a jerk from his peaceful slumber, but instead he smacked his lips, closed his mouth and slept on.

It occurred to Karl that his friend's hair would leave a dirty mark on the wall. For as long as Karl had known him, Halli had worn his thin, greasy hair in a ponytail, and the collar of the black leather jacket he wore year-round was shiny at the back. The wall was bound to suffer the same fate, but since

Karl's mother was no longer there to be annoyed, he wasn't going to lose any sleep over it. In the unlikely event that he succumbed to a cleaning frenzy, he had a sink full of washing-up awaiting him upstairs. Followed by the laundry room, the bathroom and almost the entire living area. It was amazing how quickly the place had deteriorated into a pigsty. The basement was the most presentable because he rarely brought food down here for fear of spilling it on his sensitive equipment.

Börkur shifted his leg, which he had slung over the arm of the faded chair that matched the sofa. He didn't seem very interested in the dog-eared magazine he was flicking through but at least he wasn't snoring with his mouth open. 'If nothing happens at seven, I'm thinking of making tracks.' He chucked the magazine on the coffee table. 'Unless you want to catch a movie? I could murder some popcorn.' Börkur had a unique talent for pursuing his goals by crooked paths: it was perfectly possible to get hold of popcorn without going to the cinema. Halli was no better, with his unrealistic dreams and expectations. Whenever the three of them were together Karl felt as if he were stuck in one of those stupid radio plays his mother used to listen to.

But it wasn't like Karl could swap Halli and Börkur for anyone better; they were his only friends. And it was the same for them: their friendship was based on lack of choice rather than mutual liking. They had met in their teens and in more than a decade no one better had come along. There had been four of them originally, and for a while they even had a girl in tow too. They had all been crazy about her, though she was no goddess, but unfortunately she didn't return the feelings of Karl, Halli or Börkur. It had been a different story with the fourth member of their group, however, and after

she and Thórdur got together, they had quickly made themselves scarce.

It hadn't really come as a surprise that Thórdur should drop
them since he'd never shared their hobby. That was the
problem: hardly anyone shared it. Being a radio ham just
wasn't cool. Recently, to Karl's dismay, both Halli and Börkur
had showed signs of distancing themselves from the only
interest that bound them together, a development he doubted
their friendship could survive. Perhaps part of the problem
was that they had only qualified for a novice's licence, so were
somewhat behind Karl. Actually, it was surprising Börkur had
even managed to pass that. Halli had lost interest, becoming
obsessed with the internet instead, while Börkur just slobbed
in front of the TV. They had more or less given up switching
on their transceivers and never initiated conversations about
radio matters. Karl rarely took part in their discussions about
the conspiracy theories that Halli dug up on the internet and
believed uncritically. Although Karl tried to fake an interest,
he sensed that this was the beginning of the end of their
friendship. He just hoped it would last long enough for him
to meet some other people so he didn't end up entirely alone.
Yet, against his better judgement, he had been hoping the
Icelandic numbers station might revive their enthusiasm.

'Something's bound to happen at seven.' Karl sent up a
silent prayer that he would be proved right. 'Bound to.'

'If you say so.' Börkur yawned. 'God, I need popcorn.'

There was popcorn upstairs but Karl wasn't about to admit
it. He couldn't be bothered to fetch it and Börkur would only
empty the bag, then start moaning on about wanting something else. Karl felt sure that if the equivalent of a cardiograph
existed for the human brain, it would soon lose track of

Börkur's thoughts. He certainly didn't seem to know his way round his own mental maze.

'What do you think it means anyway, this station of yours? Assuming you weren't just hearing things . . .' Börkur sniffed and brushed his overgrown fringe out of his eyes. Why couldn't Karl have friends with tidy hair?

'I wasn't hearing things.' Karl gritted his teeth to stop himself snapping. He had always tried to give Börkur's stupid ideas a sympathetic hearing and this was his reward. A headache broke through the fading, dope-induced high. 'I'm not a total moron. I listened to it several times and I know what I heard.' At first the ID numbers had been repeated over and over again, but the second broadcast had included a more complicated sequence that Karl couldn't make head or tail of, interspersed by the word 'reversed'. Seventy-five, twenty-three, sixty-three minus ninety-two, seven, thirty-two. Fourteen reversed. Sixteen, seventy-four, sixty-three minus ninety-two, fifty-two reversed – was one series that kept coming up. 'We just need to be patient. It'll happen.'

Börkur seemed unaware that he'd annoyed his friend. 'Whatever. Anyway, what do you think it means? And who could be arsed to do something like that? What's the point? I just don't get why your ID number should be mixed up in it.'

'Neither do I.' Karl's voice sounded as odd as he felt. The whole thing was deeply unsettling. The more he thought about the broadcast, the less sense he could make of it and the worse he felt. It had stopped him sleeping last night; he had lain there staring at the ceiling, listening for strange noises outside the window, though all he could hear was the rustle of dead leaves in the garden. He had peered out as warily as he could, only to see a fat neighbourhood cat waddle out from among the bushes, then make off slowly into the darkness. 'It has to be someone taking the piss. It can't be anything else.'

Börkur swung his leg up and down, making the chair creak. 'Yeah. Maybe.' He sounded sceptical. 'But who'd bother? It's not like you know many people.'

Karl coughed. 'I know loads of people. There are, like, two hundred people in some of my lectures.' No need to mention that only maybe a dozen knew his name. Karl didn't for a moment believe that any of them would waste so much as ten minutes on a practical joke aimed at him, let alone go to the trouble of setting up a transmitter. If the other students wanted to make his life a misery, they would do so in the lecture hall. 'I had the idea it might be someone from the club.'

'Seriously?' From Börkur's expression, Karl might as well have said he suspected someone from the Scout movement. Yet it was the logical conclusion. At least the members of the amateur radio club knew of his interest in numbers stations, could work a shortwave transceiver and owned the right equipment, unlike the students on his chemistry course. Yet Karl couldn't picture any of them pulling a prank like this.

None of them were the type to play tricks on him, let alone gang up to do so. As Börkur had said, what would be the point?

Börkur scratched his tousled head. 'Isn't it always the same old blokes?' He had eventually been chucked out of the club for failing to pay his subscription – for three years in a row. The committee was so desperate to hold on to their members that they'd turned a blind eye for as long as they could. Karl admitted that they were indeed still the same people. 'What about the other ID number? Who's the woman?'

'Don't ask me. I was hoping the broadcast would've changed and given me more information to go on. She's just some woman – I don't know her or have any connection to her. Her name's Elísa Bjarnadóttir. I don't know anyone called Elísa.'

'How can you be sure? Maybe she's an old aunt or some relative you've forgotten about. Could you know her by a nickname or something?'

Karl couldn't begin to imagine what this 'or something' could be. Nor could he think of any nickname that fitted with the name Elísa. 'No. She's no aunt of mine. I looked her up on Facebook. Her page is public and there are loads of pictures of her. I've never seen her before, or anyone else in her photos. She's just some mother with a husband and young kids.'

He got no further. From the amplifier behind him the numbers station began to transmit. The musical box picked its way through the opening tune that had become so ominously familiar, to be followed by the woman's voice. Its mechanical, obviously artificial, tone should have made it less spooky but had exactly the opposite effect. 'Good evening. Good evening. Good evening.' Silence. Then the voice began to recite a string of numbers.

Karl was happy, despite the sense of misgiving the broadcast aroused in him. He hadn't screwed up after all. Halli woke with a jerk and stared, transfixed, at the receiver, as if it were providing the answers to life's great mysteries – though without the key to the code, these answers were no more than a monotonous string of numbers.

Chapter 10

The liquid dribbling from the machine couldn't even be described as light brown. To think he'd dropped by the office to grab a decent cup of coffee before attending Margrét's interview at the Children's House. The grinder had made a hell of a noise but, judging by the sound, the beans must have run out halfway through. Huldar decided to make do with the thin, watery brew and let the next person refill the machine; he had more than enough on his plate already.

On his way through the office he passed members of the investigation team working under his direction on Elísa's murder. He hoped he had assigned each of them a task appropriate to their talents. Although he knew them all, he had never made any effort to learn their individual strengths. That was the job of those in more senior positions.

He had only accepted the job of leading the investigation because it seemed the easiest thing to do. Now, after the pathologist's warning, he suspected he had made a serious mistake. He hadn't exactly been given much time to think about it. According to his boss Egill, the heads of CID had had little chance to consider the matter but decided to offer the job to Huldar on the basis that he had been one of the detectives called to the scene and his name came first in the alphabetical list of candidates. Leifur was next, should he decline the position. As Huldar couldn't stand Leifur and had no intention of working under him, he didn't think twice. So now he was stuck with this unlooked-for promotion and a potential fall from grace if the investigation went badly. Well, that wouldn't be the end of the world, and even if he was successful, he might still ask for his old job back. Managing people had never particularly appealed to him. But he wanted it to be his decision, not have it forced on him by senior management.

'Great meeting.' A young female officer smiled at him as she passed. So there was at least one person who had appreciated the team briefing he'd held. Personally, he thought he'd done all right too; no worse than his predecessors, at any rate, though he felt a slight sense of disappointment because he'd intended to be so much better. He smiled back and hoped she wasn't on her way to fetch a coffee from the empty machine. Unfortunately he couldn't remember what task he had assigned her, but he hoped it was interesting. It might compensate for the lack of coffee beans.

'How's it going?' Huldar paused by Ríkhardur, and immediately regretted it. Too late now to pretend he was in a hurry. Anyway, he was sick to death of beating himself up about the situation; it was time to push it to the back of his mind.

'Badly. We're getting nowhere. Nobody has a clue how to crack this and, just to make matters worse, it turns out we have no expert codebreakers in Iceland.' One of the jobs Ríkhardur had volunteered for was to search for a way of deciphering the mysterious message discovered at Elísa's house. 'The question is, should we look abroad for help?'

'What if it's in Icelandic?' Huldar had relaxed once they started talking, his tension eased by how normal Ríkhardur seemed – or, rather, how dry, wooden and ill at ease. The fact that Ríkhardur was his usual awkward self must be a sign that he hadn't found out. Soon Huldar would be able to stop worrying altogether; after all, it was months since his encounter with Karlotta at that bar, and therefore increasingly unlikely that their ludicrously ill-advised shag in the toilets would come out. Especially now that she and Ríkhardur were getting a divorce. She would hardly use the incident as a parting shot. 'I mean, isn't it impossible to decipher a code in a language you don't understand? If it is in code?'

'Yes, I suppose so. But they might be able to give us some advice; tell us what system it's based on or suggest a way in. I have no idea how we're supposed to decipher it without assistance.' Ríkhardur pushed away the photocopied message in disgust. With no clutter on his desk to provide an obstacle, the sheet of paper slid off on to the floor.

Huldar reached down and replaced it on the desk. 'Put in a request for assistance from abroad. Interpol must have a department or expert who can take a look at it for us.' He took a gulp of coffee and grimaced. 'Until then, you'd better focus on something else. Any updates from the inquiry into the husband?'

'Same story. Nothing doing. He appears as blameless as his wife. No disputes, no enemies, nobody hates him. Or at least we haven't succeeded in proving otherwise.'

'What about at work? Anything cropped up there? Any medical errors or sexual abuse of a patient? That sort of thing?'

Breaking out of his habitual impassivity, Ríkhardur screwed up his face. 'Sexual abuse of a patient? He's a gynaecologist, for Christ's sake.'

Huldar was surprised. 'Not all gynaecology patients have STDs, you know.'

'That's not what I meant. I believe the majority of the women he sees are pregnant. He works in obstetrics.'

'Oh, yes, so he does.' How could it have entered his head that the fastidious Ríkhardur would have associated Sigvaldi's patients with herpes or gonorrhoea? Diseases like that had no place in his world. 'All the same, we'll have to look into the possibility. If memory serves, the majority of complaints that come before the surgeon general relate to obstetricians – whether they're justified or not.'

'I'll look into it.' Ríkhardur was staring unseeingly across the room. 'It's a good point. It must be terrible to lose a newborn baby or for it to suffer damage at birth that could have been prevented.'

Huldar ignored this, praying that the subject of Karlotta's miscarriages wouldn't come up again.

He had already endured a lifetime's worth of stomach pain and anxiety over the whole affair. From November, when Ríkhardur had proudly announced for the third time that he was going to be a father, until the day when he quietly stated that Karlotta had lost the baby, Huldar had felt as though he was carrying around a weight in his own belly. Especially after he'd summoned up the courage to ask how far along Karlotta was, then calculated to his horror that he could be the father. Ríkhardur's grief over the miscarriage had compounded Huldar's inner turmoil – a combination of sympathy for the couple and relief at not having to live in fear that the child's eyes would be brown like his rather than a celestial blue like its parents'. And, worst of all, the shame at having betrayed his colleague. They might not be bosom buddies but he'd worked more closely with Ríkhardur than anyone else on the force and that created a bond. The betrayal was unforgivable and, in retrospect, inexplicable, unless you factored in Karlotta's outstanding attractions.

All she'd needed to do was gaze into his eyes with that mischievous smile and he had forgotten everything but his primitive urges. He knew she was alone; Ríkhardur was on a firearms course in the countryside that weekend, so the coast had seemed clear. An opportunity like that would never come his way again. What a fucking terrible mistake. Huldar cleared his throat to overcome a sudden hoarseness.

'Yes. The surgeon general may have a list of patients who've made accusations or complaints about Sigvaldi.'

'You think? I gather he has an unusually good reputation. Karlotta tried to get an appointment with him but he was booked up. Apparently you have to plan your birth years in advance if you want him to be your obstetrician. That wouldn't be the case if he had a history of mistakes.'

'Check it out, anyway. It's a possibility we can't ignore.' Huldar straightened up. 'If the girl's right and the murderer has another woman in his sights, we need to get our skates on.'

'Why would someone who murders a doctor's wife due to a medical error resort to killing again?' Ríkhardur came straight to the point as usual. 'And anyway, wouldn't he have murdered the doctor? Why kill his wife?'

'I'm not saying the murderer definitely has a link to Sigvaldi, but we can't rule it out, however far-fetched it may seem to you.' An answer to Ríkhardur's question belatedly occurred to him. 'For all we know he may have intended to kill Sigvaldi but decided to attack his wife instead because he wasn't home. Besides, it's not only doctors who make mistakes. Maybe a nurse or midwife's implicated. What do I know?' Huldar hastened to change the subject. After all that had happened, it gave him heartburn to discuss childbirth with Ríkhardur. 'What about the tax office? We need to examine all the cases Elísa was involved in. Perhaps someone was tipped over the edge by a heavy tax bill or penalties. That sort of thing can completely screw people financially, and money troubles are a well-known motive for murder. Incidentally, have you heard any news about how that side's going?'

'No, that's not my responsibility. It was assigned to Andri and Tómas.'

Nodding, Huldar glanced across the office. Neither of the men was present. He hoped they were hard at work gathering data and statements from the staff at the tax office. His thoughts returned to what the pathologist had said during the post-mortem. 'The vacuum cleaner would make sense in that scenario.'

'How do you mean?'

'Well, I don't know how plausible it sounds but maybe the murderer wanted to make the point that she'd hoovered money out of his account, so he paid her back in her own coin. By hoovering her life away.'

Ríkhardur looked sceptical. 'Yes, right.' He moved the mouse to wake up his computer and a picture of Karlotta filled the screen. The photo had been Ríkhardur's wallpaper for as long as Huldar could remember. Since the screen was as tidy as his desk, the few icons on the desktop were arranged in a neat, vertical column on the left-hand side, which meant the picture was visible in its entirety. He quickly shut down his computer.

When Ríkhardur confided at the beginning of the year that Karlotta had left him, Huldar had been badly thrown. It had cast a dark shadow over his relief at learning of the failed pregnancy. His biggest fear was that Karlotta had left Ríkhardur in the hope that the two of them could get together, but a phone call to her had soon disabused him. When he asked, he was reassured by her dry laughter: the divorce had nothing to do with him; she and Ríkhardur simply weren't meant to be together. But Ríkhardur clearly didn't share this view and it wasn't hard to see why. They were so obviously made for each other; she was just like him, always immaculately turned out, not a hair out of place. Huldar couldn't remember ever seeing so much as a chip in the varnish on her pretty fingernails. Ríkhardur was unlikely to be so lucky second time around.

Ríkhardur carried on discussing the case as if nothing had happened. Yet he seemed unusually hesitant. 'Are you sure we shouldn't concentrate on investigating all the black men who could possibly have a link to Elísa or her husband?' When Huldar had announced at the progress meeting that he didn't think there was any reason at this stage to act on Margrét's description of the killer – it was too vague and the picture would be clearer once they had spoken to her again – Ríkhardur and several of the others had objected.

'Like I said, we'll hold fire on that for the moment. I'm going down to the Children's House later for their second attempt at interviewing the girl. Hopefully that'll give me a better idea of how seriously we should take it.' Huldar glanced at his watch: he was going to be late. 'We don't want to be accused of racism if it turns out she only saw his silhouette. But, obviously, if you come across any black men in the course of your investigation, make a point of checking them out.'

'I haven't so far, and until you give the green light I won't go deliberately looking for one.'

'No. Of course not.' Huldar smiled. Ríkhardur wasn't only exemplary in dress and manners, he was also scrupulous about following orders. Guilt about Karlotta raised its ugly head again and Huldar felt compelled to add: 'Maybe you'd like to come with me to the Children's House to observe?'

'I haven't got time. I've arranged to go over to the local shopping centre, remember? To run through the CCTV footage from the cashpoint.' Ríkhardur looked disappointed, as if he'd rather delegate the task Huldar had assigned to him that morning and accompany him instead. Particularly since his errand was unlikely to produce any results. The cashpoint was situated on one of the main approach roads to the area where Elísa had lived. If they were lucky, the camera would have caught the moment when her killer drove past, but it was far more likely that the lens had been pointing downwards and there wouldn't be any footage of the street. Nevertheless, a member of the team still had to go over there to find out.

'Of course. Never mind. Come along next time. I have a hunch this won't be our last attempt at questioning the girl.'

On his way back to the office to collect his jacket and car keys, Huldar scanned the room for someone to take with him. Someone who could act as a buffer between him and Freyja. He'd had enough of the constant dirty looks reminding him of his shoddy behaviour. The bugger of it was that he wouldn't have minded renewing their acquaintance, but her manner made it abundantly clear that this was out of the question. Then again, she had dressed up to meet him at the crime scene earlier. Maybe he was still in with a chance after all.

Chapter 11

Molly watched Freyja intently, as was her habit. Freyja sighed quietly and saw the dog's gaze sharpen. She was having a hard time getting used to having a dog. Whenever she met the alert brown eyes she felt guilty for not taking her out for more walks or feeding her better. Given the choice, she wouldn't have had a dog at all, especially not such a large one – she was sure that if you went back far enough you'd find a horse in Molly's pedigree. But of course this was exactly the type of breed that would appeal to her brother. Baldur had gone for an animal that would look good in a rap video, snarling in the background, surrounded by flashy cars and girls shaking their asses; a breed that looked capable of quenching its thirst with blood and gnawing on dinosaur bones. She wouldn't be surprised to find a tattoo lurking under the thick pelt. Only now, after sharing the flat with Molly for a month, could Freyja go near her without being in constant fear of losing a finger or even her whole hand.

The bitch gave a wide yawn, revealing rows of sharp, white teeth that seemed to extend right down her throat. Though Freyja was still on her guard around Molly, there were times when she felt reassured by her presence. These invariably came at night when she was shocked awake by shouting and commotion in the corridor outside, thanks to the wayward occupants of the depressing building. Her brother wasn't the only one living on the edge. The squalid condition of the building and flats presumably made them cheap to buy or rent – you wouldn't be able to charge much per square metre here – and these unlucky souls had ended up here for want of anything better.

Molly finished her yawn and turned her big head away from Freyja, apparently offended. Freyja felt guilty again. She had neglected the dog today; made do with letting her out early this morning to find a patch on which to urinate among the empty cans and other rubbish that decorated the garden. It wasn't the first time the demands of work had ruined her plans for the animal.

'I'll take you out later.' She shouldn't have said the word 'out'. The dog pricked up her ears and swung her head back to Freyja, her tongue lolling. Freyja groaned. She reached for the box containing yesterday evening's pizza and selected a slice with plenty of meat in the topping. 'Here.' The dog wolfed it down whole, then licked her chops with a tongue the size of a haddock fillet, gazing at Freyja in hope of another, larger slice. 'Sorry, old girl. You mustn't get fat on my watch.' Freyja tilted her head to gauge if the dog had put on any weight. Maybe – not that it mattered at this stage since Molly had been all skin and bone when Freyja recovered her from the friend of her brother's who had originally been entrusted with looking after her while Baldur was in prison.

Unfortunately, this fine, upstanding character had ended up behind bars as well, after breaking the terms of his probation. And seeing as her brother had generously lent her his flat, she couldn't really refuse to take care of his dog – though she wouldn't have agreed to take on so much as a goldfish in return for his wreck of a car. When she'd switched off the ignition earlier, the engine had emitted a death rattle that suggested she'd do well to have the number of a taxi company handy for when she had to return to the Children's House.

The clock that hung wildly askew on the kitchen wall told her it was time to head off. Huldar's demand for an interview within the hour had proved unrealistic; the girl's grandfather had refused point blank to attend at such short notice. He made the excuse that the children had finally been reunited with their father and it would be too stressful for Margrét to be dragged away from him again so soon. Standing there on the doorstep, Freyja had almost had to resort to tears to persuade him to agree to a time later that afternoon. She hadn't been invited inside or caught any glimpse of the children, their father or grandmother. The sounds of crying and raised voices had carried out through the open door, but Freyja couldn't distinguish the words. Nor did she have any desire to eavesdrop; she'd rather leave the shattered family in peace.

As she walked away she could feel the grandfather's eyes following her. The front door didn't close until she had unlocked the car, as if he wanted to reassure himself that she was genuinely leaving. Like she had any interest in hanging around outside their place until the meeting at the Children's House. Quite the reverse. It was Sunday and she'd had very different plans. Her friends were probably leaving the restaurant by now, so there was no point hurrying into town. She'd go along next time. Her plan to give Molly some attention after lunch would have to wait as well. Freyja grabbed the keys, smiling at the dog, who had followed her hopefully to the front door. When it became clear that there was to be no walkies, Molly curled her lip in disapproval, then shambled back into the flat.

Freyja wondered if she could count on Molly to stand by

her in the event of a break-in. The way their relationship was now, it didn't seem very likely.

'I hardly need stress how vital it is that everything goes according to plan this time.' They were sitting round the large conference table, watching through the glass as Silja and Margrét took their places on the small sofa. The girl was visibly more distressed than on the previous occasion; her mother's death must be sinking in. 'Our investigation will rely heavily on what she says, so I'm asking you, please, to make a special effort.' Huldar leant forward slightly as he spoke, as if trying to find his balance. He probably just wanted to ensure that Silja heard every word via the microphone in the centre of the table. The bags under his eyes were deeper, his hair more of a mess, his clothes more crumpled than they had been that morning, yet he had turned up punctually this time, accompanied by a female officer who he introduced as Erla. She said little and seemed to have no real role except to sit in silence at Huldar's side, though it was evident from her expression that she had definite views on the proceedings. Since these appeared to be unflattering, it was probably just as well she didn't say much. Now she nodded to indicate agreement with Huldar's words. 'Let me repeat, a special effort.'

'You don't need to tell us.' Freyja's tone was polite but dry. She was not amused. Who exactly did he think he was? The police had no authority here, and it would be as well to establish clear boundaries at the outset. 'We're used to children's disclosures being of the utmost importance. Nobody comes here for an idle chat. So don't worry.' Meeting his eye, she gave him an icy smile. 'Just let us get on with our job and concentrate on asking your questions.'

Before the girl arrived, Huldar had sat down with Silja to run through the main questions he wanted her to ask Margrét. He had also given her the drawing of the man outside the house and was put out when Silja refused to show it to the girl in its plastic sleeve. In the end he had accepted her argument that Margrét was more likely to be forthcoming if the drawing looked as it had the last time she saw it. Above all he had stressed that the most urgent task was to elicit anything Margrét might know about the other murder she had said was imminent.

Silja had memorised Huldar's questions but pointed out that Margrét's answers were bound to throw up new questions, so he must make sure he supplied her with these. He would also have to understand that she couldn't just pump the girl the way he'd like. She would control the pace and phrase the questions as she thought best. Like all his predecessors – judges, investigators, prosecutors – he had nodded, assuming this wouldn't be a problem. But like them he would inevitably betray signs of impatience and agitation once the interview was under way.

'You remember what we talked about – if you need Silja to deviate from your original line of questioning, you must let her know. Just stay calm and make sure you don't bark orders into the microphone while she's talking. You can trust our methods, and that we take this seriously. OK?'

Huldar shrugged, avoiding Freyja's eye, but he seemed to acquiesce. Perhaps he was simply too tired to object. 'Fine. Can we get started then?' He sat back, disappearing behind Erla.

'All in good time.' Freyja turned to the glass and listened to Silja chatting gently to the girl about the snow outside. Margrét was tight-lipped. She tucked her long red hair behind her ears in a childish gesture, then fixed her gaze on her pink socks. Although obviously upset, she was composed. The same did not apply to her grandfather.

'Let me remind you that I'm taking her out of here the moment the hour's up. That's all the time you're getting. She needs to be with her family. With her father and brothers.' It had surprised Freyja that the girl's grandfather had brought her along this time as well, but she hadn't commented. Presumably the father was too distraught, or wasn't allowed to hear his daughter's statement because he was under suspicion himself.

'The clock's ticking,' the grandfather added.

Silja signalled that she was ready. Turning to Margrét, she took hold of the girl's small hand, which lay on the cushion between them. Margrét snatched it back and stuck both hands under her skinny thighs. Silja was unperturbed. 'Right, Margrét. I know you don't want to be here and would like to go home as soon as possible. So let's get this over with.'

The girl's gaze remained fixed on her socks. Although her feet didn't reach the floor, like the countless other children who had occupied the sofa before her, she resisted the urge to swing them.

'You know, you're very important, Margrét. Of course, you always have been, but now you're more important than ever. You can help the police find out what happened to your mummy.' The child sat there like a wax effigy. 'You're a hero, you know. But sadly no one can be a hero without going through a difficult time.' Margrét neither agreed nor disagreed. 'I know it's not easy for you to remember that night – that's where being a hero comes in. If you try to remember everything you saw or heard and then tell me about it, that means you're helping the police. They want more than anything to find out what happened.'

Freyja and Silja had agreed that it was imperative not to refer to the person who was believed to have broken in. The perpetrator's gender wasn't known for certain, and even the subtlest reference to a man or woman could influence Margrét's memory. It was crucial not to plant any ideas that the little girl might come to accept as her own. 'Do you think you could tell me what happened? Just the parts you remember. If you don't remember anything, that's fine. You can say so.'

This drew frowns from Huldar and the prosecutor. The doctor and nurse who had attended the previous interview were absent because Freyja had judged their presence unnecessary, especially in view of the cost of calling them out at the weekend for a second time. The Child Protection Agency had also declined the invitation to observe.

'I put my hands over my ears.' The tiny voice carrying over the loudspeaker wrenched at their heartstrings. 'I put my hands over my ears. I didn't want to hear Mummy crying.'

Silja was disconcerted, though no one but Freyja noticed. She hadn't been expecting such a quick answer. 'I understand. That was probably a wise decision.'

Margrét spoke again, almost in a whisper now. 'I had my hands over my ears. I don't know what he said. I didn't want to hear.' They all leant forward in unison. Margrét had said 'he'.

Silja had also caught the word. 'You talk as if it was a man, Margrét. How do you know that?'

'I saw him. I woke up and needed a wee-wee. I saw him walking about in the sitting room. I tried to tell Mummy but she didn't believe me. She went to have a look.' Margrét freed her hands from under her thighs and began twisting her fingers together in her lap.

'So your mummy left the bedroom. Where were you while this was happening?'

'I was in her room. When I heard someone coming, I hid. Under the bed. I looked out and saw Mummy's feet. I was going to come out but then some other feet came in. The black man's feet.'

'So he followed your mummy into the bedroom?' When Silja stopped speaking Freyja became aware that those listening with her in the meeting room were scarcely breathing.

When Margrét spoke again, after a pause for thought, everyone inhaled at once, almost drowning out the fragile little voice. 'Yes. I didn't dare come out from under the bed.' She fell silent again, staring down at her clasped fingers. 'I should have helped. I should have got out from under the bed and run outside. I could have found a policeman or a fireman to help Mummy.'

'You know, Margrét, it's a good thing you didn't do that. There aren't any policemen or firemen in your street at night. The man would have caught you long before you could have fetched help. Your mummy wouldn't have wanted that. If you're not a grown-up, it's better to hide. Sometimes it's better for grown-ups too.'

Margrét didn't look up. Her fingers were still now but her gaze remained fixed on them as if seeing them for the first time. 'But it was a man. I saw him and I heard him talking when I took my hands away from my ears to find out if it was over.' She shifted on the sofa. 'But it wasn't over. He sounded like a man.' In one fell swoop she had reduced the number of suspects by half – the female section of the population was in the clear.

Silja waited for a while, in case the police or prosecutor

wanted to add anything. Nobody spoke, so she bent down to Margrét and drew the girl's hair from her face as if peering behind a curtain. 'Do you remember what you told me last time we met, Margrét? You said you thought another woman was in danger.'

The girl averted her eyes, shaking her hair over her face again. 'I heard a little bit. I had to take my hands away from my ears sometimes to put them over my mouth, so the man wouldn't hear me crying.'

'I see. Sometimes you can hear things through your hands, too, however hard you try to block your ears.' Silja remained perfectly calm; her voice didn't for a moment betray how much was at stake. You'd have thought they were discussing the weather. 'You might not think so, but it was probably lucky you heard something. Especially if it can help the police stop another woman getting hurt.'

'I don't want to think about it.' Margrét's voice had dropped to a whisper again. 'I don't want to. I want to talk about something else.'

'Do you remember what I said about being a hero? That you can only be a hero if you're brave?' Margrét nodded. They couldn't see her expression because she was leaning forward, her hair blocking their view, but it was easy to imagine the despair on her face. 'If you can pluck up the courage to tell me what you heard him say, you'll be a hero, Margrét. It needn't take long and you'll feel better afterwards. Sometimes it helps to clean out the bad thoughts if you talk about the thing that's upsetting you.'

Margrét's legs began to swing slowly back and forth. The movement was neither idle nor careless; she looked like a toy whose batteries were running down. She drew a quick breath, glanced up and bit her lower lip before she began speaking again. Her legs stopped moving. 'Mummy cried and asked if he was going to hurt us too. I heard that even though I had my hands over my ears, but then I took them away. I wanted to hear if he said yes. But he just said not now. There was another woman he needed to teach a lesson.' She took great care in enunciating this, then turned a questioning look on Silja. 'What did he mean by a lesson?'

'He wanted her to understand something.' Silja was flustered and shifted on the sofa as she groped for an explanation. 'No need to try and understand, Margrét. It's not always easy to work out what grown-ups mean.' She darted a sideways glance at the two-way mirror in search of help.

'Ask her if he mentioned who the woman was.'

Huldar had spoken too loud and Silja winced. She tapped her ear pointedly, then focused on Margret again. 'Did the man say who the woman was or anything else about her?'

Margrét shook her head. 'No. He just said he was going to make her suffer. Like Mummy.' Margrét broke off and took a deep, gasping breath. 'I saw Mummy. He'd covered her eyes with sticky tape.'

Silja coughed. During the briefing, Huldar had shown her a photograph of Elísa's body at the scene. It was considered unavoidable since Margrét might refer to the grisly details. Freyja had been shown the photo too and it had taken her a moment to work out what she was seeing. When it sank in, she had to look away.

'Did you come out from under the bed, Margrét?'

'No. Mummy looked underneath. But she couldn't see anything. She stroked me and said, "Ssh". Then the bad man dragged her away.'

'That was sensible of her, Margrét. She didn't want the man to know you were there. Now you can see for yourself that the last thing she'd have wanted was for you to rush out from under the bed. She wanted you to do exactly what you did. To stay hidden.'

Huldar bent suddenly to the microphone. 'Don't lose the thread. Ask if she heard anything else. That was effective.'

'After he dragged your mummy back up, Margrét – did the man say anything else?'

'Yes. A story. He wanted to tell her a story. But I put my hands over my ears. I didn't want to hear his story. I knew it would be nasty. He didn't say anything else after that. Nor did Mummy.'

Nobody could speak for a moment. Silja was the first to recover and carry on as if nothing had happened. 'Tell me something else. Did you have your eyes closed? I know you saw your mummy when she told you to keep quiet, so you must have opened them sometimes.' Silja took great care over the phrasing of this, but Margrét didn't answer.

'Ask her again.' Huldar grabbed the microphone. Silja flinched at the crackling in her earpiece. He was speaking far too loud and it didn't help when he repeated his words even louder. 'Ask her again.'

Freyja laid the flat of her hand on his chest and pushed him away from the microphone. She tried not to remember that the last time she had touched him there it had been to brace herself so she could move faster on top of him. 'Leave it to Silja. She's well aware of how important it is.'

Huldar let go and shut up. They turned back to the glass as Silja resumed.

'Did you have your eyes closed, Margrét? If you did, it's OK. If not, it would be good to know what you saw.'

'I don't want to talk about it.' There was a hint of anger in the girl's voice now. 'I don't want to.'

'All right. Shall we talk about something completely different?'

The girl raised her eyes for the first time. She peered hopefully at Silja. 'Yes. You're not trying to trick me, are you?'

'No, of course I'm not trying to trick you. I want to ask you about a picture you drew.' Silja smiled at her. She reached for the sheet of paper on the little table beside the sofa. There was a teddy bear sitting there too, with legs straight out and head tilted archly on one side, as if it had little faith in the proceedings – much like Huldar. 'You're very good at drawing.' Silja handed Margrét the picture. 'Could you tell me what the picture shows?'

Margrét pushed her hair back from her face and bent over the page. 'You can see what it shows. You said I was good at drawing.' She handed it back.

Silja didn't lose her cool. 'I can see it's a house. Is it your house?'

Margrét nodded.

'Is it your car?'

Again the girl nodded.

'What about this? Is this the tree in your garden or is it a Christmas tree you bought to put in the house?' Silja was trying to phrase her question so as to elicit a longer answer.

'It's in the garden.'

'Yes, it's very big. I can see it wouldn't have fitted in the house.' Silja asked about other details of the drawing. She was careful to ask questions that would require full sentences in reply. They all noticed that each answer Margrét gave was longer than the one before. As she relaxed, her replies were becoming more detailed. But the prosecutor and Huldar were growing restless. The former caught Freyja's eye when Silja asked about the curtains in the window, and gestured to his watch. Freyja looked away and took care to avoid his gaze after that. The two men settled down when Silja finally came to the point.

'And who's this?'

'The man.'

'Which man?'

'Just a man.'

'Do you know him? Is it your daddy?'

The girl shook her head.

'A neighbour?'

'I don't know what he's called.'

'Why did you draw him then?'

'Because I saw him.'

'Did you see him when you were drawing the picture?'

'No.'

'I see.'

Huldar bent to the microphone again. To his credit, this time he spoke with restraint and didn't touch the equipment except to press the button. 'Ask her if she saw the man near the house or somewhere else. If he has nothing to do with the house, we can move on.'

Silja nodded unobtrusively. 'Tell me something, Margrét. Where did you see this man?'

'In our street. On the pavement. And once in our garden. At night.'

Silja nodded. 'Was he often in the neighbourhood?'

'I don't know.' Children had difficulty grasping what constituted 'often'.

'Did you see him twice? Five times? Ten times, maybe?'

Freyja swore under her breath. Silja shouldn't have mentioned any numbers. The girl was bound to seize on one.

'Maybe five times. But only maybe. I didn't count.'

'That's quite often.'

'Yes.'

'When was this, Margrét?'

The girl shrugged. 'A while ago.'

'Was it after Christmas?'

'Yes. Or no. When I saw him in the garden it was still Christmas. I woke up and I was looking in my shoe to see if I'd got any presents but there weren't any. At first I thought he was Father Christmas.'

'Did you see him after Christmas too?'

'Yes, I think so.'

'What do you think he was doing?'

'Watching. He was watching.'

Huldar reached for the microphone again. 'Ask if she saw his face.'

'Did you see his face, Margrét? Can you describe him?'

'I saw him. His face was cross. He wasn't happy.' The girl suddenly began to swing her legs again. It was a sign of agitation; they swung mechanically back and forth. 'I don't want to talk to you any more.'

She focused on her socks as they swung back and forth. 'Can I stay here?' She didn't look up. 'I don't want to be with Daddy. It's all his fault.'

Chapter 12

'It doesn't necessarily mean anything. Maybe she blames her father for the murder because he wasn't home that night.' Huldar shrugged, not to emphasise his point but in an attempt to stay awake: he'd rather not keel over on his boss's desk. The fatigue that had been building up over the weekend was kicking in badly now; he couldn't hold it off any longer with coffee and nicotine gum. Since early on Friday morning when Elísa's sons had been found wandering around in the street, he had slept no more than eight or nine hours, and only in the form of cat naps in his office, either on his desk or on the little couch that was so short it was more like a chair. 'I'd be wary of reading too much into what she said. At least, that was the opinion of the psychologist who interviewed her.'

Egill wrinkled his nose, revealing a gleam of unnaturally white teeth. No one had dared to comment on the transformation when he turned up to work one day sporting a Hollywood smile. Any more than they had when his bald patch suddenly disappeared. His hair no longer stirred in the breeze except en masse and he had taken to wearing his police cap whenever he went outside. Egill's efforts to enhance his appearance had coincided with his decision to swap his old wife for a new model twenty years younger. Some of the guys in CID had bets on whether Egill would go for a face-lift, but the odds weren't that great as everyone was betting he would.

The twitching around his eyes suggested that Egill could read Huldar's mind. He coughed portentously. 'The opinion of the psychologist. Quite.' He sat behind his desk, pretending to bring the full weight of his great intellect to bear on the matter. The self-important air and empty phrases were par for the course. 'By the way, what's your impression of the Children's House? I've never actually set foot inside the place but I have my reservations about the work they do there. In my opinion, it's inadvisable to entrust forensic interviewing to amateurs. It's unlikely to pay off.'

Huldar felt overwhelmed by weariness. 'It's all right. I wouldn't describe the staff as amateurs. They have people specially trained to interview children.'

'Children, adults – what's the difference?'

Huldar's surprise must have shown on his face because Egill suddenly backpedalled.

'All right, granted, of course there's a difference. I didn't mean literally. Children are smaller and all that. But different when it comes to answering questions? I doubt it.'

Ever since Huldar had transferred to the Police Commissioner's office he had been working for this man. At first he had been so low down the food chain that he had scarcely been able to breathe for the crush of people above him. At that time he had felt an awed respect for Egill, taking his trademark look of disgruntlement as a sign of profound intelligence and insight. The man must be weighed down by all the crimes that were constantly being committed on his patch when he wasn't there to prevent them. But nothing could be further from the truth. With the passing of the years, Huldar had come to realise that Egill had been born discontented. Nothing was ever good enough for him. Nothing anyone said ever pleased him. No cases were ever solved quickly enough and, when they were solved, Huldar got the impression that Egill took most of the credit. The man was in the habit of barging into progress meetings, casting an eye over the evidence, then stating the blindingly obvious, triumphantly drawing attention to details or suggesting angles that everyone else had spotted long ago. Huldar couldn't once remember hearing anything of substance emerging from those perpetually downturned lips.

The man's forte appeared to be technology. He had an inexhaustible enthusiasm for gadgets, ranging from screen projectors to firearms. As a result, CID was unusually well equipped with the latest gizmos, but since the budget was tight, this was at the cost of other areas in which their boss had less interest. That autumn, for example, all the officers in the department had been kitted out with iPads for ill-defined purposes. It swiftly became apparent that they were mainly being used to play Candy Crush. At the same time Egill had tried to convert them to a paperless office as part of an economy drive, by removing the paper from their printers and photocopiers. Anyone who wanted to print or copy had to knock on his door to be allocated paper. Huldar knew he wasn't the only one who preferred to bring along his own supplies from home.

'The picture's bound to become clearer soon. We've got the father coming back for further questioning later today. In the meantime, I'm thinking of grabbing a quick nap at home. I've hardly had any sleep since all this kicked off.' Huldar shifted his feet to combat a sudden wave of dizziness, fighting the urge to lean on Egill's desk. He was afraid of tipping it over, scattering all the carefully arranged framed photographs of Egill in the company of various VIPs with whom he had crossed paths in the line of duty. Huldar was willing to bet that the VIPs didn't return the favour. He recovered his balance without having to reach out for support, and continued: 'There's nothing going on that can't wait or be taken care of by someone else.'

Egill emitted a deep rumble, the corners of his mouth turning down even further. 'And there was I thinking the captain was always the last to abandon ship. I hope it won't be necessary to remind you that you're in charge of the investigation and that the first few days are critical.'

Huldar felt as if he had grit in his eyes. It hurt to blink, they were so sore. 'Erla, Ríkhardur, Almar and Stefán are all hard at it. The others are performing their tasks on top of their other work, though most have gone home seeing as it's Sunday. The inquiry's progressing slowly but surely and won't stop just because I nip home for a rest. I won't be much good to anyone till I've caught up on some sleep.' He refrained from pointing out the absurdity of the captain metaphor: the investigation was hardly a sinking ship. He didn't for a minute believe that any of his predecessors would have stayed awake round the clock in the early stages of an inquiry. Quite apart from which, their working methods hadn't exactly set a good example. These days you could hardly move in the property office for members of the internal inquiry team who were busy taking everything down from the shelves in an effort to work out whether any evidence had gone missing. It was rumoured that the results of this stock-taking were not going to look good for CID.

Egill grabbed his mouse, abruptly switching his attention to the computer. Huldar was willing to bet he was in the middle of a game of Patience. There was no need for him to be in the office on a Sunday; he only turned up at weekends to avoid exercising with his young wife. She had arranged for them to cycle right round the country next summer and Egill was going to have to come up with a bloody good excuse for not taking part if he wanted to avoid a second divorce. If he did go, Huldar had every intention of driving out east to visit his family, making sure that their paths crossed. He could do with a laugh.

'Well, I just hope you're not going to let us down. It would be a pity if you cocked this up.'

This wasn't worth pursuing. 'I won't. But there's more risk of that if I work round the clock without any sleep.'

Egill kept his gaze focused on the screen. 'At least set an alarm so you don't oversleep and miss the interview of this Sigvaldi. Regardless of what the psychologist says, I believe the girl meant something by it.'

'I won't oversleep, don't worry.' He would set an alarm and as a precaution he had asked Erla to call him an hour before Sigvaldi's interview was scheduled to begin. He had invited her to be present. Although she hadn't contributed much at the Children's House, she had paid close attention to the proceedings. They had worked together on a number of cases during the three years that Erla had been with CID. She had an excellent memory and never wasted her breath. With the exception of Ríkhardur, she was the person Huldar had probably worked with most closely, since he was one of the few officers who had no objection to partnering a woman. As a result she sought out his company, and since they were both single they tended to sit together at the rare CID socials. After the Karlotta debacle, Huldar had increasingly turned to Erla in an attempt to avoid Ríkhardur, but unfortunately she appeared to have misinterpreted his interest. Why did everything related to his private life have to go pear-shaped?

Egill glowered at him; he could tell that Huldar's mind was wandering. 'Just as well. And don't be misled by the crocodile tears. The really cunning operators are capable of putting on quite a performance.'

Sigvaldi Freysteinsson shed no tears, crocodile or otherwise. He sat on the hard chair facing Huldar and Erla, head bent, shoulders bowed. His shirt was buttoned up wrong and hung out of his trousers on one side. He appeared utterly crushed. It was exhausting to look at him and the energy that Huldar's rest had restored to him ebbed away every time his eye fell on that defeated face. To make matters worse, the man appeared to have hurt himself: he had a bandage around his right hand and a black bruise merging with the dark shadow under one eye. There had been no mention of any injuries in the report of his first interview.

Huldar hadn't yet commented on the injuries, although the interview had been in progress for nearly an hour. He had warned Erla not to refer to them until he himself raised the subject, for fear the man would go into lockdown if he mistakenly believed he was under suspicion. It was better to have him on their side, to start with at least. Up to now the questions had therefore touched on matters that were easy to discuss, such as what Sigvaldi thought about the message that had been left at his house and the possibility that someone might have a grudge against him because of a mistake he had made at work.

The message appeared to be as much of a mystery to him as it was to everyone else, and he dismissed any suggestion of a link to his job. According to him, his reputation was irreproachable, though he added, drily, that it wasn't that long since he had completed his specialist training. His patients were all women and he couldn't remember a single one, whether pregnant or suffering from some ailment, who hadn't parted from him on good terms.

When it seemed that nothing of substance was going to emerge from the questions about his job, Huldar steered the interview to his marriage.

The lifeless voice echoed off the bare walls. 'As I keep trying to explain, everything was fine when I left. My relationship with Elísa has always been good. No quarrels. No tensions.' Sigvaldi's head drooped; he reminded Huldar of a grown-up version of Margrét, despite the lack of physical resemblance between father and daughter. Sigvaldi raised his eyes again, even more wearily than when he had first arrived. 'I just can't take it in. I keep praying I'll come to my senses and find out I've imagined the whole thing. Or that it's a bad dream.'

Erla leant back, jabbing Huldar in the side as she did so. He had a feeling this wasn't accidental, as she made little attempt these days to disguise her attraction to him. It was a pity it wasn't mutual but Erla simply wasn't his type. She was too hard, both mentally and physically. Viewed from the back, her honed body could have been that of a man and she had such a coarse tongue that she'd been known to shock even the most foul-mouthed veterans of CID. She also spoke in a deliberately deep voice, so it could be hard to tell her gender, especially on the phone. Huldar doubted this gruffness and crudeness came naturally to her. He suspected it was her way of trying to fit in with the guys. He often wanted to point out that the men who talked like that were far from desirable role models. For men or women. But it had proved difficult to broach the subject. And even more so to subtly convey the message that he wasn't interested.

'Would you like some water?' Huldar's side ached from contact with Erla's iron elbow. If her intention had been to turn him on, a gentle caress of his thigh would have been more apposite. The thought of sex that bore more resemblance to a combat sport, no doubt spiced with obscenities as well, did nothing for him. In fact it was a positive turn-off.

Sigvaldi declined the water. It could have done nothing to alleviate the mental suffering he had been describing.

'Sigvaldi, I have to ask you something that may be painful. It's important that you answer honestly.' Huldar fixed and held the man's bloodshot eyes with his own. 'Is there any chance that either of you were having an extra-marital affair?'

The answer came back promptly, without pause for thought. 'No. No, no and no. Not me and not her. Sure, there have been opportunities, for me at least, but since we got married I haven't looked at another woman.'

'How can you be so sure that the same applied to her?' Erla's question was a natural one; of course the man couldn't answer for his wife with absolute certainty.

'I just know. Elísa wasn't the type. We were enough for each other. If you don't believe me, talk to her friends. They'll confirm it.'

'We will be talking to them, and not only about that. It's possible she may have confided in them about something she forgot or chose not to discuss with you. Important information can often be gleaned from incidents that didn't seem particularly significant at the time.' Huldar couldn't actually call any examples to mind and hoped the man wouldn't press him for any, but Sigvaldi merely stared vacantly at the wall behind them. 'Moving on. Was Elísa involved in any disputes or altercations at work or outside it that you're aware of? It doesn't have to have been recent.'

'No. Why would you think that?' Sigvaldi sniffed. Though he hadn't shed any tears during the interview, he might well be struggling to hold them back. 'She was popular at work and among her friends. Everyone liked her.'

'Yes, that's consistent with the picture we've built up. Nevertheless, we're compelled to ask you a number of questions that may sound absurd to you, if only to eliminate certain lines of inquiry. Just because her colleagues claim everything was fine, that doesn't necessarily mean she'd have agreed. The same applies to the testimony of her friends.'

'Elísa didn't have any enemies.'

'Not many of us do. Sure, people may envy or dislike us, but fortunately real enemies are few and far between. Anyway, leaving that aside . . .' There was no point trying to persuade the man to rake up anything negative about Elísa. Right now he could only see her in a rosy glow. But everyone had their bad days and everyone made mistakes. There wasn't a man or woman alive who was universally popular. Yet, in spite of intensive questioning, Sigvaldi's interview still hadn't provided any leads. It was looking increasingly likely that the murderer had selected Elísa at random. 'How do you get on with your neighbours? Any tensions about noise or trees or blocking out light, that kind of thing?'

'No. Nothing like that.' The man looked as if a light had been switched on in his head, but he was blazing with anger not joy. 'You think our neighbours might have been responsible? Which ones?'

'We have no reason to think that. We're simply trying to examine all the angles, as I explained. So your relations with your neighbours are OK?'

The light in Sigvaldi's eyes dimmed again. 'Yes, fine. The people one door down, at number sixty-eight, are quite good friends of ours. We chat to each other over the hedge and have the odd barbecue. Elísa and Védís saw more of each other than me and Helgi.'

'So they were friends then?' Erla scribbled down the question as she was speaking. There was no need since the interview was being recorded but it was a habit she had picked up. She took constant notes, during interviews, at the scene and on her computer at work. Although Huldar sometimes wondered if he should follow her example, he didn't have the knack of writing at the same time as talking to people.

'Yes. Védís's second name is Gísladóttir, I think, and I'm almost sure Helgi's is Magnússon.' The pen skated deftly over the page as Erla noted this down. Huldar had grown so used to watching her write that he could almost guess the letters from her movements. When she had finished, he looked back at Sigvaldi. The man appeared to be mesmerised by her note-taking as well. He must have slept even less than Huldar over the last few days.

'Right, I'm going to show you some drawings by your daughter.' Huldar took a clear plastic sleeve from the pile of documents on the table. 'We gather that Margrét drew these pictures after seeing a man watching your house from the road and, on at least one occasion, from inside your garden.'

Sigvaldi carefully lined the drawings up in front of him and studied them. It was difficult to interpret his expression and Huldar and Erla had no choice but to wait patiently until he had finished. Without a word, he suddenly collected the pictures together and raised his eyes. 'These could be Margrét's. It looks like her style. But then I don't have any pictures by other girls her age to compare them to.' He pushed them back across the table. 'I've never seen them before, if that's what you're asking.'

'That's not what I'm asking.' The man's reaction had put Huldar on the alert. In the circumstances he would have expected Sigvaldi to ask about the man in the picture. 'We're interested in learning whether she mentioned this to either you or Elísa and, if so, whether you have any idea who the man was.'

Sigvaldi seemed at a loss for an answer. They watched him lick his lips and run his left hand through his untidy hair. He sighed and slumped even lower in his chair.

'Take all the time you need.' Huldar gestured to the unin-spiring refreshments on the tray. 'Would you like some water now? Or a coffee?'

'No, thanks.' There was a puzzled note in Sigvaldi's voice as if he had never heard of these drinks before and didn't know if it was safe to try them. He swallowed and his prom-inent Adam's apple bobbed up and down. Then he cleared his throat again and straightened up a little. 'Margrét's a child. Kids view the world differently from us. They have a tendency to imagine things.'

'Imagine things?' Huldar found Erla's tone a bit brusque considering that the man was the girl's father. Apart from Margrét's comment, there was nothing to link him to the murder. The description Sigvaldi had given of his marriage was consistent with the testimony of everyone they had inter-viewed and all the evidence they had uncovered so far. In the absence of any other information, they were to treat the man like a grieving husband, though of course they still had to question him about his injuries.

'Could you explain for us?' Huldar gave him a friendly smile. 'I haven't spoken to your daughter but I've seen her and she appears to be a perfectly ordinary little girl in extraordinary circumstances. The psychologists at the Children's House didn't dismiss these pictures as imaginary.' Margrét was seven, old enough in Huldar's opinion to know the difference between reality and make-believe, though she wasn't his child. He had about as much desire to have children as he had to sleep with the masculine Erla. 'Has Margrét been diagnosed with learning difficulties?'

'No, quite the opposite. She's doing well at school. Maybe she doesn't have as many friends as we'd like but she's not being bullied. Margrét's just like other children except that she's got an unusually fertile imagination. She imagines stuff; sees things that aren't there.'

'Invisible friends and so on?' Huldar couldn't disguise his disappointment. Perhaps the man in the drawings was a figment of the child's imagination. Their only lead might turn out to be no more real than Father Christmas, who, come to think of it, the girl had also mentioned. He pictured her white, china-doll face and unruly red hair. Was it possible that she hadn't actually been under the bed when her mother was attacked? Could she have hidden there in the morning after finding Elísa's cold, stiff body? After locking her own door behind her? Could she have made up all the details about the events of the night? No, impossible. 'What form does her imagination take?'

'She doesn't have visions or see figures or anything like

that. But she has a tendency to think something really happened when she only dreamt it. It's actually not that uncommon among children.'

'And you'd put this in that category?' Huldar pointed to the drawings.

'I don't know. She never mentioned any man to me or Elísa – as far as I'm aware. Where did you find the drawings?'

'In her room.' Huldar couldn't be any more specific. The officers who had been first to examine the girl's bedroom couldn't remember where the pictures had been before they had ended up scattered everywhere for Freyja to find. One had a feeling that they had been in a drawer in the wardrobe, but both agreed that they hadn't been anywhere conspicuous, and the photos taken before they'd set to work confirmed this. Since her father didn't know about them, there was no telling whether the girl had hidden them or her mother had been aware of their existence. Hopefully Margrét would be able to enlighten them herself. 'I'm not entirely satisfied with your dismissal of this as a figment of your daughter's imagination. The pictures suggest that someone was watching your house, so we need to know if they're pure fantasy. Is that your considered opinion?'

'God. No. Yes. I don't know. I'm just too confused to know what I think about anything.' Sigvaldi sighed heavily. 'Why should anyone have been watching us? Isn't it obvious that the murderer got the wrong house or chose it at random? There's no way Elísa could have been killed for any reason connected to us. We're not that sort of people. There can't have been any man outside. It just doesn't make sense.'

Further discussion of Margrét's drawings seemed unlikely

to prove productive. The best course would be to have a psychiatrist assess the reliability of the girl's statement.

'Has Margrét spoken to you at all about the night her mother died?' Huldar would have liked to ask Sigvaldi straight out why Margrét blamed him for her mother's death, but reminded himself that they needed to handle him gently. For now.

'No.' Sigvaldi looked bewildered. He gazed at Huldar and Erla in turn. 'She won't talk to me. She refuses to be alone with me and won't even look at me when we're in company. I have no idea why. God knows, she has no reason to be angry with me or frightened of me.'

Huldar nodded. Clearly the girl hadn't forgiven her father. It was time to wrap this up. 'Incidentally, what happened to your hand?'

Sigvaldi glanced down at the scruffy bandage, which obviously wasn't the work of a professional. 'I tripped over my suitcase in my hurry to pack. I was in such bad shock that I wasn't paying attention.'

Huldar nodded again. 'Did you get it looked at?'

'No.' Sigvaldi hesitated, then added: 'I had other things on my mind.' There was no mistaking the sarcasm in his hoarse voice.

'There's no mention of any injuries in the report of your first interview. Did you trip over the suitcase afterwards?'

'No. It happened when I was emptying my hotel room. I was in a hurry to leave for the airport after I got the news, obviously. It wasn't until I got home from the interview that I realised I'd hurt myself. I was met at the airport and brought straight here. That's why I didn't mention it, and the police didn't notice because there was nothing to see then. The black eye only developed after I lay down.'

'I see. We can help you jump the queue at A&E. You ought to have it looked at.'

'No, thanks. There's no need. I'm a doctor, so I know it's nothing serious. I'll recover.'

'I'm afraid you'll have to go to A&E. We need a medical certificate confirming the nature of your injuries.' Huldar didn't smile. He glanced at the clock. 'We'd better call it a day. You're not planning to leave town any time soon, are you? We're sure to need to talk to you again shortly.'

'I'm not going anywhere. Except to A&E.'

Huldar slapped the table so hard that his hand stung, then stood up. 'Right. That's it then. Unless there's anything else you want to tell us, or think we ought to know.'

Sigvaldi shook his head. 'No, nothing I can think of. You'll keep me in the picture, won't you? No one cares more than I do about seeing this sick monster caught. No one.' He lowered his eyes, then rose to his feet. Huldar escorted him all the way to the main entrance. Neither of them spoke. Then, as they stood staring out through the glass that separated them from the bitter north wind, Sigvaldi turned and held out his hand.

'Good luck. I'll be waiting by the phone.' Then an odd look crossed his face, as though he'd forgotten something upstairs. 'I couldn't give a damn if Elísa was having an affair. I just want you to find the man who killed her. Then, for all I care, you can kill him.' He headed to the electronic doors, which opened with a sucking sound. The icy air poured in but Huldar didn't move. He stayed there, watching thoughtfully, as the man walked over to his car, climbed in and drove away.

Chapter 13

Karl didn't really know why the car got on his nerves so much. His friends weren't complaining, though Halli's knees were jammed against the glove compartment and Börkur kept shifting around in the back seat in a vain attempt to make himself more comfortable. They were in no position to make a fuss, after all; neither owned a car, so they had to make do with the one Karl had inherited from his mother.

In spite of this, Karl simply couldn't reconcile himself to the vehicle. He might as well face it: almost every detail of his existence sucked, yet he hadn't been parachuted into someone else's life by mistake; he was trapped in his own. Ugly house, crap car, substandard friends. This was his world and he had better accept it. No father and now no mother. How ironic that his only 'close' relative should be the emotionally – and now also physically – remote Arnar. Could life be any more of a downer? Everyone else at least had a family – or a girlfriend. But even if the woman of his dreams were to fall out of the sky into his arms, chances were she wouldn't hang around, so there was no point chasing girls. His life sucked. The sooner he accepted it, the better. Nothing was going to change any time soon.

He could start by learning to live with the car – only it was impossible. You'd have thought the goal had been to manufacture a vehicle to meet the minimum possible requirements: bodywork, chassis, four wheels, seats and a steering wheel.

Nothing to enhance the driving experience or provide any comfort for the passengers. He also felt inexplicably irritated at the thought of the pride his mother had taken in it, the way she had cleaned it inside and out every week, and taken it for regular services as if it were an aircraft.

Shortly after she died, Karl had checked online to see how much he could get for it, only to be disappointed. The dealer he rang said it made no difference that the car was in perfect condition and that you'd never have known it was eight years old. The only advantage of its being in good condition was that it would speed up the sale. Then he had yawned hugely, as if the vehicle were beneath contempt. Karl had the impression the man was relieved when he said he would have to think about it. Of course, there was no chance of flogging the car anyway. Like the house, he'd have to split the proceeds with Arnar, and his share would only cover the cost of an even crappier model, if such a thing existed. In fact, he'd be lucky to buy a decent bike for that amount.

'Try ringing the bell.' Börkur grabbed hold of the headrests and shoved his head forward between the front seats. Karl leant back and his view of the house was blocked by Halli's head. 'Just go and ask to speak to the woman.'

'Then what? What am I supposed to say to her?' This was the worst idea so far this evening. Not that the others had been much better. 'Hello. Are you Elísa? I heard your ID number on the radio.'

'Yeah, why not?' Börkur looked from the house to Karl. 'Wouldn't you be curious if someone knocked on your door and told you something like that?'

The back of Halli's head waggled slightly as he spoke. 'Personally, I'd think he was mental. Some kind of headcase.'

Now and then there was a grain of common sense in Halli's contributions. 'She might call the cops. Or freak out and beat you up.'

Karl lost it. He felt an urge to tear down the string of beads that hung from the rear-view mirror and lash Halli over the head with them. 'What the fuck? Do you really think I'd let some old bag hit me? You might, you fucking pussy. Not me.'

Halli stared at him, flabbergasted by this violent reaction. Karl's anger evaporated, leaving behind a sensation of emptiness, and he wondered what had made him fly off the handle like that. Halli hadn't meant any harm, any more than he ever did with his gormless comments. Karl simply wasn't himself these days; the shortwave broadcasts had unsettled him and his disquiet showed no signs of fading. In fact, it was growing worse.

No doubt it was part and parcel of the existential crisis he had been going through lately. He was dissatisfied with chemistry, dissatisfied with his home, dissatisfied with his friends and dissatisfied with himself.

He had just turned twenty-three and had to face the fact he was a failure. And he couldn't see how to turn his life around. But losing his temper wasn't the solution, whatever had brought it on – general depression or his anxiety about the shortwave broadcasts. None of this was Halli's fault. Karl tried to retrieve the situation: 'Just kidding.' It was hard to tell from Halli's expression whether he believed him; he turned back to the window without a word.

As usual, Börkur was oblivious to any undercurrents. He was the only one who hadn't spotted their old fourth wheel Thórdur at the cinema earlier. Thórdur had been there with his girlfriend. Both parties had pretended not to see each other in the half-empty auditorium. There were times when it must be an advantage to be as impervious as Börkur. He slapped Karl on the shoulder.

'You could always take a chance. Anyhow, it doesn't look like anybody's home.'

Karl, silently studying the house, came to the same conclusion. All the lights appeared to be off, the drive was empty and the windows were shut. Karl immediately regretted not having shown Halli by knocking on the door. It would have been good for his image and wouldn't have had any awkward repercussions seeing as there was nobody there. He must learn to think before he opened his mouth.

'I wonder if there's a broadcast on air now.' Karl stared at the deserted house, trying to fathom why the woman's ID number should have been read out. He had long since given up trying to work out why his own had come up. Perhaps it was all a massive coincidence and the sequences hadn't been ID numbers at all.

'Dunno.' Halli was still staring at the house, his breath fogging up the window. He wiped the glass.

'Aren't you two going to try and catch it?' Karl glanced into the back seat at Börkur, who had lost interest and was now drumming his fingers on his knees and humming a tune.

'Me?' Börkur looked surprised. 'No. I haven't touched my receiver for weeks. It isn't even hooked up. It blew a fuse and I couldn't be arsed to fix it.'

Karl shifted his gaze to Halli. 'What about you?'

Halli kept his eyes on the house. 'No. I think mine's broken too. I've kind of lost interest in that radio stuff. There's so much else going on. You know what I mean, just so much other cool stuff.'

'Broken?'

'Or something. I'm thinking of flogging it anyway. Buying a new computer instead.' Halli had plunged into the online world with such enthusiasm that when, just before New Year, the police had carried out a raid on a ring involved in illegal downloads, he had been among those arrested. His IT equipment, his pride and joy, for which he had slaved for months in the supermarket warehouse, had been confiscated. At the time Karl had hoped this might force Halli to revive his old interest in radio, but no such luck. That was more than two months ago and he still hadn't encountered Halli on any frequency.

Karl was speechless. His friends had completely lost interest and not even the numbers station was enough to rekindle it. Both used to be like him – eager to communicate with foreign operators and fascinated by all the weird and wonderful transmissions out there. For years they had often chosen to sit at home by their radios, waiting for something exciting to happen on air, rather than meet up in person. But when at last, against all the odds, it had happened, they couldn't be bothered to tune in. Karl was at a loss. He opened his mouth, then shut it again, unwilling to hear their replies. It would be even worse to hear them confirm out loud that he was the only one left in the ham radio world. If they abandoned him, he would have nobody left. Not a single soul.

'Look!' Börkur pointed to the next-door house. 'There's somebody watching us.' Through the net curtain they could see a figure peering out at their car. Nothing odd about that and no reason to be afraid, but Karl felt a shiver run down his spine all the same. The atmosphere in the car became even more subdued.

The idea of checking out Elísa's house had come to them, seemingly out of the blue, after they left the cinema. They would drive first to her place, then past the house of the woman whose ID number had been added to the list in the latest broadcast. They didn't live that far apart. But seeing the shadowy figure watching them, Karl wondered if this had been such a good idea. The nosy neighbour might mistake them for burglars casing the joint, and call the police. He wondered if his licence plate was visible at this distance. No, probably not. Karl could think of many things he'd rather do than visit a police station. As a precaution, he had better empty the ashtray containing the evidence of this evening's spliffs. There was a sour taste in his mouth as he thought of the pungent smell now permeating the entire basement of his house.

Karl started the car. 'Let's go. There's nothing to see here. I don't know what we were expecting. The woman's a total stranger; I didn't need to see her house to confirm that.'

Börkur fell back into his seat as Karl accelerated away, but that didn't shut him up. 'Let's drive past the other woman's place. I mean, we've come all this way, and for all you know you may recognise her. Maybe we'll see her and she'll turn out to be from the chemistry department. Then you'll know the broadcast's a student prank.'

'Student prank?' Halli didn't take his eyes off the road ahead. From the way he was deliberately ignoring Karl, it was clear he was still sulking.

'Yeah, a student prank. Is the departmental party coming up?'

'No. That was before Christmas.' As Karl drove past the neighbour's house he regretted not having turned and driven out the other way. If the watcher in the window hadn't been able to read the licence plate before, he or she would certainly be able to now. The figure turned to follow their progress and he stamped on the accelerator.

If he sprayed window cleaner around the basement, maybe that would cover up the smell of dope.

'This has nothing to do with the chemistry department.' Ástrós Einarsdóttir, the owner of the new ID number, didn't allow public access to her Facebook page and the only pictures of her online were old and blurry. If she was enrolled at the university she must be a mature student because she was sixty-five. There was no one that old in his lectures. Unless she was studying from home or in a different department. The photos of her had been too grainy for Karl to say for sure whether he had ever seen her before. It didn't help that she had one of those instantly forgettable faces. She was about as memorable as this car.

'Whoa!' Börkur, who wasn't wearing a seat belt, slammed into the door as Karl swerved on to the main road without slowing down. He wanted to get out of here as quickly as possible. 'Go on. Swing by the other woman's place. It can't do any harm.'

Unless they ran into another nosy neighbour who might also report them to the police. Nevertheless, Karl obeyed. At least Börkur was still talking to him: he couldn't face the drive home with both of them in a sulk. He'd rather finish this disastrous evening on a high note. That way he might be able to sleep tonight instead of lying awake, fretting over his lonely future. 'OK, OK. But I'm not going to knock on her door. There's no point.'

'You could at least try.'

In the rear-view mirror Karl saw Börkur fold his arms and

turn away to look out of the side window, like a spoilt child denied a trip to the sweet shop.

Karl didn't respond and silence descended again. Luckily, they didn't have far to go, but Karl switched on the radio to lighten the tense atmosphere. They were playing a sentimental song about eternal friendship. Damn. There was no chance of changing stations as that would only draw attention to the unfortunate coincidence.

The song didn't end until they reached the other woman's address. Karl parked against the kerb. 'Right. Now what?' He bent forwards to get a better view through the windscreen. The house, a maisonette containing two flats, was lit up by a string of Christmas lights that no one had yet taken down. They had discovered by googling her that Ástrós lived upstairs – alone, apparently, as there were no other phone numbers registered at that address. Apart from this, they knew almost nothing about her.

Halli and Börkur had been little help after they heard the numbers broadcast. When Halli was startled awake by the opening tune, he had seemed distracted. If Karl hadn't known better he'd have thought Halli was ashamed of having dozed off. He'd hardly said a word, merely listened without participating in the conversation. Börkur had more than made up for this by talking so much that Karl had hardly had a chance to write down the evening's broadcast and the new ID number. After the recitation finished, they had tried and failed to come up with any plausible explanation for it. Börkur found it amusing; an unexpected adventure to break up the monotony of their lives. For Halli it seemed to be an embarrassment and best ignored, whereas for Karl it was a compelling mystery that involved him personally.

What could be more personal than your ID number?

'There's somebody home. The light just went out upstairs.' In his excitement, Halli had forgotten his bad temper. He had shaken off his earlier distracted mood once they got to the cinema, and now he seemed to be recovering from the altercation with Karl. 'Do you think it's her?'

Börkur stuck his head between their seats and peered up at the house. As he wriggled to get a better view, his foot knocked against a loose object and he reached down. 'What are you doing with this?' He held out a mobile phone. 'Was it your mum's? It was on the floor.' The phone had a sparkly cover.

Karl took it and turned it over in his hands. He had never seen it before. His mother's phone, which was still lying on her bedside table, wasn't nearly as smart. 'On the floor? I've no idea whose it is.' He tried switching it on but the battery was flat. 'Perhaps one of my mum's friends dropped it.' The phone must have slid out from under the seat when he stamped on the accelerator. It could have been lying there for months.

'Were any of your mum's friends hot?' Börkur bent down again and this time drew out a pair of women's knickers. A lacy, scarlet thong. There was no way that could have belonged to Karl's mother. Karl took it from him, turning slightly pink as his fingers touched the flimsy material. It was like trying to catch hold of a spider's web or thin air.

Halli burst out laughing but his initial amusement quickly soured. 'Have you got a girlfriend you're not telling us about? I don't mean to be rude about your mum, but there's no way these belonged to her or any of her mates. I saw a couple of them once and they wouldn't have been able to pull these over their knees.'

'I haven't got a girlfriend.' Karl carefully laid down the thong and placed the phone beside it. 'I haven't a clue who these belong to or what they're doing in the car.'

'They must have been here since your mum was using it.' Börkur picked up the phone. 'I've got a charger at home that fits this model. Like me to charge it and find out whose it is?'

Halli glared at Karl as if expecting him to decline the offer for fear that his secret girlfriend would be found out. He smiled faintly when Karl thanked Börkur and let him pocket the phone.

The lights went out in another window upstairs. And a third. Slowly but surely they all went out. In the same instant the radio news began.

'The police are still refusing to release any details about the death of a young woman last Thursday night. According to sources, the incident is being treated as murder. The woman's body was discovered at home where she had been alone with her three children while her husband was abroad. There was no evidence of drug or alcohol abuse. The Police Commissioner's office is due to issue a statement tomorrow morning.'

Karl swallowed. He didn't want to stay here another minute. He felt as if he were suffocating in the car and cracked open the window to let in some fresh air. Pain suddenly exploded in his head as though he had been struck with a hammer. He turned the key in the ignition and drove off. He couldn't be sure but as he turned out of the street he thought he heard a faint scream. Neither Halli nor Börkur showed any signs of noticing it, however, so Karl kept it to himself.

When he finally fell asleep later that night, the scream was still echoing in his head.

Chapter 14

The popcorn was too salty. Ástrós kept having to get up and refill her glass of water, which broke her concentration. She had completely lost track of the plot and only had the vaguest notion of how the people on screen were connected or who had done what to whom. The identikit actors didn't help with their big, white teeth illuminating the screen every time they smiled; the women all young, their faces like extraordinarily beautiful, immobile masks; the men too old to justify the young women's interest. She missed Geiri. He should have been sitting here beside her, dozing off whenever there was a lull in the action or she spent too much time grumbling that the female characters were only there to vie for the men's attention.

Ástrós reached for the remote control and turned down the volume for the adverts. They always seemed to be louder than the programmes, as though to ensure that nobody would miss them. Perhaps it was time to go to bed and persevere with the book she was struggling to finish. She really couldn't care less about the fates of the two-dimensional characters who were so busy cheating on one another on the TV. For all she cared, the lot of them could end up alone or dead in the gutter.

The temperature had dropped and she went over to pull the curtains across the large sitting-room window. As she drew near, she felt the cold reaching out to meet her and her skin prickled with gooseflesh. It was slightly warmer once the thick curtains were in place, shutting out the draught and the sight of the frozen world outside. Ástrós had taken a quick peek out at the deserted street. Naturally there was no one about in this weather. It wasn't actually snowing but a biting wind blew the loose snow crystals over the icy pavements and tarmac. She shivered and carefully closed every gap in the curtains. With any luck the weather would be better tomorrow. It was about time this relentless series of cold fronts went off and persecuted some other part of the world.

The advertisements gave way to trailers for upcoming programmes. This did nothing to lift the depression induced by the cold and loneliness. Better call it a night. Ástrós went to check that the balcony door was locked and to close the curtains there too. She hadn't ventured out on to the balcony since she tidied up the planter in preparation for winter, removing the dried-up summer flowers and a little tuft of weeds that was peeping out of the soil. There was no real need to check the door, but she did so out of habit. In defiance of her scientific training, she had a superstitious fear that some unexplained danger would threaten if she failed to check the door. It was no good trying to rationalise the feeling away. It was like the fear of the dark, which had afflicted her as a child and returned now that she was alone. As long as Geiri had been there, she hadn't given it a thought; once the lights were out the warmth of his presence had kept at bay any dread about what might be lurking in dark corners.

Ástrós jumped at what looked like a movement outside. She let go of the curtains. Her heart was hammering in her chest. Her thoughts flew to the doctor's appointment she had booked to check if she needed stronger pills for her blood pressure, and this raised her pulse still further. She didn't want a heart attack. She met her own reflection in the glass: the worn pyjamas visible below the skirt of her grubby dressing gown, the grey hair that had looked so neat when she had finished all the curling and teasing but was now sticking up untidily. The wide-open eyes almost lost among more wrinkles than it was fair for one face to contain. She was riveted by the sight of the loose jowls and the turkey wattle of flesh that sagged unbecomingly from her chin down to her neck. What had happened to her face? And her body? The dressing gown tied round her waist only exaggerated her shapeless figure, adding several kilos where she could least afford them.

Ástrós pulled herself together. It was pointless indulging in vain regrets about her appearance when the choice lay between growing old or dying. Her thoughts flew to the strange phone messages and the promised visit. The person in question hadn't shown up or sent any further message to cancel. As the day wore on she had gradually stopped thinking about it, put away the cake she had taken out of the freezer and emptied the coffee out of the thermos. She wasn't going to drink it that late in the evening and risk lying awake all night. Not that it mattered if she slept or not; there was nothing to look forward to in the morning. It was the thought of lying in the dark, staring uselessly at the ceiling, that she would do anything to avoid. Strange how one's troubles seemed so insurmountable at night. The tiniest problems drew strength from the darkness. The moment it grew light they shrank and became manageable again.

Nothing stirred on the balcony apart from the swirling snow that had accumulated in one corner. Ástrós felt her heartbeat returning to normal and suddenly everything appeared in a better light. As she turned away from the window, she noticed that her reflection didn't look as much of an affront to her self-respect as before. She sighed and a small cloud formed on the glass, only to vanish almost immediately. That dreadful TV drama had probably affected her more than she realised. At one point a man had crawled under the bushes along the wall of a house until he found a window to break in through. Then he had throttled one of the beautiful women with his gloved hands. The woman's death mask as she lay on the floor was as flawless as when she had been alive. Ástrós doubted she would make such a beautiful corpse herself. Irritably, she pulled the curtains over the door.

The programme resumed after the ad break. Ástrós sneaked one more look out at the balcony, jerking the curtains apart to take any potential burglar by surprise, but there was nothing to be seen. It must have been rubbish blowing around. Although an agile man could climb up there easily enough, it was unlikely that a thief would go to that amount of trouble.

The drama had lost all its charm by now. Ástrós hurried into the bathroom, leaving the TV on to avoid being enveloped in silence while she got ready for bed. She might be able to hear what happened to the beautiful people as well, but in the event the buzzing of her electric toothbrush drowned out their conversations.

When she heard an oddly muffled crash it didn't occur to her that it was anything other than another commercial break – an advert for home insurance this time. So it came as a horrible shock when she emerged into the hall to see a shadowy figure swooping towards her, its arm raised to strike. She didn't even have time to scream. Her cry was caught in her throat as the blow landed on her neck.

When Ástrós regained consciousness she was sitting more or less upright. She couldn't open her eyes. Her hands fumbled for her face. She felt it was going to burst, as if her head had been clamped in a vice. But her trembling fingers could only feel some sort of smooth, cold texture covering half her face, from the middle of her nose up to her forehead. She ran her hands over her head but could find no way of loosening it; she scrabbled with her fingernails at the bands that had obviously been wound round and round. Clawing at it was futile; it only made her forehead and cheeks sting. It felt as if a mask had been glued to her face.

Just then her right hand was wrenched from her head and she felt a familiar object being forced into her fist. It was a pencil. Her hand was roughly shoved into position over a sheet of paper on a table in front of her. She was in the kitchen, she realised. She could tell by the familiar feel of the chair and the faint smell of curry from yesterday's leftovers that she had heated up for supper.

'Do the maths.'

'What?' Her voice cracked, but to Ástrós's surprise she sounded more astonished than afraid. What on earth was happening? Her neck was agony and she remembered receiving a blow. In fact her whole body was aching, so the man must have dragged her violently to the kitchen.

'Do the maths. You're so fucking good at it, aren't you?' It was a man's voice, oddly indistinct, as though he had something over his mouth, but perhaps that was because of whatever was covering her ears. Ástrós didn't recognise the voice but could tell that the man was beside himself with rage; his voice was quivering with hatred. The pressure in her head increased and Ástrós sensed she was losing consciousness again. All she could think was that this was bound to end badly. The only question was how quickly? How long would be quick enough? Twenty minutes? Ten? Five?

Ástrós sniffed and steeled herself. If she didn't make an effort, it was sure to turn out even worse. 'Maths? What maths?' How could she do any calculations if she couldn't see? Should she ask the man to uncover her eyes? No, it was probably better not to see his face. This kindled a tiny spark of hope: the fact he had blindfolded her suggested he didn't intend to finish her off completely. 'I'll do any maths you like. Just tell me what.'

'Probability. Calculate the probability for me.'

Ástrós felt faint. What was the man on about? Probability? Perhaps he'd got the wrong house. 'I'm no mathematician. Or statistician either. I'm a biology teacher. Retired.' Her mouth was so dry it hurt but begging for water would probably be futile.

'I said, calculate the probability.'

'Of what?' Ástrós felt her eyelids stinging with unshed tears underneath the horrible wrappings. 'I can't just calculate probability at random.'

'You're so clever. Show me how it is that if there are two possibilities, you should only focus on the probability of one of them happening. Just ignore the other. I bet you find that easy, don't you?'

Her heart and lungs seemed to constrict. She grew short of breath, was close to blacking out. What did the man want her to calculate? The thing he wanted her to prove made no sense. 'I can't calculate that. It's not a proper equation. I don't know what it is.' The pencil moved and she hoped he wouldn't see the line that must now run across the page as an unforgivable blunder.

'You're telling me.'

Ástrós was silent. She didn't dare speak for fear of provoking him further.

'Go on, do the maths.'

Her fingers trembled and she almost dropped the pencil as she began to scrawl figures. She tried to visualise the paper and symbols. She didn't want to write them on top of one another and risk another blow. $1/10 + 9/10 = 1$. It was all she could think of. Giving up the attempt, she licked her dry lips. What she wouldn't give to be able to see. The uncertainty about where he was, what he was doing and whether he was about to strike her again was unbearable. She made herself as small as possible, bracing herself to prepare for the blows that were bound to fall.

'What's that supposed to mean?' Instead of hitting her, the man violently grabbed hold of her upper arm.

'The probability of mutually exclusive events with odds of one in ten plus nine in ten is one hundred per cent.' The pain in her throat flared up with every word. She hoped she had made herself understood.

'Mutually exclusive? What the hell are you talking about? I asked you to demonstrate why you should only focus on one of two possibilities when you're calculating probability. I'd have thought you knew all about that.'

This rang a faint bell. Had he come to the right place after all? But how could this nonsense ring any bells? 'No.' Her nose was leaking. She realised she was weeping, though her tears had nowhere to go. 'I'm not familiar with anything like that. It's a false assertion.'

'Let's say the probability of a negative outcome is one in four. Doesn't that mean that the probability against it happening is three in four? So which is the more probable? The negative or the positive outcome? One in four. Three in four.' The man fell silent. Ástrós sensed him beside her, then heard him move round behind her to the other side. So it didn't come as a shock when he whispered in her other ear: 'Or one in ten. Nine in ten.' She was taken aback by how cold he felt when his head touched the bare skin on her forehead. No breath, either hot or cold, had accompanied his whisper. The last dregs of rational thought abandoned her at the idea that the man might be dead. What else could explain the ice-cold flesh and lack of breath? She felt him moving away. What she heard next made her blood run cold: the familiar squeaking of drawers and rattle of steel kitchen utensils. The drawers were full of knives, scissors, tongs and other implements that could be used to inflict pain.

The clatter of steel grew louder, as though the man was rooting around in the drawer in search of the right instrument. A pathetic whimper escaped her, taking with it her last reserves of courage. She was helpless, powerless to resist the whims of this deranged man. How ridiculous that she should have clung to the hope that this might turn out well. The man slammed down a bunch of utensils on the table. Ástrós tried not to think about which ones he thought he needed and what he intended to do with them. Instead she wondered in desperation what his crazy statement about probability could mean.

'Do the maths.'

Ástrós flinched.

'Demonstrate for me how you work it out. That the probability of a positive outcome is lower than that of a negative one. You're the expert at that.'

While she desperately scribbled arbitrary numbers on the page, a memory began to stir. Was it possible? Could there really be a connection? She stopped writing. If she was right, she might be able to talk the man round. It was worth trying. Trembling, she put the pencil carefully down. Her voice shook, her throat hurt and her mouth was dry. 'One in four is a lower percentage than three in four. One in ten is lower than one in nine. But it doesn't follow that one in four or one in ten is equal to zero. It depends on the context whether the number is considered large or small. Sometimes one in four is considered a very high probability. One in ten too.'

The man let out a roar and Ástrós quailed. She had no way of avoiding the blow that now fell, making her head ring. Then everything went quiet. His footsteps receded and, straining her ears, she heard him fiddling with the light switches in the sitting room. Unable to see, she couldn't remember how she had left the room, so she wasn't sure if he was switching the lights on or off. The volume of the television was suddenly turned up. Ástrós felt her pulse quickening. This must be intended to drown out other sounds; to muffle her screams. But could it have been a mistake on his part? Wasn't there a chance that the downstairs neighbours would come charging up to complain about the noise?

A faint ray of hope cut through the pain, darkness and terror. The neighbours. If she could only escape from the flat they would be able to save her. She wouldn't have to go far to alert them. All she had to do was make it outside. Having lived here for decades, she could find her way blindfold.

Leaning on the tabletop, Ástrós pushed herself up on to her feet. She began to grope her way along the table towards the kitchen door.

'Where do you think you're going, maths genius? Self-appointed probabilatist.'

Ástrós gasped and turned her head, though she knew she wouldn't be able to see anything. She felt a pedantic impulse to point out that there was no such word as 'probabilatist' but didn't get a chance. She was flung back into the chair and her head was dragged back as far as it would go. Leather-clad fingers forced her jaws apart until she thought they would break.

She tasted metal. A hard object was forced into her mouth and down her throat. Right down her throat. She was aware of a chemical smell as she struggled not to gag, then the man started winding something round her jaws and mouth. It was sticky tape. Strong adhesive tape, intended to hold the metal object in place.

The man released her and as she fought for air she heard a clunk. He was plugging something in. Then he came closer and she heard the click of a button as he whispered in her ear: 'Serves you right.' He paused, then added: 'Soon be over.'

But he was lying.

Chapter 15

Monday

The bags under Huldar's eyes were more pronounced than ever; he thought if he squinted down he would be able to see them. Ríkhardur was sitting opposite him in the seldom-used visitors' chair. He avoided meeting Huldar's gaze, as though he'd rather not be faced with such a seedy vision first thing in the morning. He himself was neatly turned out as ever, emitting a faint smell of toothpaste mingled with aftershave. Huldar couldn't help feeling a momentary stab of satisfaction when he spotted a small patch of stubble on Ríkhardur's cheek that he had missed while shaving.

This was the second time lately that he'd noticed a flaw in his appearance. It was so out of character. Perhaps he'd left the patch deliberately, like architects in past centuries including minor defects in their buildings so as not to offend God, for He alone was perfect.

But of course the truth was that with all that was going on at work and in his private life, Ríkhardur didn't have time to be as impeccably turned out as before. Huldar found it depressing to see these outward signs of his suffering, though he took care not to let it show. It didn't help that he himself may have been partly to blame for the failure of his colleague's marriage. His schadenfreude over the patch of stubble was replaced by anxiety; what if Ríkhardur cracked under the strain, as the HR manager had warned he might? They couldn't cope without him on the investigation team.

'You haven't considered taking a few days' leave?' Huldar blurted out the words without stopping to think. Ríkhardur was clearly taken aback.

'Leave? Now?' It sounded like a curse.

'Just a suggestion. You know you're entitled to some. I was sent a summary of departmental holiday allowance and you've got a ridiculous amount left. We don't want you coming down with flu or collapsing from overwork. It would be better if you took a few days off now rather than end up taking several weeks if you get ill.'

Perhaps the HR manager had been wrong, though. Wouldn't it be better for Ríkhardur to immerse himself in work than sit at home, brooding over what he had lost? It must be a strange feeling to rattle around alone in the house he had until recently shared with Karlotta. Lately even Huldar had caught himself reflecting that he was fed up with waking alone. Though admittedly not this morning. Any woman would have packed her bags after waking up with a guy who looked this rough. His thoughts strayed back to Freyja and how he had screwed up. Why hadn't he simply told her the truth? It wouldn't have mattered what they talked about that evening – the noise in the bar had drowned out every other word so she probably wouldn't even have grasped what he did for a living. But no. Instead of waking up beside her and admitting the truth – blaming the drink perhaps – he had slunk out like an idiot. It would be a hell of a lot harder to slink back into her good graces.

Ríkhardur's face twisted into a grimace. 'No thanks. I have no intention of taking any time off.'

'Good. I'd rather not lose your talents but I'm obliged to draw your attention to all this bloody leave you've accumulated.'

Ríkhardur nodded and made a gesture as though he'd like to hurl his leave out of the window into the wide expanse of Faxaflói Bay. 'I've hit a brick wall,' he said. 'Whatever angle I take, I draw a blank. If anything, the solution seems even more remote than it did in the beginning. Neither Elísa nor her husband had any dirty secrets, as far as I can discover, or trod on anyone's toes or were involved in any feuds – this is according to her friends, neighbours and work colleagues. I'm coming round to the idea that either she was selected at random or the murderer got the wrong person. Which doesn't look good for the next victim. If there is another.'

They lapsed into silence. Huldar had an acid feeling in the pit of his stomach. He had tried to dismiss the thought that he might not catch the killer, but it was becoming ever more insistent. Every time it reared its ugly head, the idea seemed to have gained strength and become harder to deny. Added to that was the worry that the next murder might be just around the corner, with Huldar and his team powerless to prevent it. Every time the phone rang he felt a constriction in his chest, which only eased when it turned out not to be someone reporting the discovery of a second body. His most fervent wish right now was for the girl to be proved wrong.

To cap it all, he had run out of nicotine gum. It took a superhuman effort to remain calm as his subordinates sought his advice on various aspects of the inquiry. Only once did he blow his top and that was when the internet suddenly went down and it turned out that IT had forgotten to inform them about a systems upgrade. At that moment he would almost certainly have lapsed and started smoking again had there been a shop on the premises. But no such luck, so he had resorted to snapping several pencils and yelling obscenities at the ceiling panels.

'What about the girl? Can they extract any more information from her? The description of the black man with the huge head isn't helping much.' Ríkhardur caught himself hunching and sat up straighter.

'I just don't know. The bugger is that she's our only hope right now. If we didn't have her, we'd be even worse off.' Acid curdled in Huldar's stomach again. 'She should come in very handy if we nail the guy. There's a chance she saw his face outside her house – assuming she wasn't just imagining things, as her father seems to think.'

Ríkhardur frowned, either over the father or the thought of the murderer in the garden. 'Erla mentioned something about that. Let's hope we get a chance to verify her statement. We could really do with a lead.'

'You're telling me.' Huldar suppressed a groan. The evidence wasn't exactly piling up. The duct tape hadn't provided any clues, though there was more than enough of the stuff, and they had learnt nothing from the biological samples. On the plus side, the CCTV footage from the cashpoint had shown the approach road to Elísa's neighbourhood and countless cars driving past, but no licence plates were legible and Ríkhardur hadn't spotted anything useful when he skimmed through the film for the period when they assumed the murderer must have been coming or going. As for the coded message, it looked as if it was going to remain a closed book; they'd heard nothing from Interpol about possible ways to decipher it – assuming it was a code, of course.

'Isn't it time to interview Margrét in the usual way?' Hitherto Ríkhardur had refrained from expressing an opinion about the involvement of the Children's House, unlike the rest of the department who were split into two camps, for and against. Those for were in the minority. Among those who made no attempt to hide their disapproval was Erla. Her observation of the second interview had done nothing to win her round.

'No. I want to stick with it. I'm afraid the girl will go to pieces if we put any more pressure on her. Best give it another shot.' The office was too small for two grown men to share for any length of time. Huldar opened the window. Fresh air poured in, dispelling the stuffiness and reviving him a little. He turned back to Ríkhardur, feeling more positive. 'They're considering taking the girl into care for the duration of the inquiry.'

Ríkhardur shook his head. 'What?'

'Indeed. We'll see what comes of it. Actually I think it's a good idea. One of the papers has got wind of her involvement. They want to run the story to be sure of getting a scoop. By some miracle we managed to secure a reprieve and the article's being withheld for now, but I doubt that'll last long. The rest of the media's bound to sniff it out sooner or later.'

'Who spilt the beans?'

Huldar shrugged. 'Search me. Far too many people know about it. Here in CID, at the Children's House, among her extended family, the hospital pathology department, the Child Protection Agency. Really it's amazing it didn't leak out straight away. I don't need to tell you how hard it is to keep secrets in a small society like this, but we'll see what happens. Anyway, like I was saying, they're considering taking her into care and I was told in no uncertain terms that there would be no need for such drastic measures if the inquiry was making better progress.' Huldar gave a mirthless smile. 'Let's just pray for a breakthrough before they make the final decision.'

'I wouldn't get your hopes up.'

Huldar felt suddenly overwhelmed with anger and frustration. He tried to disguise the fact but the strained silence finally galvanised Ríkhardur to make a move. He had no sooner left than the next person appeared.

'Here are all the messages, e-mails, photos and Facebook stuff I can find going back six months. I filtered out anything obviously irrelevant. If you like, I can go back further.' Almar handed Huldar a memory stick. His gaze flickered to the broken pencils and away again. 'There's a massive amount of data.'

'Anything useful?' Huldar made an effort to soften the harsh expression his face had worn ever since the internet had gone down. 'Anything that could point us to the killer?'

'I'm not sure. There's loads we overlooked first time round but nothing that shouts at you. Mind you, your eyes tend to glaze over after reading a thousand status updates.' Almar shuffled his feet awkwardly. He was one of the younger members of the department. His unusual expertise in IT had drawn the attention of his superiors in the regular police, and they had recommended his transfer. However, rumour had it that the real reason for his move was that Almar was completely unsuited to ordinary police work. He had graduated from the training college with the lowest possible marks in all the areas relating to physical operations and manoeuvres, but managed to drag up his average by his strong performance in the more academic subjects.

He was shaping up pretty well in CID, though, despite a tendency to be absent-minded and slow on the uptake, which irritated some of his colleagues. In part this was due to Almar's habit of walking around with earphones on, which meant he only heard a fraction of what was going on around him. Egill's attempt to reprimand him had achieved little since they had both ended up poring over a new app that Almar had downloaded onto his phone.

He had politely removed his earphones when he entered Huldar's office. 'I've divided it into two folders: "A" contains material that might be important; "B" stuff that probably doesn't matter. Like I said, I filtered out anything obviously irrelevant.'

'For example?' It was impossible to guess what Almar might regard as irrelevant.

'The unimportant folder contains, for example, e-mails from the widows of Nigerian generals, mass mailings from online stores, adverts, notices from the children's schools and so on.' Almar drew breath to continue but Huldar interrupted.

'Good. I'll take a look at it. What about text messages? Are they here too?'

Almar's eyes widened as he raised his brows. 'No. That was kind of odd. The phone I was given was full of messages up until about two months ago. But it's like she didn't send or receive any texts after that. Maybe her phone broke.'

'Oh?' Huldar sat up. 'Are you sure it was the phone she used?'

'Well, there was a SIM card in it, so I just assumed it was. They gave it to me along with the desktop computer and laptop and told me it was her stuff. No one said anything about a second phone.'

'There may not be one.' Huldar ran a hand over his head and sighed. 'What about phone calls? Did you see if there had been any recent ones?'

'I didn't look at them.' Almar wore a hunted look, as if he'd been guilty of gross negligence. 'I was told to go through the photos and texts. Nothing else.'

Huldar put down the memory stick. 'What kind of phone is it?'

'An iPhone 4.' Almar frowned. 'It's kind of an old model, now I come to think of it.'

Huldar didn't waste time replying. He put in a call to Elísa's husband Sigvaldi, identified himself, received the man's lukewarm greeting in return and fielded his enquiries about how the investigation was progressing. This didn't take long; the only difficulty was to find a sufficiently polite phrase to explain that it wasn't progressing at all. When the man started ranting at him about Margrét, Huldar interrupted. 'The idea's being considered in the interests of her own safety. You yourself agreed to it. If you've changed your mind we'll have to accept that, but I'd advise you not to make any rash decisions. We have reason to be concerned for her safety, as you're well aware.'

'Then hurry up and solve the crime.' Sigvaldi's voice swooped and dipped. He coughed, got his feelings under control and continued, sounding flat and hollow. 'You must be able to solve it.' There was no conviction behind the words.

'Oh, we will. I promise you that.' Huldar blurted this out before he had time to think. On the desk in front of him lay Ríkhardur's report on Sigvaldi's injuries. He had gone to A&E and interviewed the doctor who had examined the man. According to the doctor, the injuries were consistent with

Sigvaldi's explanation. No signs of a struggle had been observed anywhere else on his body. No scratches or bruises to suggest that a desperate woman had tried to fight him off. In spite of this, Huldar wrote a question mark against the report. Sigvaldi was a doctor and probably acquainted with the medic who examined him, though they worked in different departments. 'Actually, I was calling about another matter. What kind of phone did your wife have?'

'She had a new iPhone. I gave it to her for Christmas.'

'What model?'

'An iPhone 6.'

'Not 4?'

'No. Her old one was an iPhone 4 but she stopped using it when she got the new one.' Sigvaldi paused. 'Why do you ask?'

'It turns out we've got her old phone. Could her new one have been sent in for repair?' While he was talking, Huldar called up on the server an inventory of everything that had been removed from Elísa's home. Only the old iPhone was listed.

'No, not as far as I'm aware. It was working when I left. I called her from the airport and she answered.'

'I see. But there was a SIM card in the old phone. Is it possible that the new one stopped working after you left and she transferred the card to the old one while it was being repaired?' Most telecom companies had taken to offering phones on loan in these circumstances but it was conceivable that she had refused one, for whatever reason.

'No. They take different SIM cards. She got a new one when she changed over. The new card's much smaller.'

Huldar rang off and turned back to Almar who was

nervously winding the fine wire of his earphones around his fingers.

'She's got another phone. An iPhone 6. She stopped using this one some time ago. Do you know where they found it?'

'Er, I think I read in the accompanying document that it was in a drawer in the kitchen. I swear there was no mention of any other phone.' Almar's eyes dropped briefly to the broken pencils as if afraid Huldar would grab one and lunge at him. News of his explosion that morning had obviously spread. Ríkhardur had taken care not to let his gaze linger on the desk any more than on Huldar's face. Almar lacked his self-control; his eyes were constantly darting round the room in search of something other than the broken pencils to fix on. 'If there'd been another phone I'd have examined it, of course.'

'I'm not blaming you. Talk to the guys who searched the house. Double check that no other phone was found, then tell them from me that I want them to go back and have another look. If it doesn't turn up, we'll have to put a trace on it. You can take care of that, can't you?'

'We can try. But if it's switched off, there's not much we can do. Either the wifi has to be on or the phone has to be connected to the GSM network.'

'So, let me get this straight: if for some bizarre reason the murderer has taken it, it would have to be switched on for us to trace it?'

Almar nodded, embarrassed, as if the limitations of the technology were somehow his fault.

'Like that's going to happen. But make arrangements, just in case.' Huldar waved Almar out and plugged the memory stick into his computer. He felt a pang of conscience that he hadn't been kinder to him when he saw how conscientiously Almar had sifted through Elísa's electronic data and the pains-taking care with which he had classified the information. Every file in folder A had been given a descriptive label to enable Huldar to view them systematically. Once immersed in the material, however, he quickly forgot about the young man and his flaming cheeks.

Elísa's life lay open before him. Barely a day had gone by in the past six months when she hadn't been in constant contact with the outside world via her computer. No doubt a similar picture would emerge when and if her phone turned up. The volume of personal messages and e-mails was absurd when compared to his own habits. The only e-mails he received outside work were sporadic messages from his sisters, scolding him for never getting in touch or for something else he'd done to displease them. They also liked sending messages about joint gifts for children's confirmations or important family birthdays – followed by angry ones when he failed to come up with any suggestions for presents.

Elísa couldn't have been more different. She welcomed all messages about gifts and parties and had, for example, responded to one about a class reunion with the words: 'Yay! Awesome! Me! Me! Me!' Huldar couldn't remember ever in his life using an exclamation mark. He noted down the date of the party in case Elísa had any enemies from her school days. Once written down, the idea seemed ridiculous. This must count as low priority even allowing for their almost total absence of leads.

He felt compelled by the depressing state of the inquiry to continue his trawling, tedious though he found it. Although he had a Facebook account he almost never logged on. What was the point? He never knew what to write and had no interest in looking at photos of his friends and acquaintances on holiday or on skiing trips. He would rather see his sisters' kids in person, especially since they were all boys – a fact that seemed like poetic justice to him, after growing up as the only boy among five girls.

In contrast, Elísa had been incredibly conscientious about updating her status – which was almost invariably about her children. Their minutely detailed antics were no doubt cute or funny if you happened to like children, which Huldar didn't. He had even less time for the updates featuring pictures of cakes and food she had variously cooked, baked or ordered in restaurants. Her friends, on the other hand, seemed to appreciate these, and every update was followed by a string of comments. He skimmed through them all, but the reason for Elísa's murder was highly unlikely to be connected to her children or eating habits. Or to her job at the tax office; the police had talked to her manager who said that although plenty of people had reason to hate the tax authorities, that hatred was unlikely to be directed at Elísa. She had worked behind the scenes, had no direct contact with those under investigation and had never been called upon to testify in court. Those fingered by the tax man would have no idea of her existence.

One thing that did emerge from his reading was how different Margrét was from her two younger brothers. Elísa rarely mentioned any funny things she had said or done. When she wrote about her daughter it was on a more serious note, to dutifully report the loss of a tooth or, more commonly, her good performance at school. Margrét didn't come across as a particularly lively or happy child and Huldar experienced a twinge of guilt when he remembered the ongoing debate about whether to place her in care. If the girl was naturally depressive, he didn't like to think about the consequences if the rug was pulled from under her feet at a time like this. Then again, she herself had asked not to be sent back to her father. But she might well change her mind at the last minute. It wouldn't surprise him.

Huldar turned from the screen to gaze out of the window at the sea and the long, flat-topped bulk of Mount Esja, looming over the scene, content with its lot, elevated above all human strife. How nice to be a mountain and never get yourself into a mess or take on a case you couldn't handle. Huldar sighed and shook his head. Were their concerns for Margrét's safety unnecessary? It was one thing to murder a grown-up but a child was another matter. Then again, it was one thing to kill a person in a conventional manner, with a blunt object, knife or firearm, but quite another to hoover all the air out of her body with such violence that her eardrums burst. The M.O. suggested that the perpetrator was a psychopath, completely devoid of conscience. Huldar turned back to the screen and started browsing through the photos that Elísa had either uploaded to Facebook or stored on her computer. In every shot his attention was drawn irresistibly to Margrét's green eyes in her colourless face beneath the dark red tangle of hair. She was the only member of the family who was careful always to look directly at the lens. The others seemed unaware that a photo was being taken. She also appeared to be much more dependent on her mother than her brothers were, since in most of the pictures she was either clinging to her or standing close beside her. Huldar thought this tendency was even more marked in the most recent photos. You'd have thought the girl had had an intuition of what was to come.

Studying these family photos that clearly weren't intended for strangers' eyes made him uncomfortable. He had seen enough to conclude that Sigvaldi and Elísa had been a normal couple who gave every appearance of enjoying life. She was smiling or laughing in almost every frame, and the pictures in which they appeared together gave the impression that here were two people who were in love and great friends. Though of course this could have been a front.

Bored as he was of ploughing through this material, Huldar persevered. He concentrated on Elísa's social life, which gave him more than enough to work with. She had been part of a large circle of friends who kept in touch and met up regularly. They exchanged countless messages about meals, children's parties, diets and trips to health spas. Elísa was always up for everything. Huldar didn't know enough about married life or women in general to tell whether this was normal or a sign of cracks in a relationship that appeared perfect on the surface. If he had to guess, he would say it wasn't normal. To him, marriage meant having less need of other people's company, but perhaps he was just hopelessly old-fashioned. Perhaps that explained why he was still single. If he hadn't been such an idiot and screwed Karlotta, he could have turned to Ríkhardur for advice. He must know a thing or two about failing marriages, but there was no way Huldar could bring up the subject of divorce with him now. It would be totally inappropriate for him to say Karlotta's name in Ríkhardur's presence. The sooner their divorce was finalised, the better. Once it was done and dusted, he hoped the memory of his cock-up would no longer come back to haunt him every time he laid eyes on Ríkhardur.

In the end there was nothing of real interest on the memory stick. Going by the bank statement Elísa had e-mailed to her accountant, the couple's finances were fairly healthy, better than most people's nowadays. Elísa's death wouldn't bring about any major changes in their circumstances. The insurance companies had confirmed Sigvaldi's claim that she had no life insurance, though it wasn't impossible that he was concealing information about a policy with an overseas company. They would find out in due course. The police had contacted those foreign insurers known to do business with Icelanders and their responses were expected shortly.

As Huldar returned to examining the photos it suddenly occurred to him that the man who had been watching the house in Margrét's drawings might have been accidentally caught on camera. He skimmed through the albums again, bearing this in mind. There was a knock and Erla put her head round the door while he was studying a picture of Elísa and Margrét. The photo had been taken outdoors and for once both were looking straight at the camera with a rare ray of sunshine illuminating their hair. Their eyes were sad, though Elísa was making a feeble attempt to smile. Margrét looked as stony as ever; not a hint of pleasure or happiness could be detected in her childish face. This made her appear older than her years. Huldar tore himself away from the photo and turned to Erla. 'Yes?'

'They've found a woman's body. Quite a bit older than Elísa. But the circumstances are more or less identical. Only nastier.'

Huldar closed the photo, switched off his monitor and

stood up. Before leaving the office he rang Egill and broke the news to him, adding that it would be advisable to move Margrét to a safe house without delay. While he was speaking, he fought an overwhelming craving for nicotine.

He would leave it up to fate to decide: whether he took up smoking again today would depend on which he drove past first, a chemist or a sales kiosk.

Chapter 16

It was hard to imagine a less inviting place than the visitors' cell at Litla-Hraun prison. It might have been deliberately designed to convey the message that crime didn't pay. The walls could have done with a lick of paint, and the worn vinyl flooring needed replacing. The room was furnished with a small table, a single chair and a narrow bed nailed to the floor, which was at present serving as a seat. No doubt it was intended for more enjoyable activities during conjugal visits, judging by the bag containing a blanket and sheet that had been placed at the head of the bed. Freyja hadn't bothered to inform the new prison guard that she was the inmate's sister, but every time her gaze fell on the bedclothes she regretted the fact. She was afraid the guard would subsequently discover their relationship and jump to unsavoury conclusions.

Freyja was a past master at worrying about imaginary misunderstandings; capable of brooding over them long after everyone else had forgotten. Once, when she was twelve, she had walked around with a knot in her stomach for weeks because she hadn't managed to answer the craft teacher's question about whether she had knitted her jumper herself. The bell had rung as Freyja opened her mouth. When, just before the Christmas holidays, she had finally plucked up the courage to correct the misunderstanding, the teacher had stared at her blankly. Perhaps the disaster of the gloves she had accidentally knitted without thumbs had helped the teacher to forget that she had ever overestimated her ability.

'How's Molly?' Baldur rested his right arm on the little table, gripping the coffee she'd brought him from the drinks machine outside. His white teeth lit up his face in a smile as he thought about his dog. Baldur had always been beautiful; as a plump baby, a mischievous boy, a lanky teenager, and now as a man. Adulthood suited him particularly well, and as a result he was wildly successful with women; more successful than could be counted healthy. At least two of Freyja's friends had slept with him and she suspected a third, though the friend had vehemently denied it, her cheeks burning, when the other two grilled her during a particularly drunken dinner party. Baldur winked at her as if he could read her mind. She couldn't help grinning back, though the memory wasn't particularly edifying.

Baldur had an innate ability to sweep people along with him against their better judgement. Had he chosen to live on the right side of the law, he would have made a consummate politician; charismatic and utterly persuasive, whatever nonsense he was peddling. Freyja had often caught herself thinking that his absurd plans weren't so crazy after all.

But she always came to her senses the moment he stopped talking. The enchantment of his words and personality were like a firework display: you were blown away while it lasted but afterwards it left you with irritating blobs of light on your eyeballs and a ringing in your ears.

Baldur had yet to hit upon a clever scheme that also happened to be legal. When he did, his life might well turn around. But the hope of his finding the right niche was fading.

He seemed ever more comfortable dabbling in shady business, surrounded by characters who knew no better. His looks were not all he had inherited from their mother: he seemed to have imbibed with her breast milk her dreams of luxury and a happy-ever-after, all achieved without effort. They both lived entirely for the moment, convinced that better times were just around the corner, so there was no need to complicate one's life with such tedious things as worries or foresight.

Baldur's smile didn't last long. 'Make sure she doesn't get fat. It's a bloody nightmare trying to get the weight off her again.'

'I'll make sure.' Freyja shifted on the mattress, trying to find a more comfortable position, and eventually settled with her back against the wall. 'She's doing fine. Don't worry.'

'You know you have to exercise her. Not just a little potter around the block but a full-blown hike.'

Freyja forced a smile. Baldur was optimistic if he thought she was going to charge up a mountain with his dog every morning and evening. 'Look, stop worrying. Molly's in good shape. But what about you? Is everything OK? In the circumstances?'

'I'm always OK. You know that.' He took a mouthful of coffee. 'There's not much time left if I toe the line. I'll probably be out in a few months.' He hastened to add: 'You can stay on in the flat even if I do come home. I'll have to sleep at the halfway house to start off with, so you can have the place to yourself at night.'

Freyja's thoughts strayed to the spare room that had been crammed full of heat lamps and propagators when she moved in. They had been used to cultivate a variety of crops other than herbs over the years and although she had moved the propagators down to the storeroom, the place still reeked of cannabis. 'I'll find a flat. It's just not going too well at the moment because people would rather rent to tourists. Understandably – they pay better.'

'Maybe I should take a look at the tourist industry when I get out.'

Freyja gave an inaudible sigh. She didn't like to imagine what opportunities Baldur might spot for making a quick profit at the expense of foreign visitors, but she was sure they were services the tourists could do without. He was currently serving a sentence for taking out a major loan with a friend, using as security a property that belonged to a man who happened to have the same name as his friend. They had spent the money before the fraud was discovered, even paying off some of the monthly instalments to buy themselves time. It was only when they could no longer cover these that the scam was exposed. As Baldur had been on probation, the remainder of his previous sentence had been added to the new one for forgery and embezzlement. Freyja could hardly remember a time when Baldur wasn't either inside or awaiting sentencing.

He winked at her again and smiled. 'So, what about you? Seeing anyone special?'

'No. No one, special or otherwise.' Freyja had no intention of telling him about the Huldar fiasco. For one thing, her love life was none of his business, and for another she didn't want him to find out that she'd let a cop into his flat, however unwittingly. 'I'm absolutely fine for the moment.'

'Absolutely fine? What the fuck's the matter with you?' Baldur scowled. In his world view everyone needed a partner to be happy, though not necessarily long term, as variety was the spice of life. 'Don't you get out at all? You won't find anyone by sitting on your arse at home.'

She felt like retorting that being banged up didn't seem to have cramped his style when it came to meeting women. How he did it was beyond her. He'd had four girlfriends in the past year. Every time the position became vacant, a new one materialised. Freyja had a constant fight on her hands to be granted a visitor permit because the current girlfriend always took precedence. It was mainly when he was between women, like now, that he had time for her. 'I'm not sitting on my arse at home. I go out. I just haven't met the right guy. Anyway, I haven't been single that long. I'm not giving up hope yet.'

'I can fix you up, if you like. No problem. I'd choose carefully.'

'No way – thanks all the same.' She tried to hide her vehemence so he wouldn't notice how little she appreciated his help. Better change the subject before he started interrogating her about her taste in men and making a list of possible candidates. 'Work's hectic at the moment.'

'Oh?' Baldur had never had much faith in Freyja's career. The jobs she had done over the years had no place in his world. He thought the Children's House was all right as a concept, but couldn't understand all the fuss when everyone knew you could deal with paedophiles with a baseball bat without having to trouble the health services or legal profession.

The sun broke through the black clouds that had loured over Freyja on her drive east over the mountains from Reykjavík. The bars in the narrow window threw symbolic shadows on the floor. Unable to tear her gaze from them, she felt a pang at the thought of her brother's situation and was seized with anxiety about his future. They had seen an older prisoner slipping into another visiting cell; a bent, scrawny figure, with faded tattoos emerging from the neck and sleeves of his crumpled fleece. Freyja couldn't bear to think of Baldur ending up like that. It mustn't be allowed to happen. Unrealistic as it was, she felt it was up to her to make sure it didn't. The feeling was a familiar one.

Ever since she could remember she and Baldur had been responsible for one another. He was there for her; he used to hit the boys who teased her during break, and help her to carry her heavy school bag. He was two years older and ever since she was a baby she had looked up to him and felt safe when he was near. Her admiration and unfailing trust had in turn boosted Baldur's self-confidence and endowed his life with purpose. But as Freyja grew older and the realisation gradually sank in that her brother was not perfect, so her hero worship waned. The truth was that he had his share of faults, which were allowed to develop unchecked. No wonder: their mother had had them both before she was twenty and was too immature to raise them properly, yet they loved her unconditionally, as children do, and she made it easy for them. Like Baldur, she was happy-go-lucky, always smiling in spite of the difficulties and chaos of their home life.

Although Freyja and Baldur didn't share a father, they had never thought of themselves as half-siblings. There was nothing 'half'-hearted about their relationship. Their fathers were peripheral figures; their mother was the centre of their world. From her they received all they needed – food, shelter, security, companionship and a refuge, however chaotic – whereas their fathers came and went without ever gaining a foothold in their life. Both were young men who had only been casually acquainted with their mother, though they did at least make feeble attempts to do the right thing. Their contributions consisted mainly of badly wrapped presents for birthdays and Christmas, the occasional trip to the cinema, visits to the bowling alley, and meals at hamburger joints, which were characterised by long silences during which they kept stealing glances at the clock. Little by little they had faded from Freyja's and Baldur's lives, vanishing for good after they married and had other children. Their mother had done nothing to encourage further contact; as long as her child support arrived on time, she couldn't care less about their participation in her children's lives. Her heart and mind were always taken up with new men and it was only a question of time before she would find Mr Right who would welcome all three of them with open arms and build them a large, detached house on Arnarnes where they would live happily ever after.

In Freyja's memory these men formed a long line in which each was allotted a brief opportunity to intrude on her and Baldur's life. They used to turn up reeking of aftershave, awkward in the presence of the children and eager to get out of the cramped flat as soon as possible, out on the town with their mother. None of them had hung around long enough to learn the brother's and sister's names or how old they were. One had given Freyja a kitten and seemed promising, but before long he had vanished from the scene like the rest.

Perhaps their mother would have managed to find herself a partner in the end, but she had dropped dead at thirty, when Freyja was ten and Baldur twelve. The beautiful, lipsticked smile, the waft of perfume, the heavily mascaraed eyes and varnished nails disappeared from their lives one Saturday evening when she went out on the town as so often before but this time failed to come home. At a party in Mosfellsbær, her heart, which had in its eccentric fashion beaten for her two children, decided without warning to pack it in. They had received the news, the sleep still in their eyes, at the unfamiliar home of an old schoolfriend of their mother's, who she had wheedled into looking after them for the night.

They didn't cry until later that evening, but once their tears had started to flow they were unstoppable. Their grief was made worse by fear about what would happen to them. They would probably have wept even more bitterly if they'd known that they would be sent to live with their mother's parents, a religious couple who had given up on their daughter and taken little interest in the family. They weren't bad people so much as emotionally stunted, and, in hindsight, worn out by a life of toil, and were ill suited to caring for children, especially a naughty, obstreperous boy. Within a short time Baldur had managed to break almost every ornament in their suburban home, but Freyja shouldered the blame half the time to protect him from their scolding.

Their life didn't really change that much; there were fewer happy times but brother and sister remained inseparable. Freyja tried to look after her brother and he took care of her. There was a lot they didn't understand, which no one took the trouble to explain to them. Their grandparents lavished all their love on a strange, invisible God who sat on His throne in heaven. This struck the children as unfair because God had millions of people to love him while they had no one but their grandparents. God was to loom large in their new home: this celestial being who had hardly impinged on their lives before was suddenly everywhere yet nowhere. Neither of them understood the first thing about their grandparents' faith but, afraid to admit the fact, they made do with exchanging glances and giggling behind the old couple's backs.

None of the pearls of divine wisdom that fell from their grandparents' lips were consistent with Freyja's and Baldur's experience, and over time they agreed that if God existed and was as old as people claimed, His eyesight must be failing. The alternative explanation for why an all-good, all-powerful God would allow injustice and evil to flourish in the world was that He quite simply did not exist. They quickly inclined to the latter explanation. It was simpler and spared them the effort of trying to grasp such nebulous concepts as the Holy Ghost or the forgiveness of sins. In spite of this, both agreed to be confirmed, too cunning to alert their grandparents to the fact that they were non-believers. That bombshell would fall later.

Soon after her confirmation, Freyja was forced to accept that Baldur wasn't academic like her. His interests lay elsewhere, and her attempts to encourage him to apply himself had less and less effect as he moved down the path towards juvenile delinquency.

And now here they were. She felt the usual regret about not having been firmer, made more effort to encourage him. But it wouldn't have changed anything.

'Have you heard from the loser?' Baldur had no need to say his name. He never referred to her ex any other way. 'Loser' could mean anyone. But '*the* loser' was Freyja's ex-boyfriend who Baldur had never been able to stand. 'You know I'll have him dealt with if he tries anything.'

Freyja wanted to laugh. 'Like what? He won't try anything. Have you forgotten that I walked out on him because he was a pain in the arse, not because he was violent?' Recalling now the perpetual nagging over the most trivial things, she was amazed she had put up with it for so long. *What's this smear on the fridge door? Did you hit the kerb? There's a dent in the wheel rim. How often do I have to tell you to tidy away your bag when you come in? Why do you have to load the dishwasher in such a stupid way?* Her present situation might not be that enviable but at least there was no danger of anyone complaining about which way round the loo roll was facing. 'I'm shot of him for good.'

Baldur stared at her. 'There are two blokes on my corridor who are doing time for attacking and raping their ex-girl-friends. I bet the girls thought they were free of them *for good* when they moved out.' He took a sip of coffee, his gaze straying to the window. 'Lock the door and keep Molly beside you. The loser wouldn't stand a chance against her.'

Freyja omitted to mention her fear that, if it came to the crunch, Molly would turn on her instead. There was no point. And the last thing she wanted was for Baldur to organise a revenge attack on her ex. The idea was more tempting than she cared to admit but the chances of a plan like that blowing up in Baldur's face were almost one hundred per cent.

'Molly sleeps on the floor by my bed. He'd be mincemeat if he tried to set foot inside.' She smiled. 'Leave him alone, Baldur. He isn't worth the risk of extending your sentence. All he did was nearly bore me to death with moaning.'

'Well, seeing as you don't want me to fix you up with a boyfriend, the least I can do is fix you up with a protector. Would you like that?'

'A protector? No, thanks, I don't need anything like that. Molly and I are good together. Stop worrying.' She could tell from his face that he was sceptical. Or didn't want to believe her. She suspected that it gave Baldur a purpose amid all the futility of life in jail to feel that he was helping her. Why couldn't that help consist of sorting out her tax return or cutting out newspaper advertisements for flats to rent? Why did he always have to go too far? 'Seriously. I don't want some bloke hanging around outside the house.'

Baldur didn't respond to this and they spent the rest of her visit chatting about other things. The sun went down and Freyja drove home under a darkened sky.

She was at the window of a drive-in burger joint when her phone rang. She tried simultaneously to answer it, hand over her card and take hold of the greasy bag. 'Hello?'

'Freyja?' It sounded like a question. She recognised the voice; he worked for the Child Protection Agency but she couldn't remember his name. When he introduced himself as Geir, she pictured him at once: a decent guy who was good at his job and whose only fault was his habit of interrupting people – which was intolerable. 'Something's come up in connection with the little girl, Margrét. Margrét Sigvaldadóttir.'

'Come up?' Freyja trapped the phone under her cheek and took back her card and a receipt for the food, then found a parking space beside the restaurant.

'There's been a major development in the police investigation. I don't know what but it's really stirred things up.' The man paused and Freyja had to listen to his breathing. Perhaps he was waiting for her to speak so he could interrupt her. She decided not to give him the satisfaction and waited for him to resume.

'To cut a long story short, we've agreed to the police's

request to take the girl temporarily into care. I gather she's still refusing to go near her father, but the main reason is that they believe it would be in her interests to go into hiding now that news of the case is breaking in the media. Reading between the lines, I think they're afraid of what the murderer might do when he learns there was a witness.'

'So? Did you want my opinion?'

'Oh, no. No need for that.'

Freyja decided not to take offence. He probably hadn't meant it to come out quite so clumsily.

'The reason I'm ringing is that we were hoping you would agree to look after her. Just for a few days. Possibly only for part of the day.'

'Part of the day?' The smell of fried food was filling the car and the windows were misting up.

'Naturally, as soon as the police have solved the case the girl can go home. I'd be surprised if they don't make an arrest soon.'

'I'm sorry. I can't do it.'

'It's not such a big deal. You'd stay in the flat we use for exactly these sorts of cases. There's no one there at the moment.'

'Why can't she go to Bogga?' Bogga ran a fostering service for children who had been removed from their parents until a permanent solution could be found for them.

'She's completely full. Already has two more kids than she should.'

'Sorry, no can do – I'm dog-sitting. I can't leave the dog alone at home.'

'We could pay to send it to the kennels.'

'Jesus, isn't there anyone else who can do it? What about

Dísa or Elín?' She didn't mention any of the men as that would be out of the question. It was policy that men were never allowed to be alone with children under the agency's protection, not because they were thought to constitute a risk but because some of the children were so broken that there was a danger they would read too much into it if a man was kind to them. Of course this applied to women as well, but not nearly to the same extent. 'Aren't they at work? Or Silja? I know she's not on leave.'

There was a humming and hahing at the other end. Eventually the man came out with it: 'You're the only one who's single. Everyone has their own children. Except you. We want Margrét to have her carer's undivided attention. It's much more difficult for mothers to drop everything and move to the flat.'

So, she was the only woman who was suitable because she had no life. Great. She lost her appetite for the contents of the bag on the passenger seat.

'And the guy in charge of the investigation specifically asked for you.'

'Huldar?'

'Yes. Don't ask me why but you're are the only one he trusts with the girl.'

Freyja frowned. He didn't know her at all, if you overlooked the single night they'd spent together. Surely he didn't base his professional opinion of people on his personal sexual experiences? If that had been the purpose of their one-night stand, the results of her personality test would presumably place her in the rampant and insatiable category. She turned pink and was grateful that videophones had never become fashionable. 'I'm sorry. There must be another solution.'

'No, we've exhausted them all.' His tone was final.

Although Freyja continued to raise objections, she knew how it would end. Before the evening was over the girl would almost certainly be in her care. Hopefully she'd have eaten by then. There wasn't enough in the bag for two.

Chapter 17

Karl felt no particular guilt about missing his lectures. No one monitored attendance, so it was entirely up to him whether he went in or not. Now that his mother was no longer there to fret, nobody cared about his education, not even him – most of the time. It was a depressing thought, though he took advantage of his freedom, taking as much time off as he liked. If no one cared about his results, what did it matter how well or badly he performed? But it wasn't really that simple. To meet the Student Loan Authority's conditions, he had to stick at it. Had it not been for that, it was doubtful he would have attended any lectures at all or handed in a single piece of coursework. But if he wanted a study loan to live on he had to pass his exams, and if he wanted to pass his exams he had to apply himself.

Today, however, he was going to ignore the faint twinge of conscience. He deserved some time off. He had so much on his mind and finally, finally, he had found the energy to sort out his mother's possessions. Halli and Börkur's visit had been the catalyst and now he was going to make the house his own. For too long it had been like an outsized memorial to his mother – like the mausoleum of a dead pharaoh.

The realisation had sunk in that he was going to have to find himself some new friends, but there was no way he could invite people round to this grannyish house – always supposing he found anyone to invite round in the first place. Still, he'd had an idea that was bound to make him popular. His fellow students were always having trouble finding venues for parties. The offer of a house, a crate of beer and a few bags of crisps might help to get him noticed.

Transforming the place needn't cost much; the ugly furniture could stay, so long as he removed most of the knick-knacks from the surfaces and took down the pictures from the walls. Tore down the window dressings and dumped every last net curtain in the bin. It was time to make his mark on the house, even if only by removing all traces of his mother.

He began by taking down Che Guevara from the entrance hall and stuffing him in the black plastic bin under the sink. One of the revolutionary leader's eyes and half his military cap could be seen poking out of the rubbish as Karl closed the cupboard. Next he decided to tackle his mother's bedroom with a view to moving in there himself. It was absurd not to use the room when it was so much larger than his. At the moment it was almost exactly as she had left it and that in itself was a little creepy, as though she might come home any minute.

He had closed the door some time ago to avoid having to see inside every time he went to the bathroom. The sight of his mother's old dressing table covered in face creams and cosmetics was particularly disturbing, combined with a whiff of the heavy perfume that used to follow her around like a cloud. Of course no scent could carry from the closed bottles out into the passage, but that didn't stop him imagining it. Strange that his mother's smell should linger in his memory when he could hardly picture her face any longer.

When Karl opened the door the musty air in the room

tickled his nose. He fetched some loo paper and blew it. He thought briefly of stuffing cotton wool into his nostrils but, abandoning the idea, decided to start in the bathroom instead. He went and fetched a plastic sack, swept all the cosmetics off the bathroom unit and carried them out to the dustbin. Among the objects he disposed of was a hideous white soap-dish on gilt legs that his mother had been very fond of. Karl had always thought it tasteless, implying as it did that they dreamt of a bathtub with claw feet but had to make do with a soap-dish. An expensive electric toothbrush, brand new – a Christmas present to his mother from Arnar – went into the bag as well, along with a mother-of-pearl hairbrush, an old confirmation gift that she'd kept for special occasions. Karl should have taken some of these to the Good Shepherd charity shop but he was terrified of losing momentum if he started trying to sort the stuff. Into the bin with it. It would all end up at the tip sooner or later, so what difference would a brief interlude with a new owner make?

There was a loud bang as the heavy sack landed on the bottom of the empty dustbin. It had an uncomfortably final ring; nothing that went into the bin could ever be retrieved. This dampened Karl's zeal and he closed the lid with less of a flourish than he'd opened it with. It was insulting to his mother's memory to dispose of her belongings like any old trash.

He went back inside. The bedroom was full of the worldly goods on which his mother had lavished such loving care. He had the odd notion that they welcomed his arrival, as if they had been waiting for someone to admire them again. But that wasn't the plan.

Some objects only have value in their owners' eyes; to others they are junk. With an odd sense of pathos, Karl realised this was true of everything his mother had owned. There had never been much money left over for buying nice things; the expense of rearing two boys had seen to that. All those foreign textbooks of Arnar's had cost a bomb; all the books he amassed while he was deciding which subject to study at university. He wasn't like Karl, who had chosen the subject he hated least. Oh, no. Instead of doing the bare minimum to pass his school-leaving exams, Arnar had devoted his time in the sixth form to methodically researching the syllabuses of all the subjects he thought might suit his needs.

Salary was the motivating factor. He intended to choose the field in which he was most likely to excel. He had no truck with mediocrity; he wanted to shine in a profession that was well remunerated. Arnar had been insufferably smug about this long-term goal, whereas all Karl had wanted in those days were comics, which his mother only bought for him in those months when Arnar didn't require expensive new textbooks.

Karl repressed a sudden wave of grief for his mother; of nostalgia for a past that hadn't really brought him much happiness. Though at least he hadn't been alone then. He had to look forward, not back. Perhaps starting in his mother's bedroom had been a mistake. It was as if her possessions had noticed the rubbish bag and were mourning their fate. Clearing out the house was proving to be much harder than he had expected.

Karl tried to pull himself together, keen to preserve the illusion, at least in his own mind, that he was less affected by their mother's death than Arnar was. For once in his life he wanted to surpass his brother in some way, especially now that he had decided to cut all ties with him. From today their relationship was over – apart from discussions about the will. Arnar had shown that they were brothers in name only. That had become abundantly clear during yesterday's phone conversation.

The memory still stung. Karl had swallowed his pride and rung Arnar against his better judgement. He had been driven by an idea he couldn't shake off, an idea that had occurred to him before but that he'd always dismissed until now. But in the growing sense of disquiet created by the shortwave broadcasts the idea wouldn't leave him alone, so without stopping to think he had taken the plunge and phoned. To avoid speaking to the awful Alison, he had dialled Arnar's mobile number and for once the connection had been disconcertingly clear, as if Arnar was in the next room. This only made the conversation more difficult, as he couldn't hide behind the usual crackling, delays and echoes.

Karl had let slip his diffident request, every word bringing him closer to the rejection he had been dreading – and received. He wasn't even given a chance to finish. The instant Arnar realised that Karl was testing the waters about coming over to stay with him and go to university in the States, he cut him short. Maybe later. Not now. Alison was trying to get pregnant and it wasn't a good time. Besides, it would make far more sense for him to apply to the famous, big-name schools on the east coast, which were much closer to home.

As if Karl would have any reason to go back to Iceland.

It went without saying that he could always visit them in the holidays. Well, not this Christmas actually, as they were going to Hawaii, and preferably not in the summer because they wanted to be able to drop everything and get away at a moment's notice. By this point in the conversation even Karl couldn't fail to grasp that all his brother's words amounted to was a big, fat no. No, thank you. Don't come. Not to study or on holiday. Don't come. Ever.

His cheeks burning, Karl had only just managed to say goodbye and hang up before the tears of rage spilt over. His humiliation was complete.

Well, for all he cared Arnar could go fuck himself. He hoped Alison would leave him and he'd die alone in a hotel room in Hawaii. If he called and asked Karl to come over, he'd slam the phone down. Laughing. What a pity their mother had already emptied Arnar's room. If she hadn't, Karl could have started the clear-out by taking all his junk to the tip. Or making a bonfire of it in the garden.

The kitchen cupboard was overflowing with all kinds of tea that his mother had been more conscientious about buying than drinking, but there was no coffee in the house. Karl fetched the plastic sack and dumped the whole lot in it. It was a small victory; he was back on track and this time nothing would stop him. In the absence of coffee he drank a glass of water and immediately felt himself losing steam. His body craved caffeine but there wasn't much he could do short of knocking back some of the vitamins his mother had accumulated like tea, for all the good they had done her. They were unlikely to give him the boost he needed, though, so he added the bottles of health supplements to the bag and knotted the top.

Two empty shelves met his eye as he closed the cupboard, feeling pleased with himself. It was good to have an occupation to take his mind off Arnar. And those sinister shortwave broadcasts. He felt ready to tackle the bedroom now.

His resolve deserted him at the door. Last time he'd set foot in there had been with his mum's cousin, looking for clothes to bury his mother in. The cousin had inspected each garment in turn, holding dress after dress against herself to help Karl choose. He had feigned interest and resisted the temptation to ask her to lie down on the bed and try out the dresses in that position. After all, it wasn't like his mother would be upright in her coffin.

In the end the cousin had opted for the dress she liked best. During the viewing of the body, only his mother's collar and shoulders had been visible, so she could have been wearing pretty much anything. He would have done better to give some thought to his own outfit. His jeans hadn't made too good an impression on the handful of mourners who had bothered to turn up.

Karl felt the soft pile of the carpet between his toes. It had been there as far back as he could remember and his mother had cared for it so well that it looked like new. Nothing had been allowed in her bedroom that might stain the carpet. The only drink permitted had been water, and he never once remembered seeing her take a snack to eat in bed. He kicked himself again for forgetting to buy coffee. Drinking it on the carpet would have been the perfect way to mark the dawn of a new era. A far more symbolic gesture than clearing out her bedroom. Or the funeral. The mourners who did turn up had mostly been people his mother hadn't cared for; in fact, he'd never seen or heard of half the congregation before – or since.

Two sweeps of the arm were all it took to clear the cosmetics – jars, tubes and bottles – off the dressing table and into the refuse sack. Karl felt no compunction. It all belonged in the bin. Who in their right mind would want to use a dead person's leftover creams or perfumes? After he had knotted the neck of the bag and flung the window open, the room smelt less musty. He drank in the fresh air and felt the dull pain in his head receding. His mother must have had a permanent headache, walking around covered in all that muck. The fumes were bound to be toxic; maybe they had caused the cancer that had finished her off – in record time. He pushed the window as wide as it would go, then chucked the bag out into the hall.

At first he made good progress. With the same deft movements he emptied a chest of drawers full of socks, underwear and colourful scarves that he never remembered his mother wearing. Into the rubbish with it all. Then the bottom drawer, which was crammed full of children's clothes that must once have belonged to him and his brother. Why she had kept them was a mystery to Karl; the fabric felt stiff and odd to the touch, so they would hardly come in useful for the next generation. Besides, it didn't look likely that he would be increasing the human race any time soon, and if Arnar and Alison had children, his sister-in-law would sooner dress them in bin bags than in dusty old clothes from her husband's childhood home.

She had once visited Iceland but instead of staying with her future mother-in-law, she and Arnar had packed up after two nights and moved to a hotel. Karl had been only too glad to see the back of them, especially his sister-in-law's permanently disapproving face. She couldn't take so much as a sip of water without carefully inspecting the glass first. His mother, who had talked of nothing else since Arnar first announced their plan to visit, had been hurt, though she tried to disguise it. After they relocated to the hotel, she kept trying to find excuses for their sudden departure, the most pathetic of which was that Arnar didn't want to inconvenience her. Yeah, right.

He was brought up short by the sight of two clear plastic bags of clothes right at the bottom of the drawer. Both contained sets of children's garments, one of which he recognised. His mother had taken them out on occasion and told him he had been wearing these the first time she laid eyes on him. Little dungarees and a top. The first time she showed them to him they had stirred up memories of a dark-haired woman lying under the covers in a hospital bed.

This time he didn't experience anything. His former life was completely lost to him. The clothes went into the sack. He didn't even bother to take them out of the plastic first.

The other bag contained trousers, a top and a cardigan, all of which were soiled. He hadn't seen these before. Karl grimaced, puzzled, because it was unlike his mother to put dirty laundry away in a drawer. He turned the bag over in his hands, trying to work out if they had belonged to him or Arnar. Arnar probably. He didn't recognise them, but then he had few memories from early childhood. He guessed the clothes had belonged to a boy of four or five, but what did he know about children's sizes? Impelled by curiosity, he took the garments out instead of throwing them straight in the sack. A fine dust rose and tickled his nose.

As he sat there contemplating the clothes, he wondered why on earth their mother had hung on to them. They must be the outfit Arnar had been wearing when he arrived or the first time she saw him. It was the only explanation. Apart from his own dungarees, all the rest of the clothes in the drawer were hand-knitted or for special occasions. These were neither. A cardigan, top and trousers, the material worn and bobbly. Karl ran his fingers over it, recoiling when he encountered a hard stain. He picked up the top and examined it all over. There was some crusty substance on the other clothes as well, but the cardigan was too patterned and the trousers were too dark for him to see the marks. The white cotton, on the other hand, showed everything. The top was clean on the back but had stains on the front. These varied in size but were mostly round. It looked as if someone had spattered the child with brown liquid. Karl sniffed at them but could only smell the inside of the drawer.

As he stared, mesmerised, at the brown spots, it occurred to him that they could be blood. Old, dried blood. How had he or his brother got blood all over him? And why had their mother kept the clothes as a reminder? He shuddered over the stained material. It must be something else. But what? All he could think of was some form of baptism into a weird cult. But surely the children wouldn't have been sprinkled with some nasty substance?

He stuffed the clothes into the bin bag. If they were his, he had no memory of them. If they were Arnar's, he couldn't care less. The whole lot went into the sack and by the end the chest of drawers was empty. Karl stretched, pleased with his achievement. He was getting on brilliantly.

On top of the chest were photographs of the brothers at various ages. Karl put aside the pictures of himself but threw out those of Arnar. He gloated as the earliest photos of his brother vanished into the bag: they had been taken on film and the negatives had long ago been lost. His six-year-old brother's gappy grin met his gaze as he closed the sack, and Karl felt a stab of guilt but it soon passed. Neither of them was wearing the stained clothes in any of the pictures. He shrugged off the problem. Why puzzle over a mystery that would never be solved? The only person who could have provided the answer was dead. And there was no way he was going to ask Arnar. He was as dead to him now as their mother. Anyway, he knew instinctively that their mother would have discouraged him from digging up the past. Karl didn't care – but Arnar did.

The wardrobe was going to be a massive job. It contained the bulk of his mother's clothes, along with countless boxes of all sizes, full of clobber she had thought worth keeping. The clothes wouldn't present much of a problem; the only question was whether he should chuck them out or donate them to charity.

He decided to bin them and assuaged his guilt by reflecting that there were unlikely to be any women poor enough to want dowdy, shapeless clothes that stank of mothballs and stale perfume. One by one the garments ended up on the bed until only the bare hangers remained.

Only after the clothes had gone did he notice the large yellow envelope right at the back of the wardrobe. As he extracted it, he discovered that it was quite thick. He debated whether to throw it away without opening it. But rather than recipes or ancient newspaper cuttings it might contain a will, title deeds or other important documents. It would only take a moment to flick through the contents.

Karl pushed aside the mountain of clothes to make room for himself on the bed. A few garments slid off but he ignored them. They were destined for the dump anyway. He pulled a sheaf of papers out of the envelope. Bingo. Adoption papers. Documents that were akin to sacred relics in his brother's eyes. Whereas to Karl they were simply bits of paper that had transformed the brothers' lives, removing them from their biological parents and placing them with the woman they had known ever since as their mother.

Naturally the papers dated from different times; Arnar had been adopted nine years before Karl. These looked like the originals, with signatures in blue ink and red stamps in the corner. To think of the efforts Arnar had made to track down this information at the National Register and various other institutions. All in vain.

Arnar had been informed that his situation was not unique; records were destroyed in exceptional cases. The fact that their mother had been a social worker and worked on child-protection cases may have been significant. Her job had included assessing whether children should be removed from their parents. Karl doubted she would have had to move mountains to push through the adoption, unlike those outside the system. The same would have applied in Karl's case.

He felt a faint sense of trepidation, though his interest in his origins had long ago cooled. The identity of the boys' real parents had been a forbidden topic. Their mother would probably never even have told them they were adopted – would perhaps have invented stories about their absent fathers – were it not for the fact that Arnar retained hazy memories that prompted him to question her again and again, with increasing urgency. In the end she had caved in and admitted that they were adopted, but not another word would she add.

One day at the breakfast table, shortly after Karl started school, Arnar had informed him in a loud voice that he was adopted. Karl hadn't understood at first, but when he did he was glad because this meant he had a father after all. He would be able to inform his classmates and stop their speculation. But then Arnar had sneered at Karl that his parents hadn't wanted him; that's why he had ended up here. So there was no point in his dreaming of ever meeting them. His real parents had other plans and probably had new, better children by now. For once their mother had lost her temper with Arnar and assured Karl that it wasn't true: his parents were dead. At six, he hadn't known which was worse.

She would reveal nothing else, except that the brothers shared neither father nor mother, which pleased Karl no end.

Unlike Arnar, Karl hadn't pressed her for any more information. He had accepted his mother's statement that his parents' story was better forgotten. He had interpreted this as meaning that they hadn't been the kind of people he would want to know or be associated with.

Sometimes it was best to know as little as possible.

Cowardice was another reason why he hadn't been as insistent as Arnar. He was afraid of the truth. It was bad enough feeling that you were useless at everything, but even worse to know that you had been useless from birth.

Arnar was a different story. He excelled at school and although he was a bit of a loner like Karl and had few friends, things always went his way. He won an overseas scholarship, graduated summa cum laude from a respected American university and was offered his pick of highly paid jobs at home and abroad. The time he had devoted at school to choosing the right career path had more than paid off.

He was living the good life and his origins could do nothing to alter the fact. He had proved himself.

In fact, Arnar's only defeat in life was his failure to persuade his mother to tell him about his family. She hadn't even promised to tell him later or at least to think about it. Her answer was always the same: 'No, out of the question.' No matter how often Arnar cited the law on a child's right to know its origins, she wouldn't budge, and since the information appeared to have been lost in the system, Arnar was forced to accept his repeated failures.

Karl smiled. He was holding in his hands the very documents his brother had been seeking all these years. It was in his power to give him the long-desired information. His smile grew.

Would he give Arnar the papers?

Would he hell! Arnar should have treated him with a little more generosity last night.

Karl returned the papers to the envelope. He wasn't tempted to acquaint himself with their contents straight away. It would keep until he was in a better frame of mind. He had seen the names of his biological parents but felt no urge to look them up online. It could wait. He could do without any bad news right now. Though no way was he throwing them out. The knowledge that he possessed the papers and was withholding their contents from Arnar gave him a sense of triumph. He ran his fingers tentatively over the cold envelope, then stood up, feeling more pleased with himself than he could ever remember. The crappy old mattress yielded as he pushed himself up and more clothes fell on the floor. He'd pick them up later; there was no rush. He had already decided to skip tomorrow's classes as well; it would give his teachers the impression he had been ill, especially if he turned up wearing a scarf. Nobody was ill for just one day. Although attendance wasn't compulsory, his teachers might be more lenient towards him in the exams if they thought he'd been diligent in his studies.

There was a faint thud from the basement. Karl's stomach lurched and all his self-confidence vanished in an instant. Putting down the envelope, he strained his ears. Nothing. But the moment he moved towards the door he heard the same noise again, slightly louder this time but not much more distinct. There was somebody in the basement, but the only way in was through the house. Unless the noises were coming from the shortwave receiver? But surely he had turned it off last time he was down there? Perhaps he had left it on, intending to go back later and listen. All he had to do now was switch it off.

The basement was in darkness. Karl tried to ignore the thought that this implied he had come upstairs yesterday evening with no intention of going down again. But he wasn't some sad old-age pensioner, stuck in the same routine. He must have turned off the lights but not the radio. That was all there was to it. As he descended the stairs a broadcast started up. The moment he heard the familiar soulless voice he realised that it was tuned to the Icelandic numbers station. That wasn't right. He clearly remembered forcing himself to stop listening to it for fear it would keep him awake in the night. The last thing he had listened to was a lonely broadcast from an amateur operator in Australia, late the previous night. He slowed his steps. 'Hello?' His voice sounded human and vulnerable, unlike the robotic tones of the shortwave transmission.

'Hello?'

No reply. It was absurd calling out like this. If a burglar had broken in he was hardly likely to answer. And anyway there was no one to be seen and nowhere to hide. Well, an intruder could conceivably have squeezed behind the sofa but he would have to be on the skinny side. And it was equally ridiculous to imagine that a fully grown man could fit inside the cupboard at the back of the room.

'Hello?'

No one answered. The amplifier continued to churn out numbers.

By the time Karl finally summoned up the courage to enter the room his heartbeat had steadied. He must be going crazy. Surely the burglar from last year wouldn't come to the house a second time. There were far too many others to choose from, which had contents that were actually valuable. Thieves wouldn't have a clue what the radio equipment cost, and even if they did, they would find it impossible to offload because the only buyers in the market for such gear would immediately recognise it as stolen goods. The group who practised this hobby was so small that a single e-mail to the club would be sufficient to put everyone on the alert. What an idiot Karl was to imagine the worst. Perhaps his conscience was punishing him for having thrown away those photos of Arnar. He would have to toughen up if he meant to excise his brother from his life like a tumour. Next time Arnar phoned out of a sense of duty or to ask him a favour, he mustn't answer. He must be strong.

Karl reached over to the shortwave receiver. On the table in front of him lay a bracelet he didn't recognise – a band of colourful beads with a silver elephant dangling from the clasp. There was no way it could have belonged to his mother. She had favoured jewellery made of large wooden beads in earthen colours, the sort of hippy shit that made him think of poetry readings and 1970s protest marches against the NATO base at Keflavík. This bracelet was far too cheerful. But it didn't arouse any answering mirth in Karl. Somebody had been in the basement. Somebody who had no business in his house. His fear returned with a vengeance and the relentless stream of numbers hurt his ears.

'Thirty-nine, eight, ninety-two, sixteen, twenty-two minus fifty-three, eight, three minus fifty-three, sixty-three minus ninety-two, nine, eighty-six minus seven, eight, twenty-five minus seven, forty-two minus eight, sixty-three minus ninety-two.'

Karl fetched a pen and paper. Absorbed in the numbers, he didn't hear when the same dull thud that had brought him down here sounded again behind him.

Chapter 18

Sigvaldi sat watching his sons playing on the sitting-room floor with the old cars that had once so enthralled him and his brother. The cars showed signs of rough use, their bright paint chipped in places, the metal showing through. The shiny patches reminded him of the violent collisions that he and his brother used to stage when they had grown bored of pushing the cars around on the parquet. The frequent crashing sounds rising from the floor indicated that some things didn't change.

Little Stefán, his younger son, glanced up. 'When's Mummy coming?' He was only just four and seemed incapable of understanding what had happened. He was probably too young. He seemed to think that if he asked often enough the answer would change. The question grew no less painful for Sigvaldi with repetition.

'She's not coming, sweetheart. Remember what I told you?' The answer now came automatically.

Stefán met his father's gaze but seemed to look right through him as he slowly nodded, his face preoccupied. 'I'm going to show her what I can do when she comes back.' His small fingers grabbed a car and raised it aloft. 'Look.' He mimicked a noise that Sigvaldi knew was meant to represent the wheels spinning – he'd been given the same demonstration over and over again. Then the boy hurled the car away to crash into the wall next to a painting at the far end of the room. Normally Sigvaldi would have spoken sharply and told the boy off. But what did it matter now?

Bárdur, who was nearly six, raised frightened eyes to his father. He was unusually sensitive at the moment since he understood more than his younger brother. He also knew that if you threw toys at the wall, grown-ups were supposed to lose their temper. When they didn't, something was very wrong. Sigvaldi made an effort to perform his paternal duty but couldn't manage any more than: 'Stefán. No.' He hoped the boy would understand.

'Come on, Stebbi. Let's find Granny.' Bárdur stood up and led his little brother out of the room, leaving Sigvaldi on his own. He watched them go, the same thought going round in circles in his head: how on earth was he supposed to cope without Elísa? The boys' hair was too long and now it was up to him to take them for the appointment their mother had booked at the salon. Today. She had meant to take them today.

He remembered more things she had said she was planning to do while he was abroad. Everything she'd mentioned had only made him gladder to be going away. While she was tramping all over town with the kids he would be in the States, relaxing between conference papers. Swilling whisky in the hotel bar, trying out the sauna in the basement, taking in a round of golf with his colleagues, relishing the absence of snow and not having to start the day by scraping the windscreen.

There would be none of that now and probably not for the foreseeable future. He was a single father with three kids who he didn't even know that well. Elísa had looked after most of their needs. He had ended up on the sidelines somehow, a full-time provider and part-time scolder. The household disciplinarian.

'Has something happened?' Sigvaldi heard his mother ask behind him. He turned for politeness' sake, though all he really wanted was to go on staring at the wall where the car had struck it. He felt a sort of empathy with the plaster on suddenly receiving such a deadly blow.

'No. Nothing.' Sigvaldi studied his mother. She had always been a striking woman; tall and slender, with strong features that wouldn't have looked out of place on a Grecian coin, whether dark-haired and red-cheeked as she was in his memory or pale-complexioned beneath a mane of grey hair as she was now. But the shock had left its mark on her; she seemed on the point of buckling beneath the weight of her grief. He was aware he looked no better himself.

'The boys are a bit subdued.' She leant against the door-post, her arms folded. 'If you ask me, you should get up off that sofa and devote some time to them. Go into town, see a film, visit the zoo, buy them ice-cream. Anything. They need fresh air and a break from grief. Your grief. Obviously they'll carry their own with them wherever they go.'

They stared one another in the eye without speaking, and Sigvaldi saw for the first time how alike they were. It was almost like looking at himself. Ever since he could remember people had been saying he had his mother's eyes. He hadn't been able to see it until now. Perhaps it was their shared pain that had pulled their eyelids down in exactly the same way. 'It would do you good to drag yourself out too. We all have to get up and carry on. Whatever happens.'

His mother had always pushed him, possibly aiming too high at times. She had really gone overboard when he was slaving for his medical degree; you'd have thought he was a young soldier on his way to the front when he left the house in the morning during his exams. As if she didn't expect him to return. But this time she was quite right. Sigvaldi forced a smile. 'I'll take them for a drive. I can't really face the sweet shop or ice-cream parlour where I'd have to interact with other people.' He added hurriedly before she could retort with some guff about 'no man is an island': 'It'll be better tomorrow. A little better. Then better still the next day, and the next. In the end it'll become bearable. That'll have to do.' His back hurt from sitting hunched on the sofa. 'Thank you for taking us in. I know we're not easy company at the moment.'

His mother made a dismissive gesture. 'Don't talk rubbish. You know you're welcome to stay here as long as you like.' Her face hardened. 'Your father was saying there's talk of taking Margrét into care. I sincerely hope you haven't agreed to that.'

There was a toy car lying at Sigvaldi's feet; he fixed his gaze on it. 'I wouldn't put it like that. The police are concerned for her safety. They're worried it might leak out in the press that she was there that night. That she might have seen something.'

'So what if it does? Do they think that's the worst the child has to face? That people might start spreading rumours about her?'

It was the red car, the one he and his brother used to fight over. Both had wanted to play with it because it was a convertible with lightning bolts painted on the sides. He remembered that cool as the car looked, it didn't actually move very well as one of the rear wheels was crooked and it had to be pushed along by hand. There was a moral there that the brothers had failed to learn: the things you desire most don't always live up to expectations. 'It's not the gossip the police are worried about, Mum. They're afraid the murderer will come after her. That he'll be scared she might identify him, so he'll try and silence her. She'd be easy to track down here or at home. It'd be much harder if she was at a safe house.'

His mother gasped and her glamorous face crumpled. 'What are you saying?'

'Only what I was told. I'm incapable of inventing anything or embellishing what other people tell me at the moment. They want to take Margrét to a safe house. Temporarily, just until they've caught this sick bastard.' He spat out the last word.

His mother opened and shut her mouth like a fish on dry land. Then shuddered and tried to get her bearings. 'Who do you think did it? Some psychopath?'

Sigvaldi couldn't answer that. On his way home from America he had racked his brain to think of anyone who could have wished her harm. But he couldn't. Not friends, not family. They weren't involved in any disputes, either with their neighbours or at work. Admittedly, he knew little about her job but she would have confided in him about any problems there. That was the sort of relationship they had. He remembered the police asking if either or both of them had been having an affair but couldn't remember how he had replied.

It was easier to remember the first interview; the second was a blur.

You'd have thought they had timed it to coincide precisely with the moment when the finality of it had hit home. He had only just managed to stop himself slumping forward on the table, screaming, sobbing and tearing out his hair. The strain had been so great that it was a miracle he'd managed to answer any questions at all, and afterwards he was afraid he had come across as cold and detached. This couldn't have been further from the truth. He'd known that if he allowed the least emotion to slip through, the dam would break.

He had only a vague memory of the murderer's message that they had forced him to read. This wasn't surprising since, from what he could recall, it had been nothing but a meaningless jumble of numbers. As incomprehensible as the other actions of the person who had cut out the numbers and glued them to the paper. 'I haven't the faintest idea who it could have been. Only that it must have been a stranger. Nobody who knew Elísa could have done that to her.'

'Then how are the police supposed to catch him?'

Now it was his turn to mouth helplessly as he cast around in vain for an answer. In the end he gave up. 'I don't know.'

'Margrét needs to be with us. Not with strangers.'

'I don't know if Dad told you but she wants to go.' It was so hard to say it out loud. He felt a sudden fury at his mother for forcing him to do so. 'Perhaps it'll help reconcile her to me.'

'Reconcile her to you? What have *you* done?' His parents behaved as if there were nothing odd about the way Margrét was reacting to him. They hadn't once commented on the fact that she spent all day reading in the bedroom that used to be his brother's and hardly ever emerged. Even when she was forced to join them at mealtimes, she made a point of never looking in his direction, and her grandparents made an equally determined effort not to notice. To compensate, they spoke unnaturally loudly and cheerfully. The only ones who behaved normally were Stefán and Bárdur. Except when Stefán asked if Mummy was hungry and if she was coming to eat with them. Then Bárdur behaved like the rest of them. Those were the times Sigvaldi found hardest.

'I haven't done anything. But she seems to blame me. She's only a child. She probably thinks I should have been there to save her mother.'

'Have you tried asking her why? Do you want me to talk to her?'

'Yes, I've tried asking and no, she won't talk to me. I think she just needs time to recover. The women at the Children's House have recommended therapy to help her get over it.'

'Therapy?' His mother's tone was so scandalised you'd have thought he wanted to send Margrét to rehab.

'Appointments with a psychologist. A child psychologist who specialises in trauma counselling. There's nothing wrong with that. What are you worried about? That it might be harmful?'

His mother didn't answer. It was her usual reaction when she disagreed with the person she was talking to but didn't want to quarrel. But she couldn't disguise her anger when she spoke again: 'If she's sent away from us she's bound to need trauma counselling. I've never heard such nonsense. To tear a child away from her family after she's just lost her mother! I swear some of these so-called specialists aren't right in the head.'

'Actually, the suggestion came from the police. And nothing's been decided yet.' At that moment his phone rang. He didn't recognise the number and wondered whether to answer. What if one of his patients had gone into labour? It wouldn't be the first time a woman had rung him directly. He dithered, then eventually picked up. If it was a pregnant woman, he would direct her to speak to the doctor on duty in the maternity ward: he was on leave. He almost burst out laughing at the inadequacy of the word.

It was a policeman on the phone, the detective who had interviewed him on the second occasion, Huldar. He didn't introduce himself with his full name and Sigvaldi couldn't remember his patronymic, not that it mattered. He listened, said 'yes' once, then goodbye. Slumping back, he took to staring blankly at the wall again. 'That was the police. They're coming to fetch Margrét later.'

'You didn't even try to object.' His mother came to stand in front of him, blocking his view of the textured white paint.

'No. It's the right thing to do.' Sigvaldi let his arm fall onto the soft sofa cushion. The phone slipped from his grasp.

The phone call had sapped his last reserves of energy.

'There's been another murder. Same guy.'

With an effort he managed to pull himself upright. He had to get his act together. There wasn't much time; the police and a social worker were due in two hours. He wanted to talk to Margrét, explain the situation and try to work out if this was really what she wanted. If so, he would help her to choose clothes and toys to take with her. If not, he would call the police and revoke his consent. In that case he would just have to take the kids into hiding himself. In some remote shepherd's hut in the highlands, if necessary.

Perhaps she would give him a chance to explain how terribly hard it was for him that he hadn't been at home when it happened. Perhaps he could convince her that he wasn't in any way responsible for the ghastly fate of her mother – of the woman he had loved as much as she had.

Sigvaldi squared his shoulders. 'If it means Margrét'll be safe, we'll just have to go along with it. I'm not losing her as well.'

Stefán's ruffled head appeared in the doorway and Sigvaldi almost broke down when he repeated the question that was preying on his mind: 'Daddy, when's Mummy coming home?' The childish pink lips turned down. 'She didn't kiss me bye-bye.'

Chapter 19

The sickening stench of charred flesh intensified as the evening wore on. It was impossible to become inured to it. In the brilliance of the portable floodlights, no one even noticed that the fleeting portion of daylight had long since ceased to filter in through the curtains. The blue-white glare turned people's eyes black in unnaturally pale faces, giving them an exaggerated appearance of shock. They spoke more slowly than usual, in lowered voices, clamping their hands over their mouths in a vain attempt to prevent the smell from coming into contact with their tongues.

Soon forensics would be ready to pack up and the body could be removed; only then would it be possible to open a window. But it would take more than a blast of fresh air to purge their minds of what they had seen.

Huldar was among those who had been there longest, having accompanied the pathologist and forensics team to the scene, but he doubted he was the only one suffering from claustrophobia. Erla seemed to have lowered all her defences for once and forgotten to play the hardboiled detective. She said little and her face expressed the weariness and despair shared by the rest of the team. Ríkhardur too had hardly uttered a word since he'd shown up.

Huldar regretted having summoned them. Both had been working all weekend and had a right – a need – to knock off early. Yet neither had protested or tried to make excuses. Erla had been in the changing room at the gym, with one sock off. Ríkhardur had been on his way to Mosfellsbær, the little town to the north of Reykjavík, to visit his parents but had immediately turned round.

They showed no sign of resentment at being dragged back to work. Erla had arrived first and as a result was given her choice of tasks. When Ríkhardur eventually appeared there had been no need to give him his orders. He sensed what was required and got on with the job, without saying anything on the rare occasions when his colleagues conferred in muted voices. Nobody took exception to his silence: they were all pretty despondent.

They could do nothing now to change the fate of Ástrós Einarsdóttir. Instead, all their efforts were focused on the perpetrator, on ensuring that he was brought to justice. Their anger had ceased to flare every time they caught sight of the woman's maimed body lying dead on the kitchen floor, yet their outrage was palpable. Huldar felt as if his fury was winding itself round his head and squeezing tight.

'Any chance we could cover her up?' Erla asked the pathologist, who had been crouching over the body for nearly an hour. 'I can't look at that face any longer.'

'Nearly done.' The pathologist carried on recording information about the victim without raising his eyes. Then he put down his notebook and began taking photos again. 'It's not as if you can see much.'

In a nightmare repetition of Elísa's killing, the woman had been blindfolded with shiny, light grey duct tape that had been wound repeatedly around the upper part of her head. Perhaps it had been a mercy that she couldn't see. The same tape had been used to secure the electric appliance in her mouth, the appliance that had brought about her death and presumably prevented her from screaming. Little flesh was visible; only the top of her forehead, nose and ears, and the odd glimpse of her cheeks between the lengths of tape. The way her shortish, bristly hair stuck out of the top made it look as though she had died of an electric shock. If only; it would have been a much more merciful end.

The pathologist took one more picture, then stood up. 'You can take the body now. Is the ambulance here?'

Huldar told him it was and everyone's relief was palpable. The worst was over and soon they would no longer be confronted by the gruesome sight.

For some reason it was the woman's fingers that affected Huldar most. They were clenched as though she had been groping for some way of preventing the inevitable, of pulling the gadget out of her throat and stopping the unspeakable agony that must have accompanied her death throes. From the signs, the pathologist deduced that the murderer must have pinned down her hands with his feet. There were a number of kitchen utensils on the table, including a large knife and a pair of scissors that had probably been used to cut the tape. Whether and for what purpose the murderer had intended to use the other implements was unclear. To frighten the woman, perhaps. But the murder weapon would have been horrifying enough on its own.

Huldar had been trying to interpret the scene in terms of what was there. In addition to the kitchen utensils there was an overturned chair, and beside it on the floor a single sheet of paper covered in strange jottings. These consisted of random numbers and calculations whose logic was obscure.

They didn't resemble the coded message left at Elísa's house; for one thing, they were written in pencil, not cut out of a newspaper. The pencil had been found on the floor beside the kitchen unit.

The woman had in all likelihood been sitting on the chair before she died. It wasn't immediately obvious whether it was her or the murderer who had scribbled the sums, but given the clumsiness of the figures, it was probably her. It looked like the writing of a person who couldn't see what she was doing. When her death struggle began, Ástrós had jerked sideways and fallen on the floor. According to the pathologist, the pain of her unprotected landing would have been completely eclipsed by the agony in her mouth and throat. It was unlikely she would even have noticed the fall.

'You can take the paper, the pencil and these kitchen utensils. And unplug that bloody thing. I want the extension lead too. Don't detach it, just wind it up carefully and put it on top of this.' The pathologist pointed to the black handle protruding from Ástrós's mouth, half hidden by tape. 'Make sure you use gloves – when you unplug it as well. And bag up any loose items.' He removed a large bag made of strong transparent plastic from his case. 'You know how to mark them, don't you?'

Again, Huldar had to answer for his team. The others had spoken little and then only to answer questions directly addressed to them. Even without Ríkhardur's usual dampening presence the atmosphere would have been gloomier than at any funeral. They were all upset, though none of them had known the dead woman. Huldar was satisfied with their reaction: he wouldn't have wanted to work with people who could shrug off a murder, particularly one as grisly as this.

'What have you discovered?' Huldar watched as the pathologist removed his mask and tugged off the gloves, which seemed glued to his hands.

'Well, I can't state anything categorically but her body temperature gives an estimated time of death of around midnight. All the indications are that the cause of death was burns to the throat, though I'll need to conduct a full postmortem to establish what happened and what actually killed her. She may have suffocated due to obstruction of her upper airway as a result of the burns. Or haemorrhaged and drowned in her own blood. There are various possible scenarios but I have no comparable cases on which to base a verdict. It's not every day that people are despatched with a pair of curling tongs, if that's what they are.'

Huldar and Erla stared, transfixed, at the black handle. The odour of charred flesh grew stronger again and Erla rubbed her nose in a feeble attempt to block it out.

The pathologist shook his head sombrely. 'I'm afraid her death was neither painless nor quick. Alas.'

Huldar and Erla both made faces. Ríkhardur turned away from sprinkling the shelves of a kitchen unit with fingerprint powder, his face wearing a similarly pained expression. The pathologist continued unperturbed: 'But, as I said, the postmortem will clarify the picture and may also provide us with a more precise time of death, though that's going to be a bit of a challenge. It would help if you could find out when she last ate, but that could be tricky – she lived alone, didn't she? Assuming this was her flat.'

'Yes. So I'm told.' Huldar had talked to the dead woman's sister, who had reported the murder. She was almost too shocked to speak but he had managed to glean some basic information, including the fact that she had come round because Ástrós wasn't answering the phone. Between sobs she had explained that she was worried her sister might have had a heart attack and been lying unconscious on the floor. She'd suffered from high blood pressure. 'According to her sister, Ástrós was widowed two years ago, so we can be certain she didn't have supper with her husband. They had no children. There's a cake in the fridge with only one slice missing, so it doesn't look as though she'd been entertaining. There's a saucepan, plate, knife and fork in the sink, also indicating that she ate alone. But there are two glasses. I suppose one could have been used earlier in the day, but given how clean and tidy the place is, she doesn't appear to have been the type to let the dirty dishes pile up.'

'Have you collected it all? The cake too?' The pathologist had a reputation for thoroughness. Huldar knew from experience that he wouldn't leave the scene until he was satisfied that all the evidence had been bagged up and nothing had been missed.

'Yes. I'm hoping there'll be fingerprints on the glasses, but they'll almost certainly prove to be hers. I get the impression the killer's too careful to be caught out like that. Did you find any prints on the body?' Huldar already knew the answer. He had been watching the pathologist attentively and couldn't have failed to notice any significant discoveries.

'I found nothing on her front during the provisional examination. Naturally it's possible I've overlooked something but I'm not optimistic about finding any prints on her clothes, given the way she's dressed.' The woman had quit this world clad in a thick towelling dressing gown, a threadbare T-shirt and checked cotton pyjama bottoms. Her top had ridden up as she fought for her life, revealing a pale, flabby stomach. Her dressing gown was open and the flaps lay spread out at her sides like misshapen wings. 'We'll know more once I've conducted an exhaustive examination at the lab. The back of her neck may be covered in prints but I doubt it. The tape is our best bet but I'm not getting my hopes up about that either. We found nothing on it last time and whoever the murderer is he seems to be incredibly careful. Assuming it's the same man.'

Huldar didn't comment, though he believed it was. There were too many similarities for it to be a coincidence. Two women, murdered a few days apart in almost exactly the same, grotesque fashion. The tape on its own was enough to convince Huldar that they shared a killer. They had little enough else in common, aside from the detail that neither had apparently been raped and the circumstances didn't point to a sexual motive. As far as he knew, there was nothing in either of the women's lives that provided any reason to suppose that someone would want them dead: Elísa, a thirty-something mother of three children, who worked at the tax office; Ástrós, a widow in her sixties, who used to teach biology at sixth-form college and had few interests apart from watching television, if her sister's description was to be believed. The flat bore witness to the woman's humdrum existence: there were photos of her and her husband posing together in a variety of situations: on beach holidays, picnicking on the Icelandic moors, at festive dinners. Although the photographs had been taken at lengthy intervals, the couple had changed little; she invariably wore her short, thin hair combed back from her rather colourless face; he had fleshier cheeks and his hair had receded a little more in every picture. Ordinary people. Neither Ástrós nor Elísa appeared the type to attract the attention of a deranged killer. Yet the fact remained that they had.

Huldar needed to keep all his senses alert so as not to miss any important details, but this was proving hard as the odour of singed flesh kept forcing his thoughts back to the macabre scene in the kitchen. From now on, the sight of duct tape would always bring an acid taste to his mouth and he assumed that the same would apply to all the others who had set foot in the flat that day.

Huldar bent down to the socket and carefully unplugged the extension lead. With gloved hands, he rolled up the lead and placed it gently on top of the body. His head swam and he took care to straighten up slowly for fear of fainting and keeling over on top of the poor woman. She had suffered enough when alive; there was no cause to visit any further indignities on her corpse.

While he waited for the dizziness to subside, he tried to discipline his thoughts in a way that he had failed to do since he arrived. It was so easy to fall into the trap of concentrating solely on the tape and electric appliances. But despite their similarities, the two murders exhibited a number of differences too. Huldar knew he should keep an open mind about whether it was the same perpetrator. Better men than him had been badly burnt by taking such things for granted and in the process overlooking obvious points that didn't fit in with their theory.

Elísa had been found in bed, not on the floor like Ástrós. In the former case, the murderer had waited for the victim to go to sleep; in the latter he had burst in on the woman while she was awake. Huldar had a feeling that this was a symptom of growing confidence, but it was only a hunch. It was also possible that it wasn't the same man. While the detail about the duct tape hadn't been reported in the news, it could conceivably have leaked out. A number of people, not just within the police, were aware that tape had been used in Elísa's murder, and it was quite possible that more than one person had confided this detail to a spouse, family member or friend. In normal circumstances it wouldn't take long for that sort of information to spread.

Huldar rubbed his face hard. His hands needed employment, but when he lowered them again he felt no different. He missed the days when it had been somebody else's job to worry about the progress of the investigation. When some officer above him in the pecking order had to wrestle with the question of who would resort to such an act and whether the method provided any clues to the murderer's motives. Now there was no escaping the responsibility. He studied the grotesque spectacle of Ástrós's head, exhaling slowly. It had to be the same man. It was inconceivable that two psychopaths with an almost identical M.O. could exist in a small place like Iceland.

The pathologist snapped his case shut and Erla, who had been standing in a daze against the wall, almost jumped out of her skin. It had been a long day. Too long. Huldar had not only fatigue to contend with but a splitting headache as well. The harsh lighting caused spots to dance before his eyes, forcing him to abandon the attempt to focus on anything. His phone rang in his pocket but he didn't answer, just as he hadn't when it had rung before. He hadn't even bothered to check who was trying to reach him; the crime scene required his undivided attention. Murders, rare as they were in Iceland, thank God, had to take priority over everything else. The first time his phone rang, everyone had paused in the middle of what they were doing and looked at him, startled. Now no one took any notice when he didn't answer.

'Did you take the suction cups and glass-cutter?' The pathologist's voice hinted that even he was not having the best of days. He massaged his face where his mask had pinched it.

'Yes.' The phone went silent as Huldar spoke. His headache receded slightly. The attacker had entered through the balcony door. This was indicated by a kick mark on the wall beside it, footprints in the snow on the balcony and tracks leading from the door to the hall. The footprints were left by shoes in a common man's size but the pattern on the sole was too indistinct to analyse.

The balcony door had been opened by cutting a hole in the glass. A suction lifter had been used for the task but it appeared that the murderer wasn't entirely familiar with the device as the suction cup had fallen inside the flat when he tried to free the round of glass, which had then shattered. After that it had been an easy matter for the intruder to reach in and open the door from the inside. He appeared to have attacked the woman in the bedroom hallway. This was indicated by the black lines on the floor, which started outside the bathroom and led to the kitchen where her body had been discovered. The lines were assumed to be rubber marks left by the woman's slippers as the killer dragged her behind him. After this the sequence of events was unclear.

The pathologist was removing his paper overalls. 'There's something you need to bear in mind. If this turns out to be the same man, he won't hesitate to kill again. Of course, he might be satisfied with these two, but after this it won't really affect his sentence how many more lives he takes. All it would mean is twenty years instead of sixteen. It's a sobering thought.'

The atmosphere grew oppressive again. 'Let's just hope the killer is concerned for himself. Presumably he doesn't want to be caught, but every murder increases the chances that he will be. Always assuming it's the same man.' Huldar hoped this logic would serve to encourage the team: they had to believe that the worst was over.

Personally, though, Huldar doubted it was, and his colleagues seemed to be of the same opinion. Ríkhardur turned back to the shelf he was dusting and Erla lowered her gaze and folded her arms. He decided to send them home; they had done well. He could finish things off with forensics. Their relief was plain, though they tried not to show it. But when Huldar asked Ríkhardur to drive past Freyja's place on the way home, the man's impassive mask slipped a little, betraying his exhaustion. He seemed grateful when Huldar explained that she lived on Grandi, not far from his own home in the west end. He was even more grateful when Huldar stressed that he needn't go inside, just take a look around from the car and make sure all was quiet. Now that Margrét had been moved to Freyja's flat, it was best to keep an eye on things. There weren't many people he could ask; apart from the senior officers who had arranged it, Ríkhardur and Erla were the only members of CID who knew about the plan to send the girl there.

Erla scowled, obviously feeling slighted, but Huldar was too tired to think of any job for her to do on the way home. Unless she could drop by the chemist and buy him some painkillers. But he doubted that would be sufficient to smooth her ruffled feathers, and didn't have the energy to point out that it made no sense to send her to Freyja's since she lived on the other side of town in Breidholt. She should just be thankful for the chance to go home and maybe even catch the evening news. Instead, he was silent and merely hoped she would realise how ridiculous it was to think he favoured Ríkhardur over her. The situation would never have arisen if only he had refused his promotion. Yet again he bitterly regretted his decision. But this only made his headache worse.

It was freezing outside and grateful though he was for the fresh air, Huldar half wished he was inside in the warmth again. He still had to talk to the downstairs neighbours but all he could think about was how badly he needed a cigarette. He pressed the doorbell and held it down, though he knew this would have no effect on the ringing inside. He pressed it again. The occupants were home; another car had appeared in the parking space. He rang the bell a third time.

One ciggie. It would rid his nostrils of the nauseating smell. All right, two. He had managed to stay off tobacco, had actually forced himself to drive past two kiosks before he reached the chemist. Since then he had been chewing nicotine gum non-stop. He spat out the exhausted gum and replaced it with a new piece. When the door opened, he introduced himself thickly, and asked to have a few words with the occupants.

'Hello. Has something happened?' The woman pulled her cardigan tighter as if to shield herself from bad news.

'I need to ask you and any other people living here some questions about the events of yesterday evening.' Huldar slid the gum into his cheek.

'Yesterday evening?'

'That's right. Were you home?' The words emerged more distinctly now the gum was out of the way.

'Yes. My husband and I were home from about five. Our children have flown the nest.' The woman turned her head over her shoulder and bawled: 'Gunni! It's the police.' She turned back to Huldar. 'We were watching television. The ten o'clock news.' Her manner conveyed the message that his visit was extremely inconvenient. Evidently she would much rather watch the news than be involved in it.

The door opened wider and the husband appeared. He seemed no more pleased by the interruption than his wife. 'What's up?' He stuck his head outside and peered around as if he expected to find the explanation in the street.

'I need to know if you heard any unusual noises from the flat upstairs yesterday evening, or noticed anyone coming or going, in the garden or inside the house.'

The couple seemed indifferent. They didn't display any concern or curiosity about his reason for asking. 'Yesterday evening, you say?' The woman furrowed her brow and glanced at her husband. 'Was it yesterday or the day before that I heard that crash?'

'Last night, I think.'

'Crash? What time was this?'

'Well, I fell asleep around half past ten, so some time after that. About two, maybe. It woke me up and I looked out of the window but couldn't see anything. Was there a break-in at Ástrós's place?'

Huldar didn't answer. 'Are you sure the noise came from there?' This didn't fit with the estimated time of death; by 2 a.m. Ástrós would have been dead for a couple of hours. It couldn't have been the balcony door they heard because the murderer must have broken in considerably earlier. Perhaps he had lingered to admire his handiwork or obliterate any possible traces. He may have knocked over a vase or some other object, though no sign of any other breakage had been found.

'I'm not sure. I was woken by a noise and I was confused. I didn't check the time because it didn't occur to me that it was linked to a burglary. If it had, I'd have made more effort to remember.' Even so, the woman had been concerned enough to look out of the window, but Huldar let this pass. He was merely relieved that the couple had fixed on the idea of a burglary. They had obviously failed to notice the body being carried out to the ambulance.

'What about during the evening? Were you aware of anything then?'

The couple said no, but corrected themselves after a brief exchange, and concluded that around ten o'clock they had heard voices coming from Ástrós's flat and what sounded like wailing or crying but it could equally have been laughter. They hadn't paid any attention as Ástrós was always having visitors round. This last was uttered in a censorious tone. When Huldar questioned them about the gender and possible number of the visitors, they retracted and said maybe it had only been the TV or radio.

After disagreeing with each other for a while they eventually concurred that it must have been a radio programme or play because there had been no background music or advertisements. The woman added that sound carried easily between the flats. Her resentful expression implied that this was a source of tension, but she abruptly shut up at an unobtrusive poke from her husband and let him take over. He scratched his sparsely covered scalp and racked his brain until it came back to him that he too had heard odd sounds like weeping or wailing from upstairs when he woke to go to the toilet some time after midnight. But he hadn't thought Ástrós was ill or in trouble, just sad. She had lost her husband two years previously and relations had been rather strained since then, so they would never have dreamt of phoning to ask if she was all right. According to the man, since being widowed she had tried to wriggle out of her share of the upkeep of the property. The choice of colour for the exterior paintwork had been the final straw; Ástrós had insisted on yellow whereas the couple wanted grey. Huldar guessed that the moment they learnt of her death they would seize the chance to paint the house before a new owner could become involved.

Huldar's phone rang twice while the couple were busy denigrating their deceased neighbour. He ignored it. In a few minutes he would be back in his car, at leisure to return any urgent calls. In the meantime he listened to them droning on, taking it in turns to rake up all Ástrós's alleged failings as a neighbour. Their tales became progressively pettier until finally they ran out of steam and lapsed into an awkward silence.

Deciding there was nothing more to be gained from the couple, Huldar took his leave, explaining that they would be asked to provide an official statement some time in the next day or two. He was about to enter their mobile numbers into his phone when he noticed that the most recent call was from Freyja. Hastily he took the couple's numbers and said goodbye. The cold and the soreness of the chewing gum in his cheek were forgotten, replaced by much more serious concerns. Freyja was unlikely to be calling him merely for a chat, and he had promised to be contactable day and night.

'Hey!' The husband was still at the door. 'There's something you might want to see.' He vanished and returned after a brief interval, which seemed endless to Huldar in his impatience to call Freyja. He would never forgive himself if something had happened to Margrét because he failed to answer his phone. It was probably a minor matter; he hadn't heard from Ríkhardur so it couldn't be anything major. Then again, it must be half an hour since he had driven past and there could have been any number of developments in the interim.

Huldar had no choice but to push aside his fear and wait. The husband reappeared, looking shamefaced, and held out an envelope covered in what appeared to be tomato ketchup. 'Sorry but I threw it in the bin. The envelope was stuck under my windscreen wiper this morning. When I opened it I thought it was some kind of nonsense. You can throw it away if it has nothing to do with the burglary. I've no idea who the hell it's from.'

Huldar put on his latex gloves and gingerly took hold of the envelope. The man and his wife, who had also returned to the door, watched this precaution wide-eyed. Huldar ignored them. If this was what he thought it was, no further proof would be necessary: Elísa and Ástrós had been killed by the same man.

Turning away from the couple, he drew the note from the envelope, scanned its contents, then carefully replaced it. Here was the evidence: two victims, one killer. Huldar raised his eyes to the man's face. 'I'll need to take your fingerprints.' Then he turned to the woman. 'Yours too, if you've touched the envelope or note.'

The couple's faces were the picture of bewilderment.

Chapter 20

Margrét got on much better with Molly than Freyja did. The dog followed the little girl everywhere, refusing to leave her side; when Margrét sat down, Molly would settle at her feet. She lay with ears pricked, though her eyes were closed and she appeared to be asleep. It was as if the dog instinctively knew the girl needed protecting. She was right. Naturally everyone was hoping that their fears for Margrét's safety would prove groundless, but no one dared take any risks.

Geir from the Child Protection Agency had stressed this when he rang Freyja back to inform her of the final decision about Margrét's placement. He had made it very plain that they expected Freyja to accept the responsibility, and seemed far more concerned about maintaining good relations with the police than hearing her views on the subject. And since the police and social services had agreed to try this solution, she had no choice but to comply.

She didn't give in without a fight, though, pleading the problem of Molly. But it turned out that in their eyes the security provided by the dog was a big advantage. Freyja's description of the flat didn't help her case either; on the contrary, they assumed no one would dream of looking for the girl there. Clearly, there was nothing she could do but resign herself to the inevitable.

Two inspectors were sent round to evaluate both flat and

dog. They appeared as soon as she'd hung up and she suspected they had been waiting outside in their car for her to give in. They inspected every inch of the flat under Molly's watchful eye. The dog behaved impeccably and, bizarrely enough, they judged the flat perfectly acceptable. It helped, no doubt, that Freyja had hurriedly removed any incriminating objects that could get her brother into hot water. Luckily, she had moved the heat lamps out of the spare room several weeks ago when it had been her turn to invite the girls in her sewing circle round. They were unlikely to have met with the approval of the inspectors, or indeed of some of her girl-friends, though most would probably have smiled and one or two might even have shown an interest in the harvest.

As a result, the storeroom in the basement was crammed to bursting and the wardrobe in the bedroom was overflowing with paraphernalia decorated with cannabis leaves and other drug-related designs.

She was surprised by how cheerless and empty the flat appeared after this tidy-up. It matched Margrét's dull eyes as she stood there with lowered gaze after the men had delivered her to the door. The girl didn't say a word, simply took off her anorak and only reacted when Freyja told her not to bother taking off her shoes: the floor was always rather dirty from the dog and her socks would soon turn black if she walked around in them. The girl had glanced up then and from her anxious expression it seemed she thought Freyja was setting her a test or a trap. Freyja grinned and pointed to her own shoes. The men seized this opportunity to hand Freyja two bags of clothes and a DVD of the film *Frozen*, then made off without escorting the child inside, moving quickly away down the corridor to the head of the stairs.

Some time later Freyja was standing in the doorway of the bedroom, which she had vacated for Margrét. She herself was planning to make do with the sofa in the living room rather than sleep in the little room that had housed the heat lamps. That would have involved removing the shutter her brother had fitted over the window, not to mention the other objects that didn't belong in a bedroom, such as the collection of dumb-bells and other weight-lifting gear. It was this that had deterred the inspectors from insisting she sleep in there; neither of them fancied having to lug the weights out to make room for her.

'Shall I make some cocoa?' Freyja asked 'I make really good cocoa, you know.' She smiled at the girl. 'Or would you prefer coffee?'

Margrét looked up from her book. She was sitting on the bed, unnaturally upright, as if propped against an invisible wall. Her thin legs dangled over the edge, the slightly-too-large socks showing below her jeans, and her shoes lay kicked off on the floor. Her face bore the stamp of grief. 'No, thank you.'

'Are you sure?' Freyja was suddenly worried that the child wasn't eating or drinking. She had declined everything since she arrived and it was now 8 p.m. 'I've got fizzy drinks too, if you like. And there's water in the tap.'

'No, thank you.' Margrét's lips barely moved. She looked like a doll, her china-white face only enhancing the impression.

'Would you mind helping me feed Molly then?' Freyja glanced at the dog that was lying curled up at Margrét's feet. 'I'm afraid she won't want to come to the kitchen otherwise. She's taken such a shine to you that she'll refuse to leave your side.' Freyja smiled again. 'It's quite unusual for her, you know. She's certainly not very keen on me.'

'Isn't she yours?'

It was the first time Margrét had offered an opening for conversation.

'No, my brother's. This is his flat. I'm just looking after it and dog-sitting for him.'

'Where's he then?' Margrét sat there poised like a ballerina, arms at her sides, back ramrod straight.

'My brother?' Freyja frantically racked her brain for a suitable reply. She couldn't possibly tell the child the truth. 'He's living in the countryside at the moment but he'll be moving back to town soon, and I need to find myself a flat before then. I don't want to share with him.'

Margrét moved her head for the first time. She nodded, with feeling. Then she lowered her feet to the floor and forced them into her shoes. 'I'll help you. Molly's hungry.' As soon as the dog heard her name she rose to her feet and stationed herself beside Margrét. The girl patted her head and scratched her behind the ears, and the animal closed her eyes like an overgrown cat. Freyja had never managed to elicit that kind of response, despite her frequent attempts to pet her. Molly would merely shake her head as if to get rid of an annoying pest. Who knows – maybe Margrét's family could be persuaded to look after the dog? Absorbed in these thoughts she hardly noticed when Margrét sighed. A sad little sigh.

'Are you all right, Margrét dear? Is there anything I can do?'

'No.' The girl's voice was harsh and uncompromising. But she continued more mildly. 'I feel bad inside. In my head.' She stated this without emotion, as though it were her duty to report the fact. 'Like everything's broken down.'

'Have you got a headache?' Freyja had to ask, though she was well aware that what ailed the child could not be cured with painkillers.

'It's not like a headache. It's more like I've hurt myself, but inside my head, so you can't put a plaster on it.'

'I know what you mean.'

'No, you don't. Nobody does but me. It's my head, not yours.'

Freyja wasn't offended by this; she knew the feeling only too well from her own childhood. She had felt the same when grown-ups talked to her with sympathetic faces and feigned understanding in their voices after her mother died. They hadn't a clue what she was going through. Not a clue. 'Shall I tell you a secret, Margrét?'

The girl looked up. Secrets always held an allure, however difficult the situation.

'My mummy died when I was only a tiny bit older than you. So I might not know exactly how you feel but I do have some idea.'

Margrét scrutinised her face to satisfy herself that Freyja was telling the truth. 'Was she killed?'

'No. Not directly. She died because she didn't look after herself properly.' Freyja wanted more than anything to stroke the curly red head but didn't dare for fear the girl would resent the caress. Like Molly. She made do with a wry smile. 'You had a much better mummy than I did. But I still miss mine terribly. So I don't know exactly how you're feeling because you're bound to feel much worse than me – but I almost know.' She paused, sensing she was getting through to Margrét and unwilling to break the tenuous thread that now connected them. 'Come on. We don't want Molly to die of hunger.'

The kitchen was small since the building dated back to the days when little importance had been placed on food and cooking. In spite of this, her brother had managed to fit in a table and two chairs by the window, as well as finding room for a set of huge bowls for the dog. It was quite a squeeze for the three of them.

'I'd have to be absolutely starving before I'd eat that. How about you?' Freyja watched the girl carefully pouring dried food into a bowl from a half-full bag.

'Maybe I'd want it if I was a dog. But I'm not a dog.' Margrét struggled to lift the heavy bag on to the table. Her voice was unnervingly devoid of emotion, though she had at least begun to respond to Freyja's questions.

It was only to be expected. Nothing Freyja said could drive out the pain. Only time could do that. Freyja forced a chuckle. 'No, luckily. It's more fun being a girl.' She managed to grab the bag in the nick of time before it tipped over. 'You know what they say about a dog's life – it can be pretty miserable.'

'I'd rather be a dog. At the moment, anyway.' Margrét stared at the lino, avoiding Freyja's eye. 'Dogs don't care about their mummies and daddies.'

'Yes, I expect you're right.' Molly certainly gave no sign of missing her parents. Freyja handed Margrét the bowl she had filled. Molly's eyes followed it and when the food was placed on the floor she began to wolf it down to the accompaniment of rattling as her collar banged against the dish. It was pointless trying to talk over the din, which was just as well, because Freyja had to be careful what they discussed. Not only was the girl desperately sensitive but Freyja didn't want to inadvertently influence her statement.

Silence fell once Molly had finished. Freyja feigned surprise. 'Gosh, she must have been hungry. Shall I tell you something?' Margrét didn't answer but appeared to nod. 'Molly's always hungry. The instant we take the bowl away she'll be hungry again.' The dog gazed at them both in turn, licking her chops. She emitted a low whine as if she knew she wouldn't be given any more but thought it worth a try.

'Now we need to take her out for a little walk. Are you up for that?'

'All right.' It sounded as if a walk was no better or worse than anything else.

Freyja pushed aside the incongruously frilly, old-fashioned kitchen curtain. Huge flakes of snow were falling outside. A police car drove slowly past; presumably one of the patrols they had promised. Although it crawled by at a snail's pace, it was hard to see how this was supposed to deter any potential attacker. The deterrent would surely only work while the car was in the street. The thought unsettled her and Freyja hoped it didn't show. 'We'd better wrap up warm. It's snowing.'

Freyja had little experience of dressing children and wondered as they stood at the door whether she had overdone it. Nothing of Margrét could be seen apart from a glimpse of green eyes between her scarf and woolly hat. 'Do you think you'll be too hot?'

'I don't care.' The voice emerged rather muffled through the scarf.

Molly couldn't contain her joy and slammed her tail noisily against the wall as they descended the stairs. She capered around them when Freyja opened the front door, tugging hard on the lead. Although she had meant to let Margrét take the dog, Freyja realised this was too risky. She didn't want to return the child with injuries, though it was hard to see how she could hurt or graze herself through all those clothes. In spite of this, Freyja took care not to walk too fast on the slippery pavement, though Molly was in a tearing hurry and half dragged her along. There was no sign of the patrol car or of any other vehicles or pedestrians.

The snowflakes floated slowly down to earth. They seemed to absorb all sound and the few words that Margrét and Freyja exchanged sounded oddly muted, as though wrapped in cotton wool.

Down by the sea, Freyja let Molly off the lead. She hurtled away and vanished in the thick whiteness. For once Freyja wasn't worried about the dog getting lost or throwing herself at strangers. People seemed to have agreed to stay indoors this evening. She and Margrét stood side by side, watching the swarming flakes that had swallowed Molly up.

'Do you believe in God?'

Freyja was glad the girl wasn't looking at her face when she answered. She didn't want to tell the child what she really thought in case a belief in heaven and life after death was the only thing keeping her going at the moment. But neither did she want to tell an outright lie. 'Sometimes. Sometimes not.' Feeling this was rather feeble, she added: 'What about you?'

'Sometimes. Sometimes not.' They fell silent again and when the phone bleeped in Freyja's coat pocket it seemed like an insult to the tranquillity. Out of habit she took out the phone, which glowed in the dark. The text had been sent from a number she didn't recognise which at first she assumed belonged to the police – to Huldar. He had promised to be in touch but she had heard nothing. Typical. She had read his character right when he did a runner that morning. Underneath that handsome exterior was an empty shell.

But the message could hardly be from him. 'THINK I CANT DEAL WITH THE DOG?' Freyja's heart began to pound as she spun round, expecting to see someone standing behind them. She couldn't hide her agitation. The child was bound to be frightened. But there was nothing there except the snow, falling ever more thickly. She seized Margrét's hand. 'Molly! Molly!'

Margrét had noticed her panic. 'What's wrong?' The small gloved fingers struggled in Freyja's grasp.

'Nothing. But we'd better get back before the snow's up to our knees or Molly's tummy will get cold.' She was talking nonsense as she tended to when trying to conceal her dismay. 'Molly! Here, girl!' Freyja shifted the phone in her fingers, wondering whether to release Margrét's hand and call the police. Before she could make up her mind they heard a bark, followed by a pathetic whine. 'Molly! Molly!'

The dog reappeared as suddenly as she had vanished and Freyja heaved a sigh of relief. 'Molly! Come here!' As the dog limped over to them Freyja saw that she was leaving a bright red trail on the white snow. By the time she reached them there was no question where the blood was coming from; there was an ugly gash on the back of her thigh. Since there was little they could do for the dog on this godforsaken footpath, Freyja clipped on her lead and set off walking as fast as she dared.

It was a blessing in disguise that the dog was limping or Freyja would have raced home, pulling the little girl along with her and betraying the terror she was trying to hide.

She thought she heard the echo of footsteps in the thick silence behind them.

Chapter 21

Molly opened her eyes drowsily but apparently didn't like what she saw because she immediately closed them again. 'You can leave her here if you like. She can sleep it off in the back room.' The vet, a woman of about forty who didn't look easily daunted, was watching Freyja, waiting for her answer. The pristine white coat she had put on to receive them was now decorated with a spray of fine red spots.

Freyja avoided looking down at her own clothes, aware that she was in no better state. Tempting though the thought of a night without Molly was, she declined the offer. She knew herself well enough to realise she would be overcome by remorse before she was halfway home. Her brother doted on the dog like a child, and she would never have abandoned a child of his in hospital just to go home and rest. She was already dreading having to call him to explain what had happened, and only prayed he wouldn't launch a series of crazy reprisals against the person who had injured his dog. The problem being that it was by no means certain he would take as much trouble over establishing the guilt of the suspected perpetrator as he would over organising a fitting punishment. 'No, thanks. I'll take her home. Though maybe you could give me a hand getting her out to the car.' Fit though Freyja was, Molly was so heavy she wasn't sure she could carry her unaided. Nor did she like to think what sort of state her clothes would be in afterwards. Molly's coat on her wounded side was dull and sticky with half-congealed blood and other mysterious fluids that had poured out of her when the vet set to work with scalpel and needle.

'Is there anyone at home who can help you carry her inside?'

'No.' Freyja felt the blood mottling her cheeks. What was wrong with her? There was nothing to be ashamed of about living alone at her age. Countless other women over thirty were divorced or unmarried. The vet had shown no curiosity about Freyja's bloodstained trousers and wild hair, or the traumatised child she had in tow, so the woman was unlikely to raise her eyebrows over her marital status. Besides, since when had Freyja given a damn what strangers thought? It must be delayed shock. She was longing to relax in a hot bath but would have to make do with a shower since she had a child in her care – a child and an injured dog. For the first time since she had walked out on her ex, she missed him. He'd had his good moments. More than she cared to remember. 'There's no chance Molly'll recover on the way?'

'I recommend you wait a bit. Now she's started opening her eyes it won't be long before she wakes up. You don't want to risk her coming round in the back seat of the car while you're driving. I'll find you a surgical collar, some painkillers and antibiotics, and sort out the bill. If the dog wakes up in the meantime, you can take her with you, otherwise she stays here tonight.'

There was no alternative but to agree. Freyja wasn't looking forward to the bill. On top of the normal cost there was bound to be an additional charge for the late call-out. When the vet had asked if the dog was insured, Freyja had almost burst out laughing, so unlikely was it that her brother would have arranged such a thing. The only reason he'd take out insurance was if he saw some way of cheating the system, but it was difficult to see how this could be achieved with pet insurance. No doubt she'd be saddled with a sky-high bill to pay. Still, no point worrying about that: the wound would never have healed on its own and she couldn't have done the stitches herself. She had briefly considered asking the doctor at the Children's House for help but decided against it. If there was anything she disliked more than extortionate bills, it was being beholden to people.

Molly stirred, opened one eye and kicked her back leg. Then she seemed to doze off again, though her eyes were moving under their lids. There were ten gleaming sutures in the shaven patch at the top of her thigh. According to the vet she had been stabbed with a sharp knife, apparently deliberately. The wound wouldn't have been as deep or clean if the dog had merely bumped into something. The vet had explained this while she was cleaning and stitching the gash. Freyja would have preferred to wait out front, but outside normal opening hours pet owners were required to assist with operations. Apparently most of the vet's time was spent manipulating the owners into the recovery position after they had fainted mid-operation. Freyja had narrowly avoided this humiliation, chiefly by looking away whenever the world began to spin before her eyes. She found herself thinking about Margrét's mother and wondering how her murderer could bring himself to kill another human being in such a barbaric fashion. This only made her dizziness worse and she had to step away from the operating table and lean against a cupboard until she recovered.

She decided to take the chance that Molly wasn't about to

surface, and opened the door to the waiting room where Margrét was sitting looking at the pictures in a dog magazine. 'Want to come and see? The operation's over. Poor Molly's still asleep but she's about to wake up. I'm sure she'd rather see you than me when she opens her eyes. But you mustn't be sick at the sight of the stitches.'

Margrét laid the magazine carefully down. She smoothed it out as though to obliterate any sign that she had ever been sitting there. Freyja tried to read from her face whether she was suffering any ill effects from their adventure earlier that evening but she didn't seem to be. Unless her stony expression meant that she was still in shock. They had made it home without anyone blocking their way or chasing them. While Molly lay on the floor with the blood pumping out of her thigh, Freyja had tried repeatedly to get hold of Huldar. There must have been a major incident because the police station refused to put her through or tell her where he was. She couldn't help feeling annoyed, especially as she had been forbidden to speak directly to the regular police. She gathered this was to guarantee that as few people as possible knew of Margrét's whereabouts.

'Look at the poor thing.' Freyja led Margrét into the surgery. 'She's had ten stitches.' She watched as the girl gently stroked the dog and thought she saw her rigid jaw soften into a faint smile. 'Hopefully she won't be in any pain when she wakes up.'

'Does the woman know what happened to her?' Margrét moved her small fingers towards the wound. Freyja braced herself to grab her hands but this proved unnecessary. The girl stroked tenderly and warily all round the shaven area but didn't touch the stitches. 'Did she say anything about it?'

'No, she couldn't be sure. Molly may have caught herself on something sharp that was hidden by the snow, or been hit by a cyclist. It's hard to say.'

'What would you do if someone could tell you who had hurt her?'

Freyja took a deep breath. It was possible Margrét was sounding out her views, so it would be as well to answer with care. 'That would depend on whether it was deliberate or an accident. If it was an accident I'd make the person who hurt her say they were sorry. That would do. But if it was deliberate, saying sorry wouldn't be enough. It would be much more serious, so I'd talk to the police and leave it to them to deal with the guilty person so they'd get their comeuppance.'

'What's a comeuppance?' The girl's green eyes narrowed doubtfully, as if she suspected Freyja of inventing the word.

'A comeuppance is when people get the punishment or telling-off that fits what they did wrong. It's very important as a way of stopping them from doing wrong again and also of stopping others from copying them.' Freyja hoped this short speech would impress on Margrét how vital it was that she tell them everything she had witnessed on the night of her mother's murder. The next interview was due to take place tomorrow and it would save time and effort – and anguish for Margrét – if she could be persuaded to open up. Unless, that is, she didn't have any more to tell.

'If someone hurt Molly I think he deserves to be hurt back. Only worse.'

'That's how it used to be in the old days, Margrét. And still is in some places.' Freyja stroked Molly's ear, which had begun to twitch as if it were being tickled by a piece of grass on a summer's day. 'But it's been shown that that kind of punishment is no good. Ordinary people slowly become bad inside if they start doing the same thing as those who hurt others deliberately.'

'Not if you only do it once.'

'No, maybe not. But there are better ways of punishing people who do bad things to other people.'

'Like what?'

Freyja wondered what on earth was keeping the vet. She had no wish to engage in further conversation about crime and punishment with a child whose mother had died in such traumatic circumstances. Her thoughts went to her brother and she wondered what the little girl would think of someone like him. 'Prison. No one wants to go to prison, Margrét.'

'Yes, they do. The people who are dead. The ones the bad men kill. They'd rather be in prison than dead.' The girl fell silent and ran her eyes over the sleeping dog. 'At least, that's what I think.'

Margrét had a point. It was clear now where her thoughts were leading.

'I'm sure you're right. But sadly that's not possible.' Once again Freyja fought an urge to stroke the cloud of curly red hair, which was alive with static electricity from the little girl's hat. 'But, take it from me, it's better to lock up the people who commit such wicked crimes than to kill them. Much, much better.' She was aware how lame this sounded. If she were honest, the world would be better off without some individuals. But the call wasn't for her to make – or anyone, probably. She wondered if she should explain to Margrét that the main problem with the death penalty was that it was impossible to reverse if the person turned out to have been innocent, but she didn't get a chance. The door opened to reveal the vet.

The woman was holding two sheets of paper that Freyja assumed was the bill. She was alarmed to see that one sheet had not been sufficient. The vet asked Freyja to step outside with her for a moment, telling Margrét to look after Molly in the meantime. No sooner had the door to the surgery swung shut than she shook the papers at Freyja. 'This was lying on the reception desk. It's the medical notes for a dog brought in earlier today and the description of the incident is suspiciously similar to what happened to yours.' The woman gave Freyja a sharp look. 'Do you live in Grafarvogur? According to your ID number, you live next door to the dog that was stabbed there.'

'No. I live in the centre of town, like I told you. Out on Grandi.' On the other hand, her ex still lived in the flat they used to share in Grafarvogur. If the neighbours hadn't moved, she thought she knew the dog in question. It was an infuriatingly noisy animal that used to make a terrible racket in the communal garden where it spent its days tethered to a post. It was as large as Molly but had seemed mostly harmless. Struck by a sudden suspicion that her ex could have been behind the incidents, she flushed. It must have been her brother's comments that had given her the idea. Her ex had taken their break-up pretty hard and said some ugly stuff. But could he really be so angry that he would resort to harming Molly just to scare her? And practise on the neighbour's dog first? The very idea made Freyja's blood boil and from the heat in her face she guessed she was blushing again. What made it worse was that the woman didn't seem to believe a word she said. 'I moved ages ago but haven't got round to changing my address with the National Register yet. My ex-boyfriend still lives there.'

'I see.' Whatever it was the woman saw, it did nothing to improve her opinion of Freyja, judging by the look in her eye. 'Is this his dog, by any chance?'

'No. He has absolutely no claim on her. This has nothing to do with any dispute about custody of the dog.'

'What is it about then? It's not every day that dogs are subjected to this sort of attack in Reykjavík. Two similar incidents in short succession are more than a little suspicious. The injuries are almost identical and it wouldn't surprise me if the same person was responsible. Anything else would be too much of a coincidence.' The vet put her hands on her hips. 'I've half a mind to report this to the police. If your ex was behind the incidents and is planning to carry on like this, we need to stop him right now. Are you sure you didn't see him at the scene?'

'No, I didn't. Please believe me when I say that I wouldn't shield him if he was hurting animals. By all means call the police. You'll save me the trouble.' The conversation was cut short by a feeble bark from the surgery, although it was plain that the vet had not said her last word on the subject.

'I couldn't answer but I came as soon as I saw your messages. As soon as I could, anyway.' Huldar was standing at the door of Freyja's flat. He looked ready to drop but showed no sign of being ashamed, which, to Freyja's chagrin, implied that he had a perfectly reasonable excuse. It was intolerable when your righteous anger turned out to be groundless. Beside him stood a young woman who introduced herself as Erla. She looked no less weary but her eyes were more alert, which made her seem less shattered than Huldar. Freyja recognised her as the police officer who had accompanied him to the second interview at the Children's House, though now she was dressed in civilian clothes. As a result she appeared smaller and had lost the air of authority that went with the uniform. She seemed to have come straight from home, her wet hair suggesting she had just stepped out of the shower. Freyja could sense the woman's dislike, though they hadn't exchanged a word since they were introduced at the Children's House. Goodness knows what she had against her. To avoid being flustered by Erla's inexplicable hostility, Freyja pretended she wasn't there and focused her attention on Huldar instead.

He was still making excuses. 'There's been a development.'

Freyja didn't know what he expected her to say. She had called his mobile twice, sent a text message and phoned the police station as well, so it was pointless to pretend that it didn't matter and that everything was fine with her and Margrét. But politeness kicked in and instead of snapping that he wasn't the only one to encounter unforeseen problems, she replied drily: 'Don't worry. We managed in the end.'

Before Huldar could respond, Erla cut in. 'Mind if I ask you something?' She was surveying the corridor critically as she spoke. The duty of cleaning the communal areas was supposed to be shared among the residents, but as far as Freyja was aware, no one but her had picked up a vacuum cleaner and cloth since she arrived. It was now three weeks since it was last her turn to clean. To do Huldar justice, he didn't turn up his nose in disgust at the state of the place, any more than he had on that other, happier occasion. But Erla was another story. 'How come you're living in a shithole like this? Is the pay at the Children's House that bad?'

Freyja was furious. 'Why, are you planning to organise a

whip-round?' There was no way she was going to tell them about her brother or explain that the accommodation was temporary. It was none of their business. She certainly wasn't ashamed of Baldur and she had no intention of betraying him by discussing him with two police officers. As far as her brother was concerned, they belonged to the enemy; he would regard their visit as sacrilege as it was. She just hoped he never got wind of it.

Erla's face darkened but a murderous glance from Huldar prevented her from retorting and she clamped her lips shut. Huldar turned back to Freyja and spoke in a more conciliatory tone. 'I'm sorry; where you choose to live has nothing to do with us, obviously. We're both knackered. As you must be too.' He held her gaze for longer than was strictly necessary and she read in his eyes a plea not to refer to their earlier acquaintance in front of Erla. Perhaps they were a couple. Perhaps he had been using a false name because he was cheating on her. What a cliché.

Freyja's manner became even drier. 'No problem.' She didn't know which of them she was angrier with, him or this rude young woman. Him probably. Nevertheless, she avoided looking at Erla and reminded herself to behave as if she wasn't there. Next time Erla opened her mouth she wouldn't dignify her with an answer.

It was unusually quiet in the corridor. Her neighbours must have spotted the police car and decided to lie low or else sensed danger in the air. A visit from the police constituted a very real threat to the occupants of this block. Freyja wouldn't have been surprised if a warning bell had jangled in the corridors when the patrol car pulled into the drive.

'Could we maybe come in? I need to see for myself that

everything's OK. We need to talk to you too and I'd rather not do it out here.'

Freyja realised she had been considering his request for an embarrassingly long time when Huldar began to shuffle his feet. Erla, on the other hand, stood with legs apart and hands on her hips, as though she had been ordered to adopt a formal stance. In uniform the effect might have been impressive but in civilian clothes it looked mildly ridiculous.

'Please, come in.' Freyja stepped aside for them, annoyed with herself for giving way. Erla inspected the hall and what she could see of the flat with a supercilious air, while Huldar studiously ignored his surroundings. He was doing a bad job of acting like a man arriving somewhere for the first time. He wiped his feet thoroughly, then took off his shoes as a sign that he was coming further inside. Erla copied him, looking livid. Freyja decided to let them dirty their socks.

'How's the dog doing?' Huldar glanced down at the blood-stains that Freyja had yet to wash off the floor. 'Will it recover?'

'She's still a bit woozy from the anaesthetic and unhappy about the surgical collar but I gather she's going to be OK.' As if sensing that people were talking about her, Molly appeared at the door of the bedroom where she had been dozing under the watchful eyes of Margrét. The dog bared her teeth and emitted a low growl, the menacing effect of which was somewhat diminished by the cone-shaped plastic collar. 'Hush, Molly.' Freyja pushed the dog back into the bedroom. Margrét was sitting on the bed with her book, just as she had been the last time Freyja looked in on her. She couldn't be persuaded to watch the film she had brought along. 'The police are here about Molly. I'm going to close the door so she doesn't bite them. She doesn't understand that they're trying to help.' She smiled at Margrét who didn't respond. As Freyja closed the door, the eyes of both girl and dog rested on her as if they were hiding something and couldn't believe that they had got away with it. Freyja was tempted to fling the door open again and catch them red-handed. Instead, she turned back to Huldar and Erla. 'You should be safe now.'

Huldar dropped his eyes from the poster in the hall, which he had been studying to avoid inadvertently catching sight of the bed. The poster had only just avoided the purge before Margrét came to stay. It was an advertisement for a gig by a heavy rock band that Freyja wouldn't be caught dead listening to: she'd rather stand next to a pneumatic drill. Huldar seemed surprised to see it there. Freyja didn't remember having mentioned whose flat it was during their night together. They'd been otherwise occupied. She decided not to correct the misconception that she was a heavy metal fan.

'Could we maybe sit down?' he asked diffidently.

'Fine by me.' She showed them into the living room where she took the only chair, forcing Huldar and Erla to sit side by side on the sofa like kids on a school bench, their hands on their knees, as if ready to leap up at any moment.

'I received a phone call from the animal hospital. It was put through to me when your name came up.' Huldar didn't beat about the bush. 'I understand you have an estranged ex who they suspect of stabbing the dog. The vet who rang mentioned that another dog had been injured as well. Apparently its owner lives in the same building as your ex.'

Freyja sent up a silent prayer of thanks that Margrét wasn't in the room. The girl was still under the impression that Molly had probably hurt herself in a fit of exuberance. 'I'd be extremely surprised if he had any connection to this.'

'You didn't mention any ex when they discussed placing Margrét with you.' Huldar had the presence of mind to stop himself adding that she hadn't said a word about him that other time either. After all, he was hardly in a position to complain that she hadn't disclosed certain details about her private life. 'If he's violent, we'll have to reconsider the decision. It raises doubts about the advisability of leaving Margrét with you. I think it would be safer to station a police car outside until we've proved otherwise.'

It didn't occur to Freyja to refuse the offer of protection. If this surprised him, he didn't show it.

'Fine.' Far-fetched though it was that her ex-boyfriend could have attacked Molly, all the indications were that the culprit knew her. He'd had her phone number, after all. Though admittedly she was in the telephone directory, so it would have been enough for him to know her name. 'Although I very much doubt my ex poses any threat to Margrét, there's no question that she's in danger. Someone slashed Molly with a knife and I received a text message at the same time. Look. This morning I'd have said Margrét was safe here with me. Now I'm not so sure.'

Huldar read the message, showed it to Erla, then handed back the phone. 'There's no denying this business with the dog doesn't look good. The only reason for doing a thing like that would be to get the animal out of the way to make it easier to attack you or Margrét. I assume the dog would leap to your defence.'

'Yes, I expect so.' Freyja wasn't about to confide in him her doubts about Molly's loyalty.

'Did the dog use to belong to both of you or did you acquire it after you separated?'

'After.' Freyja didn't elaborate. 'And we weren't married.'

'I see.' Huldar's sigh was hard to interpret. 'It's only right you should know that we're calling him in for questioning – tomorrow morning probably. I don't expect anything to come of it, unless he makes a full confession, but I think it's best to let him know we've got our eye on him.'

'Definitely. Give him the third degree. It can't hurt.' Freyja leant back in her chair. 'But he's very unlikely to be involved. At least I'd be amazed if he was. He wouldn't have the guts to take on one big dog, let alone two.'

'Well, we'll see what emerges. We'll have the text message traced and if it turns out to have been sent from his phone, that'll clarify matters. Though I doubt he's that stupid. The text is bound to have been sent from a disposable SIM card, in which case it'll take longer to trace. But that's our problem. At present, the most obvious assumption is that it's from your ex and, if so, the situation could escalate.' Erla couldn't suppress a grin as Huldar said this. It took all Freyja's self-control to ignore her. 'Any intervention from us can have the effect of provoking stalkers. It can make them even angrier with their victim because they tend to blame them for the humiliation of being questioned by the police.'

The word 'stalker' always struck Freyja as inappropriate, with its associations with deer-stalking in the highlands. The reality was far, far worse, as she knew from her work with the children of women who were being persecuted by their ex-husbands. She bit her lip and answered calmly: 'We'll just have to wait and see.'

'Well, you can rest assured that nothing'll happen while there's a patrol car parked outside.'

In other words, as soon as they found a new safe house for Margrét, the car would disappear. She would be left alone with Molly who couldn't bite because of the surgical collar. Perhaps the person who attacked the dog had been after her, not Margrét. She felt her palms sweating. 'Was there anything else?'

'Yes, actually.' Huldar's gaze was fixed on the coffee table. 'The case has taken an unexpected turn. It's right you should hear it from me rather than reading it in tomorrow's news.' He met her eye. 'Another woman's been murdered. Same M.O. Naturally that alters the situation. Margrét was right when she said there would be another victim and I don't need to explain to you how incredibly important it is that we get the whole story out of her tomorrow.'

It took Freyja a moment or two to recover. What did it mean? That the person who had hurt Molly might be the man who had murdered Margrét's mother? Exactly how much danger was the girl in? And herself too? 'Are you sure it's the same man?'

'Without a doubt. We found the same type of message as he'd left at the scene of the first murder.'

'Message? What kind of message?' The question was involuntary. She had no real desire to know about the killer's message. She just wanted the pair of them out of her flat and to be able to turn the clock back to how things had been before. More than anything she longed for something ordinary, like a phone call from her friend Nanna to moan about her children's earache. Right now it seemed unbelievable that she should ever have found it boring to listen to Nanna's complaints. 'What did it say?'

'That needn't concern you.' Erla had found her tongue but evidently not her manners.

Huldar ground his teeth in an effort to control his temper. 'I'll fill you in before the interview tomorrow,' he told Freyja. 'We may need to ask Margrét about the messages in case she heard something that could shed any light on them. We still can't make head or tail of either of them – the one found at her house or this latest one. Assuming there is anything to understand.'

The pleasure at having got in a dig at Freyja was stripped from Erla's face. She breathed out heavily like a bull about to charge.

'Fine. If there's nothing else, I'd like to put Margrét to bed now.' Freyja was seized with such a longing to throw them out that she twisted her fingers into a knot. They got the message.

Once Margrét was in bed and everything was quiet, Freyja went and stood by the living-room window. It had stopped snowing. The neighbourhood appeared utterly peaceful under its pristine covering of white. It seemed impossible to believe that somewhere out there lurked a man who would want to harm her or Margrét. A policeman had emerged from the car that was parked outside, and was leaning against the driver's door, smoking. Glancing up, he spotted Freyja watching him and waved. Embarrassed, she dropped the curtain without returning his wave.

Neither of them noticed the movement in the garden across the street. The figure that had been standing there backed away and melted into the darkness.

Chapter 22

Tuesday

The ringing sounded uncomfortably shrill in the quiet house. Karl stared at the phone, its strident jangling filling his ears while he tried to make up his mind. Should he answer or leave it to ring? He knew who was on the other end and his hand hovered over the receiver while he vacillated. He had promised himself never to speak to his brother again. Don't answer. Yet he was desperate to talk to someone, even Arnar. Go on, answer. Both were equally tempting.

Ever since he'd woken up he had been enveloped in silence and a chilling sense of loneliness. Now that he had removed all his mother's clutter, the place felt bleak and cheerless, like a stage that had yet to be dressed. The windows seemed larger since he had torn down the curtains and without the nets the world outside looked drab and desolate.

Most of all he missed the pot plants that had withered and died, one after the other, since he'd stopped watering them. It wasn't hard to identify with them. Without the plants, the ugliness of the furniture was unrelieved. And the paler patches on the wall where the pictures and decorations used to hang looked like shadows of the past.

It was too late for regrets – he was stuck now with this stark version of his home. The bulk of the ornaments, curtains, paintings, pictures, old electric appliances, flower pots, decorative china and other superfluous objects had gone to the dump. In the end it had taken three trips, with the car filled to bursting each time. The staff had watched in astonishment as he threw away one perfectly good item after another, and on the second visit his attention had been politely drawn to the charity bin provided by the Good Shepherd. Red in the face, he had moved to another spot and disposed of the remainder there. On his last trip the member of staff in question hadn't been around so Karl had chucked the rest of the contents in the general skip. It had felt so much more final.

Now the empty flat echoed, the naked walls making it feel as though he were rattling around in a metal container. Not that he generated much noise; now that his mother's radio and the clunky TV had been disposed of, and he had no one to talk to, he existed in almost total silence. He didn't like the solitude, although he should have been used to it by now, but his attempts to get hold of Börkur and Halli had been unsuccessful: Börkur's phone just rang unanswered; Halli's seemed to be dead. Every now and then he nearly jumped out of his skin when he heard knocking sounds from the basement, but when he went down to check, there was nothing to be seen. In the end he had persuaded himself that the sounds must be coming from outside and stopped being scared witless when he heard them. But he hadn't actually gone out to see if there was anything knocking against the wall; he was too afraid of finding nothing there.

The ringing persisted, sounding, if possible, even more peremptory. Perhaps it was a sign that it was the last ring before Arnar gave up. Karl's hands felt clammy. He longed to hear a voice, a human voice, the voice of someone who actually wanted to talk to him. If he wanted to communicate with strangers he could go down to the basement and seek out other lonely radio hams. No doubt he would be sitting there now if the equipment wasn't a continual reminder of the creepy numbers broadcasts. Then there was that bloody knocking too. It was bad enough hearing it from upstairs; up close, in the basement, it was unbearable.

The ringing seemed to be fading out. Karl couldn't afford to dither a moment longer. He snatched up the receiver.

His brother sounded surprised, as if he'd been expecting someone else. 'Hello, Karl?'

'Yeah.' He did his best to sound indifferent, neither angry nor pleased. He had to convey the message that he couldn't care less about his brother.

'I was about to hang up. It's Arnar. Have you just got in?'

'What? No. I didn't hear the phone.' Karl immediately regretted not having grasped the proffered excuse and lied that he had just walked in the door. You couldn't fail to hear the phone anywhere in the house, as Arnar was well aware.

'I see.' Arnar let a pause develop and Karl pressed the receiver closer to his ear. Silence in America sounded no different from silence in Iceland. Oppressive. But it didn't last long. 'I just wanted to check you were OK after our last chat. You know.' There was no need for him to elaborate.

'What do you mean?'

'Oh, I just wanted to check you hadn't misunderstood. It may have sounded like I didn't want you to come over.' Arnar was uncharacteristically hesitant and his tone of voice kept changing, as if he didn't know how to be nice and was struggling to strike the right note. 'Anyhow, that wasn't the intention.'

'I never thought it was. Like I said, it was you who misunderstood me. I'm not interested in trekking all the way over to the west coast.' This feeble lie sounded no more believable now than when he had resorted to it during their last conversation. 'No worries.'

'OK.' Arnar's relief was so obvious it was almost embarrassing. 'By the way, one question.'

'What?' Karl considered hanging up. The receiver felt uncomfortable pressed against his ear like this. The blood had rushed to his face when it dawned on him that Arnar hadn't even tried to encourage him to come over. If he hadn't chucked out the big mirror in the gilt frame that used to hang above the phone, he would have been able to see his scarlet face. He fixed his eyes on the white rectangle the mirror had left behind.

'Have you been through Mum's stuff?'

'Yes.' Better restrict himself to monosyllables so as not to betray his anger and hurt.

'Did you find any papers or documents?'

Karl hesitated. For the first time in their relationship he had the upper hand and he wanted to use it to his advantage. 'Yeah. Loads.'

'Loads?'

'Yeah, a whole pile of all kinds of old papers.'

'Have you been through them?'

'Yeah.'

'All of them?' Arnar obviously couldn't bring himself to ask the burning question. With so much at stake he wanted to defer any potential disappointment.

'Yes, all of them.' Karl had no intention of making this easy for him.

'And?'

'And what?'

'And . . . did you find any adoption papers? *My* adoption papers?' Yet again Arnar had revealed his self-centredness; he couldn't care less about Karl's origins. *He* was the only one who mattered.

Karl took a deep breath, then, grinning to himself, he said: 'No.'

'No?' There was no disguising Arnar's disappointment. Nor the embarrassing wishful thinking contained in his next questions. 'Nothing else? No letters, certificates, that sort of thing? It doesn't have to be formal records of adoption.'

'No, nothing.' Karl grinned to himself again. 'Nada.'

'I see.' Arnar fell silent as if he needed time to digest this disappointment – and total defeat. 'Send it all to me anyway. I want to look through it myself in case . . .'

Karl leant back and raised his eyes to the ceiling. What luck that he had answered. He couldn't have ended his relationship with his brother on a better note. 'Oh, I threw it all out,' he said casually. 'Yesterday. You should have rung sooner.'

'Threw it out? Where? In the bin?'

'No, I took it all to the dump. All the papers too.' Karl closed his eyes. 'There's no chance of finding them now. They'll have gone into landfill with the rest of the rubbish. Though maybe you could ask where they threw that day's stuff and try looking for yourself – if you were in the country. I doubt it would do any good, though.'

'I see.' Arnar sounded like a completely different person. The smug, bullying note had left his voice, which had dropped to little more than a whisper.

'Was there anything else? I've got to get on.'

'What? Oh. No.'

'Well, so long.' Karl hung up. He no longer felt lonely or jumpy. Quite the reverse – he felt bloody great. It was like sinking back into a comfy sofa when you've just taken a drag on a big fat joint. So this is how winners felt. A guy could get used to this.

The envelope lay on the kitchen table with the documents arranged around it. Karl had carefully laid them down, one after the other, after reading their contents. Although the names had been omitted from some of the papers, he had gleaned enough information to know who his and Arnar's real parents were.

His own parents' names told him nothing: Gudrún María Gudjónsdóttir and Helgi Jónsson. Like everything else connected to him, the names were neither impressive nor memorable, just ordinary. He regretted having given in to his curiosity but it had been too tempting to discover the kind of information about his biological family that Arnar was so desperate for on his own account. When Karl drew the papers out of the mustard-yellow envelope he had imagined that for the rest of his life he would walk a little taller, feel a little more reconciled to his lot, in the knowledge that he alone possessed this information. Now, however, he wished he could wipe the knowledge from his memory. But that wasn't how it worked.

The fan in his cheap laptop whirred into life as if to prompt him; remind him that he had to finish this now that he had started. Karl ran his hands through his hair. His palms came away shiny with grease. As he studied them, it occurred to him that either Gudrún María or Helgi must have been faced with the same hands every day. Broad, flat nails, unnecessarily long ring fingers, thick thumbs. They must have come from somewhere.

Pushing the papers aside, he pulled the laptop towards him, keeping his eyes on the black keyboard instead of looking at the screen as he usually did. For some reason he didn't want to see the names materialise letter by letter. He never normally looked at the keyboard, so only now did he notice how badly the letters had faded. The M had completely disappeared and so had half the S. Only small white lines remained of the A and R. It was a bit like his memory of his adoptive mother; her features were growing ever hazier and he could no longer remember her voice. Since there was no recording of her speaking, her voice had been quite literally obliterated from the universe.

Raising his eyes to the screen, Karl began his search. Like Arnar during the phone call, he had decided to stall a little. He would hunt for his brother's parents first. That way he could continue for a few more minutes in blissful ignorance of his own depressing origins, while clinging to the hope – against all reason – that they might not turn out to be so bad. After all, his mother had presumably kept them secret to shield him from the ugly truth.

Mind you, from what he remembered, their mother had been more focussed on withholding information from Arnar. Perhaps that was because he had been more insistent than Karl, yet he had a hunch that that wasn't the reason. Arnar's origins must have been worse than his own, so it seemed logical to dig around for his family first. It would lessen Karl's own pain to know that others had worse to contend with. He would just have to discipline himself not to blurt the secret out, however terrible it was. Far better to hug the knowledge to himself for the foreseeable future than to fling it in Arnar's face in order to savour his shock. His brother wasn't the type to dwell on disappointment and before you knew it he would have bounced back and be walking tall again, towering over Karl – more intelligent, more smugly self-satisfied than he deserved to be. No prehistory could be sufficiently devastating to crush Arnar for long – Karl must never forget that.

But there was another reason why Arnar's background was of more interest to him now than his own sorry history. According to Arnar's birth certificate, his mother was called Jóhanna Hákonardóttir. The box following her name contained an eight-digit number; there were no ten-digit ID numbers on the document because these hadn't yet been introduced in 1983 when Arnar was born, but the number had struck Karl as familiar. He was convinced that the same sequence had been broadcast over the radio the previous evening – he remembered scratching his head over it for ages because it resembled nothing that had hitherto been transmitted by the station. After the broadcast had ended, he'd searched for the eight-digit sequence but nothing had come up. It was almost certainly the same number, though, and to make sure Karl had even gone to the trouble of fetching his notes from the basement. He was right: Arnar's mother's old social security number had indeed been read out.

It was no good trying to persuade himself that it was a coincidence. The chances of a random eight-digit series co-inciding exactly with this woman's number were sufficiently remote, even without the additional fact that the ten-digit series in a previous broadcast had tallied with his own ID.

There was no avoiding the conclusion that the person

responsible for the broadcasts had deliberately drawn him and Arnar into his or her dark designs. Karl couldn't begin to fathom what it all meant. Perhaps he could unravel the mystery if he could find out something about this woman.

None of the numbers broadcast so far had been linked to Arnar's father, whose name, according to the birth certificate, was Thorgeir Bragi Pétursson, so Karl was less interested in him.

The search shed little light on the matter. It threw up 30,000 results but the women with the same name listed at the top were still alive. He repeated the search with Jóhanna's birth date and this greatly reduced the results. Among them was the notice of her death. She had died on 12 February 1987 at her home on the farm of Gráhamrar in the Hvalfjördur district, aged twenty-three. She was described as a housewife and that was it. There was no mention of a husband or son, or of any surviving relatives or in-laws. An obituary turned up by the search engine provided no further details. The name underneath was Thorgeir Bragi Thorhallsson, Arnar's father, but he had made do with sending in a poem that didn't seem immediately relevant.

> *O Lord, I pray, keep watch upon*
> *My poor beloved little son;*
> *Grant that he may sweetly sleep;*
> *Grant that he may never weep.*
>   Benedikt Th. Gröndal

Given the subject of the poem, Karl would have expected to see a reference to their son Arnar, but no. The decision to put him up for adoption must already have been taken and the only possible interpretation was that this Thorgeir Bragi had declined to take in his son.

Where was the scandal? The photo of Arnar's mother that accompanied the obituary showed a perfectly ordinary-looking young woman. It was a rather bad passport picture that appeared to have been taken in her teens; her childlike face prompted Karl to work out how old she would have been when she gave birth to Arnar: nineteen. Could that be the dreadful secret? That she'd had him so young? What a let-down. That wasn't remotely scandalous. Disappointed, he closed the obituary.

The window containing the death notice reappeared. Karl was about to close this as well when towards the bottom of the screen his attention was caught by the heading of another death announcement. Hákon Hákonarson had died on the same day as Jóhanna, 12 February 1987, also at home in Gráhamrar in the Hvalfjördur district.

Karl sat back, frowning at the screen. Hákon must have been Jóhanna's father; Arnar's grandfather. But, as with his daughter's death notice, there was no mention of any surviving family. He appeared to have died alone and friendless like her. On the very same day.

Karl turned next to the newspaper archives to see if there were any reports of an incident that could have caused both their deaths. His immediate thought was a house-fire or a car crash, though the latter explanation didn't fit with the information that they had both died at home. An avalanche? None was reported, although he scoured the papers for the weeks either side of 12 February. A shroud of secrecy seemed to hang over the deaths of father and daughter.

Before giving up altogether, Karl decided to find out more

about Thorgeir Bragi Pétursson, Arnar's father. Perhaps he could ring him and ask him about Hákon and Jóhanna's deaths, though that would be risky. What if the man was suffering from remorse and wanted to contact Arnar? His fear proved redundant, however, since it transpired that Thorgeir had died two years previously. Unlike the mother of his child, he had left behind a large family: a wife, sister, parents, four children and several grandchildren. As a result, there were lots of obituaries from which it was possible to learn that he had been born, raised and lived out his life in the village of Akranes, on the other side of Faxaflói Bay from Reykjavík. Although the cause of death was not stated, the authors of the obituaries made frequent references to a diffi-cult illness and gruelling battle. There wasn't a single word about Jóhanna or Arnar.

Karl shut down the computer. He wouldn't find the answers online. The most likely source of further hints would be the numbers station. It was ten to five. He stood up and hurried downstairs. When the broadcast commenced on the hour he intended to be ready and waiting, armed with pen and paper. His own past would have to wait.

In the basement, the faint knocking began again.

Chapter 23

There was an unusual hum of activity at the station. The focus of the inquiry had shifted from the murder scene to the incident room, as the majority of the data collected in the course of the investigation was now in-house. As a result, most of the team were present, almost every desk was occupied and people were tapping away at computers on all sides. The rattling of keyboards didn't quite drown out the other sounds but it formed a constant, purposeful backdrop whenever conversation ceased. The atmosphere was more like that of a newsroom than CID; the smell of coffee hanging over it all only enhanced the effect.

The midday sun crawled over the horizon and shone directly through the huge picture windows, making it almost impossible for people to see their computer screens. In consequence, many of the blinds were drawn and the resulting gloom gave the impression that it was much later in the afternoon. For most of them the day's work was half over, whereas for Huldar it was only just beginning. The leader of the investigation had to arrive first and leave last. It was an unwritten rule. If he went home at four it would convey the message that it was all right to slacken off the pressure, and the next day the team would start drifting away by 3 p.m. He had even cancelled a dentist's appointment made six months ago for fear that it would detract from his colleagues' dedication. His urgently overdue haircut would also have to wait.

They were in the process of reviewing and analysing the information that had already been collected in connection with the two murders, trying to make sense of the mass of data and searching for the thread that would eventually lead them to the culprit. In a modern society every individual leaves a digital footprint, a trail of electronic transactions and other data generated by everyday activities. Once arranged in order and systematically compared to witness statements, this evidence can reveal the last few days of a person's life in extraordinary detail. Most of the information can be acquired with minimum effort: for example, by examining the use of bank cards, phone calls, e-mails and social media activity. The main problem lies in isolating what matters from the vast tide of information available.

After skimming through the data Almar had found on Elísa's laptop, Huldar had delegated to others the task of sifting through the files on her office computer. There was plenty of other work to do, and besides he was afraid of falling asleep on his keyboard. The group had now finished piecing together the majority of Elísa's movements in the lead-up to her death and were busy trying to build up a clear picture of Ástrós's final hours.

Elísa had woken early and got the children out of bed with her husband's help. She had glanced through the news head-lines on her laptop while the kids were eating breakfast, and e-mailed the school to request that Margrét be kept indoors during break because she thought she might be coming down with a cold. The couple had then split the children between them; Sigvaldi had driven Margrét to school while Elísa took the boys to kindergarten. She had turned up to work at the tax office ten minutes late and rushed straight to an internal meeting on changes to the tax laws. The meeting had lasted for two hours. This was followed by routine tasks until midday; she had composed a paragraph in a report on tax loopholes in the tourist industry and read over a section compiled by a colleague. At lunchtime she had popped out to a restaurant in the town centre with two female colleagues where she had a Caesar salad, washed down by a Pepsi Max. She had posted a picture of the meal on social media. Seeing this dreary fare, Huldar wondered if she would have chosen something more sinful had she known that the calories she ingested would never be converted to fat.

After just under an hour off for lunch, Elísa had returned to work on the report. You couldn't exactly describe her as industrious, however. Her computer revealed that she had spent a disproportionate amount of time online, where her browsing had included looking at shoes on Amazon and offers on a discount site. On the latter, Elísa had booked a family offer at a burger joint that would have been a good bargain, only they were unlikely to take advantage of it now. Almar had gone to the trouble of printing out the confirmation and giving it to Huldar with the request that he should pass it on to the family. It was still lying on his desk, from where it would eventually find its way into the bin.

At two, Elísa had recorded on the office Lync system that she had to pop out but would be back before three. Shortly afterwards she had bought a ticket for the flybus, which tallied with her husband's statement that she had picked him up from home and given him a lift to the central bus station as they had agreed that morning. While she was buying the ticket, he had carried his luggage out to the bus. They had kissed goodbye, then she had hurried back to her computer.

Elísa had left work just before four and collected the children from kindergarten and school. She had stopped by a supermarket on the way home where she had done a big shop, at least by Huldar's standards. Then the gang had hurried home with the shopping, with a brief stop at a petrol station where they had filled the tank and purchased three ice lollies. The cashier said he remembered Elísa because the kids had been impatient and there had appeared to be a lot of squabbling going on in the car. The ice lollies had been an attempt to pacify them. One detail of the cashier's account didn't fit with the known sequence of events. He claimed that Elísa's husband had been with them and that he had filled the tank.

Countless customers passed through the garage every day, so the obvious explanation was that he had mixed up two different sets of people. The petrol had been bought at about the same time as Sigvaldi was boarding his plane. At first Elísa's sons had shrugged when asked if they remembered the trip to the petrol station and whether there had been another person in the car with them, then Bárdur, the elder boy, had vaguely recalled a garage attendant filling the tank. This was considered more plausible than the idea that Elísa's killer had been a passenger in the car and returned home with them from the filling station. Védís, the woman next door, had seen the family arrive home. At that point it had just been the four of them – Elísa and the three kids, no one else. It was possible that Margrét might be able to shed more light on the matter when they spoke to her later.

The next electronic transaction on Elísa's credit card was a payment to a locksmith for opening the front door.

According to him, she had lost the house key, her husband was abroad and the spare key was locked inside. Huldar and other members of the investigation team had put a question mark by this incident, suggesting, as it did, that the murderer could have got hold of the key that day. There was no sign of a break-in, so logically either the man must have used a key or Elísa had forgotten to lock up. Although the front door had been found locked the following morning, that wasn't necessarily significant. For all they knew, the killer could have locked it behind him when he left, even if it had been open when he arrived.

Elísa hadn't wanted the locksmith to change the locks, assuring him that this had happened before and there was no cause to worry. She had a spare key inside; her key ring was old and the key must have fallen off somewhere: at work, at the school or kindergarten, in the shop or the petrol station. The police had conducted searches at all these places without success.

Once they were inside, Elísa had logged on to Facebook and 'liked' several of her friends' status updates. She posted that Sigvaldi was in the States, so that her circle of friends would know that she was alone at home with the kids. She also informed the world that she was going to cook spaghetti and received countless 'likes' for that. Huldar couldn't tell if it was the spaghetti people liked or the fact she was alone. The police had taken the precaution of checking that no weirdos had infiltrated those who liked the update, but the comments all came from friends Elísa had been in contact with for a long time. That aside, the evening had not been recorded as minutely as the rest of her day. Nevertheless, between 7 and 11 p.m. Elísa had accessed Facebook and

Twitter several times. Her final update in this life could be read on Facebook: *Good night – new day tomorrow, going to do everything right for a change!* But of course this had never been put to the test.

Given the countless updates Elísa had made to these sites during her lifetime, Huldar couldn't help wondering what she'd have posted if the murderer had handed her a computer during her death throes. *You're never going to believe this but a man is trying to hoover the spaghetti – which was delicious, by the way – out of my stomach.* Or simply: *Help! Somebody. Help me!*

Far less was known about Ástrós's last movements. She hadn't been nearly as active as Elísa on social media and seemed to have been less outgoing generally. She had also retired two years previously, so her work colleagues were no longer in the picture. As far as they could tell, she had stayed at home all day, unless she had gone for a walk at some point. Her car, a small Toyota, was parked in the garage and she had noted down the mileage when filling it with petrol the day before. Taking account of the distance between the petrol station and her flat, they concluded that she had driven straight home and not touched the car again after that. Her credit card showed only one transaction on the day she died and that was a direct debit to a charity. She had made three phone calls from home during the evening, one to the phone company, another to her sister and the third to a friend. The call to the phone company hadn't been about anything important, according to the customer service representative who spoke to her. He couldn't remember any details, only that it had involved a fault or virus on her mobile phone. There was nothing to suggest that this conversation had any connection to the murder. Ástrós's friend said they had discussed a book Ástrós had lent her and the friend's planned Mediterranean cruise. Her conversation with Ástrós had lasted seventeen minutes and it took the police officer at least seven minutes to get her off the phone. By then he felt he had heard all he wanted to and more about the imminent cruise.

The phone call to her sister had been of a similar duration, at around nineteen minutes. The sister said they had discussed some confirmations of relatives' children that were due to take place in the spring, a new shop in the Smáralind shopping centre that they were keen to try out, and also a visit Ástrós had been expecting that had come to nothing. She had been unable to give her visitor's name and her explanation had been rather muddled. From what the sister could remember, Ástrós had received a text message announcing that someone was coming round, but she seemed to be mixing it up with some other messages she had been sent that she thought either hadn't been intended for her or were somehow dubious. She hadn't explained what these texts contained and her sister hadn't taken much interest as she'd been late for the theatre. Weeping, she informed Huldar that the play had been a disappointment and she should have talked longer to her sister instead.

Ástrós's mobile had been found at the scene. This time the police had been careful to verify that it was the one she used, to avoid repeating the blunder over Elísa's phone, which had still not turned up. Whoever had it hadn't switched it on yet and seemed unlikely to do so now. The phone company had handed over a list of the calls and texts Elísa had received in the days leading up to her death but none of the messages resembled those they had found on Ástrós's phone.

The texts sent to Ástrós were being analysed. There were four from an unknown sender, three of which were incomprehensible:

39, 8, 92 · 5, 3–53, 8, 8, 66 · 83, 43, 1
39, 8, 92 · 75 · 10, X, 65–5
66–39, 8 · 90, 63–92 · 42–8, 85, 108

The person working on the coded message left at Elísa's house was now wrestling with these as well, but Huldar wasn't holding out any hope for a solution. The man was also trying to crack the message that had been found in the envelope on Ástrós's neighbour's car: 22, 90–1 · 9, 8, 86–7 · 73, 90–1. Huldar had thought the regular sequence that appeared in two of the texts might facilitate their decoding, but it didn't seem to have helped at all.

They had seized on the 'X' as the only letter among the numbers, but this hadn't led to any breakthrough either. Huldar's main hope was that Interpol would be able to crack the code, but so far all their request had resulted in was some paperwork for him to fill out. It had better not turn out to be a waste of time.

The fourth text on Ástrós's phone consisted of an announcement by an unknown individual of his or her imminent arrival. The police had no idea of the person's identity and neither had Ástrós, to judge from her conversation with her sister.

Not long till my visit – excited?

Huldar wasn't the only one who believed that the texts had been sent by her killer. Absolute priority had been given to tracing the number they were sent from; with any luck he would have it by the end of the day. At last the murderer seemed to have slipped up. A disposable SIM card had been used, of the type bought mainly by foreign tourists or the odd local who used them for dodgy purposes. Retailers were supposed to record the names of the purchasers but the records for those sold at hotels proved to be patchy at best. It should nevertheless be possible to trace the card to a specific sales outlet and check their records. While it was too much to hope that the man would have given his real name, the card might have been bought recently, in which case there was a chance the sales assistant might remember the buyer or that he had been caught on CCTV. The SIM card did at least offer a faint chance that the solution to the case might be imminent.

What with the lack of potential suspects, especially any with links to both women, they could use some encouragement. Most officers – including Huldar – inclined to the view that the victims had been selected at random, but they avoided discussing the fact as it would be the worst scenario. How were they to find the murderer if there was no logic to his killings? Especially when he operated with such methodical care. To make matters worse, neither Elísa nor Ástrós seemed to have stood out from the crowd in any way, which made them unlikely targets for an individual so filled with hatred that he resorted to butchering complete strangers.

Nothing in Elísa's or Ástrós's lives or deaths appeared to hold the key to the mystery.

Nor had the evidence gathered at the scene yielded anything useful. So far they had found no fingerprints or trace evidence at Elísa's house or Ástrós's flat to provide a lead. This wasn't necessarily significant, however, as both places were teeming with biological specimens, only a small percentage of which had been analysed so far. Perhaps the right fingerprint or human hair would be discovered at any moment. But every sample that turned out to have an innocent explanation reduced the likelihood that clues from the crime scene would help solve the case. It wasn't that surprising since anyone who watched TV nowadays would know the pitfalls to avoid. A sufficiently clued-up teenager should be able to commit a crime without leaving a trace.

Huldar sighed. He knew the lack of progress would have a depressing effect on the team sooner or later, with the exception of one or two individuals whose response to every disappointment was to redouble their efforts. Ríkhardur belonged to this select group, if the undimmed energy in his voice was anything to go by. And judging by his productivity over the last couple of days he must be one of the most effective. But the strain was evident in further flaws in his otherwise neat appearance, like the button left undone on his shirt or the tiny but unmistakable coffee stain on his sleeve.

Even his dark hair looked a little dishevelled, though it was tidy by Huldar's standards. As if he could read Huldar's mind, Ríkhardur ran a hand over his head and every lock fell neatly back into place. 'They have nothing in common,' he stated flatly. 'No friends, no relatives, not even a connection through work. In fact you'd be hard pressed to find two other people in Iceland with less to link them. They're different ages, unrelated, never attended the same school, were never neighbours, never even shopped at the same supermarket. Extraordinary, really.' He sounded confident of his facts as he handed Huldar the report. Erla, who had worked on it with him, was leaning against the doorpost.

She had forgiven Huldar after he called and invited her to accompany him to Freyja's place the previous evening. Although this meant having to drive halfway across town, Erla had done so gladly, apparently regarding it as levelling the score in her absurd rivalry with Ríkhardur. She had treated Freyja with appalling rudeness, but then what had he expected? That they would fall into each other's arms and swear eternal friendship? He was only grateful that Erla didn't suspect the truth; that this was the second time he had used her as a buffer in his dealings with Freyja. Though buffer wasn't really the word, since she wasn't there to shield him from mocking comments so much as to prevent their being uttered in the first place.

Huldar glanced over the report enumerating potential links between the two women, which had all turned out to be dead ends. 'So, no connections whatsoever? Not even indirectly?' Despite his disappointment at the outcome, he was pleased to see how thorough Ríkhardur and Erla had been. They had spoken to dozens of people, mostly over the phone, and some of these conversations must have been difficult so soon after the women's deaths. He was willing to bet that Ríkhardur had made the majority of the calls. The man had a gift for tackling emotionally sensitive issues without diverging from his naturally wooden manner, though admittedly his approach could come across as a little heartless. 'Well done anyway.'

'Thanks.' A rare smile crossed Ríkhardur's face. It was the first genuine smile Huldar could remember seeing him give since his divorce. He made a mental note to praise Ríkhardur more often – when he deserved it. But the smile disappeared so quickly that Huldar wondered if he had imagined it.

'Pity it didn't get us anywhere.' Ríkhardur sounded dispirited.

'Well, at least now we know they weren't connected.' Erla shifted a little to favour her left shoulder. She had been injured during a call-out six months ago and forced to take two weeks' sick leave. Seldom if ever had an officer been so pissed off about being sent on leave. She seemed ashamed of her body's fallibility. On her return to work no one had dared ask how she was feeling. Huldar had been no exception. As a matter of fact, he had forgotten the incident. So, staying true to form, he pretended not to notice the grimace of pain she was trying to control.

'What do you want us to do?' she asked. 'Move on to some other shit or carry on searching? There may be a link somewhere that we've overlooked.'

Huldar pondered. Further research was unlikely to produce any results and their time would be better spent elsewhere. 'No, you can stop looking for the moment. Perhaps we should wait until we can compare their debit card transactions and so on. We haven't received all Ástrós's bank records yet, so let's hold fire for now.'

'What should we do then?' Ríkhardur straightened his back. His military bearing had always irritated Huldar, and never more so than now that he was his boss.

'I'm updating the list of people we still need to interview. When I've finished, there'll be plenty to occupy you. As your analysis shows, the women have no contacts in common. Since the murderer appears to be their only connection, it's clear there's going to be quite a bit of overtime for the foreseeable future.'

Erla grinned and Ríkhardur seemed cautiously pleased as well. Whatever their faults, you had to give them their due: they weren't afraid of hard work, and the thickness of their wage packets had nothing to do with it.

'Though I've still got to get Egill's consent for the overtime.' Huldar didn't exactly relish the prospect of discussing the matter with his boss. Egill was the only person unaffected by the frantic activity around him. Instead of doing his bit to help, he was immersed in a stock-take of the office equipment and checking that maintenance had been carried out in accordance with policy. Egill had never worried about such things before, simply bought new gadgets to replace the old ones. Presumably the National Audit Office had started asking awkward questions and he was stressed about having poured money into equipment for an already well-equipped organisation. Huldar was dreading a barrage of questions about the registration and loan of gear. On the plus side, as long as his boss was occupied with searching for mislaid and obsolete bugging devices, thirteen pairs of protective footwear and two riot shields, and puzzling over the calibration of distance-measuring devices, he wouldn't have time to interfere with the investigation. If he managed to finish his stock count, Egill could always busy himself with collecting up the new iPads and hiding them from the auditors.

'Are either of you interested in coming to the Children's House with me? They're making another attempt to interview Margrét.' Glancing at the clock, Huldar saw that it was nearly time to leave. He had no intention of being late, especially since he had used the interview as an excuse not to attend the post-mortem on Ástrós. The pathologist had been very nice about it and refrained from comment, although he knew full well that Huldar was chickening out. Instead, he had promised Huldar an especially thorough report. Even the thought of that was enough to make Huldar's skin crawl. When the duct tape had been removed and the appliance extracted from the woman's throat, it had indeed turned out to be a pair of curling tongs. He could just imagine the sort of damage they had done. 'I want to get there on time so we can brief the interviewer properly.' This might also give him a chance to have a coffee with Freyja and attempt to make his peace with her. In retrospect, he wished he could retract his invitation to the others, recalling too late how badly she and Erla had got on. It wouldn't help his case to have Erla there, directing snide remarks at Freyja. That is, unless it made him look good in comparison. He hoped Ríkhardur would pre-empt her.

'I'm up for it.' Predictably, Erla was quicker off the mark. 'Fuck, I need a break from my desk.'

Ríkhardur closed his half-open mouth, swallowing what he had been about to say. He was too uptight to admit that he would have liked to go, but his look of consternation gave him away. 'I can stay behind. Apparently we've received a ton of tip-offs. I can go through them while there's nothing more urgent to do.'

Huldar had been intending to ask Ríkhardur to have a go at deciphering the cryptic messages, but tip-offs from the public were one of the most tedious aspects of any inquiry and it was rare for people to volunteer to take them on. He couldn't afford to decline the offer. 'OK. Good.'

The bulk of the tip-offs were invariably a waste of time. In their desire to help, the public failed to grasp that the police had nothing to gain from following up their intuitions and fantasies. Yet because this kind of information occasionally led to an arrest, the police couldn't afford to discount it. They were just lucky it wasn't a missing-persons case or one that involved asking the public to identify an individual from CCTV footage: an unknown man in a hoodie could result in a deluge of phone calls that proved almost impossible to halt even after the case had been solved. He imagined that fewer people would ring in if they put out an urgent appeal for news of a black man with an unusually large head. Then again . . .

'Try to filter out the time-wasters.' Huldar saved his work and closed his open files. 'I'll find someone to relieve you when we get back.'

'No need. Once I've started, I might as well finish.' Ríkhardur looked as sour as if he had bitten into a lemon.

'Well, we'll see. Apparently they're unusually colourful this time. I gather the paranormal gang have started calling in.' When Huldar said this, the sour expression intensified. Poor guy. Maybe that would encourage him to assert his real wishes for a change.

'The paranormal gang, what the fuck?' Erla frowned. Instead of leaning against the doorpost she was now digging her hands so deep into her pockets that it was lucky she had a good hefty belt on. Perhaps she was doing it to relieve her shoulder.

Huldar fumbled for the car keys. 'You know the kind of thing – psychics, crackpots claiming they can help us by contacting the dead or through dreams and so on. They always crawl out of the woodwork when there's news of a murder. Though strangely enough they never seem to beat the media to it.' He located his keys and stood up. 'That kind of bullshit can go straight to the bottom of the pile as far as I'm concerned. Concentrate on the tips that might contain a grain of sense.' He smiled at Ríkhardur in an attempt to jolly him along. After all, he owed him. 'Good luck. I'll look in when I get back. I'd like you to join me when I haul in Freyja's ex-boyfriend to question him about the attacks on those dogs. We need to shake him up a bit; make sure he leaves her alone.'

Erla scowled; she didn't even bother to hide her jealousy. Honestly, she and Ríkhardur were like a pair of children. Huldar regretted having broken all his pencils; he could happily have snapped a few more right now.

Why couldn't they be like they used to be? Before he was promoted; before he stupidly cuckolded Ríkhardur. If only he could turn back the clock to the days when they were all on the same level; when he didn't have to turn away, shame-faced, on the rare occasions when Ríkhardur confided in him about his grief over Karlotta and his lost dream of starting a little family. Even if it were only for the duration of the inquiry. Once it was over, he could deal with this, try to improve their relations. He simply didn't have the time now.

He felt like a man playing hopscotch in a minefield. Things couldn't go on like this.

But any good intentions Huldar had about coming clean led to an impasse. Why should he salve his conscience at Ríkhardur's expense? Hadn't the guy suffered enough? If Huldar confessed to him about his and Karlotta's terrible mistake, it would be like spitting on Ríkhardur's memory of a perfect marriage, which was, at the end of the day, no better than many others. And that was quite apart from the reper-cussions it would have for their relationship at work.

Erla interrupted these thoughts with an aggrieved complaint. 'Why the hell are we wasting time on Freyja and her ex? We're rushed off our feet as it is – surely she's capable of sorting out her own problems? For fuck's sake, she's a psychologist, isn't she?'

Huldar slammed down the car keys, took out his nicotine

gum and popped two pieces in his mouth, chomping until he felt the drug dissolving and flowing into his capillaries. Only then could he trust himself to speak. The gum didn't entirely conceal his rage but at least his colleagues didn't recoil from him in fright. 'As long as the girl is staying with Freyja we have a duty to prioritise any possible threats to her safety. Someone needs to give Freyja's ex a talking-to, and I don't want to hear another word on the subject.' So much for his dream of restoring them all to an equal footing again.

He stomped off towards the lift, Erla following silently in his wake. On the way they passed the offices of the two men who would have been the most likely candidates to head up this inquiry if they hadn't been grounded in their offices until the public had forgotten the scandal over their misconduct. Both glanced up as he walked past, and tried to look busy though they weren't fooling anyone. Neither acknowledged him.

Chapter 24

Molly couldn't get used to the plastic collar. Before the interview began she roamed restlessly around the meeting room, colliding with people and furniture. Huldar's calves, which seemed to hold a particular attraction for her, were feeling distinctly bruised. He faked indifference, while nursing a private desire to drag the dog outside by her collar and despatch her to the police car. But Margrét had become so attached to Molly that they hoped the animal's presence would have a calming effect on her. If the dog helped the little girl to open up, she was welcome to bash into his shins as often as she liked.

Nothing had come of the coffee with Freyja. From the moment Huldar and Erla arrived, the task ahead had claimed all their attention. There had been some debate about whether Silja should continue the questioning or hand over to Freyja. While Silja had not had much success in persuading Margrét to talk, the girl was at least used to her presence on the sofa beside her. On the other hand, Freyja had reached a good, if fragile, understanding with Margrét, but there was a risk the girl might retreat into her shell if Freyja suddenly switched roles. Huldar and Erla stayed out of the discussion.

Eventually, it fell to Freyja to stick the tiny speaker in her ear and thread the wire down her back to the battery that hung from her waistband. Meanwhile, Silja sat on the other side of the glass, distracting Margrét with small talk. Today the girl was wearing a top with a picture of a panda on it and jeans decorated with sequins in flower patterns, which made her look even younger than her seven years.

Huldar watched Freyja, struck by the contrast between her delicate handling of the equipment and the way police officers behaved when donning a wire. Unlike them, she made no show of puffed-up heroism, nor was she likely to indulge in any chest-beating once everything was in place. Of course, she wasn't facing the same kind of situation as a police officer in full riot gear but he didn't think that was the reason. Erla would have shoved the piece in her ear with enough force to pierce her eardrum, then roughly yanked the wire through her shirt and no doubt stamped her foot to help it on its way.

'OK. I'm ready.' Freyja refastened her belt and loosened her ponytail so her hair fell over her ears. 'Anything specific you want me to focus on? Any particular order of priorities?' She directed her question at Huldar as he prepared to take the same seat as last time. The group in the meeting room followed suit. Erla sat down beside him, arms folded across her chest like a sulky child. They had driven to the centre in silence and no doubt the drive back would be the same. She had a short fuse but wasn't the type who was equally quick to shrug off her anger.

Huldar dismissed Erla from his mind. 'Naturally we're particularly keen to learn about anything she may have seen or heard. Anything that could help us identify the killer. It would also be interesting to find out why she blames her dad, as that might be significant. And we need to know if she remembers the trip to the petrol station the day before the murder and can tell us if there was a man in the car with them. Plus, if we have time, I'd like to ask her about the message that was left at her house. But that's less urgent.'

Freyja nodded and left the room. They watched her swap places with Silja. Molly, who had followed her, began frantically wagging her tail the moment she spotted Margrét, her plastic collar flapping about wildly. They had only been parted for quarter of an hour: Huldar couldn't imagine how the dog would greet her after a longer absence. 'Right. Here we are again.' Freyja settled on the sofa beside Margrét. 'We weren't that long, were we?'

The girl shrugged. 'No.' Putting her hand inside the plastic cone, she stroked Molly's head. The dog reacted with pleasure.

Freyja indulged in some brief small talk, mainly about the dog, discussing whether they should take her for a walk around the block afterwards or go out to Geirsnef. Freyja's comment that Molly might be embarrassed to be seen in the collar by other dogs brought a smile to the girl's lips and her back relaxed slightly, but she stiffened up again the moment Freyja got down to business.

'Now, Margrét, you know the police are looking for the man who hurt your mummy. They really want to put him in prison so we can make sure he won't hurt anyone else.' The decision had been taken to shield the girl from the news of Ástrós's death. It might upset her and derail the interview. Margrét nodded gravely. She seemed to accept the seriousness of the matter. It was a good sign. Freyja continued: 'But to be sure of catching him quickly, the police need to know who he is. Otherwise they won't have a clue who they're looking for.'

'Murderers aren't like us.' This emerged almost in a whisper.

'No, they're not. Not on the inside. But they can look just like the rest of us on the outside.'

'Not this murderer.'

'No. The way you described him, he sounds very unusual-looking.'

'Not really.'

'Oh? I don't know anyone with a very big head. White or black.' Freyja raised her hands to sketch an oval in the air the size of a basketball. 'Was it this big?'

'Yes.' Margrét's voice was barely audible and the audience round the table had to crane towards the speaker. She seemed to have realised how unrealistic her description had been. 'It was like that.'

Freyja seemed momentarily at a loss for a suitable follow-up question so Huldar bent to the mike. 'Ask what his hair was like. Perhaps his head looked unusually big because he was wearing a wig or had a strange hairstyle that confused her in the dark.'

Freyja began speaking the moment he finished. 'Do you happen to remember what kind of hair the man had, Margrét?' She didn't explain why she was asking this or give any examples of possible hair colours or styles. Huldar had learnt enough about their techniques at the Children's House to realise that this was deliberate. She didn't want to risk influencing the girl's memories.

'He didn't have any hair.'

The answer caused a stir; everyone exchanged glances. All except Huldar, who knew that no hairs belonging to the perpetrator or artificial fibres from a wig had been found at the scene. The consensus was that the murderer must have hoovered the bed with a small handheld vacuum that he had brought along specially to remove any biological traces. For obvious reasons, the family vacuum cleaner wouldn't have been available for the task. It had been the same story at Ástrós's flat; no alien hairs had been found. When they opened up her vacuum-cleaner bag, it had contained only her own hair. This had increased the likelihood that the man had come equipped with a handheld vacuum. But if he had no hair, that would also explain it.

'Was he bald?' Freyja managed to ask the question in a perfectly neutral voice. Margrét mustn't be able to detect the slightest hint of a desire for a yes or no.

'I don't know.' The girl sounded agitated or confused. She fidgeted on the small sofa, avoiding Freyja's eye. 'He had a shiny head, I remember that.' Margrét frowned. Then looking at Freyja she added in a tone almost of enquiry. 'He didn't have any ears.'

Erla swore. Huldar felt a stab of anger and hoped the sound hadn't carried to Freyja. But he checked an urge to look daggers at Erla; it wouldn't do any good and would only delay the interview. Instead he bent to the mike again. 'Ask her if the man she saw in the garden looked the same. With no ears and so on.'

On the other side of the glass Freyja crossed her legs and nodded so faintly that Huldar barely caught it. 'Margrét. You remember the pictures we showed you last time? Did the man in your drawing look like the man you saw in your house that night? With a big black head and no ears?'

Margrét twisted a strand of red hair round her fingers, looking thoughtful. 'Yes. I think so. But I don't know. He had a hood.'

'What kind of hood? An anorak hood or a balaclava?'

Margrét furrowed her brow. 'A balaclava? What's that?'

Freyja smiled. 'It's a hat that comes all the way down to

your neck, with a hole for your face or small holes for the eyes and mouth. Sometimes there's no hole for the nose. If you saw a man wearing a hood like that in the dark you might think he had a black head and no ears.'

'Don't they have holes for ears?'

'No. I don't think so.'

'Well, he wasn't wearing one of those. It was a hood. An anorak hood.'

'Was the man you saw in your house that night wearing an anorak hood?'

'No.' The answer came straight back.

'A balaclava then?'

'No.' Again the girl answered without hesitation.

'All right.' Freyja gave a sideways glance at the two-way mirror and Huldar took this to mean that she needed a prompt.

'Ask her about the trip to the petrol station.'

'Margrét, do you remember when you all went to fill up with petrol last Thursday?'

Margrét shook her head.

'Tell her that her mother bought them ice lollies. That might help her put it in context.'

'Your mummy bought ice lollies for you and your brothers.'

Margrét nodded. 'Oh, yes, I remember that. Stebbi and Bárdur were being naughty. They were fighting over the Spider-Man.'

'I see.'

Freyja's smile transported Huldar back to their night together. He coughed behind his hand in an attempt to block out this inappropriate flashback. God, he was an idiot to have walked out on her. Freyja stopped smiling and resumed her questioning, which recalled his attention to the task in hand.

'Who was in the car when you went to the petrol station?'

Margrét looked irritated. 'I just told you. Me, Stebbi and Bárdur. And Mummy, of course.'

'No one else.'

'No, I'd have said so.'

'Of course you would.'

Huldar interrupted. 'Ask her who filled the car with petrol.'

'Who put the petrol in the car? Can you remember?'

'It wasn't me.'

'No. I didn't think it was, and I don't suppose it was Stefán or Bárdur either.'

Margrét snorted like an old lady. 'They couldn't do it. They're too little and clumsy.'

'So who did?'

'The man. The man from the petrol station.'

'The pump attendant? Was he wearing the petrol-station uniform?'

'No, he was just wearing clothes. Not a uniform. Anyway, I don't know what a petrol-station uniform looks like.'

'An overall the same colour as the petrol-station sign. With the logo on the front.' Freyja patted her left breast and again Huldar had to discipline his thoughts to prevent them from straying. 'Was he wearing something like that?'

'No. Just ordinary clothes. A jacket and trousers. And gloves.' She stole a quick glance at Freyja, her face grave. 'Not a balaclava. Just a hood. Like the man in the garden.'

'Ask if she thinks it was the same man.'

Freyja shook her head unobtrusively, by turning it slowly once to either side. Silja explained to Huldar: 'Not a good idea. If she asks that, Margrét might start to believe it. And if that happens, you'll never get her to change her mind even if it turns out to be wrong.'

Huldar leant forward to the microphone again. 'Forget that. Just ask if she saw his face or heard him speak. And if he went inside the petrol station after he'd filled the car.' Huldar turned to Silja. 'If so, he might have been caught on the security camera in the shop.'

'Did you see the pump attendant's face, Margrét?'

'No. He had his hood up, like I told you.'

'What exactly did he do? Can you remember?'

Margrét wrinkled her nose. 'He came over when Mummy got out of the car and took the keys from her. Then he went and opened the little door of the petrol tank and put in the nozzle. I didn't see him do it, I only heard it. But I wasn't really taking any notice because I had to tell off Stefán and Bárdur. I took the Spider-Man off them.'

'You remember it very well. What then?'

'When he'd finished he came and opened the door and put the keys on Mummy's seat. Then he went away.'

'Did you see his face when he opened the door and reached inside?'

'No. He had his hood up like I told you. I keep telling you that. And I was sitting in the back with Stebbi and Bárdur. I'm not allowed to sit in the front until I'm ten. Or twelve, I can't remember.'

'We can check that later if you like.' Freyja adjusted her hair over her ears. 'Where did he go then? After he'd shut the car door.'

'He went away.'

'Into the petrol station?'

'No. Just away.'

'Did you see where?'

'No. Stefán snatched the Spider-Man from me. I had to fight him to get it back.'

'All right. You can't see everything.' Freyja reached for the jug of water on the small table and poured herself a glass. 'Would you like some water?' Margrét shook her head and Freyja took a sip. 'There are just two more things we need to talk about, Margrét, to finish off, but it won't be easy. Shall we get them over with? Then we can take Molly out and maybe buy some ice-cream. Or hot chocolate. Maybe it's too cold for ice-cream.'

'It's never too cold for ice-cream.'

'No. You're right.' Putting down the glass, Freyja leant back again. 'Shall we get this over with?'

'Can I choose what comes first?'

'Sure you can.' Freyja hesitated, picking her words carefully. 'Which would you rather talk about first: the night the man hurt your mummy, or about your daddy?'

Margrét started fidgeting again, unsurprisingly: the choice wasn't an easy one. 'I want to talk about that night first.' Suddenly she raised her eyes to Freyja. 'But you're only allowed to ask one thing. You're not allowed to ask two questions. Just one about that night and one about Daddy. Then I want to go.'

'All right. It's a deal: one question about that night and one about your daddy.' Freyja took another sip of water. 'Then I'll begin. How did you know the man was going to hurt another woman – did he say so?'

'Yes.' Margrét closed her mouth and met Freyja's eye with a mulish look.

'That's not a fair answer, Margrét.'

'Yes, it is. I answered.'

'That's like me taking you to the ice-cream parlour and only letting you have an empty cone. You have to tell me what he said.'

'Then do you promise not to ask me any more about it?' Freyja agreed and the girl took a deep breath. 'He said there was a woman he was going to get even with. He said she did her maths wrong.' Margrét stopped speaking and stuck her hands under her thighs. The jolly panda on her T-shirt looked absurdly out of place.

Huldar bent quickly to the microphone. 'You have to ask her more about it. We found paper covered with calculations at the other victim's house, so this is vital.'

Freyja grimaced at the glass. 'She can't,' interjected Silja. 'She promised not to ask any more. You'll have to accept that. Unless you want to drop the question about her father.' Freyja gave a tiny nod to show she agreed with Silja.

'No. Ask about her father.' Huldar couldn't hide his frustration but no one seemed to mind.

To be fair to Freyja, she was trying to give Huldar what he wanted. Though sadly she was doing it for the investigation, not for him. Whereas there were plenty of things he wouldn't mind doing for her . . .

'Can I ask you another question about this woman and the maths, Margrét?'

The little girl shook her head.

'Then I'll move on to the other thing. It's actually harder because it's about your daddy. But you're such a good girl that you'll be brave and answer, then you can start thinking about whether you'd prefer vanilla or strawberry ice-cream.'

'Chocolate. I want chocolate flavour.'

'Then it's yours. Let's finish this, then it's time for ice-cream and a walk with Molly.' The dog, which had been lying quietly at Margrét's feet, now peered up through the cumbersome collar and searched both their faces hopefully before lowering her head again. 'Why do you think your daddy's to blame? Did the man say something that made you think that? And you're not allowed to answer just yes or no.'

Again Margrét drew a deep breath. She dropped her gaze and looked as if she'd like to shrink inside herself or be swallowed up by the sofa. When she spoke again her voice was low and filled with grief and despair. The audience all bent as one towards the speaker in the middle of the table. 'I didn't want to hear his story.' Margrét paused. Breathing heavily, she went on. 'But I heard it anyway. I heard him talk about Daddy. He told Mummy it was his fault. She had to die to punish him. The man said Daddy was the murderer, not him. But he killed Mummy anyway.' Margrét looked up, her cheeks wet. Her small body was trembling as she wiped the tears away. 'It's all Daddy's fault.'

The interview was adjourned without any attempt to show Margrét the message containing the series of numbers. Freyja reached into her pocket for the tiny transmitter and switched it off. For a while there was silence in the meeting room while they pondered the implications of all they had heard. It seemed they would have to suspend the investigation into Elísa's life and concentrate on Sigvaldi instead. Huldar didn't for a moment believe that the man had actually committed murder, though of course he couldn't rule it out. By far the more plausible explanation was that he had lied to them about his job. He must have been responsible for the death of a child or a mother or another patient at some point during his career. At least, that's what Elísa's murderer seemed to believe.

Huldar rose to his feet. 'I'd like to take the recording with me, if I may.' He wanted to listen to the whole thing again at his leisure. He needed time to digest everything that had been said. Then all of a sudden it dawned on him. A big, shiny, black head. No ears.

The man had been wearing a helmet. A motorcycle helmet.

Chapter 25

Wednesday

The odour of wet coats filled the lecture hall. They hung from the backs of seats, the melting snow forming shining puddles on the floor below. Every time the lecturer paused to draw breath you could hear the sound of dripping.

Karl was finding it impossible to concentrate. However hard he stared at the PowerPoint slides, he found himself distracted by straining to hear the next faint plink. The drips proved infinitely more fascinating than the lecture. The harder he tried to understand, the more confused he became. It had been the same with all his studies for as long as he could remember; like being caught up in a race he couldn't win. Just as he was finally grasping a point, the next would arrive. He could never catch up. So what chance did he have now when he couldn't even concentrate? Worse still, this was a key lecture; the teacher had announced at the beginning that the next part of the course would be based on today's material. Which made it all the more bloody frustrating that he couldn't follow it.

The screen of his laptop was as blank as his mind; he hadn't managed to take any notes. It was little comfort that the same was true of the students sitting in front of him. In fact, that only made matters worse because it meant he wouldn't be able to scrounge their notes afterwards. He would have to make do with the lecturer's slides, which would prove no more illuminating when puzzled over at home.

'This element, named after the Swedish town of Ytterby, was discovered in 1843 when the Swedish chemist Carl Gustaf Mosander managed to separate gadolinite into three materials that he named yttria, erbia and terbia. At the time the similarities between erbia and terbia led to their being confused by scientists and . . .'

Karl had lost the thread. Far from taking in the significance of the discovery, which had clearly been of such magnitude that the lecturer's voice was trembling with excitement, his mind was preoccupied with the shortwave station. Rather than ID or old-style social security numbers, yesterday's broadcast had consisted of an incomprehensible sequence that meant absolutely nothing to him. The numbers flew around in his head as if they had sprouted wings and turned into buzzing flies. His attempts to marshal them into some kind of order were in vain, and yet there was something indefinably familiar about them. Try as he might, though, he couldn't put his finger on what.

9, 92, 6, 19, 39, 8, 92. There was no logic to these seven numbers – and since no alphabet contained over ninety letters, the digits couldn't represent individual letters. Three times he had experimented with writing down the standard Roman alphabet, arranging it so that each letter represented three different numbers, but no sense emerged from it, not even when he factored in the extra Icelandic characters and re-numbered the whole thing.

It was complete gibberish.

He shouldn't have been surprised. He had been listening to foreign numbers stations for years without ever being able to make sense of a single sequence. Without the key, it was impossible to decode them. So what on earth had made him think the Icelandic station would be different? Yet he couldn't rid himself of the suspicion that it *was* different, that he ought to recognise these numbers and what they signified. After all, he had picked out the ID numbers and social security number, so it followed that he ought to be able to understand other parts of the broadcast. Deep down he knew it was meant for him. So he must be able to interpret it. Why else would anyone have gone to all this trouble?

If the numbers had been completely alien, he would have found it easier to dismiss them from his mind. It was this tantalising feeling that he was on the verge of comprehension that was driving him mad. Not helped by his growing conviction that the messages held some deadly serious significance.

Either for him or for Arnar.

Karl stared blankly at the lecture slides, which might as well have been written in Mayan hieroglyphics for all the sense he could make of them. Until he got to the bottom of the mystery, he wouldn't be able to think about anything else, least of all chemistry. Again, Karl had the sense that the solution was on the point of breaking through into his consciousness but it seemed to have become entangled in his cerebral cortex and refused to penetrate any further.

The lecturer had speeded up; his slides were flashing by as if he were paid for the number he got through. It was a sign that the hour was almost up; yet again he had tried to cover too much material. For once, however, Karl wasn't relieved at the prospect of escaping the lecture theatre. His problems would follow him wherever he went. Even the girl he fancied couldn't engage his interest, though she was sitting right in front of him, no doubt taking it for granted that he was gazing adoringly at the back of her head. With a sudden movement she tossed aside her hair as if to remind him of her presence. Usually he would have been thrown into confusion by the flying locks and faint fragrance of shampoo but this time he was oblivious.

The final slide appeared on screen and the lecturer started intoning about homework and preparation for the next class. Karl caught none of it. Emulating those around him, he rose to his feet as soon as the time was up, while the lecturer carried on talking to deaf ears. The girl glanced round as she was stuffing her textbook into her bag and seemed miffed when he paid her no attention. Even this small victory in the uneventful tale of their relations failed to raise Karl's spirits.

The girl slung her bag over her shoulder and left the hall, swaying her hips provocatively. Out of the corner of his eye he noticed her look round to see if he was watching. When she realised that for once he wasn't, she reverted to her normal gait.

The next lecture was due to start in fifteen minutes. Karl dithered. Should he go along or skive off? Skive off or go along? While the alternatives were fighting it out in his mind, his legs continued on their way. Before he knew it he was outside the building; his body had taken the decision for him. The wind was whirling up the loose snow that had fallen that morning. Small, hard flakes stung his eyes and he squinted at the car park, cursing himself for not having dressed more warmly. When his phone rang, he answered without even peering at the screen.

'Have you seen the news?' Börkur sounded out of breath. It was only eleven; he was never usually up this early.

'What news?' Karl tasted snowflakes on his tongue. He had

a good idea what Börkur was referring to but didn't want to say in case he was wrong. Talking to Börkur was unlikely to help him straighten out his chaotic thoughts.

'Her name! The woman's name!' Börkur sounded highly agitated. 'She's dead. And that's not all – they think she was murdered.'

Karl was silent. He had read the name of the dead woman in the newspaper that morning over a bowl of rather dry cereal – there had only been a drop of milk left in the fridge. The cereal had turned to cement in his mouth when he saw that it was Elísa Bjarnadóttir, the woman whose ID number had been broadcast on the shortwave station. Swallowing with difficulty, he had read the rest of the item. It referred to earlier news releases about the woman's death to which he had paid scant attention. The police were refusing to disclose any details or confirm whether an arrest had been made. All the journalist had been able to establish was that an inquiry was under way and that further information would be provided shortly. Newspaper sources were quoted as claiming that the police hadn't yet made any arrests or discovered any leads, which would explain why they were urgently appealing for witnesses who had been in the area of the woman's home last Thursday night. Karl knew the brief report almost by heart. 'I saw.' He didn't mention the still briefer news item that had compounded his dread: another woman had died in suspicious circumstances. The woman's name could not be divulged at present and the police were refusing to comment. There was no point causing Börkur even further alarm, especially since Karl had no idea whether or how the second murder was linked to him. 'I read about it this morning.'

'So? What does it mean?'

This was the question that had been plaguing Karl ever since he had flung his half-finished bowl of cereal on the pile of washing-up in the sink. 'I don't know.' Karl's thoughts flew to the bracelet. He had scrutinised all the photos of Elísa on Facebook in the hope of spotting it on her wrist. Actually, 'hope' wasn't the right word. It had been a load off his mind when none of the pictures showed her wearing any jewellery that resembled it. The bracelet was still lying beside his computer. He hadn't been able to bring himself to touch it again, though he was almost sure it couldn't have belonged to Elísa.

'Are you going to call the cops?'

'Yes. No. Not sure.' Reaching his car, Karl trapped the phone between cheek and shoulder so he could open the door. 'What am I supposed to say? That I heard her ID number on the radio?'

'Yes. Why not? Then they can find out who's been sending the messages.'

'Oh yeah? And just how are they supposed to do that? It's no joke trying to trace that kind of broadcast. And anyway, do you really think they'd launch a search based on some crazy-sounding bullshit that I come out with?' It was even colder inside the car than out. 'I don't have any recordings and Halli was half asleep that time you heard it. We're the only two real witnesses.'

'Two are better than one.' Börkur sounded deflated, as if it had belatedly dawned on him that he didn't count for much in Karl's eyes. 'And it's not like Halli could have been a witness anyway. You know what I mean.'

'Yes, I know.' Was it possible that Halli's arrest would disqualify him? But it wasn't as though he had been arrested for perjury or bearing false witness. Illegally downloading and circulating music and videos surely didn't count as a serious offence, on however large a scale it was done? Personally, Karl thought he would escape with no more than a fine, but Börkur and Halli liked to wind each other up about it, as though Halli faced a long spell in jail. Listening to their overexcited conversations, in which Halli's imagined sentence grew ever longer, was like overhearing an auction. Perhaps Börkur had a point, though; Halli wouldn't be considered a particularly reliable witness with this blot on his record.

'Hey.' Börkur seemed to have recovered his spirits. 'The cops are bound to employ someone who can decode the messages. A codebreaker or cryptologist or whatever they're called.'

Karl's teeth were chattering so badly by now that he could barely answer. 'Huh, I doubt it. Why should the cops employ a codebreaker? It's not like Icelandic criminals go in for secret codes. Isn't that more the kind of thing you get with international espionage? Who do you think would bother to spy on Iceland?' Karl inserted the key in the ignition. The thought of going home made him so apprehensive that he was suddenly grateful for Börkur's phone call. 'Are you busy?' The chances of Börkur being busy were so slim that the question was redundant.

'No. Not really.' Displaying an unusual degree of perspicacity, Börkur added: 'Shall I drop round?'

'I'll be home in ten. See you there.' Karl started the car and although the heater pumped out cold air, he knew it would soon warm up inside. Things could only get better.

After hanging around in the car outside his house for ten minutes, Karl gave up. Börkur could turn up any moment or not until long after midday. It was impossible to predict and

Karl couldn't afford to leave the engine running in order to keep the heater on. He peered yet again at the big sitting-room windows, feeling himself stiffen in anticipation of seeing a movement. But the black glass presented a blank face to the world. Of course there was nobody inside, but Karl couldn't rid himself of the notion that there was; that the person was standing just out of sight. He felt a momentary regret that he had thrown out the curtains.

Squint as he might, he could make out nothing but glass and the faint reflection of the surroundings. It was ridiculous to be afraid of entering his own house. But even worse was the suspicion that the problem wasn't about to go away and that it would be a long time before he could feel comfortable alone at home. This was how his mother had reacted after they had that break-in, just before she fell ill. Next to nothing had been stolen but the fall-out had been similar to what he was suffering now. His mother hadn't felt safe and was constantly on edge in case the burglar returned. According to her, the worst part was when she arrived home and opened the front door. It made no difference that the policeman who came round had told her that burglars very rarely struck twice in the same place. Although Karl hadn't been present at the time, he suspected that the officer had been referring to houses like theirs, which were hardly worth burgling once, let alone twice. He wished he had been more sympathetic to his mother instead of rolling his eyes whenever she brought up the subject of burglar alarms and three-point locks. He would have been grateful for those now.

Pulling himself together, he turned off the engine. He had to stop being such a pussy. Chances were he would be living alone for the foreseeable future, so he had better nip his fear in the bud before it developed into a full-blown phobia. There must be a simple explanation for the knocking sounds and the bracelet materialising on his desk. There were no signs of a break-in and the door had been locked. He was just being pathetic. Steeling himself, he stepped out of the car, but took the precaution of slamming the driver's door loudly to alert any potential burglars to his presence. The last thing Karl wanted was to come face to face with an intruder.

'Hello?' No reply, no sound of retreating footsteps. Karl stuck his head round the door and shouted again: 'Hello?' No answer. Aware that he wasn't going to feel any more reassured than this, he stepped inside.

He was met by the familiar smell. He was too used to it to be able to guess how it struck other people, nor could he work out its components. Yet he sensed that the odour of dusty curtains and dead pot plants, which had become noticeable after his mother died, had begun to recede. No doubt it would soon fade altogether. Karl chucked the keys on the chest of drawers in the hall. They landed with a rattle and clanged against an ugly china vase. The vase had only escaped the general purge because there had been no room for it in the last cardboard box and Karl couldn't be bothered to assemble another one. The vase toppled over, and although he couldn't care less if it broke, his eyes shot instinctively to the source of the noise.

The vase rocked back and forth on its belly, between unopened envelopes and an old, half-empty can of Coke. The can didn't fall over but it wasn't concern about a spillage that drew Karl to it. Sweeping the envelopes aside he picked up the Coke can, the vase and several credit card receipts, a half-empty packet of chewing gum and other rubbish. But he couldn't find what he was looking for – his mother's keys, which he was sure had been lying there ever since she was admitted to hospital. He checked that they hadn't fallen on the floor or slipped into a drawer. A search of the kitchen produced no results either, and he knew for certain, following the clear-out, that they couldn't be in her bedroom.

The keys had disappeared.

Karl's anxiety returned with renewed force. When had he last seen them? The bunch had included a key to the outhouse on the basement level, from which he had fetched the winter tyres just before Christmas. He hadn't needed his mother's keys since then. But they had been lying here. A week ago. Two weeks ago. He could have sworn.

When the doorbell rang his insides seemed to turn to stone. He was so shaken that he didn't care what Börkur thought but asked warily before opening: 'Who is it?'

'Whoa! You expecting the bailiffs?' Börkur was shivering out on the steps. He was hopelessly underdressed for the wintry weather, in a windcheater that would hardly have kept out a summer breeze. 'Aren't you going to let me in?'

'Sorry. I don't know why I asked.' Karl pointed at the chest of drawers. 'Do you happen to remember seeing a bunch of keys on here? Last time you came round or any time recently?'

Börkur gaped at the chest. 'Keys? There's a bunch there now.'

'Yeah, I know, those are mine. I'm looking for the spare keys. They're on a ring with all kinds of fobs. A lion – Leo, you know, like the zodiac sign. And a whistle. The kind you blow.'

Börkur shook his head with an enquiring expression. 'Nope. Haven't seen them. Ever, as far as I can recall.'

There was no need to attach too much importance to this. Börkur wouldn't have noticed the key ring if it had been dangling from the end of Karl's nose.

In no hurry to go down to the basement, Karl dragged Börkur into the kitchen instead. He didn't care what his friend thought of the house now that it had been stripped bare of clutter; in fact, he wondered why he had ever been worried about his opinion in the first place. It wasn't as if Börkur was exactly classy or had a palatial home. He still lived with his parents in a high-rise that could have done with redecorating ten years ago. Karl had rarely been invited in but on the few occasions he had he'd hung around in the dark entrance hall while Börkur was getting ready, surrounded by countless shabby coats and an acrid smell of cigarette smoke that permeated every nook and cranny. Inside he could glimpse a threadbare, swirly-patterned carpet. The hoarse smokers' voices of Börkur's parents as they called after their son matched the seedy surroundings. In comparison, Karl had no reason to be ashamed.

Börkur sat down at the kitchen table while Karl was making coffee. He'd found an ancient, open packet during his tidy-up. It would have to do. The resulting brew turned out to be stale and flavourless, and it didn't help that the milk Börkur asked for had run out. As they sat sipping the bitter sludge, Karl confided in Börkur that someone had entered the house the previous night. It was unclear from his reaction whether Börkur believed him.

Nor could Karl interpret his expression once they were down in the basement. 'This is the bracelet.' Karl indicated the desk where he sat on the rare occasions when he opened his textbooks. He watched Börkur examining the piece of jewellery.

'Whose is it? The burglar's?'

'Unlikely. All I know is that it's not something my mum

would've worn, so it can't have been put here by her or me.'
Karl stared at the bracelet as Börkur deftly toyed with it, the
gaudy beads slipping through his fingers like a rosary.
Suddenly Karl remembered the phone that had turned up in
his car. 'Could you get that phone to work?'

'Oh, shit! I plugged it in to charge, then totally forgot about
it.' Börkur put the bracelet down. The bright colours clashed
with Karl's gloomy mood. 'I'll try and remember to check
later. Though it's bound to be password protected, so don't
get your hopes up. Maybe you should advertise it on Facebook.'

Karl struggled to suppress his irritation. It wasn't as if
passwords were a new invention. Why hadn't Börkur
mentioned this snag in the first place? The phone would
probably be back with its rightful owner by now if Karl had
advertised it straight away, or rung his mother's closest friends
and asked them about it. No chance of doing that now as
he'd disposed of her tacky clamshell phone containing her
list of contacts. Still, no point wasting breath on talking about
things that couldn't be changed. 'Well, be sure to let me know,
or bring the phone back. Then I'll see what I can do myself.'

It was just past the hour. Karl switched on the Collins
shortwave receiver, glad to have his dopey friend there, for
all his shortcomings. It was much pleasanter than listening
alone. Even the knocking had ceased in his visitor's honour.
'Let's hope we hear something. Then I can record it on my
phone so I have some concrete evidence if I do decide to call
the police.'

'If?' Börkur lost interest in the bracelet and flopped down
on the sofa. The rickety frame creaked in protest. 'You've got
to call them, man.'

Before Karl could answer, the tinny notes of the musical

box began to echo round the room. The receiver was still tuned to the same station as yesterday evening but he seemed to have turned it up much louder than usual. Karl reached for the button to lower the volume but snatched back his hand when the familiar female voice began the recital. He took out his phone in readiness but forgot it as he listened. The same series of numbers was repeated over and over. No letters, no minuses or pluses. Seventy-four, one, sixty-eight, ninety-nine, one, thirteen, three. It sounded so familiar yet Karl couldn't place it. He listened again. And again. Seventy-four, one, sixty-eight, ninety-nine, one, thirteen, three.

Sixty-eight. Sixty-eight. Sixty-eight. A light dawned on Karl. He put down his phone, ran to his desk and started scribbling down the numbers. Seventy-four, one, sixty-eight, ninety-nine, one, thirteen, three. Think. Think. Think.

Slowly he wrote down the letters he thought the numbers signified. He mouthed the result to himself, then gasped.

'Börkur. Have you heard from Halli at all?'

'Er, no.' Börkur was bemused by his actions. 'Aren't you going to record it?' The broadcast abruptly went silent, as if by pre-arrangement.

'When did you last hear from him?' Karl didn't wait for an answer. He selected Halli's number with trembling fingers. The phone rang but nobody answered. The voicemail announced that the owner of the number was unable to take his call at present but please leave a message. Karl hung up. He turned back to Börkur.

'Where's Halli?'

Chapter 26

Huldar noticed out of the corner of his eye that an automatic message from Accounts had popped up on his computer screen. He withdrew his attention momentarily from Ríkhardur and Erla: *You have 12 invoices awaiting authorisation.* Damn, why had he let himself be distracted? There was no time to deal with this now and he would only receive the same prompt tomorrow with the addition of several new invoices. The inquiry was top priority. He wondered why on earth the invoices couldn't be offloaded onto the senior officers who were currently spending their days exploring the outer limits of the worldwide web. And while they were about it, they could also take over responsibility for the staff appraisals, which were the latest addition to his to-do list. Egill had briefed Huldar on how to help his team set their objectives and come up with ways of realising them. He had produced a list of questions that Huldar was supposed to fill in for each member of the team, before comparing his version with the answers provided by the relevant employee. After that he was to hold a meeting with each team member to discuss the outcome.

Huldar had never heard such a nonsensical idea. He pictured himself suspending the investigation in order to sit down with Ríkhardur and compare their answers about where he saw his career heading in five years' time.

Personally, Huldar hoped that by then he would still be finding ways of dodging the necessity of authorising invoices and scheduling objectives meetings. Perhaps that was the solution: to hold the interviews in five years' time and save himself the bother of speculating about his team's future prospects. By then they would be obvious.

Egill had shown Huldar no mercy when he pleaded that the timing was extremely unfortunate. He had merely bared his blindingly white teeth and handed him a thick bundle from HR containing his team's CVs, an overview of their timesheets for the year and other relevant information.

This had included a document comparing the employees' and previous manager's responses to last year's objectives forms, which Huldar was to compare with this year's comparisons.

He was still wondering if he had heard right.

Shaking his head, he turned back to Ríkhardur and Erla. 'Do either of you know how to switch off automatic reminders from Accounts?'

Erla was quickest off the mark. 'No. Ask Almar. He helped me stop the reminders about timesheets.'

Ríkhardur tipped back his head and made a face. He achieved the sudden movement without disturbing a hair on his head or creasing his shirt. 'I've a better idea. Why not just fill in your timesheets? It only takes five minutes at the end of the day.'

'Yeah, right.' Erla smiled, banishing her habitual harsh expression and resembling once more the young woman who had joined CID three years ago. It occurred to Huldar to call her in for a performance review and ask why she was so hell-bent on emulating the grumpy old gits at the station. But he checked the impulse and let her continue. 'At the end of the day. The *end*. When every minute counts. I don't know about you but I look forward to going home after work.' The moment she had blurted this out, she realised. 'Oh, shit. Sorry, you know what I mean.'

Ríkhardur didn't answer and the walls seemed to close in on them. What was it about this divorce that had them all walking on eggshells? Erla turned red and Huldar became suddenly very interested in his stapler. He wouldn't be discussing Ríkhardur's personal affairs when and if his objectives meeting took place, that much was certain. Though the bugger of it was that the guy was bound to know precisely which areas were supposed to be covered, including the employee's well-being and life outside work. Huldar felt as if his mobile was burning a hole in his pocket from the text message he had received from Karlotta just before Ríkhardur appeared in the doorway: *I need to talk to you. Call me.* If he hadn't known better he'd have interpreted it as a come-on, now that she was single. But the snatches he could recall of their sexual encounter gave him no reason to believe she would be desperate for a repeat performance. In every scene that paraded before his mind's eye, they were clumsily banging into the partition between the cubicles. Really it was a wonder it hadn't collapsed on top of them. Still, what did he know? Perhaps it had been a refreshing change from her fastidious sex life with Ríkhardur.

Putting down the stapler, Huldar cleared his throat. 'Right, back to business.' Although the digression had ended in awkwardness, the thought of bringing the conversation back to the case filled him with gloom. He had hardly thought or spoken about anything else for days. The worst part was their total lack of progress. They were no closer by the end of the day than they had been first thing that morning. He let out a long breath, trying to marshal his thoughts and focus on essentials. He had lost sight of the big picture – of who was doing what – and needed to rethink the order of priority. Up to now they had been following routine procedure for a murder inquiry but they had hit a dead end and he had no idea where to go from here.

They had scrutinised every detail of Sigvaldi's work record, spoken to the Director General of Public Health's office and the senior consultant in the gynaecology/obstetrics department at the National Hospital. Neither had received any complaints about Sigvaldi's performance. Assuming their information was correct, no women had died in childbirth and no one had held him responsible for any stillbirths. They were still awaiting a response from the Karolinska sjukhus in Sweden where Sigvaldi had completed his specialist training six years ago, but Huldar doubted this would provide them with any leads. It was too long ago and the majority of the patients would have been Swedish. Sigvaldi had confirmed that Margrét didn't understand Swedish as she had only been one when they moved home, so logically the murderer must have been speaking in Icelandic.

The police had gone through the list of everyone with conceivable links to each of the two victims and Sigvaldi to find out how many had a motorbike registered in their name. Very few, as it turned out, and again none with links to both women. They had also checked whether anyone in Elísa's, Sigvaldi's or Ástrós's circle of friends, relatives or work colleagues had a criminal record for violence. Six names came up, all but one of whom had been charged with assaulting other men. The sixth had been charged with rape ten years previously but had watertight alibis for the nights of the murders.

The job of combing through these lists had been extremely time-consuming since Elísa had worked for a large organisation and came from a large family as well. The same applied to Sigvaldi. Added to this were a host of friends and acquaintances, especially in Elísa's case. Ástrós's list had been much shorter. Huldar didn't like to think how many hours had been squandered on this effort.

Whichever way they turned, they drew a blank. No forensic evidence had been recovered from the crime scenes: no fingerprints, no DNA, no clues. Nothing of interest had emerged from interviews with friends or from the paperwork they had obtained. The police had knocked on doors in both victims' neighbourhoods but nobody recalled noticing a motorbike at around the time the women were killed. Elísa's phone still hadn't turned up; either it had been destroyed, was lying around somewhere with an empty battery, or was still in the murderer's possession. The SIM card used to send the texts to Ástrós's phone turned out to have been sold at a hotel in the town centre and the police had managed to trace the person who bought it – a British citizen called Mike Linane who not only existed but acknowledged purchasing the card while holidaying in Iceland. He claimed his phone had been lost or stolen on the last day of his stay. Since it had been an old model and the card would have been no use to him outside Iceland, he hadn't bothered to report the theft, if theft it was. A trip to the Blue Lagoon had proved more tempting than a visit to the police station. If necessary, his friends who had been travelling with him could back up his story. As the man had not left Britain in the intervening period, their confirmation would not be required.

The police had also visited every retailer known to stock duct tape but no one could recall a bulk purchase over the last few months. Or indeed before that. From this they deduced that the murderer must have bought the rolls in small quantities to avoid attracting attention. Or imported them from abroad in his suitcase.

One building supplies company reported the disappearance of a whole box in a warehouse burglary before Christmas more than a year ago, but various other goods had been taken as well, which suggested that the tape had not been the primary object. The warehouse manager explained that they hadn't even noticed until later that the duct tape was missing. A new member of staff had put the rolls in an empty box that had previously contained USB sticks, so the matter hadn't come to light until after the stock-take at New Year. The thieves must have been under the impression that they were making off with far more valuable items.

Huldar had looked the burglary up on the police database and spoken to the investigating officer who was convinced that it was a professional job. The incident was still unsolved and the police had no suspects. Huldar couldn't decide if there was a connection. The clumsy use of the suction cups and glass-cutter at Ástrós's flat implied that the murderer was an amateur at breaking and entering; on the other hand there would have been enough rolls of duct tape in that box to wind countless times round the heads of the two victims and several more into the bargain.

And the use of suction cups, along with the phone theft and the break-in, implied that the murderer had links to the criminal world. Several members of Huldar's team were now poring over lists of burglars in search of possible candidates. The search criteria were links to assaults or other violent incidents.

While new doors were opening, others were closing. It had been established that no foreign life insurance company had Elísa on their books, so that seemed to rule out murder for money. The same was true of Ástrós; they hadn't yet received confirmation from abroad but they had ascertained that she wasn't insured with any Icelandic company. Since Ástrós was childless, her three siblings stood to inherit, along with her late husband's two brothers. Although there was no mortgage on her flat and she had died with money in the bank, it stretched credulity that any of these people would have killed her for their share of her estate.

The CCTV footage from the petrol station, dating from the Thursday when Elísa's key was thought to have been stolen, had turned out to be faulty; some clever dick, possibly even the murderer, had jogged the camera by the pumps so it was pointing at the roof. Footage from inside the shop showed Elísa enter, grab some ice lollies and wait by the till while the car was being filled. She kept peering out at the forecourt, presumably checking on the kids and the pump attendant, then paid by card, said goodbye and left. No one else came in immediately before or after her. On the basis of the footage and Margrét's statement, Huldar concluded that Elísa had been unacquainted with the man who had filled the car. According to Margrét, she had handed him the keys but hadn't spoken to him or greeted him in a friendly way.

The more ground they covered in the inquiry, the more doubtful Huldar became that the end was in sight.

'I can check the colours of these guys' helmets, if you like,' said Erla. 'Perhaps one of them will turn out to have been acquainted with both women after all.' She ran her eyes down the list of motorbike owners. 'Though I have a hard time believing that a bike owner would be dumb enough to use a motorcycle helmet as a disguise to commit murder.'

'That doesn't alter the fact that we need to run thorough checks on them.' Huldar rubbed his dry eyes. 'We've asked Customs to provide a list of people who've ordered helmets from abroad online, in case someone bought a helmet specifically for this purpose.' He dropped his hands from his eyes. 'We've also contacted all retailers selling helmets in this country and asked them to provide a summary of the last six months' sales. Luckily, there aren't many of them, so the information should be ready by tomorrow or the day after. I gather we've also tracked down four adverts on classified sites offering second-hand helmets for sale.'

'Or he could have stolen it.' Ríkhardur flicked some invisible fluff from his shirt.

'Would you mind looking into that?' Huldar knew Ríkhardur was growing bored with following up tip-offs from the public. Having been lumbered with this job more than once himself in the past, he knew it was like tidying up the kitchen: you had no sooner turned on the dishwasher than a dirty mug appeared from nowhere and before you knew it the place was a mess again. By the time you had dealt with one call, the next would have come in. And another wave could be expected once Ástrós's murder hit the news. After that things should quieten down, but until then Ríkhardur would just have to persevere. 'How are you getting on with the tip-offs, by the way?'

'Fine . . .' Ríkhardur tried to sound upbeat but his eyes told a different story. 'Nothing of any value yet. But you never know.'

'What's been the funniest or weirdest shit so far?' Erla asked, leaning towards him.

'I hear it's been unusually colourful stuff.' Huldar chuckled. 'They had a call earlier from one of the paranormal gang claiming to have been receiving coded messages via the radio.'

Ríkhardur looked uncomfortable. 'Yes, so I gather. Actually, none of it's made much sense. A woman reckoned she'd seen Elísa getting off a coach full of tourists at the Blue Lagoon and claimed the party left without her. She'd obviously got the wrong end of the stick because she thought we were appealing for any news of Elísa and suggested we dragged the lagoon for her body. Then there was the guy who claimed to have spotted her having an altercation with a traffic warden on Laugavegur. According to him it ended with them both being arrested – the day after she died.'

'Well, I hope you followed that up.' Huldar wondered if calls from the public were becoming less crazy these days. If these were the worst Ríkhardur had to contend with, he didn't deserve any sympathy. Perhaps the crackpots were now channelling their energies into commenting on web forums instead of bothering the police. 'Has anyone trawled through the online comments about the case? There's always a chance we've missed something there.'

'I haven't paid any special attention to the internet.' Ríkhardur appeared to regard this as a serious oversight on his part. Swallowing awkwardly, he added: 'In fact, it turns out that nobody has ever been arrested in Iceland as a result of an argument with a traffic warden, so Elísa's alleged arrest can't even have taken place when she was alive. Of course, I don't need to tell you that Elísa appears to have been a model citizen. Like Ástrós.' A fact he clearly approved of. He wouldn't exactly have bent over backwards on their account had the two women been public nuisances.

'What about the radio messages? That must have been a giggle.' Erla shifted closer to encourage Ríkhardur to elaborate.

'I haven't got that far. I decided to take you at your word, Huldar, and leave calls like that till last. Somehow I can't imagine anything useful coming out of it.'

'Well, you never know.' Huldar paused. At this point, it was impossible to judge what was important and what was a complete waste of time. The only course was to follow up every lead, even bonkers tip-offs from the public. 'We shouldn't forget that the genocide in Rwanda was triggered in part by orders over the radio. The Hutus were told to kill all the Tutsis they could get hold of. And we're all aware of the consequences.'

Ríkhardur looked put out. Presumably he had been hoping to avoid having to investigate this call. Handling matters with a tenuous link to reality wasn't his forte. But much of what landed on their desks would seem incomprehensible, irrational or far-fetched to the general public, so he had better get used to it. The world wasn't all as straightforward as he was.

'Of course I'll follow it up. It's just that I remembered you saying anything linked to the paranormal could be sent to the bottom of the pile.'

Ríkhardur was plainly offended but Huldar had neither the time nor the energy to cope with his touchiness now. He heaved a sigh and shook his head in exasperation, then, unable to think of anything to add, changed the subject. 'Tell me, do you two agree that despite all the indications to the contrary, there must be some connection between the murderer, Elísa and Ástrós? Or between him, Sigvaldi and Ástrós?'

Huldar didn't like the glance they exchanged. He interpreted it as a sign that they would rather he displayed more confidence.

'I guess so.' Erla got in first and Ríkhardur nodded.

Huldar tried to compensate by adopting a more forceful tone. 'The only plausible explanation for all the trouble the murderer took is that he wanted to punish the women or, in Elísa's case, possibly her husband. If we knew what it was about, we'd be in a better position. I'm assuming it's retribution for some crime he believes they or Sigvaldi committed – against him personally perhaps. The murders aren't associated with sexual psychosis, despite the sadistic element.'

Erla coughed. 'Ahem. Wouldn't any old victim do for a sick fuck who kills to satisfy his sadistic urges? What does it matter who's doing the suffering if what motivates him is the desire to inflict pain?'

'I'm inclined to agree with that.' The blood mottled Ríkhardur's white cheeks. He clamped his lips into a pale line. While it violated his natural subservience to contradict his superiors, he found it hard to speak against his own convictions. 'What does it matter to a man like that who he tortures?'

'Nothing, I suppose. Unless he gets a kick out of inflicting pain on certain types. But Elísa and Ástrós didn't look alike and were different ages. They had virtually nothing in common apart from the fact they were both women – and let's not forget that Margrét overheard the murderer telling Elísa that it was really Sigvaldi he was punishing. Still, leaving that aside, what I meant is that the motive for the killings is unlikely to have been sadism pure and simple. The man must have known them or crossed paths with them at some point. If he'd simply wanted an outlet for his need to inflict pain, wouldn't he have spent more time on it? Spun out their ordeals as long as possible? According to Elísa's post-mortem, her death followed relatively quickly after he switched on the vacuum cleaner. It was different with Ástrós as it took a while for the curling tongs to burn her windpipe so badly that it closed, causing her to suffocate. It would have been easy to kill them both by another, slower method if sadism had been the primary motive.' Huldar tried not to think about the horrific details he had read in the pathologist's reports.

'You mean by torturing them for longer? For days, even?' As usual Erla came straight to the point.

'Yes, that's exactly what I mean. Obviously, I find the methods the murderer used as despicable as you do. But they don't resemble any of the foreign cases I've read up on in which women were murdered purely in order to satisfy sadistic urges. In those cases the killer almost invariably kidnaps the victim – lures her into his house or car – and takes her to a remote spot where he draws out her death for as long as possible. He doesn't finish her off in a hurry during a break-in, like our guy.'

'Do you have any examples?' Erla asked, grimacing.

Huldar opened his mouth but couldn't bring himself to elaborate. It was bad enough to have researched this stuff; he'd almost expected blood to start oozing from his computer screen. 'Take it from me, they're sickening. To be honest, I doubt some of the details I read were true.' He glanced at the watch given to him by his father when he graduated from police training college. Though most people had stopped wearing watches these days, he persisted in honour of his old man.

'Then there's the business of the messages.' Ríkhardur could recite those connected to Ástrós by memory but had to pull a note from his pocket to remind him of the one left at Elísa's house. '"Twenty-two, ninety minus one, point nine, eight, eighty-six minus seven, point seventy-three, ninety minus one," and "So tell me: fifty-three, sixteen, point fifty-three, ninety minus one, point four, forty-three minus six, sixty-five minus five, sixty-eight, point forty-three minus six, eight, point one hundred and six minus sixteen, fifty-three, twenty-three, sixty-three minus ninety-two, point ninety, eighty-nine minus six, seven, point forty-three minus six, eight, point seventy-five, fifty-eight, fifty-three, twenty-three, sixty-three minus ninety-two"?' He raised his eyes again. 'Doesn't that suggest the perpetrator felt he had some business, so to speak, with the women?' Ríkhardur shifted in his chair, relaxing his upright posture a little. But the new pose he adopted was just as stiff.

'There's something suspicious about those messages, if you ask me.' Erla was as hunched as Ríkhardur was straight-backed. A few months ago Egill had brought in an ergonomics expert with the intention of creating a healthier working environment, but it had mainly involved wasting people's time. The staff had found it hard to concentrate on their job while a man armed with a measuring tape and notebook hovered over them. Two days after the assessment and the accompanying course on how to improve their posture, everyone had lapsed into their old habits; Ríkhardur sitting straight as a ramrod, everyone else slouching, round-shouldered. Gel mouse-pads ended up in drawers and footrests were kicked into the corner. Erla hadn't even waited two days, in spite of her shoulder injury, or perhaps because of it. 'I mean, why the hell leave a message in the first place? And don't say that deep down the fucker wants to be caught. I'm not buying that.'

'You've got a point.' Huldar rooted around in the piles of paper on his desk in search of copies of the notes found at the scene. 'Maybe he's taunting us. Thinks he's so superior to the police that he can get away with it.'

Erla frowned. 'You reckon? I think it's much more likely he's doing it to fuck with us. Has anyone stopped to consider that?'

'False messages?' Ríkhardur looked as if he'd encountered a bad smell. 'Isn't that a bit far-fetched?'

Huldar didn't immediately reply: Erla's idea wasn't so crazy. 'You may well be on to something. It would fit in better with how careful the murderer is in every other respect. I mean, how come he's so concerned to leave no trace but then provides notes that he must know will end up in our hands? He can hardly imagine we'd fail to notice them. Besides, that wouldn't make sense. In that case, why leave them behind at all?' Huldar realised he was losing his thread. 'If the messages are linked to the motive for the killings, they could help us nail him in the end. Which would be a major blunder on his part and totally out of keeping with the rest of his M.O. That was a good point you raised, Erla.'

'Unless the other theory's correct.' Ríkhardur carefully avoided looking at Erla; presumably he didn't want to see her expression of triumph. 'That he's taunting us. Thinks we're a bunch of morons.'

'If we don't start making progress soon, he'll have a point.' Huldar stood up. 'I need a coffee.' He noticed yet another memo flash up on his screen. This time it was an announcement that he hadn't yet completed his manning schedule for the next six months. He switched off the monitor. He felt as if he were drowning in forms. 'I'm thinking of calling it a day. I just can't concentrate any longer. You two should knock off early as well.'

The idea didn't receive the reception he'd expected. On the contrary, they were regarding him reproachfully as if he had let them down. He felt a stab of irritation but, if he were honest, this had more to do with the knot of fear in his stomach over the state of the investigation than any short-comings on their part.

'I'll see you tomorrow. Call me if anything comes up. And let me know if Interpol gets back to us about the messages. On second thoughts, you'd better text me, as I doubt I'll be picking up any calls.' He had decided to drop in on Freyja. Which was none of their business.

Chapter 27

There was no point shedding any more tears. They had nowhere to go and weeping only made his eyes sting. Rubbing his head against the rough concrete had achieved nothing either, apart from grazing the small amount of his skin that wasn't covered in tape. Halli didn't know how many times the man had wound it round his head; he'd stopped counting after six when the pressure became so bad he could no longer think straight. It was clear to him now that the thick tape was far too tightly wound for him to be able to scrape it off without the use of his hands. His right ear had suffered worst. It felt like it was on fire. When he escaped he was probably going to need plastic surgery . . . if he escaped.

The tears welled up again. They not only stung his eyes but filled his nose with mucus, which meant he kept having to unblock it. He had to breathe through his nose because his mouth was stuffed with padding and taped shut. He didn't want to suffocate in his own snot.

Didn't want to suffocate full stop.

It was worth reminding himself of this now when he felt the temptation creeping over him to surrender to sleep and be free of the pain. He ached all over. But whenever he did nod off, the pain was worse when he woke up, so he was better off staying conscious. The heat contributed to his suffering too, exacerbating his discomfort until it was unbearable.

He could no longer even feel his hands. They were lashed behind his back with plastic ties that cut deep into his wrists. To be on the safe side, the man had also wrapped more of the bloody tape so tightly around his hands that it would be impossible to use his fingers even if he did find something to cut his bonds with. At first this had given him hope – it must mean there was a sharp object of some kind in here that he could use. But after shuffling around the room several times on his sore buttocks he had almost ruled out this possibility.

Yet he couldn't be entirely sure. Blindfolded and unable to grope around with his hands or feet, he hadn't been able to search effectively. His ankles were lashed together with more plastic ties and his knees were tied or wound together with tape as well.

Perhaps he had missed something. Perhaps it was worth forcing himself on one last exploratory shuffle. But his mind recoiled from the thought of the pain. Halli blew violently through his nose and felt the mucus shoot out and land on his chest. He didn't care. He was only afraid that if a stranger opened the door and saw the state of him, he or she would slam it and hurry away again without investigating further.

He sucked in air through his nostrils and felt a little better. Tried to savour the feeling, but it didn't last. Inevitably, snot started collecting again. He shifted, causing the agony to flare up in his wrists. That was all right because at least it told him his hands hadn't gone entirely numb.

How long had he been here? Twenty-four hours? Thirty-six? Probably not that long or he would be hungrier. It would have been impossible to feel any thirstier. How long could a person live without water? Two days? Three? Four or five? Probably not that long. Was that the man's plan? To leave him to die of dehydration? He hadn't shown up for a long while and although Halli would have given a great deal never to see him again, the fear that he had abandoned him was even worse.

If only the man would come back one more time, remove the gag from his mouth and give him a drink, then Halli would promise never ever to shop him if he was allowed to go free. Somehow Halli would make the man understand that he could be relied on; remind him that after all he had nothing to gain by reporting him.

Maybe it would be better to skip the last part, suggesting as it did that Halli might change his mind and rat on him. He should probably be preparing what to say when the man came back instead of shuffling around on his arse, searching for implements that weren't there. That is, *if* the man came back. And *if* he removed the tape from Halli's mouth.

Halli cleared his nose with such force that the snot flew out in the air instead of landing on his chest. Perhaps he'd hit his trouser legs or shoes. A wave of self-pity washed over him. His body twitched and for a while he was afraid he was developing epilepsy or a feverish chill. He wasn't actually too sure what a chill involved but imagined it probably made sufferers shiver so violently that it was like having an electric shock. Could you die from a chill? That would be ironic, given how hot it was in here. If anything, he was more likely to die of a fever, unless he died of thirst before he could succumb to either. Or would he be granted a chance to talk the man round?

The tears welled up again and he was helpless to stop them. This was so horrible. And so unfair. What had he done to deserve it?

Was this his punishment for taking part in a silly conspiracy? He hadn't really done anything to deserve this fate. He had sold the man his equipment, taught him how to set up a timed broadcast and planted the phone and woman's knickers in Karl's car. Oh, and nicked the bunch of keys. That was all. The man had told him it was just a little prank that someone close to Karl was playing, and made him promise not to give the game away.

But he should have known this man wasn't what he seemed; his voice alone had made it plain that any betrayal would have serious consequences. And to make matters worse he had withheld half the fee he had promised Halli for his help and equipment, telling him he would get the rest afterwards. But only if Halli kept his mouth shut. That had been enough to prevent him from breathing a word of it.

Now, though, he had been forced to face up to what he had suspected all along – that this was no joke. He had realised when the man fetched him from home, persuaded him to get in his car, and drove off. When they reached their destination he had forced Halli to send his parents a text saying he was going to a holiday chalet that had no mobile phone reception. At that moment it had been glaringly obvious. If he hadn't been so stunned he would have refused, jumped out of the car and made a run for it. How could he have been so stupid? And why on earth had he opened the door to the man when he turned up at his room?

In his heart of hearts he knew the answer. He had longed to hear the man tell him not to worry, that the prank was nearly over and he would get the rest of his money soon. He needed it so badly. He had already spent the first half on paying off his debts, buying a new coat and shoes and putting down a deposit on a computer that would be ready for delivery shortly. At that point he would need to pay the remainder. That was why he had opened the door. It was that simple. Money. That was why, ignoring all his misgivings, he had agreed to play this trick on his friend.

These thoughts now gave way to another: could Karl be in the same boat as him? Had the man's plan all along been to get to him? Shit. What for? To kill him?

Halli tried to push away the idea that the man might be capable of murder. If he was, then Halli himself was in deep shit and so was Karl. There was no guessing why someone would want to kill his friend but that was beside the point. What mattered more right now was that the man had a clear reason to want Halli himself out of the way. After all, Halli could report him. Even though he was unlikely to be believed, there was always a chance, and the man wouldn't want to take that risk.

He simply had to find a way to reason with the man. He'd promise to keep his trap shut and would stand by his promise. Even if the man killed Karl. Halli would remain silent as the grave, keep his head down, not say a word. If only he could find a way to convince the man of this.

He pricked up his ears. What was that? The rumble of an engine? Then he heard a key inserted in the lock and the clanking of the chain that had been wrapped round the two door-handles when they arrived and the man had tricked him into going inside. He had claimed the radio transmitter was in here and wouldn't work; Halli had to help him sort it out and would be paid extra for his trouble. Once again greed had been his undoing.

Before the door opened, Halli hastened to unblock his nose.

He'd prefer not to have to do it in front of the man. Stupid, of course, but he couldn't help the feeling.

There was the click of a light switch. Halli deduced from this that he had been sitting in darkness and, oddly enough, the thought comforted him. It was easier to reconcile himself to his inability to see anything than if he had been sitting here blindfolded in bright light.

He heard the man's footsteps approach and come to a halt in front of him. Halli guessed the man was bending down. He waited with frantic impatience for him to speak. Hopefully to say he was going to give him a drink.

'There you are. Lucky I ran into you.' This sarcastic note was new and Halli didn't know how to interpret it. Could it be a good sign? Halli started making noises behind his gag to indicate that he wanted to talk but ended up sounding like a muzzled pig having a stand-off with a slaughterhouse worker.

'Your ear's almost torn in two.' Now the man's voice sounded more like his usual self, but oddly muffled, as though he were talking through a mask. Halli's attempt to make a noise emerged as a pathetic whine. 'You won't need the top half any more. Or the bottom, for that matter.' The man seemed to sigh. 'Or anything else.' He fell silent and after a moment Halli heard footsteps again, this time moving away. Then there was a click that Halli thought at first was the light switch, indicating that the man was leaving again without offering him a chance to beg for mercy. He almost swallowed the padding in his mouth in a desperate attempt to attract the man's attention and make him come back. But then his brain processed the sound more accurately and he thought that instead of switching off the light, the man had plugged something in. But what?

The footsteps came nearer again and without warning the man was right beside him. Halli began to tremble, first from fear, then from pain as the man tore at his injured ear. He was being horribly clumsy if his intention was to put a bandage or plaster on it. But that wasn't what the man had in mind at all. Halli felt something icy against his sore earlobe; not just cold but sharp as well. He whimpered as loud as he could but of course this did nothing to help. Falling silent, he made an effort to keep still; perhaps his uncontrollable shaking had caused the man to jab him in the ear. Surely he couldn't be intending to damage it any further? Perhaps it was just scissors he was going to use on the tape. Perhaps Halli would get a chance after all to beg for mercy. He made a superhuman effort to control his shaking and moaning. He must be able to. There was so much at stake – everything was at stake.

He sat there quietly, holding himself still.

'That's better. Thank you. That makes my life much easier.'

Halli expected to feel a knife or scissors being inserted under the tape and starting to snip. But the touch when it came was not where he had expected and turned out to be very different in nature. The stinging of his earlobe was forgotten, replaced by a searing agony inside his head. He heard a click and everything that had gone before paled into insignificance.

Chapter 28

Karlotta wasn't picking up. After six rings Huldar felt he had done his duty and could relax. She would see that he had returned her call, and with any luck she'd leave it at that, forget her errand and let him off the hook.

Sadly, though, it was unlikely that the sorry tale that had begun in that grubby toilet cubicle would end so easily. Karlotta was probably in a meeting or otherwise busy and would call back as soon as she had a moment. Huldar was dreading the conversation; he was filled with remorse at the mere thought of her. It was nothing personal; the fault lay with him.

Karlotta reminded him of what a shit he had been.

He had successfully avoided her since it happened and would happily go to his grave without having any further contact with her. The mere fact that she had phoned him had given him indigestion. He knocked back a couple of heartburn pills but they did nothing to relieve the acidic churning in his stomach. He followed them up with some nicotine gum and immediately felt a little better. Well enough to think about moving. He stepped out of the car into the dark winter's evening.

Instead of heading straight to the front door, he decided to sneak round the back and see if he could slip inside unobserved by the policeman on guard duty. From what he had seen, it shouldn't be difficult. The uniformed officer was sitting in the patrol car in front of the main entrance. So far so good, but the blue glow reflected on his face suggested he was busy surfing the net.

Huldar had parked at a discreet distance, and managed to approach the rear of the property unobserved via the two neighbouring gardens. They were divided by low fences that came close to collapsing when he clambered over them. Freyja's building clearly wasn't the only one around here in a state of disrepair. But the neglect was noticeably worse in her garden; rubbish poked up out of the snow and a small gas barbecue – the cheapest money could buy – lay on its side in one corner. A rusty old swing rocked gently in the breeze. No wonder she'd been attracted to a certain carpenter from Egilsstadir called Jónas. Had he existed, he could have made a real difference here.

Having reached the corner of the building, Huldar peered cautiously up the street. The policeman was still engrossed in his phone. Huldar made it into the entrance lobby unseen, as he had suspected he might. Rather than ringing the bell, he went back outside, deliberately making a noise this time.

The police officer gaped at him, phone still in hand. He stuttered as he returned Huldar's greeting, making frantic efforts to turn off his phone without dropping his gaze. 'Were you inside?'

'No. I came to see how the surveillance was going.' Huldar nodded at the policeman's phone. 'Something good on YouTube?'

'Er, no. I just got distracted for a moment.' The young officer was scarlet in the face.

'Well, would you mind concentrating on your job? I'm going

inside to check on the situation and talk to the woman. When I come out I don't want to have to bang on the window to attract your attention.'

'No, of course not. I won't take my eyes off the house.'

As he walked away, Huldar heard the window rolling up. He glanced round before entering, to reassure himself that the young man hadn't immediately reverted to playing with his phone. No, he was staring at Huldar with fierce concentration.

There was hardly anywhere to tread among the piles of free newspapers in the lobby. Huldar kicked them aside to reach the doorbells. Freyja's name was there, on a new-looking label. Again he wondered why on earth she was living here but he couldn't possibly ask after Erla's unforgivable rudeness last time. He could have done on his first visit in the guise of Jónas the carpenter, but he hadn't been in a fit state to notice anything unusual at the time. A memory surfaced of her asking his advice about the bathroom door, which was sticking. He had run his hand up and down the frame, trying to look knowledgeable. Luckily, at that point she had hiccupped and lost concentration, and soon they'd had other things on their mind than DIY. He really hoped she wouldn't remember the incident.

'Hello?' Freyja's voice sounded hollow and tinny on the entryphone.

'Oh, hi. It's Huldar. I'd like a few words. Is this a good moment?'

There was no answer and he'd started to think she wasn't going to let him in when the door suddenly buzzed. On his way upstairs he rehearsed what he was going to say. It was essential to make a better impression this time.

Freyja was standing in the doorway, arms folded, her expression forbidding.

She was wearing tight jeans, a T-shirt, stripy socks and pink, fluffy slippers. Her wavy blond hair was drawn into an unflattering bun on top of her head, which made her look taller. Evidently, she hadn't been expecting guests. 'Hello.'

Huldar smiled, pretending not to notice the chilly reception, 'Hi.' He walked over and stood there like an idiot. 'Any chance I could come in? I need to go over a few things. I promise it won't take long.'

Freyja narrowed her eyes, apparently wondering whether to believe him. She was a trained psychologist, so he had every reason to fear she would see right through him. But she stepped aside and ushered him in. He wasn't sure if she had been taken in by his lie or simply couldn't be bothered to stand there arguing. Never mind, he was inside. She told him not to bother removing his shoes. While he was taking off his coat, Molly appeared. She kept banging into his leg with her collar in her attempts to sniff at him. Only then did a smile light up Freyja's face. It wasn't the animal's clumsy overtures but his winces of pain that amused her. Oh, well, he knew he deserved it.

As he entered the hallway, Margrét appeared at the bedroom door. She stared at him, head on one side, which did nothing to relieve his discomfort.

'Hello.'

'Why are you here?' Margrét's face remained stony. 'You're the cop.'

'Yes, I'm a cop. I don't know about *the* cop.'

'You're the cop. I remember. The cop who pulled me out from under the bed.' It was impossible to guess from her expression whether she was grateful or angry. He knew enough about children to be aware that their thought processes didn't always follow the same paths as those of adults. She might be under the impression that none of this would have happened if only she had been allowed to stay under the bed.

'Yes. I'm that cop. Quite right. You're an observant girl.' He remembered how she had screwed her eyes shut and kept them closed even when he dragged her out of her hiding place and held her in his arms, face pressed to his chest so she couldn't see her dead mother on the bed. She had refused to look at him so she had probably never seen his face; it must be his voice she recognised. Huldar smiled at her but received no answering smile. He didn't blame her.

'I saw those shoes. When I was under the bed.' She stared at his feet, then raised anxious eyes. 'There was a man in the garden just now. I saw him out of the window.'

Huldar darted a sidelong glance at Freyja who was listening to their conversation, no doubt grateful not to have to talk to him. He swallowed, groping for the right note, then answered brightly: 'That makes sense. It was me.'

'You?' Freyja glared. 'What were you doing in the garden?'

Margrét bit her lower lip, retreated into her room and slammed the door behind her.

'You frightened her. Have you forgotten the man she saw in her garden at home? You could have warned me so I had time to make sure she wasn't by the window. Now there's a risk she'll think you're him.' Her voice dropped to a whisper. 'Or the murderer.'

'I was conducting an experiment.' The words sounded feeble when spoken aloud. 'I was testing how well our officer on guard duty is doing his job.'

'And?'

'And?' Huldar stalled.

'And how did the experiment turn out?'

'I expect you'd rather not know.' Huldar hesitated, then said it anyway. 'I made it into the lobby without him noticing.'

'Jesus.' Freyja exhaled. 'Why did you come round? To conduct your experiment?'

'No, that wasn't the only reason. I wanted to tell you that we've spoken to your ex-boyfriend and established that he couldn't have attacked the dog.' Molly swung her head round and peered at him through her plastic collar, before returning her gaze to the closed door. 'The message wasn't sent from his phone and it turns out he had a watertight alibi.'

'What, was the National Society of Jerks holding a meeting?'

Huldar grinned. He had taken Ríkhardur along to the interview and regretted it the moment he saw the square-looking type waiting in the corridor of the police station. Like Ríkhardur, he was wearing a suit and in their company Huldar had felt like a hippy straight out of Woodstock. As if the guy's smooth appearance hadn't been bad enough, he had turned out to be insufferably obnoxious too. The man had wiped the chair before sitting down and made a face every time he replied to a question. His eyes kept travelling distastefully around the room as if he expected to see lice jumping out at him from the corners. 'No, as it happens. But it wouldn't surprise me to hear he was chairman, secretary and treasurer, all rolled into one.'

Freyja thawed visibly. 'What was his alibi?'

'I'm sorry, I'm not at liberty to say. But it's rock solid.' Huldar didn't want to mention that the man with whom she had until recently been cohabiting had gone out for dinner with his new live-in girlfriend. He added, a little shyly: 'You're well shot of him.'

That seemed to do the trick. 'Would you like to sit down?' Freyja waved a hand towards the small living room. 'I'm just going to see if Margrét's recovered.'

Huldar passed the heavy metal poster he had noticed last time. Having met her ex, he was confident it wasn't a relic of her previous relationship. You wouldn't catch that guy listening to anything but refined classical music. He resolved not to ask her about it or say anything that could be misconstrued or make her uncomfortable. He was determined to watch his step now that he had been given a second chance.

Well, sort of.

She hadn't exactly welcomed him with open arms; all she'd done was invite him to take a seat on a dirty, threadbare sofa with the stuffing bulging out in several places. He left plenty of room in case she wanted to sit beside him, and tried to relax. For a while he focused on two colourful cardboard cartons on the coffee table, one empty, the other half full of melted ice-cream. Then, tiring of this, he let his gaze wander over the floor until it encountered a block of parquet that didn't seem to have been properly fitted. By the time Freyja entered the room he had been staring at it so long that the straight lines of the block were beginning to bend.

'There's no reasoning with her, poor thing.' Freyja flopped down in the chair facing him.

'I'm sorry. It didn't cross my mind. I'd never have done it if I'd known she was at the window.' Huldar was careful not to gaze too intently at Freyja. He kept dropping his eyes to the cartons on the table, then realised this might make him appear nervous or just plain weird. 'Would you like me to talk to her, to explain or apologise?'

'No, absolutely not,' Freyja replied too quickly and vehemently. She tried to take the sting out of her words by adding: 'She's afraid of you as it is. It's only natural – she's not herself. Better leave her alone for a while. You weren't intending to stay long, were you?'

'No, of course not.' Huldar pointed at the floor. 'Unless I can try my hand at mending that block. I do sometimes undertake the odd spot of DIY.' He smiled warily.

Freyja didn't seem to know how to take this. 'You're not touching the floor, Jónas,' she said, deadpan.

'All right. I promise.'

'Was there anything else apart from the attack on Molly?'

'Yes, actually, though it involves her too.' He swallowed. 'I mentioned that the message wasn't sent from your ex's phone.' She nodded apprehensively. 'It came from the same phone as the texts sent to the second victim. It looks like it was the killer. That's why I wanted to test the guard. Seeing how that turned out, I'm not sure what to do. But one thing's certain: Margrét can't stay here.'

'Where's she to go then? Surely not to her grandparents? It wouldn't be hard to track her down there.'

'We're looking for a solution. I'm going to add a second officer to the guard for the evening and night shifts. If it's OK with you, I'd rather one was posted inside; he could sit in here so he wouldn't be in your way.'

'I sleep on this sofa, so I'm afraid he would definitely be in the way.'

Huldar sensed she was holding something back. 'What?'

'Oh, I was just wondering what'll happen to me when

Margrét leaves. Presumably the police car will leave then too. But what if the murderer thinks she told me something?'

'I can keep a car parked outside. But I'm not sure we'll be able to spare two officers.'

'Forget it then.' Freyja looked anything but happy. Two deep, bracket-like furrows appeared between her eyes. He memorised the sign, in case their paths crossed again after the investigation was over, unlikely though that seemed.

'No way. I'll take care of it myself if no one else is available. At night, I mean. I need to spend the day trying to hunt down this bastard. If I succeed, there'll be no need of police protection, for you or Margrét.'

'Please do. But forget about sleeping in the car outside. I can look after myself.' Freyja put her hands on the arms of the chair, preparing to stand up. 'Was there anything else?' The brackets were still there.

Huldar's phone rang in his pocket, preventing his reply. He took it out, in spite of a rather dirty look from Freyja, and his stomach lurched again when he saw that it was Karlotta. He switched off the call.

'Aren't you going to answer?'

'No.' Best say as little as possible. A scream from the bedroom rendered further words unnecessary.

Freyja stood by the living-room window, phone held to her ear. She parted the blinds. On the other side of the garden she could see the dancing beams of torches where police officers were searching for the person Margrét claimed to have seen skulking out there. Huldar was outside too but naturally she couldn't tell his torch from the others. Unless his was the beam bouncing most frenetically of all in the darkness.

The reason the incident was being taken so seriously was the girl's insistence that it was the same man as the one she had seen watching her home in the weeks before the murder. Though whether they should put any faith in that was doubtful.

Freyja listened in silence to her brother's angry tirade. It was best to let him blow off steam.

'Police car? Parked outside? Four guys from the building have already called me about it and I'm telling you they are seriously pissed off. I assured them there was no way it could have anything to do with you. Now what am I supposed to tell them?'

'The truth. That the car is here because of me. But it'll probably be gone by tomorrow like I said.'

'Why didn't you tell me? I need to watch my reputation. I can't risk people thinking I'm in cahoots with the pigs.'

'You aren't.'

'Are there cops in the flat too?'

'No.' Luckily it was true at that moment, but it wouldn't be long before the search was over and Huldar returned. He would probably demand to sleep on the sofa tonight and she'd end up sharing the bed with Margrét. Although Freyja didn't relish the thought of coming face to face with him when she woke up, nor did she want to risk having the murderer break in with no one there to protect them.

'You should have trusted me. Don't you think I can take better care of you than the pigs can? For fuck's sake.' Baldur paused to draw breath. 'Believe me, I can.'

'I do believe you, Baldur. It's not me they're looking after; it's the girl. I've already told you that.'

There was a long silence.

'Freyja. Promise not to freak out.'

'Freak out? Why should I freak out?'

'There's a gun in the flat. I want you to sleep with it beside you. Keep it in your bag during the day. Don't carry it around in your pocket or people'll notice.'

'A gun? Are you crazy?' Freyja dropped the blinds again. Her voice dropped to a whisper for fear Margrét would over-hear. 'Jesus Christ, where is it?'

'In the living room. There's a loose floorboard with a cavity under it. I keep it there. Promise me you'll take it.'

Freyja paled as her eyes fell on the uneven parquet. What would have happened if she'd accepted Huldar's offer? If he demanded to stay over he might well try and repair the floor in a misguided attempt to get into her good books. She would have to remove the gun before he came back. 'Baldur, I've got to go. I'll check out the gun, I promise. Don't worry about me.'

'I won't. I know you're going to be OK.'

Freyja hung up and hastily fetched a screwdriver to lever up the block. She reflected on Baldur's parting words. What exactly did he mean? How could he be so sure she wasn't in any danger? She knelt down and set to work.

Chapter 29

The girl looked as though she had just woken up but her jaws were working away vigorously, emitting loud smacking noises through her open mouth. They were treated to frequent glimpses of noxious pink bubblegum. The label above the doorbell said 'Linda'. In place of a second name, a small pink heart-shaped sticker had been applied, slightly askew, by a careless hand.

Karl suspected it was the girl herself who had done it; her slovenly appearance indicated a disregard for detail. Her bleached hair was yellow rather than blond and the dark roots had been allowed to grow unchecked. She had scraped it back in a greasy ponytail, revealing a high, shiny forehead covered in pimples. Below it, the two coal-black eyebrows might have been drawn on with a marker pen.

Her hand kept wandering up to her forehead and rubbing the coarse skin, drawing attention to the dark blue nail varnish that had begun to flake, showing the dirt underneath. Her clothes were in keeping with the rest of her appearance; well overdue a wash, but the thin T-shirt barely concealed a pair of incongruously perky, voluptuous breasts. It took all Karl's self-discipline to look her in the eye, and even then his gaze kept slipping downwards. Börkur, less polite, subjected her bust to an unblinking stare.

Linda didn't seem to notice. She stretched out the pink

gum, winding it round a grubby thumb, and pushed it back into her mouth with a loud pop. 'Who? Halli? Does he live here?'

'Yes. In the room diagonally opposite you.' Karl pointed to the plain door that looked indistinguishable from the other eight in the corridor. The doors led to the kind of cheap, unlicensed rental accommodation for which there was a huge demand. 'He's tall. With dark hair.'

'Dark hair?' It sounded like a question, as if the concept was foreign to her. Perhaps her desire to be blond was so all-consuming that she had forgotten any alternative existed. She shook her head. 'Nope. I dunno who you're talking about.'

Karl tried in vain to remember any distinguishing feature of Halli's that might jog the girl's memory. 'He wears a black leather jacket. Rides a bike.'

The girl's face lit up in a wide smile. Her teeth, which were large and white, improved her appearance no end. 'Oh! The bike guy. Why didn't you say so?' Instead of waiting for an answer she frowned suspiciously. 'Why are you looking for him? Are you debt collectors?'

'God, no. I'm a friend of his. I need to get hold of him. He's not answering his phone.'

'Oh. Have you tried knocking on his door?'

The question was so daft that even Börkur raised his eyes incredulously to the girl's face. Karl answered as patiently as he could. 'I've already tried. Didn't you hear the racket?'

Linda shook her head. 'Nah. I was listening to music. You know.' She tugged at one of the white earbuds that hung around her neck. It emitted a shrill buzz of music. 'I saw his bike yesterday though.'

'But not him?' Karl and Börkur had spotted his bike when

they arrived. It was sticking out from under the staircase that led to the upper floors where the rooms were located. Other floors appeared to be rented out as office space to small companies, most of which didn't seem to have much of a turnover, judging by the way their owners had made do with sticking a sheet of paper bearing the company's name on the door.

'No. Not that I remember.' Linda was becoming bored with the interrogation. She craned her neck to peer down the corridor, apparently checking to see if there were any more of them. 'I saw him the other day though. I admired his new coat. It was *fierce*.'

'Er, are you sure it was him?' Börkur finally found his voice, while keeping his eyes trained on her breasts. 'He always wears the same jacket.'

Karl waited for confirmation of his suspicion that she had remembered wrong or misunderstood. Halli was so skint he had trouble scraping the money together for a cinema ticket let alone a new coat. Especially a *fierce* one. But Linda was adamant. 'Yeah. It was him. I asked what he paid for it because I want one like that. I was hoping it was on sale but no such luck. It was definitely him.'

Karl saw that there was no point pursuing this. 'If you see him, could you maybe let him know we're looking for him? Ask him to give Karl or Börkur a call.'

'Oof, I'll never remember that. But I'll try.' Linda folded her arms over her breasts, ruining Börkur's view. Frowning again, she leant backwards a little as if planning to retreat by degrees into her room. With her face in shadow it was easy to see how she might look passable by the dim lighting of a bar or club. 'Are you sure you're not here about money? I'm not helping any debt collectors.'

Karl couldn't help smiling. 'Do we look like debt collectors?' Their combined weight wouldn't add up to that of a single steroid troll. 'We're his mates. He'll be glad to hear we wanted to get hold of him. I promise.'

'OK.' She still wasn't entirely convinced. 'The thing is, I've seen this bloke hanging around outside his place a couple of times at least. He was waiting by the door and he didn't look like he was there for fun. I thought maybe he'd sent you two.'

'Did you talk to him at all?'

'God, no. He wasn't the type you'd say hello to.' Linda furrowed her brow and thought hard. 'He was wearing a baseball cap and kept his head down both times I came by so I couldn't see his face. But it was obvious he didn't want to chat.'

'Do you know if he got hold of Halli?'

'Nah, haven't a clue. I just went into my room and locked the door.'

Karl failed to extract any further information from her. They said goodbye and she closed her door without replying. They tried knocking on several other doors but no one opened, although they could hear movement inside three of the rooms. Going by Halli's description of the tenants, they were mostly either people who had fallen on hard times or foreign migrants who lived hand to mouth on irregular, badly paid cash-in-hand work. Presumably none were expecting a visit from anyone they wanted to see.

Karl had one last go at banging on Halli's door, so violently this time that the other doors in the corridor vibrated. Nothing happened. He tried the handle but of course it was locked. As he was about to leave his gaze fell on the worn doormat. A cloud of dust rose when he lifted it. Underneath was a key.

'Are you going to use it?' It was impossible to tell from

Börkur's expression whether he was in favour of this. 'Isn't that breaking in?'

Karl shrugged. 'We're not breaking anything. We've got a key. I'm just going to take a look inside and check he's not lying there injured or unconscious.'

'Unconscious? Why would he be injured or unconscious?' For the first time a flicker of anxiety crossed Börkur's face. He had only accompanied Karl in the first place because he lacked the initiative to refuse or come up with an alternative suggestion.

'How am I to know how he could have injured himself? I just want to check. To make sure.'

The room contained a bed, a small kitchen counter with an electric ring and cupboard, a wonky wardrobe with one door missing and a desk that was too large for the space. There was also a tiny bathroom containing a shower, sink and loo.

Halli had invited Karl round a couple of times so he was prepared for most of what he saw: the rubbish littering all the surfaces; old instant noodle packets, Coke cans and sweet wrappers lying around a small waste-paper bin where Halli had chucked them across the room and missed. The rumpled duvet hanging half off the bed. And next to the bed countless scrunched-up tissues and an open porn mag. Karl looked away, directing his attention instead at the desk that in contrast to the rest of the room was almost free from clutter. The only things on it were Halli's computer, some Coke cans and an empty popcorn bag. There were two dust-free rectangles beside the computer.

Börkur peered over Karl's shoulder. He seemed unmoved by what he saw. 'He's not here.'

'No, he's not here. Nor's his transceiver.'

'You what?' Börkur shoved Karl aside to get a better view. 'Hey, you're right. His gear's gone.' He took a step backwards. 'Could he have been robbed? I wouldn't put it past the types living in this building.'

Karl groaned silently. 'Of course he hasn't been robbed or they'd have taken his computer.' Though now that he came to look at it closely, he realised this wasn't necessarily the case. In place of the expensive computer that had been here last time he visited, there was an ancient machine with hardly enough memory to run the clunkiest game. Presumably this piece of junk had replaced the turbo equipment the police had confiscated. 'He must have sold his transceiver. That explains how he could afford a new coat. Maybe he did it so he could buy a new computer too.' After taking one last glance round the room, Karl shut the door.

Börkur gaped at him. 'Why didn't he tell us? He said the equipment was broken, didn't he? So he can't have sold it. Mine isn't working and I know I'd get nothing for it unless I had it repaired first, which would cost money.'

Karl replaced the key under the mat. 'He was lying. The radio was working. He's flogged it.'

'Why? Like we'd give a shit?'

'Search me.' In fact, Karl had his suspicions. One of the reasons Halli had kept quiet about it might be that the disappearance of his equipment was linked to the genesis of the numbers station. Had he been behind it all along? Alone or in collusion with somebody else? And, if so, who?

He and Börkur left the building, none the wiser about what had become of Halli. In a final attempt to account for his disappearance, they stood staring stupidly at his bike, clueless as to what information it could be concealing.

Eventually, disappointed, they went back outside into the icy grip of winter.

It was warm in the café and the air was fragrant with cinnamon. It was a popular spot with hipsters, though at present they all seemed to be otherwise engaged. Most of the customers were uncool types, so Karl and Börkur fitted right in. Only one person stood out, a glamorous young woman who had finished her coffee a while ago and sat flicking through magazines or staring out of the window. Karl knew what that meant: she'd been stood up.

After their visit to Halli's place, Karl had felt the obvious course was to go back to his house but he couldn't face sitting there, acutely aware of the shortwave receiver in the basement. It exerted an uncomfortably strong pull on him; he alternated between wanting to smash it to pieces and take up his post to wait for the next message. He didn't know which impulse was the more powerful, so it was better to stay away altogether. The worst part was his suspicion that Halli was mixed up in the broadcasts. When you only had two friends, you expected them to stand by you, even if you were beginning to drift apart.

'They don't know anything.' After considerable effort he and Börkur had succeeded in tracking down Halli's parents. Unfortunately he had one of the most common patronymics in the country: Jónsson. But they recalled that his parents lived up north in the village of Dalvík and this had reduced the number of men called Jón who could be his father from five thousand to thirty-seven.

The third man Karl got hold of was able to tell him which Jón he wanted, based on Karl's description of Halli and the fact he had a sister with Down's syndrome.

Börkur sipped from the absurdly large cup. It left a white moustache on his upper lip. 'When did they last hear from him?'

'His mum said she spoke to him on the phone several days ago. He'd sounded upbeat so she didn't seem worried. Apparently his dad got a text from him the day before yesterday saying he was going to a holiday chalet with his mates and probably wouldn't be in touch till he got back.'

'When was he coming back?' Börkur licked off his moustache and stirred the froth into his coffee.

Karl hadn't asked this and could have kicked himself when he realised his omission. 'What does it matter? He hasn't gone to any holiday chalet. I mean, who are these mates he's supposed to have gone with? Can you name a single person he's friends with apart from us? Are we at a holiday chalet?'

'Chill out. I only asked.' Börkur adopted the petulant expression that didn't suit him. 'Maybe he's with Thórdur.'

Karl couldn't be bothered to point out that Thórdur hadn't acknowledged Halli either when they ran into him at the cinema. It was unthinkable that their former friend would have changed his mind, called Halli and invited him to the country with him and his girlfriend. Unthinkable. Even so, he felt a creeping sense of doubt and envy. What if it was true? He could understand that Thórdur wouldn't want to be lumbered with Börkur but what about him, Karl? If Halli had rekindled his friendship with Thórdur and his girlfriend, then Karl would be left with no one but Börkur. Perhaps they'd invite Börkur into their circle too and Karl would be all alone in the world. Depressed, he turned his cup round and round on its saucer. 'Halli isn't at any holiday chalet.

Anyway, I doubt there's a single chalet in the country that doesn't have mobile reception.'

Börkur shrugged. 'There must be some hut in the middle of nowhere that doesn't have coverage. Maybe he's gone there. I mean, where's he supposed to be otherwise?' Suddenly he brightened up. 'We could always call the police.'

'I doubt that'd do any good. Not after their reaction when I rang about the shortwave broadcasts. They probably think I'm a nutter. If I call again, they'll decide I'm one for sure.'

'I could call. They don't know anything about me.'

Karl passed over his phone. As usual, Börkur had run out of credit. 'Go ahead. One, one, two.' While Börkur was making the call, Karl stared first at his cup, then at the other customers in the café. Most were around his and Börkur's age but few appeared to appreciate being surrounded by their mates. They pored over their phones, only paying attention to their companions when they came across a particularly funny or cool picture or comment. To give Börkur his due, at least he was never buried in his phone, but then there wouldn't have been much point since he never had any credit. Karl's spirits rose a little and his mood had almost returned to normal when Börkur said thanks and hung up.

'That was a disaster.' Börkur handed the phone back to Karl. 'They didn't think I was the right person to notify them. I bet his parents would've had more luck. But even if they did call, apparently it's too soon after he went missing for the cops to take any action. It would be different if he was a kid or ill in some way.'

Karl became aware of a nagging pain in his head. 'His parents won't call. Not straight away. They obviously don't have a clue how unlikely it is for him to be invited to a holiday chalet. I couldn't bring myself to tell his mum. If they're kidding themselves that he's got loads of friends here in Reykjavík I'm not going to be the one to disillusion them.'

'Maybe it was relatives who invited him. Or old friends from up north. He could have mates from there that we don't know about.'

Karl had to admit that it was possible Halli had a life outside their small circle. Just because he himself had virtually no cousins his own age, that didn't mean other families were the same. That was a good point about old friends from Dalvík too. It was a pity Börkur hadn't come out with that before Karl rang his parents, or he could have pumped Halli's mum for the names of his old friends and spoken to them himself. He considered phoning back but decided it was a bad idea. If Halli didn't get in touch, he needed to be able to call his parents again and urge them to contact the police, so it was essential not to give them the impression he was weird or paranoid. Karl had to accept that for the moment there was nothing more he or Börkur could do.

Nothing but go home and sit in front of the shortwave receiver and wait for the next broadcast. The suspicion crept up on him that now he had the key to the code the messages would become darker. Instead of walking around feeling triumphant at his ingenuity, his accidental discovery of the solution had only increased his misery. It forced him to acknowledge that the messages were intended for him. First his ID number, then the link to chemistry, his subject. Though he couldn't be entirely sure, he doubted it would have struck him at all if he'd skived off his lecture this morning. It had been the slide about the chemical element erbium that had provided the light-bulb moment. Erbium, atomic number sixty-eight, symbol Er.

It hadn't taken him long to read today's message once he had worked that out. For every atomic number he simply had to find the relevant chemical symbol from the periodic table.

74, 1, 68, 99, 1, 13, 3.

W, H, Er, Es, H, Al, Li – Where's Halli?

The earlier broadcasts were also decipherable if they were converted into chemical symbols, and this banished any lingering doubts that he had found the key.

75, 23, 63–92, 7, 32, 14 reversed, 16, 74, 63–92, 52 reversed: Re, V, Eu–U, N, Ge, Si reversed, S, W, Eu–U, Te reversed – Revenge is sweet.

9, 92, 6, 19, 39, 8, 92:

F, U, C, K, Y, O, U – Fuck you.

70–5, 8, 92, 16, 65–5, 8, 71–92, 99–16, 87, 8, 25–7, 42–8, 99–16:

Yb–B, O, U, S, Tb–B, O, Lu–U, Es–S, Fr, O, Mn–N, Mo–O, Es–S – You stole from me.

But was he any better off for this knowledge? The messages didn't make sense. What had he stolen? Nothing. The only thing he had ever ripped off in his life were downloads. It was inconceivable that someone would have gone to all this trouble over a few downloads. Then again, Halli must be mixed up in it somehow. Could the broadcasts be in revenge for his arrest? Was he under the impression that Karl had grassed him up? Nothing could be further from the truth. He'd had absolutely nothing to do with it.

And hadn't listening to an incomprehensible string of numbers been preferable to a message he understood but would rather not hear? What could he expect next? On the one hand, he was itching to find out; on the other, he was desperate for the broadcasts to stop. Of course, the means were available to him; all he had to do was switch off the radio if he didn't want to hear them. And he didn't, yet part of him did.

Karl stood up. He couldn't hang around here for ever. He would have to go home eventually, so better get it over with. 'Come on. I'm going home to listen to the radio. I want to know if there's a new message.' He was surprised by the confident ring to his voice. It was pure bluff.

Chapter 30

The pizza had fused to the cardboard box. Karl tried to pick off the melted cheese stuck to the bottom but all he got for his pains were greasy fingers that now also stank of pepperoni. The slice refused to budge without taking a layer of cardboard with it. Frustrated, he watched Börkur shovel a piece into his mouth, chomping and spitting out bits of cardboard before he swallowed. Karl gave up trying to prise the pizza loose. He had satisfied the worst of his hunger; he was just being greedy. Instead he drained his Coke and occupied himself with crushing the can against the edge of the table.

They had ordered pizza when their hunger began to bite and they were fed up with hanging around in the basement, waiting for the numbers station to come to life. It remained stubbornly silent. Perhaps the Post and Telecom Administration had traced the broadcast and closed it down. Karl very much doubted that the broadcaster had applied for a licence, but the sporadic nature of the transmissions and their short duration would have made them hard to pinpoint. Unless they had begun long before he started hearing them. Whatever the reason, Karl felt relieved, yet in spite of everything some part of him missed them. Just a little. It wasn't really loss so much as the sense of a void in his life now that this strange adventure seemed to be coming to an end. When it did, he would go back to being an ordinary, dull person who nobody cared about. Troubling though the broadcasts had been, they had at least made him feel important on some level; given his life a purpose that now seemed to have evaporated – if the station really had been silenced for good.

Börkur took another mouthful and had only just started to chew when suddenly he spluttered as though he had just had a revelation. 'Hey!'

Karl was treated to a sight of half-masticated pizza that he could happily have done without.

'I brought you the phone.' Börkur stood up, wiped most of the grease off his fingers onto his trousers, then darted out into the hall. He reappeared looking triumphant with the mobile in his hand, banged it down on the table and helped himself to another slice, untroubled by the cardboard that came with it.

Karl turned the phone over in his hands. He had only had a quick glimpse of it in the car the evening Börkur found it but it looked no more familiar now in the bright light of the kitchen. The pink case, covered in crystals, proved beyond doubt that it belonged to a woman or girl. 'This thing isn't cheap.'

'You can say that again.' Having finally eaten his fill, Börkur leant back with a contented face. The tomato sauce at the corners of his mouth looked unsettlingly like blood, as if he'd bitten unawares into a piece of glass. 'Maybe it belongs to some rich bitch who's bought herself a new one because she can't be arsed to look for it. Typical.'

Börkur had a peculiar attitude to the rich – inherited from his parents, Karl suspected. On the rare occasions when wealthy people cropped up in their conversations he would blurt out sentiments like this that had little relevance to anything. As a rule Karl couldn't be bothered to contradict him; after all, he didn't exactly feel driven to defend those who were better off than him. 'Yeah, maybe. Though I still reckon she'd be pleased to get it back. There's bound to be all kinds of stuff on it that can't be replaced. Photos and so on.'

Börkur snorted, then frowned and rubbed his nose. 'Is there a bad smell in here? Like something's burning?'

Karl sniffed. 'No.' He sniffed again. 'Hang on, you're right. Ugh. Is it burning or the smell of piss? It must be coming from outside.' He closed the kitchen window. 'Shit, a cat must have sprayed the wall or something. Gross.' He turned on the phone and the screen lit up. 'It's asking for a PIN.' Of course it was.

'Try one, two, three, four.'

Karl did, assuming no one would be idiotic enough to use such an obvious combination. 'No good.' He tried several other combinations without success. 'This is pointless.' He put it down. 'I'll take a photo of it and advertise it on Facebook. If no one recognises it, I can take it to the police.' He had thirty-three friends on Facebook, most of whom were other chemistry students who had created a group to share homework and notes, which was the reason he had joined the site. Only time would tell whether he would acquire any other friends. But the chances were slim that any of these thirty-three would be able to solve the mystery of the phone.

He would have to dig up one of his mum's friends on Facebook and send her the photo to share. He didn't relish the prospect as it was bound to elicit a flood of questions about how he was doing. Still, he could spare a few minutes to invent answers that would paint a rosier picture of his life than the reality. He couldn't stand their fake solicitude. On the rare occasions that he bumped into one of them he could tell they were itching to go and ring the others and gossip about how wretched and peaky poor Karl had been looking.

Suddenly his own phone rang. Karl checked the screen, dreading a call from Arnar but hoping it might be Halli. The number that flashed up belonged to neither. 'Hello?'

'Good evening. Who am I speaking to, please?'

Karl didn't recognise the voice. 'My name's Karl. Have you got the wrong number?'

'No. My name's Ríkhardur and I'm calling from the police. I gather you rang us in connection with the murder investigation that's in progress.'

'Yes. That's right.' Karl mouthed the word 'police' and Börkur seemed to cotton on, though you never could tell: he was notoriously slow on the uptake. 'Do you want me to come in and give a statement?'

'No, no need for that. Let's start by establishing what it is that you feel we ought to know.' The man's delivery was oddly robotic, reminding Karl of the readers on the numbers stations. Every syllable was given equal weight. If the man ever quit the police he could get a job as the speaking clock. 'I understand the radio has been talking to you.' The man's voice betrayed no hint of contempt or incredulity. A dry delivery had its advantages. When Karl had originally contacted the police, the person he'd spoken to had found it hard to suppress his laughter.

'Where do you want me to begin?' Karl tried to order the events into a coherent narrative in his head but it was no good; he didn't need to put it into words to realise how absurd it sounded.

'At the beginning, if you would.'

'Well. I own a shortwave radio receiver and I came across an Icelandic numbers station.'

'Numbers station?'

'A station broadcasting series of numbers. In code. For spies and smugglers mainly.'

'I see. Someone's spying on you, are they?'

'No. Not on me. They can be broadcast between continents. They originate abroad. They're nothing to do with me.'

'Didn't you say it was Icelandic?'

'Yes. This one is. Which is really unusual. That was where I heard them read out the ID number of the woman who I saw on the news was murdered last week. And my ID number too. That's how I worked it out.'

'So this Icelandic station is spying on you.'

'No.' Karl paused and made an effort to collect himself. If he blew his top the man would lose interest and ring off. The conversation was going badly enough as it was. 'Nobody's spying on anyone.'

'Why have a spy station then?'

Karl took a deep breath. 'Look, I'm not crazy. It's a method of communicating messages so they can't be traced. It's more secure than phone calls or e-mails.'

'Have I understood you correctly that you're talking about a radio broadcast?'

'Not just one. Lots. On shortwave.'

'In what way are radio broadcasts more secure than phone calls? Surely anyone can listen in? Or are you the only person who can hear them?'

The man kept forcing him into a corner. 'No, of course I'm not the only one who can hear them. Anyone with a shortwave radio can tune in to these stations. What makes them secure is that the broadcasts are unintelligible.' Karl didn't need Börkur's look of horror to tell him he was making a hash of this. Unless his friend's expression was a reaction to the unpleasant smell that still lingered, despite the closed window. 'I'm telling you, I heard this woman Elísa Bjarnadóttir's ID number read out, then mine, then the ID of a woman called Ástrós. I can't remember her patronymic but I could dig it out.' He omitted to mention Jóhanna Hákonardóttir as that information belonged to him alone. If the police started investigating her link to the affair, there was a risk the information would get back to Arnar. On no account must that be allowed to happen. Karl had even taken the precaution of tearing the form with her name on it to shreds and throwing it away in a dustbin on the university campus. Along with the birth certificate. He didn't need it to remember the names. However absurd it was, he wanted to ensure that Arnar wouldn't find anything if he turned up out of the blue. He was perfectly capable of jetting over to Iceland to comb the dump for the papers Karl had thrown out.

'Ástrós?' At long last the voice at the other end betrayed a hint of interest. In the background Karl could hear a crescendo of noise and excited voices as if something was happening at the police station. The man paused, then asked Karl to wait a moment. The noise cut out. Karl closed his eyes and tipped his head back. He should never have called the cops. It would take a much cleverer person than him to explain the situation in a way that would make them take it seriously. Perhaps he should have hired a PR person. The man came back on the phone. 'Where are you, Karl?'

'Where? At home.' The man read out his address and asked

if the information was correct. Karl said it was, then heard the man put his hand over the receiver again. 'Is something wrong?'

The hand was removed and a sound of rustling and quickened breathing followed. 'No, not at all. Carry on. You were talking about ID numbers.'

'It's not just ID numbers. It's messages too, in a code that I've managed to break.' He couldn't keep the note of pride out of his voice. There weren't many who could boast of having solved such a puzzle.

Karl's pleasure proved short lived, however. When the police officer spoke again it was in a patronising voice, as though he were talking to a child. 'You're good at that, are you? At solving puzzles, I mean?'

Aware he was making a complete mess of this, Karl felt a rising tide of panic. Not that he'd ever had the upper hand in the conversation. 'No, I'm not good at them. It was a coincidence. I'm studying chemistry and that's how I worked it out. It was the periodic table.'

'Right, I see. So you used chemistry to break the code. That was clever.'

'You don't believe a word I'm saying, do you?'

'What I believe is irrelevant. My job is to write down what you say and try to understand it. There's no rush, just take your time and if you feel I've misunderstood, tell me.'

Karl sat up and rubbed his eyes. It occurred to him to tell the man the whole thing had been a big mistake. Or a prank. Would that make them wipe it from their records or would he be prosecuted for obstructing a murder inquiry? He could share a cell with Halli when he was sentenced. The pizza was sitting like a stone in his stomach and he couldn't rid his nostrils of the stench from outside. 'I'm trying to explain how it happened.' He opened his eyes and stared at Börkur. 'Anyway, I wasn't the only one to hear it. My friend was with me on two occasions. He can confirm that it really happened.'

At last he seemed to have wrong-footed the man. He wasn't as quick to reply this time. 'I see. May I ask if you were under the influence of alcohol or drugs when this happened?'

'No, we weren't.' No way was he going to admit that they'd shared a spliff. That had nothing to do with it; he had often listened to the broadcasts while his head was clear. Börkur hadn't, though. His anxiety increased again. Would Börkur tell them the truth if he was questioned? The thought wasn't encouraging. Börkur would begin well but soon unravel under interrogation. But did they interrogate ordinary witnesses? Surely not. It wasn't as if either of them was suspected of criminal activity. He corrected himself. Börkur wouldn't be suspected, only him. 'Do you want us to come down to the station? Both of us? It would be easier to explain face to face.'

'No, that won't be necessary at this stage. Just continue with your explanation, then we can make a decision about how to proceed. It's not up to me to invite you in for questioning. Others will take that decision, if necessary.'

The conversation continued along the same lines, with Karl explaining and the man querying every sentence. Karl got the discomfiting impression that the man was deliberately spinning out the call, as though he had been given orders to speak to him for a certain length of time. But why? Perhaps the call was being used for training purposes. But the man sounded too authoritative to be a new recruit.

By the time the doorbell rang, his phone was bleeping to warn that the battery was low.

'I've got to go. My phone's nearly out of juice and there's someone at the door. I don't think I have anything more to say anyway.'

'Oh, we'll see about that.'

Karl was disconcerted by the sudden note of mockery in the hitherto dispassionate voice. But before he could respond, the man had hung up.

'God, that was . . .'

Leaving Börkur groping for the right word, Karl went to the door. He never got a chance to hear what his friend was going to say. The men standing outside shoved some form of ID at him that he couldn't see to read.

'Karl Pétursson, we're arresting you on suspicion of being involved in the murders of Elísa Bjarnadóttir and Ástrós Einarsdóttir—'

'What?' Karl stumbled backwards and the men barged in after him holding their ID badges aloft like Catholic priests brandishing crucifixes against the possessed. This couldn't be happening.

To make matters worse he had developed a crippling headache.

Chapter 31

Thursday

The atmosphere at the station was like in an American cop show. All that was needed to complete the picture was a couple of hookers in handcuffs.

Unable to contain their euphoria, members of the investigation team were sitting around on their colleagues' desks with mugs of coffee, loudly swapping stories about their own part in solving the case. Some of their claims were true, others exaggerations or outright lies. People slapped one another matily on the shoulder, roared with laughter and knocked back their coffee as if it were beer.

Huldar surveyed the scene, wondering if the celebratory atmosphere was the same at other workplaces on the successful completion of a major project. Probably, though the situation wasn't really comparable. In conventional offices people could be unrestrainedly jubilant in the happy knowledge that their future was assured, payment was secure, the hard work lay behind them. But in a murder inquiry, the apprehension of the culprit didn't put the world to rights again. While the affair would gradually fade from the memories of the investigation team, the witnesses and lawyers, life would never be the same for the victim's next of kin or the perpetrator's family – and least of all for the perpetrator. Huldar felt no desire to join in with the general rejoicing.

He watched Ríkhardur and Erla talking to a young man who had taken part in the search of the area around Freyja's building. They were both smiling. It was a long time since he had seen Ríkhardur look genuinely happy. He hoped it wasn't only due to the outcome of the inquiry but a sign that he was also coming to terms with his divorce and would now be able to move on. But Huldar knew he was being over-optimistic; the guy was simply enjoying the moment.

After all, he was the hero of the hour.

While Huldar and the others had been engaged in a wild-goose chase in the streets and gardens around Grandi, there had been a breakthrough in the case. Elísa's phone had been switched on and they had managed to trace it. Ríkhardur, overhearing the discussion in the background, had realised that the location tallied with the address of the man he was talking to on the phone. With typical efficiency, he had already noted down the speaker's details. When the man mentioned not only Ástrós, whose name had yet to be released to the press, but a secret code as well, Ríkhardur had put two and two together, and successfully kept the guy talking while he alerted his colleagues. The suspect had still been standing there, phone in hand, when the arresting officers knocked on his door.

There was no nicotine left in his gum. Huldar spat it into a green bin. One lump more or less would hardly derail the recycling process. He headed over to Ríkhardur and Erla; it was essential to show the team that he wasn't resentful or disappointed that the honour of solving the case hadn't been his.

Although he had been informed at once that Elísa's phone had been traced, he hadn't reached the scene until after Karl Pétursson's arrest. By then the suspect was sitting open-mouthed in the back of a police car, his friend Börkur Thórdarson in another. Huldar's first task had been to order the officers to move one of the cars so the two men couldn't communicate by sign language through the closed windows. In the event, their statements had proved so inconsistent that it was clear they couldn't have agreed on a story. Huldar had taken charge at this point, discovered the mutilated body in the outhouse, then organised a systematic search of the property, which had been completed early this morning.

In contrast to the meticulous care with which Karl had covered his tracks during the murders of Elísa and Ástrós, he had accumulated a hoard of compromising evidence in his house, which appeared to eliminate all doubt that he was the culprit. It was remarkable to find such a treasure trove of rock-solid evidence; so remarkable, in fact, that it bothered Huldar. He reminded himself that the young man had obviously been in the middle of emptying his home of incriminating material; he had already removed most of the loose furnishings, though it wasn't at all clear why he thought this necessary, especially in view of what he had failed to throw away. Perhaps he was one of those killers who delighted in taking trophies from his victims. His motives would no doubt become clearer when he and his friend Börkur were questioned.

They had both been left to kick their heels in the cells overnight and Huldar's first action that morning had been to check on them.

Karl had been sitting rigidly staring at the door, in such a state of shock that he neither rose to his feet nor showed any other reaction when their eyes met through the hatch. He had been clutching at his head like a man in agony, as if his brain were about to explode.

His friend Börkur had been lying down, apparently asleep.

Huldar decided that as soon as he got a chance he would ask Freyja which behaviour was the more indicative of a clean conscience. It would give him the excuse he needed to call her, though he didn't really require anyone to tell him that the sleeping man more obviously demonstrated the calm of innocence.

'So. Did you two sleep well?' Huldar himself had only managed to grab three hours. He had crashed out the moment his head hit the pillow and enjoyed a dreamless sleep. It wasn't enough to make a dent in the accumulated exhaustion of the last week, but in spite of that he felt like a new man.

'Hell, yeah.' Erla turned to him. 'Any more news? What did the search of the property throw up?'

'What didn't it throw up? We found the phone, a bracelet that has been identified as belonging to Ástrós, rough drafts of the cryptic messages, remnants of the papers he'd cut the letters out of, a pair of Elísa's knickers, a black motorcycle helmet, a pair of gloves we believe were used for both murders, and several rolls of duct tape. Unused. Which might indicate that he was planning more attacks.'

The tape, helmet and gloves had all been found beside the body in the outhouse. The newspapers had been lying in the dustbin, though the bin appeared to have been emptied in the time since the notes were found at the victims' homes. This was a little odd, given that one would have expected the suspect to have disposed of the incriminating papers as soon as possible. But then what constituted normal or rational behaviour for a man like that? The bracelet and pages containing the rough drafts of the messages had been found in the basement, and the knickers in his bedroom along with a roll of kitchen towels, several of which had been used. Clearly the man had masturbated over them. So it seemed that the murders had been sexually motivated after all. In a grossly perverted way.

'What about the body in the shed?' Erla made a face. 'Is it true the victim was killed with a soldering iron?'

Three hours' sleep had not given Huldar the energy to elaborate on the gruesome details. He still had a bad taste in his mouth from the stench of urine, excrement and fried brains in the hot, enclosed outhouse. The smell had been noticeable even before they opened the door, but once they went inside it had been almost unbearable. 'Yes, it's true.' He left it at that, making it clear that he had nothing further to say on the subject.

'Do we know why the fuck he killed the guy? And the two women?' Erla stole a glance at Ríkhardur that Huldar could have sworn was flirtatious. It all looked very promising but he made an effort not to grin too broadly. He had to be careful not to come across like an idiot; a smile was a singularly inappropriate reaction to the subject under discussion.

'No. Hopefully today's interviews will shed some light on that. I'd thought of asking you to accompany me, Ríkhardur.'

Ríkhardur's smile grew even broader; the man obviously couldn't care less if he appeared crazy. He looked like his old self again; impeccable, not a hair out of place, the creases in his trousers perfectly straight. With that smile he could have passed for a mannequin in a shop window. 'Count me in. What time?'

'As soon as the lawyer shows up.'

Karl had chosen a lawyer from a list that had been shoved under his nose before he was taken to the cells yesterday evening. He had asked no questions, merely pointed to a name at random. He had vomited on his way to the cells. When asked if he had taken some drug he had denied it with a croak and pointed at his head. He had vomited again in his cell when they took a blood sample. Again he had gestured to his head. The nurse had shrugged and said his temperature and blood pressure were normal; it was probably just stress.

'Did he pick a good one?' For once Erla didn't seem affronted that Ríkhardur had been favoured. He had earned it, so there was no reason for resentment.

'Yes, for what it's worth. Frankly, his problems are so insurmountable that it doesn't really matter who his counsel is.'

Huldar told Ríkhardur that he would give him a nudge when it was time to head downstairs, and returned to his office. This brief exchange would have to do as a sign to his team that there were no sour grapes on his part.

Before they began interrogating Karl, he had two calls to make: one to Freyja, one to Karlotta. The latter would be difficult, but if he was to put the past behind him, as Ríkhardur seemed to be doing, he had to get it over with. And never look back. He'd learnt his lesson. Never again, however wasted he was, would he mess around with a married woman, let alone the wife of a colleague.

His old chair welcomed him into its warm embrace; he'd brought it with him when he left the open-plan office on his promotion. The other furnishings were less familiar: the desk, the new computer and the bare walls on which he hadn't yet dared to hang any pictures in case he screwed up the investigation. This would be the ideal time to impose his personality on the space, since he was unlikely to be thrown out on his arse now. It was a pity he didn't know what to put up; a heavy metal poster, maybe?

Freyja answered on the third ring. Her manner was a lot friendlier than it had been yesterday evening when he'd knocked on her door to say goodbye and inform her that they had made an arrest. He had asked her to keep Margrét for the night, until the picture was clearer. There was no time to make alternative arrangements. The police would continue the hunt for the man Margrét thought she had seen, but Huldar himself had to leave. It seemed highly unlikely that the man in the garden was connected to the murders but two officers would remain on guard duty outside the building just in case.

She had said goodbye to him at the door with a frozen smile, nodding her head repeatedly like one of those stupid dogs people put on their dashboards. At first he thought she was hiding something behind her back, but then he caught sight of the loose block of parquet and realised what was going on. Obviously she had attempted to repair it herself to prevent him from tinkering with it if he followed through with his threat to stay the night. She must be holding a hammer behind her back. Although she didn't want his help, clearly she could have done with it: the parquet block looked even looser than before.

'I just wanted to let you know that they're coming to collect Margrét. You're off the hook.'

'Has the murderer been caught?'

'It looks like it.'

'Can I tell her?'

'No, I'd wait a bit. We still need to question the suspect so you'd better not, just in case he turns out to be innocent.'

'Hasn't he confessed?'

'No. We haven't interviewed him yet. But there's so much evidence stacked up against him that it's almost a formality.' Huldar pulled over his mouse and woke up his monitor. 'Could you do me a favour?'

'That depends.'

'Could you go onto Facebook and open Arnar Pétursson's page?'

'Who's he?'

'The suspect's brother.' Huldar opened the page himself. 'Try showing Margrét a picture of him; see if he looks at all familiar to her.' Freyja didn't reply, so he continued. 'I'll take the blame if it confuses her. Her testimony isn't as important as it was. We've got a pile of evidence, so it may be possible to spare her the necessity of testifying at all. We've got some good recordings of her too. If she's already identified the man, there's less likelihood that the defence counsel will want to haul her into the witness box. He'll want to steer clear of her altogether.'

'OK. On your head be it. Though I doubt it'll harm Margrét.'

While Freyja was fetching the little girl, he searched for a photo of Karl. The albums that Huldar had examined last night on Karl's Facebook page were empty. His profile picture was a cartoon character with headphones and a microphone, so that wasn't much help. His brother's page wasn't much more informative, though at least there were a few photos, mainly of himself and his wife. But there was one of both brothers, with Arnar's wife between them. That was in the album labelled *Iceland summer 2014*, so the picture was suitably recent. Karl looked the picture of misery. Huldar shook his head. His brother and sister-in-law didn't look much more cheerful. There was something unsettlingly familiar about the brother but Huldar couldn't work out where he had seen him before.

'I'm back.' The rattle of a keyboard. 'Which photo do you want us to look at?'

Huldar described it, then listened to what passed between Freyja and Margrét. She spoke soothingly to the girl, telling her she wanted to show her a photo of a man who might be the person Margrét had seen in her garden. But that didn't necessarily mean he was the man who had hurt her mummy. Freyja stopped talking and there was the sound of a mouse clicking. Huldar pressed the phone to his ear. For a long time he could hear nothing, but when the silence was finally broken it was Margrét who spoke. 'I don't know. I think it's him. It's him. I think. He's very like him. Though he hasn't got a hood on.'

Then Freyja took over, thanking Margrét and saying she could go to the kitchen and help herself to biscuits.

'Thanks. Not quite as positive as I'd been hoping for, but it'll do for now.'

'Well, it's not like she sat down to dinner with him. She saw the man out of the window, mostly in the evening or at night.'

'I know. It was fine. Thanks very much.'

'Who is the man anyway?'

'Hardly more than a boy. A student at the university.'

'Why did he do it?'

'We don't know. Yet.' Huldar had the feeling something remained unsaid but couldn't think what. Freyja had nothing to add, so he said he'd talk to her later and rang off. He couldn't tell from her response how she felt about this.

It was no problem selecting Karlotta's number from his contacts list but much harder actually to press the button to call her. Finger in the air, he looked out through the glass wall of his office to where Ríkhardur was still standing talking to Erla and the young detective. Two other people had joined the group. Evidently they all wanted to hear Ríkhardur's story first hand. What would he do if Ríkhardur tore himself away from the others and barged in on him in the middle of the phone call? Hang up? Of course. He would have time to say goodbye and end the call. Karlotta of all people would understand that he didn't want to talk to her under her soon-to-be-ex husband's nose.

Taking a deep breath, he pushed the button. If he didn't call her now, it would have to wait until tomorrow. It was nearly 9 a.m. and he wanted to speak to her before she became too busy but when she didn't have unlimited time to chat. He'd give it six rings, then hang up.

Karlotta answered almost immediately. Behind her he could hear activity and people talking, just as he had planned. 'Hi, Karlotta. It's Huldar.'

'Oh . . . hang on a minute. I'm just going to move.' He heard the sound of footsteps, the click, click, click of her inevitable high heels. Then a door closed and she spoke again. 'Sorry about that. Thanks for calling back. I didn't want to talk to you with other people around.'

'No. I'm alone too.' He was staring directly at Ríkhardur,

who showed no sign of budging. 'I don't know how long I'll be left in peace, so we'd better be quick.'

'Yes, same here. I'm expecting a client in ten minutes.'

Huldar cursed himself for not having waited another five. He couldn't keep up a conversation with her for ten whole minutes. 'Look, I know I should have rung you ages ago. I owe you an apology for . . . you know. I've no excuse except that I was totally wasted. Which is no excuse, of course. When I phoned after Ríkhardur told me about the divorce I didn't have the wits to say it. At the time I just wanted to know if you'd told him anything. Totally selfish of me. So I'm sorry about that as well. But mainly for dragging you down to that level in the first place.'

'No need for you to say sorry. I'm the one who should be apologising.'

'You?'

'Yes. Are you surprised? What on earth did you think? That I had no will of my own?' She sounded genuinely astonished. 'That I was helpless in the face of your charms?'

'No.' Huldar didn't let himself take offence. He had asked for it, and worse. 'Of course I didn't think that. I wanted to apologise to you because I can't apologise to the person who really deserves it. You know who I mean.' Huldar watched Ríkhardur enjoying himself, surrounded by his colleagues. He didn't throw back his head with roars of laughter or wave his arms about or show any other normal signs of elation. Only someone who knew him well would be able to tell that he was over the moon. 'I wish I could, but for his sake it's better he doesn't find out.' He paused, praying she would agree. What if she got a bee in her bonnet about wanting to make a clean breast of things? Had he been too eager with his regrets and apologies?

Apparently not. Karlotta was an intelligent woman.

'For Christ's sake, don't say anything to him. He's got enough on his plate.'

'Is there any chance of you two getting back together?'

'No.' Karlotta took a deep breath. 'No.'

'He misses you.'

'Don't.'

'Sorry. It's none of my business.'

'Look,' she continued, 'I'd better go ahead and say what I meant to say when I finally plucked up the courage to call.' Huldar was silent, so she carried on: 'Did Ríkhardur tell you about our problems having children?'

'A little.'

'The whole thing was a tragedy from beginning to end. I just didn't seem to be able to carry a child to full term. Ríkhardur found it terribly hard to face up to the fact that we weren't perfect. Then I got the idea of trying another way.'

'Another way?'

'Yes. Getting pregnant by another man. I became obsessed with the idea that it was his fault. He was being stubborn about going for tests, refusing to accept that anything could be wrong. The evening I bumped into you I was on the lookout for a likely candidate. At first I tried to find a man who looked like Ríkhardur but by the time I'd trawled a few bars and downed a few drinks I'd forgotten about that. I just couldn't bring myself to do it with a complete stranger. The thought disgusted me. I was drinking for Dutch courage. Then I spotted you.'

'Me? You went into the toilets with me just to get pregnant? Because I wasn't a total stranger?'

'Yes.' Her voice suddenly held a quality that reminded him

of Ríkhardur. Emotionally repressed, that was it. 'That's why I wanted to apologise. I should never have done it, seeing as you two are friends. I was horrified next day when I realised what I'd done. Then, when I turned out to be pregnant, it was an odd feeling. Both good and bad. Good because if the child was yours, then Ríkhardur and I would have more chance of becoming parents; bad because I was terrified the child would look like you or we'd be found out. And also because the child might be Ríkhardur's after all, and I wouldn't be able to undo what I'd done.' She paused for breath, then went on: 'Anyway, you know how it ended. There was no child that time either.'

'Why are you telling me this? It's none of my business. You're just making matters worse.' Huldar closed his eyes. His rage subsided a little and, opening them again, he resumed more calmly. 'Karlotta, what's done is done. It's over. Your fault, my fault – it doesn't matter.' He saw Ríkhardur crane his head round the group and look over at him. Their eyes met and his colleague smiled more warmly than Huldar deserved. He faked an answering smile. 'Look, I've got to dash. Thanks for telling me. In spite of everything, it's good to know. I feel slightly less of a shit than I did.'

Chapter 32

Millimetre by millimetre, almost imperceptibly, the walls of the small interview room were closing in on the four men. Karl was the only one who seemed to notice. But then the room was more or less empty, so there was nothing to use as a reference point. The whitewashed walls were bare, the table and chairs plain and functional; a single light hung over the centre of the table.

He avoided looking up because the glare made his headache worse and he was afraid of throwing up again. Not that he had anything left in his stomach. He had puked up yesterday evening's pizza and he'd been feeling too sick to eat this morning's unappetising breakfast. The tray had been laid on the floor of his cell: cold porridge in a disposable plastic carton, a glass of water, two yellowing slices of apple and a watery, yellow juice of unknown origin. When he tried to drink it he had started retching and had to gulp down the lukewarm water on which a black hair had been floating. The hair had got stuck in his throat, and this made him decline the water that one of the policemen kept pushing towards him now, with increasing concern.

'Have some water. You'll be ill if you don't drink.'

Karl's lawyer answered on his behalf, scrupulously following his client's orders in everything. 'He doesn't want any water. He's already said so. If he changes his mind, no doubt he'll have some.'

Karl kept his eyes facing straight ahead as he had for the last hour, to save the necessity of moving his head for the questions that really mattered. He only spoke when it was unavoidable. The problem was, he could no longer sense what did or didn't matter.

All he could really think about was the agony in his head.

Slowly turning it now, he saw that all three men were staring at him: the balding, middle-aged lawyer at his side, who looked at least eight months pregnant, and the two policemen who sat facing them. If he hadn't known better he would have assumed that one of the cops was a lawyer and his lawyer was a cop. The officer in question was wearing the smarter suit and behaved in a manner that Karl judged more fitting for a solicitor; he wasn't constantly leaning forward on one elbow or blowing his nose after every important question like his own counsel. But few would have mistaken the other cop for a lawyer; his hair was too long and he was constantly chewing gum.

'Are you all right, Karl?' The cop slid the gum into his cheek. 'Are you ill?' Karl moved his head gingerly to the right and then to the left. The cop turned to the solicitor. 'Is he feverish?'

'How am I supposed to know? He says he's OK.'

The cop with the hair leant forward and felt Karl's forehead. Karl didn't move; he didn't have the energy, nor did he care. 'His temperature seems normal. Are you on something, Karl?'

Karl neither replied nor moved his head. He had already answered this several times. Always in the same way: no.

'We found dope at your house. Are you on something stronger? Something you made in the chemistry lab, maybe?'

Karl had answered this more than once as well: no.

The cop frowned and addressed the lawyer. 'We'll take a

short break. You can go over matters with your client in the meantime, but I'm going to call in a nurse. There's something wrong with the boy.' He rose to his feet. 'Unless he's a bloody good actor.'

Karl watched as he and the well-dressed cop left the room.

'There's no point pretending to be ill. It won't help. If you don't want to answer their questions, there's not a lot they can do about it.' The lawyer slapped the table with the flat of his hand. 'Though judging by the answers you gave at the beginning, I can understand if you'd rather stay mum. It's not looking good. Not looking good at all.'

The fog in Karl's head lifted slightly. 'I haven't killed anyone.'

'No, right.' The lawyer seemed to regard this as irrelevant. 'It's up to you how you want to play it. There's plenty of time to reconsider later, but you should take into account that they seem to have incontrovertible evidence of your guilt.'

Karl managed to nod. He would listen, gather strength, and then answer. There was no hurry. They had applied to remand him in custody and according to the lawyer their application would almost certainly be granted. In the first instance they would hold him for two weeks. When Karl had asked whether he would be released afterwards or they would apply for an extension, the lawyer refused to discuss it, telling him to concentrate on his present predicament rather than worrying about what might happen. Karl decided to follow his advice; his present situation was bad enough.

'All right, son. I understand you're feeling bad; naturally, you're in shock. Let's go over this again. Stop me if I've got it wrong or you didn't explain it right or your answer was misunderstood. If you can provide a rational explanation for everything, they'll let you go. The police have no power to detain you if you can prove that they've arrested the wrong man. But things haven't been going too well so far. Sometimes it's better to say less rather than more.' The man fixed and held Karl's gaze. 'Let's start with the positives. They still haven't managed to prove that you had any connection to the two women, but it's another matter with the young man, your friend. Is there any risk they'll be able to link you to the women if they keep digging?'

Karl shook his head. The pain redoubled and for a while no thoughts could penetrate it; he had to concentrate all his energy on breathing. Eventually, it eased a little, but he still didn't feel up to pointing out that judging by the way the police twisted everything he said, they might well succeed in inventing some connection. The words were just too complicated to articulate.

The lawyer continued. 'Fine. That's good news. Though it's a pity about your friend.' He ran his eyes down the notes he had taken during the interview. 'You're quite sure that it's your soldering iron?' He raised his eyes to Karl who nodded faintly. 'I see. Not that it would have changed much if it wasn't, seeing as they found your prints on it.'

Karl contemplated his blue fingertips. His prints had been taken when he arrived at the police station yesterday evening, after which he had been photographed from the front and sides.

'And of course it's also bad that the victim was found on your property. You live alone in the house, so it's hard to see how a stranger could have used the premises without your knowledge, seeing as there's no sign the outhouse was broken into. It was locked, after all.' The lawyer fell silent and continued reading in silence. 'This bunch of keys you claim went missing; was the key to the outhouse on it, by any chance?'

Karl nodded. He hadn't had the presence of mind to mention this when the police asked him about the outhouse. It wasn't the headache that had made it difficult to answer but the thought of Halli, trussed up in there, only a few metres away from him; Halli with a soldering iron in his ear – Karl's soldering iron.

'Why didn't you say so?' The lawyer didn't seem to care whether he replied. 'Well, that's good to know, anyway. And your friend Börkur will confirm that the bunch of keys had gone missing?'

Karl nodded, though with little confidence. You never knew with Börkur. If the police could muddle Karl that badly, they would be able to spin Börkur round in circles until he didn't know whether he was coming or going. Before it was over he would be confessing to every unsolved murder in the book. Or pinning them on Karl.

'Let's hope so. And that he can confirm that he heard the broadcast, as you claim. That's absolutely vital. Apart from him, I don't suppose anyone else will have heard it. Your other friend didn't live to tell the tale, of course.'

Karl forced himself to speak. He was growing numb; he could hardly feel one of his arms. 'Maybe. Maybe other radio hams. They've got a club. You can ask them.' Why hadn't he gone to the meeting and told them about it? Then they'd have tuned into the station to listen. They were unlikely to have stumbled across it on their own account since none of them were interested in numbers stations and they tended not to explore the relevant shortwave frequencies.

'Yes. At any rate I drew the police's attention to that.' The lawyer made a note, then scratched his neck. 'Since you claim you're innocent, do you have any theories about who could have killed these people?'

Naturally, Karl had been racking his brain about this all night but he hadn't come to any conclusions. It was impossible to conceive of who could have wanted to harm Halli and the women in this way. And himself too. 'It occurred to me it might have something to do with illegal downloads. Halli was arrested in a police raid and all I could think of was that he might have squealed. Ratted on the person who was in charge of the downloads or something.' Or something. The theory sounded even dumber when spoken aloud than when he had turned it over in his own mind.

'I see. Not very plausible but who knows?' Again the lawyer jotted down some points, then smiled at Karl. 'See how much more progress we make when it's just the two of us?'

Karl tried to return his smile but only achieved a grimace, like a dog baring its teeth over a bone.

The man stopped smiling and resumed his questioning: 'You say you've never seen this helmet before, and since they didn't mention any fingerprints, I doubt they've found any.' He glanced at his notes, then back at Karl. 'One question. Do you happen to remember when you last saw your soldering iron? If what you say is right, then someone must have nicked it.'

'No.' Karl took a deep breath but the sour, stale air did nothing to alleviate the torment in his head. 'Maybe in the burglary. We were burgled. When Mum was still alive.'

'When was that?'

'Before Christmas. Around the middle of November. I don't remember exactly when.' Karl grabbed the table and sat up a little. 'I'll try and remember – just not now. The soldering iron could have disappeared then.'

'Good, good.' The lawyer jotted this down but when he looked up again his expression was no longer as optimistic. 'Is it possible that they'll find more fingerprints? At Ástrós Einarsdóttir's place, for example?'

'I've never been to her place. I don't know her.'

'No.' The man glanced at what he'd written. 'Yet her name was found on a piece of paper at your house. In your handwriting. Elísa Bjarnadóttir's name too.'

'I've explained that.' The words sounded as if they had travelled across a rough lava-field on their way up his throat. He looked at the glass of water, then reached for it and took the tiniest possible sip. It made him feel a bit better, so he took another, larger one. At this he felt sick again and put down the glass.

'So your only explanation for this is that you looked up their names after their ID numbers were read out on the radio?'

'Yes.'

'Then how do you explain that Elísa's neighbours saw your car driving past?' The man corrected himself. 'No, you were parked outside.' He blew out, looking concerned. 'It just doesn't sound plausible that you and your friends decided to see where she lived after the business with the ID numbers.'

'Börkur. Börkur can back me up.'

'Börkur, yes. He'd better have his story straight because you're relying on him to back you up on rather a lot of things.' The lawyer attempted to lighten the atmosphere. 'Still, could be worse. Sometimes people have no one at all to back them up. Though I have to say I've never come across such a bizarre case. It makes everything I previously thought odd look positively normal in comparison.'

Karl behaved as if he hadn't heard. Idle comments like this were a waste of time.

The man didn't seem to mind Karl's lack of response. 'We haven't discussed whether you've ever suffered from delusions.' He fixed Karl with a stare and waited.

'No, never.'

'Nothing in your childhood or maybe even recently that you might not have realised was a delusion – just thought was a bit strange?'

'No.'

'Nothing in connection with drugs that you didn't want to mention in front of the police?'

'No.'

'No one's interested in nailing you for drugs – this is far more serious than a trivial offence like that.' He gave Karl a searching look but Karl's expression didn't change. Any movement was beyond him now. The lawyer shrugged. 'What about your family history? Has anyone in your family suffered from delusions or paranoia? That could be to our advantage.'

'I don't know.'

'Nothing you remember?'

'I'm adopted. I've never met any of my relatives.'

The lawyer's eyes gleamed for the first time. 'What?!'

Karl didn't bother to repeat it; he needed to save his words for what mattered.

'So it's quite possible that someone in your family has suffered from hallucinations or violent behaviour associated with a mental illness? What about abuse or bad treatment you might have suffered as a child?'

'Dunno.'

'I'll have to find out.' The man's pleased expression vanished when he saw Karl's lack of enthusiasm for this plan. 'Can I tell you something, son?' He continued without waiting for an answer. 'People generally get sixteen years for murder in Iceland. For one murder. Conventional murder. But there's nothing to say they can't receive longer sentences – the penal code allows for the possibility of a life sentence. It's never happened – there's only been one instance of a harsher sentence than sixteen years and that was twenty. But the person who killed these three people could set a new precedent and receive the longest sentence in Icelandic history: life imprisonment.' He paused and looked Karl straight in the eye. 'Let's say we don't manage to prove your innocence. You're twenty-three. Icelandic men have a life expectancy just short of eighty. If you get life you could sit inside for more than half a century. That's more than twice the amount of time you've already lived. Whereas if you receive a conventional sentence you'll get sixteen years. You'd be out in ten and a half. That's forty years' difference. Forty years. Anything that could possibly generate sympathy for you would help – in the event you're found guilty.'

'I'm innocent.'

The lawyer ignored this. 'You're going to have to let me examine your family history. Do you know the names of your biological parents? It could save you forty years in prison.'

This argument was good enough for Karl. 'Gudrún María Gudjónsdóttir and Helgi Jónsson.' He had been thinking about his parents while he sat or lay in his cell, unable to sleep. Would they regret having put him up for adoption? Especially if they heard about the predicament he was in? He had begun to feel disappointed that he hadn't made the effort to find out more about his background and contact them.

There was no knowing when he'd next have access to a computer, and now that everything seemed to be falling apart around him only family members could be expected to stand by him. Though it would have been better to make contact with them before he was arrested; if he rang from prison they almost certainly wouldn't want anything to do with him.

He had no one. Absolutely no one at all.

Arnar would disown him completely, announcing to anybody who would listen that they weren't blood relations. He was perfectly capable of testifying against Karl. The head-ache receded briefly when Karl remembered that he had thrown away all the paperwork relating to Arnar's parents. There was no reason for their names to appear in the official documents. The police would no doubt see from his browsing history that he had searched for people with those names but he would invent some lie. He had plenty of time to come up with something plausible.

'Thanks, I'll check them out. You never know.'

'Will you tell them I'm innocent if you get hold of them?'

'I'll do that, yes.' The lawyer looked thoughtful. 'Have I understood right that you have no next of kin except the one brother? Apart from distant relatives, that is?'

'Yes.' Karl gulped. His throat was dry as a bone. 'He lives abroad and knows nothing about this. You mustn't speak to him. I forbid you.'

'I'm not sure that's wise. The police are aware of his exist-ence and are bound to contact him. The picture of you they say they showed the girl was on his Facebook page.'

The pain in Karl's head suddenly intensified and he stopped speaking until the worst was over. 'I can't understand why she says she recognises my picture. I've never seen her and she hasn't seen me. Definitely not in her garden or inside her house, like they claimed.'

'I wouldn't worry too much about that. You heard how vague they were. I'm pretty sure that means the girl couldn't give a positive identification. If she had, they'd have been more confident instead of contenting themselves with dropping hints.'

Karl nodded listlessly. 'I still don't want you talking to Arnar.'

The lawyer, who gave the impression that he'd seen it all, asked no further questions on this point. Lowering his eyes, he continued to read his notes. 'Getting back to the main issue. Did you understand their references to dogs?'

'No.' He had been bewildered by the questions. The police had wanted to know if he'd attacked two dogs, one in Grafarvogur, the other out on Grandi. He had also been grilled about how he had known where the girl Margrét was staying and how he had tracked down Freyja's name and address. In fact, he had been relieved by the questions because they were so absurd that they were bound to help establish that he wasn't the man they were after. 'I know nothing about any dogs.'

'No. I thought they reacted a bit oddly when you couldn't answer, as if they doubted their own theory. But that's not saying much. Perhaps we should concentrate on the most important issues. Can you remember anything that would provide you with a proper alibi for the Thursday night when Elísa was murdered? Did you ring anyone or receive any phone calls? Were you up when the papers were delivered unusually early? Anything. If you were online it would be possible to trace the fact on your computer. Anything at all. The same applies to the evening Ástrós was killed. You heard what they said – the time of death was probably shortly after you claim to have dropped off your friends. That doesn't look good.'

Karl felt as if his mouth was full of cotton wool. 'I was asleep when Elísa was killed.' What was so difficult to understand about that? A sleeping person wouldn't go online or talk to paper boys or use the phone. Karl coughed and thought his head would split. Then the acute pain retreated again, leaving behind a peculiarly hot, nagging ache. He tried to ignore it. 'I went home after dropping off my mates the evening Ástrós was killed. I went to bed. I didn't go online.'

'I see. Can you try and remember in more detail?' The lawyer sounded discouraged. 'It didn't sound too good when you said you'd driven past Ástrós's house the evening she was murdered. Let alone the business of the scream you claim to have heard. They didn't believe you. It would be better if you ran that sort of thing past me before saying anything to them. That's what you should have done when they presented you with those numbers. Not help to decipher them. They're almost certainly connected to the murders and there was no need to show them you understood that peculiar code.'

They both glanced inadvertently at the sheet of paper on which he had deciphered the messages for the police once they had provided him with a copy of the periodic table. Their expressions as he slowly worked his way through the sequences had registered first astonishment, then eagerness, like the faces of children in a sweet shop.

53, 16 · 53, 90–1 · 4, 43–6, 65–5, 68 · 43–6, 8 · 106–16, 53, 23, 63–92 · 90, 89–6, 7 · 43–6, 8 · 75, 58, 53, 23, 63–92

I, S · I, Th–H · Be, Tc–C, Tb–B, Er · Tc–C, O · Sg–S, I, V, Eu–U · Th, Ac–C, N · Tc–C, O · Re, Ce, I, V, Eu–U

Is it better to give than to receive?
39, 8, 92 · 5, 3–53, 8, 8, 66 · 83, 43, 1
Y, O, U · B, Li–I, O, O, Dy · Bi, Tc, H
You bloody bitch.
39, 8, 92 · 75 · 10, X, 65–5
Y, O, U · Re · Ne, X, Tb–B
You're next.
66–39, 8 · 90, 63–92 · 42–8, 85, 108
Dy–Y, O · Th, Eu–U · Mo–O, At, Hs
Do the maths.
22, 90–1 · 9, 8, 86–7 · 73, 90–1
Ti, Th–H · F, O, Rn–N · Ta, Th–H
Tit for tat.

Karl looked up. 'I understood the messages because of the shortwave broadcasts. Same code.'

'Maybe you did. But you're a chemistry student and the key to the code is connected to chemistry, which means one thing to them: you wrote the code.'

'No.' Karl had nothing to add. What could he say? Wasn't the truth enough?

'They seem convinced that the scraps of paper with numbers on them that they found in your basement are messages you intended to use for the next murders.'

'Those were the numbers read out on the radio station. I wrote them down after I'd worked out the code. To find out what they said.' Karl couldn't understand the point of endlessly repeating himself. Perhaps it would be best to stay silent.

His defence counsel raised his brows sceptically, then sighed. 'I don't think you should have told them you can't stand blood or violence either. They seem to have some theory that the killer has a phobia about blood. Or finds it disgusting.'

'Was I supposed to lie?'

'No. You should have asked for permission to confer with me in private. As I keep telling you. But never mind.' The man had almost finished going through his notes. He rapped his knuckles on the final page, then closed the pad. 'We'll have plenty of time to go through all this later. They'll be back any minute. If you turn out to be ill, it may be possible to start the interview afresh. If you were delirious, for example . . .' The lawyer regarded Karl hopefully.

'I've got a headache.' Karl reached for the glass in the hope that the water would relieve the hot ache that was spreading through his head. But he missed the glass. His hand moved in a completely different direction from what he had intended. He tried again, with no more success. Karl realised he could only see out of one eye. Perhaps that was the reason, but when he tried to tell the lawyer about this sudden blindness, he produced a stream of gibberish. The pain in his head redoubled. Everything else seemed to have stopped working, as if his body was no longer connected to his head.

In the very moment that Karl toppled off his chair the door opened and the two policemen re-entered. With his one good eye he registered their horrified expressions – even the smartly dressed one. They both opened their mouths and seemed to be exclaiming but Karl couldn't hear a thing. A woman who had been standing behind them pushed them aside and rushed over to Karl. She touched his face but he couldn't feel her fingers. Or anything else.

He closed the eye that could still see.

Chapter 33

A week later

Huldar hadn't yet got round to hanging the picture in his office. He had put off buying it, convinced he would be demoted after Karl Pétursson collapsed during questioning. The incident was being described as one of the worst blunders in Icelandic police history and Huldar had started surreptitiously looking for situations vacant in the state sector.

The matter had not been clarified until two days later and during that time he had felt like a leper: no one in the office dared so much as look at him. Even Erla had been avoiding him for fear of being infected by his notoriety.

Worse still was that Ríkhardur had shared his fate. Although he hadn't borne the same responsibility for the suspect's welfare as Huldar, he had nevertheless taken part in the interrogation, and this made him complicit in everyone's eyes.

Having entered the interview room as the hero of the hour, Ríkhardur had left it in disgrace. His fall had been dramatic but he weathered it with his habitual stoicism, apparently indifferent to being cold-shouldered by his colleagues. That wasn't to say he took the incident lightly, though; Huldar had no one else to talk to at the station and couldn't fail to notice the impact Karl's fate had had on Ríkhardur.

The frame was scuffed where the picture had fallen over.

He had propped it against the wall too close to the door, which had banged into it when opened. The damage wasn't too conspicuous but he would have to hurry up and find a hammer and nail before worse befell it.

The picture was nothing special; he had bought it at a tourist shop in the centre of town on his way home from watching a match at a pub with his mates at the weekend once things had calmed down. It was a photograph of sunrise over the Reynisdrangar sea stacks, which filled him with optimism and at the same time with dread. It didn't require much insight to work out why: the sun with its promise of a new day sparked a hope of better times, while the sheer, black pillars of rock rearing out of the sea were a reminder that life wasn't all plain sailing.

Before him lay a report on items that had gone missing from the police property office. Today's task was to go through it, now that the murder case was as good as solved. He wasn't a hundred per cent satisfied on that count but had to accept that Karl was no longer capable of giving his side of the story; he was in intensive care and every day could be his last.

There was sufficient evidence to implicate Karl, so Huldar would just have to accept that some aspects would never be fully explained. A series of experts had listened to the recording of his interview and come up with the theory that Karl had used the various appliances to murder his victims in order to avoid having to stab or wound them. All he'd had to do was press a button, which saved him from having to dirty his own hands. Huldar had raised his eyebrows when he read that. How was it possible to conclude that the murders merely involved pressing a button? Plenty of violence had occurred in the lead-up to the actual killings.

Karl's physique also gave him pause. He was a complete runt; it was hard to imagine how he was supposed to have overpowered his much bigger, stronger friend. Why, even Elísa had looked tougher than him. Only Ástrós was unlikely to have been able to take on a man so much younger than her. Admittedly, rage and hatred could lend people strength, but the problem with this was that it was impossible to see what could have inspired Karl with such hatred towards two women he didn't even know. He had taken the explanation with him into his coma. A further mystery was how he had found out that Margrét was with Freyja and that Freyja wasn't living in Grafarvogur as indicated by the phone book and other official records. According to his computer, Karl hadn't googled her name in search of the information. It was possible he could have done so from a public terminal at the university but, if so, they hadn't managed to locate it yet. Nevertheless, it was believed that he had found the Grafarvogur address and attacked the dog there to get it out of the way, unaware that it wasn't actually Freyja's dog. Then he seemed to have realised his mistake and attacked the right dog close to the right address. How he had managed this and how he even knew of Freyja's existence and the fact she had a dog was unexplained. Perhaps it always would be.

If he hadn't suffered a stroke, Karl was bound to have confessed in the end – they all did. Especially after his friend Börkur had disintegrated under questioning and there was no one left to back up Karl's account of mysterious numbers stations and other such nonsense.

Huldar tried to remember whether Arnar Pétursson, Karl's brother, was leaving the country today or tomorrow. A strange individual, he had proved far more informative about his brother than the experts who had studied the recording, which was hardly surprising as he had known him all his life. But Arnar was unable to explain how, in the years since he had moved abroad, his brother had changed from a very ordinary boy with few friends and an obsession with amateur radio into a ruthless killer.

Arnar's theory was that Karl had suffered a nervous break-down when their adoptive mother flatly refused to tell the brothers about their biological parents. At first Huldar had suppressed a smile at this odd idea, but as the man elaborated, he found it more plausible. If Arnar's own desperation for information about his birth family was anything to go by, it might well be correct that the disappointment had tipped his brother over the edge.

In fact, Huldar was a little taken aback by Arnar's burning obsession with uncovering the identity of his own parents. Their adoptive mother had wanted to shield Karl from the knowledge that his mother had a genetic predisposition to stroke. She'd had him young after a casual encounter with a roadworker, and had fallen ill shortly after giving birth. By the time Karl was two she had no longer been well enough to look after him. The authorities had approached his father but he hadn't felt capable of bringing up a small child, so Karl had been put up for adoption.

Karl's mother was now dead, having eventually succumbed after suffering repeated strokes. Not long afterwards his father had been killed in a work-related accident. Since neither of them was alive to tell the tale, it had taken considerable effort to piece the story together. At first the police only had the names of Karl's parents, which his lawyer had handed over without being asked. The man had been as shocked as Huldar and Ríkhardur by Karl's collapse in the interview room and seemed eager to dissociate himself from the case. He had handed over his notes from the interview as well as several points he had written down while he and Karl were alone together. Huldar had glanced through these and thought there was little to be gained from them, not least since some parts were illegible, especially the comments the lawyer had scribbled down at the end.

The mother's name had led them to her brother who was alive and in perfectly good health. Eventually he had agreed to tell them the story as he knew it. His initial reluctance had been due to a sense of guilt and shame that he hadn't taken in the little boy himself. He confided in Huldar that at the time he'd had enough of watching his loved ones die. Now that he was older, though, he realised that we're all doomed to die in the end, regardless of our genetic inheritance.

They learnt from him that in those days it had been impossible to tell whether Karl had inherited the gene and in consequence few people were willing to adopt a child with a fifty-fifty chance of dying before he was thirty. But according to Karl's uncle, a woman who worked within the system had come forward and expressed herself willing to adopt the boy as long as his origins were kept secret. She didn't want him to grow up knowing that he had a sword of Damocles hanging over his head. Huldar found her attitude understandable: not only was it uncertain whether Karl carried the gene but even if he did it wasn't inevitable that he would have a stroke. They had verified that the paperwork relating to Karl's birth had been destroyed. It transpired that this was not uncommon practice in the past, especially when the adoptive parents were social workers or otherwise well connected. Nowadays, however, a child's right to know its origins was enshrined in the law.

If Karl's brother's history was anything like Karl's, you'd have thought he would be better off not knowing. But Arnar wouldn't stop asking questions, so desperate was he to discover how Karl had unearthed his biological mother's name. He had come to the station on more than one occasion to check if any papers had been found during the search of the house but unfortunately they couldn't help him. He said the same thing every time he left: *Ring me if you find something, whatever it is.*

Seeing Ríkhardur walk past the office, Huldar called out to him. After his phone conversation with Karlotta he had managed to lock away his guilt at the back of his mind. Well, perhaps not entirely, he still got a glimpse of it now and then, but enough for him to be able to behave naturally in Ríkhardur's presence. For that he would be eternally grateful to Karlotta.

Ríkhardur also appeared to be recovering. He had taken off his wedding ring and in time the white circle on his finger would fade or be covered up by a new ring. Perhaps his new girlfriend wouldn't be as perfect or tailor-made for Ríkhardur as Karlotta, but maybe that wasn't a bad thing.

Sometimes, when a couple were too alike, their relationship just didn't work.

Erla had destroyed her chances with him by shunning them both when they fell out of favour – if she had ever been interested. And a stubborn type like Ríkhardur would never forgive something like that, which made it all the more imperative that Karlotta's adultery with Huldar should never come to light.

Huldar wondered whether to suggest they hit the town together at the weekend, but on second thoughts it would only cramp his style. Beside the flawless Ríkhardur there was little chance he would pull. Perhaps he should make a last-ditch attempt to ask Freyja out instead. Up to now she had refused his requests for a date, initially with a snort of laughter, then wearily, and finally with a hint of pity. Now he could ring and say he wanted to invite her out to celebrate the fact that the case was closed and they wouldn't be meeting again. That might work.

Ríkhardur paused at the door as if afraid Huldar was going to dump some tedious chore on him. There were a few outstanding matters that needed to be tidied up.

'Do you remember if Karl's brother's flying back to the States today or tomorrow?'

'Tomorrow.' As ever, Ríkhardur had all the facts at his fingertips. 'Were you planning to call him back in for interview?'

'No.'

'It's your last chance. I doubt we'll receive funding to travel to America if it turns out we've forgotten something.'

'No. If anything comes up, we should be able to deal with it over the phone.' Huldar rested his gaze on the picture of the Reynisdrangar stacks and wondered if he should ask Ríkhardur to help him choose a place for it. Then he decided the picture would just have to go wherever it was easiest to bang a nail in the wall; not too high, not too low. 'By the way, has anything turned up that could help him trace his parents?'

'No. I'm going through the records that IT provided of Karl's computer activity over the last few weeks but I still haven't come across any clues. I've not actually finished, but I doubt there's anything there. Perhaps Karl knew nothing about Arnar's parentage.'

'Well, don't waste too much time on it. I doubt the guy'll be any better off for knowing the information, in the unlikely event that it does turn up.'

'No, perhaps not.' Ríkhardur sounded unconvinced. 'Still, one can understand why he's so anxious to know. It may be his last chance. It's clear now that the official documents about his background were destroyed, so it's not as if he can find out by the usual methods.'

'Even more reason to leave well alone. They won't have destroyed the information simply to please his mother. She didn't have that much clout. There must have been something in his history that people agreed would be better forgotten.'

'Isn't it just that he's inherited the stroke gene as well?'

'I doubt it – from what I understand the brothers aren't related, so it would be an extraordinary coincidence if he had. No, it must be something else. Maybe an illness, maybe something to do with his parents.'

'Wouldn't you want to know? I would.' Ríkhardur smoothed down his shirt. 'However sad it was.'

'Luckily for me that's not something I have to think about.' Huldar thought he knew what was behind this: Ríkhardur wanted to be granted permission to continue the search. After all, Arnar was a man after Ríkhardur's own heart; highly educated and preternaturally calm considering the situation – no tears, no messy emotions. In other circumstances they could have become best friends, if men like that were capable of such a thing. Were Ríkhardur and Arnar to go out clubbing together, it would certainly be a lot harder for women to choose between them than if Huldar went along. 'As far as I'm concerned you can hunt for the information as long as you like. Finish going through the computer files, then take a look at the few documents we found at the house. Karl threw away almost every single scrap of paper so it shouldn't take long. I've leafed through them myself but couldn't see anything of interest.'

'I'll do that.' Ríkhardur appeared pleased, as Huldar had guessed he would. Before he left, Ríkhardur glanced at the picture on the floor and asked if he was going to hang it up.

'Yes, it's probably safe to now.'

Ríkhardur evidently didn't understand this reply and walked away looking thoughtful.

Huldar got up to fetch a hammer and nail. The inquiry was now focusing on matters of such secondary importance that surely nothing else could go wrong. It was highly unlikely he would be thrown out of his office any time soon.

When it came to it, though, Huldar hesitated about hitting the nail into the wall. He still wasn't quite satisfied and decided to deal with the last few loose ends first. The humiliation of having to take the picture down again and carry it back to his old workstation was too great a risk. He was expecting to sign off on the case by the end of the day and the picture would surely survive on the floor till then. It wasn't as if he had many visitors; some of the team had already been transferred to other cases and Erla was avoiding him, apparently ashamed of the way she had betrayed him. He meant to seek her out and reassure her that it didn't matter and that he quite understood. Well, sort of. But that could wait, like the picture. The nail in the wall and reconciliation with Erla would mark the end of his first big case.

He pulled over the lawyer's notes and began to read them for the second time. After this they would be sent to the archives, scanned and saved in digital form as part of the case file, and probably no one would ever look at them again. There would be no need. The interview had been recorded and the notes contained nothing new. The only part that might be of interest was what the lawyer had written down at the end when he and the suspect had tried to scrape together anything that could possibly improve his position.

Huldar came across a word he couldn't decipher; it appeared to begin with an H or a B and end with a Y. In between were what might be an L, a U, an A or O and possibly an N. It was followed by several question marks. Instead of pushing the pad away, Huldar decided to ring the lawyer. That way, if the investigation was reviewed in-house, he wouldn't be left looking like an idiot but could claim to have thoroughly acquainted himself with every detail.

The lawyer was disappointed when he realised who was on the line. He had probably been hoping it was a defendant seeking a solicitor. Unless he had had his name taken off the list of defence counsels as he had threatened to after the debacle of Karl's interview. His name had cropped up frequently in the media storm sparked by the near-death of a suspect in police custody. Attempts had been made to question his conduct. One headline had read: *Lawyer's meteoric fall from grace*. This had misfired after the media coverage took a different direction and afterwards perhaps he was even tickled at having for once in his life been described as a 'star lawyer'.

'*Burglary*. It probably says *burglary*.' The lawyer had told Huldar there was no need for him to scan the relevant page and e-mail it to him; it was engraved on his memory, alas.

'What burglary?'

'Karl said they'd had a break-in shortly before his mother died. He thought the burglar might have stolen the soldering iron. I can't say I found it very plausible but I thought it wouldn't hurt to look into it.'

'I see.' Huldar pushed aside the hammer and nail. Why hadn't this emerged after Karl's arrest? He'd lived at the same address all his life, so the incident should have been immediately obvious on the police database. Perhaps no one had run a search on his address. They'd had other things on their mind. Karl's guilt was not in doubt and the team was busy trying to discover a motive for the murders and to link Karl to the purchase of a helmet and duct tape, to no avail. No one had wasted a minute on checking whether Karl could conceivably be innocent; the evidence to the contrary was too compelling. Far too compelling. Why the hell was he even thinking about this now? So what if there had been a break-in at Karl's house? How could it possibly be linked to the killings? The answer was simple: there was no link. It was just that he couldn't accept that the case had been solved. It had occupied all his thoughts for too long for him to be able to let it go.

That must be the explanation.

Suddenly his phone rang. He stared at the screen, wondering what the Children's House wanted with him. Perhaps they were drafting an invoice for him to approve. *You have one large bill waiting in the system.* But that could hardly be the reason; no settlement of that type would be necessary between two state institutions, any more than he would send an invoice to the victims' families for the cost of the inquiry. He cheered up when he heard who it was. Perhaps Freyja had been thinking along the same lines as him about celebrating the closure of the case. But her tone of voice suggested otherwise.

'I hope I'm not ringing at a bad time.'

'No, not at all.' Huldar instantly regretted having been so quick off the mark, afraid that she would picture him with his feet up on the desk, whistling idly. 'I'm just tying up some minor loose ends relating to the investigation, but they can wait. I'm hoping it'll be formally signed off later today.'

'Actually, that's why I called. Did you have anything particular in mind in connection with the end of the inquiry?'

'How funny – great minds think alike.' Huldar smiled broadly. His repeated attempts seemed finally to be paying off: she wanted to celebrate with him and he didn't care if it was only out of pity. It was a start.

'What do you mean?' She sounded astonished.

Huldar closed his eyes. Damn. 'Sorry, I misunderstood. Go on.'

'Do you need a report from us?'

Huldar opened his eyes and shook his head, cross with himself. 'Yes, that would be great. Presumably you'll describe the interviews and what emerged from them?'

'Yes. We have a fairly standard form. If you don't mind, I'd like to add a section on Margrét's welfare. It might have an impact on our future collaboration if the police can see in black and white just how important our services are for the children who end up in this sort of situation.'

'Absolutely.' He wasn't about to disillusion her by pointing out that no one but him would read the report. He knew his colleagues. And he himself would only read it because he was obliged to as head of the inquiry.

'As I already know Margrét quite well, it was decided that

I should assess her need for further therapy. She's been to see me several times.'

'And?' Huldar wasn't sure where this was leading but clearly it wasn't out for a drink with him.

'There's an issue I wanted to run by you. I don't know whether to leave it out or include it in the report. You see, it might be embarrassing for you.'

'Embarrassing for me?' Huldar's curiosity was piqued. The vision of the two of them alone together in a quiet bar evaporated.

'Yes. A bit. At least, I think so.' She paused, then continued. 'Margrét is adamant that you're the murderer.'

'Me?' Huldar burst out laughing. 'What on earth gave her that idea? What about the photo? Wasn't she satisfied that it was Karl?'

'She retracted. Now she's claiming she was confused. The man just happens to look a bit like the one she saw and anyway she didn't get a good view of him.'

'She can hardly think I look like the man in the garden?'

'She won't be drawn on that. I was going to have another go at getting her to explain and wondered if you'd like to come along and observe. She's due for an appointment with me later today and I could hold it in the interview room if you like. You'd have to make sure you arrived first so there was absolutely no chance of her seeing you.'

'I'll be there.'

'It's at three. In two hours' time. Hopefully it'll either clarify things or I'll manage to talk some sense into her. Margrét can't possibly go back out into the world in the belief that her mother's killer is not only still on the loose but, to make matters worse, is a policeman.'

'I'll be there at half two.' Huldar hung up. Clearly that picture wasn't going to be hung today.

In the meantime he would concentrate on the report about items missing from the property office.

It made for more interesting reading than he had expected.

As did the details on the police database about the burglary of Karl's mother's house.

Not to mention the report on Halli's illegal downloads, which Huldar had only skimmed before but now read right the way through.

Chapter 34

Huldar understood now what it meant to see red. He felt as if his eyes were bleeding; everything appeared to him through a pink haze. His thoughts were boiling and churning in his head.

But he had to swallow his rage and force himself to sit still and watch Freyja. For some time now she had been chatting to Margrét about how she was feeling, without once referring to the murder. Although he was well aware that the questions had to follow a certain pattern and were gradually increasing in seriousness, his impatience was killing him. Under the table his foot twitched up and down, its tempo increasing with every irrelevant question.

Margrét's father was sitting across from him. This time it was Sigvaldi who had accompanied his daughter to the Children's House. According to Freyja, the little girl was more or less reconciled to his presence again.

Huldar couldn't really object but he was cross with himself for failing to foresee this. What had he thought? That Margrét would come alone on the bus?

Last time they met, Sigvaldi had been distraught, angry and grieving, trying to come to terms with his wife's death. Now he seemed chiefly put out at having to share a room with Huldar and was no doubt cursing himself for not having accepted Freyja's invitation to remain in the waiting room.

He could have sat there drinking coffee and reading the papers instead of awkwardly shifting further and further away from Huldar by rocking his chair backwards, an inch at a time, after his initial attempt at small talk had been met with nothing but an angry hiss from Huldar.

If Huldar didn't concentrate there was a risk he would lose track of what was being said on the other side of the glass. It was too easy to become distracted by his fury with everything and everyone, but chiefly with himself for having missed so much and been made to look such a fool. He had to keep his head if he was to see his plan through and close in on the person he now believed was guilty.

While Margrét was replying to a question about how she was getting on at school, Huldar's thoughts wandered, in spite of himself, to the discoveries he had made in the last two hours. All that was lacking to complete the picture was Margrét's testimony. Everything else fitted in with his new theory – and not one shred of evidence pointing to Karl's guilt would stand up to scrutiny.

A phone call to the Post and Telecom Administration had confirmed that the shortwave broadcasts Karl mentioned had taken place. The member of staff Huldar spoke to was eager to help him get to the bottom of the mystery since they themselves had been trying to discover where the broadcasts were coming from after they received a complaint from Reykjavík's domestic airport. Apparently the frequency had been too close to the one assigned for communications with aircraft, resulting in interference on the channel. They'd had no success in tracing their origin, however, because the broadcasts had been too brief and irregular. The person responsible had had the sense not only to go off air in between broadcasts but to switch off the transmitter as well. The complaint had taken a while to reach the authorities, however, and shortly afterwards the problem had gone away with the cessation of the broadcasts. Nevertheless the man was very curious to know where they had come from since it was extremely unusual, in fact unprecedented, to encounter an Icelandic numbers station. It seemed that no one else apart from Karl and his friend Börkur had been aware of its existence.

Huldar's mobile rang and his foot ceased its twitching. He answered Ríkhardur's call after moving away from the conference table. 'I can't talk now. I'm at the Children's House – something's come up. Can I call you back later?' His words came out sounding terse, not helped by the necessity of whispering. He didn't dare leave the room in case Freyja finally guided the conversation round to the murder.

'Of course. Is there a new case?' Ríkhardur sounded eager. There was nothing else to look forward to; no prospect of another major investigation any time soon.

'No. I'll fill you in afterwards.' Huldar heard Freyja ask Margrét if she felt up to talking about what had happened to her mother. 'Got to go. Catch you later.'

'Should I come along? Who else is there?'

'Erla's not here, if that's what you're worried about.' Huldar spoke quickly. 'Nearly done here. I'll be back at the station shortly. Wait for me, if you can.' He ended the call without giving Ríkhardur a chance to respond. Margrét had said yes to the question. Huldar didn't bother to sit down again but took up position at the end of the table. Pretending not to notice him, Sigvaldi shifted almost imperceptibly closer to the glass.

'I'm quite sure it wasn't that man. The man at the hospital.'

Margrét fiddled with a stretchy bracelet on her wrist. 'Are there prison-hospitals?'

'No, not in Iceland. Though in other countries they have big prisons that might have hospital wards for prisoners who are ill. But I don't think there's any such thing as a prison-hospital.'

'Then it's a good thing he's not the bad man. Daddy says he'll have to stay in hospital forever. All his life. So he won't be able to go to prison. I want the man who hurt Mummy to go to prison.'

'Yes, that's what we all want.'

'The bad man doesn't.'

'No, apart from him.' Freyja ran a hand over her hair. She was wearing it loose as she had at the last interview, her blond locks resting on her shoulders. 'Since you're sure it wasn't the man who's ill, who *do* you think hurt your mummy?'

'The man in the shoes.'

'The man in the shoes?' Freyja tapped lightly on the concealed microphone at her bosom to warn Huldar that now they were getting somewhere. Perhaps she was afraid he might have dozed off. 'Can you describe him a bit better? After all, most people wear shoes.'

'He was at your flat. He said he'd been in the garden. But he was in my house too. I saw him from under the bed. I saw his shoes. I remember them.'

'Do you remember who pulled you out from under the bed, Margrét? In the morning? That was him.'

'Yes.' The girl didn't seem quite as sure of herself.

'That was a long time after the man who hurt your mummy had left.'

'Yes.' Margrét seemed to have lost interest in the conversation. She took off her bracelet and started stretching it between her fingers. 'But he was the one who hurt Mummy too. They were the same shoes. I know. I saw them.' She paused, then repeated, 'I saw them.'

Huldar stooped to the microphone. 'Would you mind asking what exactly the man said about her father? It's absolutely crucial.' He ignored Sigvaldi's look of horror.

'Margrét. What did the man say about your daddy when he claimed it was his fault?'

At first it appeared Margrét wasn't going to answer. Then she sat up, leant towards Freyja and started whispering. As she was right beside the hidden microphone, her words could be heard more clearly than before. 'Don't tell anyone.'

'I can't promise that, Margrét.'

Huldar groaned. Couldn't Freyja simply lie?

'I don't want anyone to know.'

'Sometimes people need to know things. Even if they're bad or nasty. Sometimes they're not as bad as you think.'

'This is very bad. Daddy did a very bad thing. But I don't think he meant to.'

'I'm sure he didn't. And what the man said might not have been true. Perhaps he was making it up. If you don't tell anyone, you'll never find out if it was true.'

Margrét deliberated again. Then she whispered to Freyja, fortunately loud enough for the microphone to pick up every word: 'The bad man said Daddy had killed his baby. It was Daddy's fault he was going to hurt Mummy. Suck out her life like Daddy sucked out his baby.' Margrét sat back again, her face twisted in sadness and revulsion. 'I think it must have been by mistake. Don't you?'

Sigvaldi emitted a peculiar snorting, gurgling noise that went on and on.

Huldar rested his knuckles on the table and bent his head for a moment, eyes screwed shut, grinding his teeth. It fitted. Then he raised his head so quickly he felt dizzy. With trembling fingers he fished the nicotine gum from his trouser pocket and shoved two pieces in his mouth for good measure.

In the report about objects missing from the police property office Huldar had recognised a number of familiar items. These had included a black motorcycle helmet, a mobile phone, a glass-cutter and a set of suction cups. Eight rolls of duct tape were missing from a box that had been full. The phone and tape were part of a haul of stolen goods uncovered during a house search. The phone had contained a prepaid SIM card that had not been traced. It was a cheap model and as nobody had reported it stolen, no attempt had been made to find the owner. No one had reported the theft of the tape; the shop it came from hadn't bothered to notify the police subsequently when the USB sticks turned out not to be missing after all, perhaps in case this reduced the insurance payout. The glass-cutter and suction cups had been confiscated when a burglar was caught mid break-in. The helmet related to an old drugs case and had never been claimed as its owner was still behind bars.

When Huldar looked up the burglary of Karl's mother's house on the system, it wasn't the incident itself that caught his attention. A few minor possessions had been taken and the house owner was described as upset but also as behaving rather oddly; the police officer who investigated the break-in had thought she seemed chiefly interested in him.

The police database also contained information about the

investigation of illegal downloads in which Halli had been involved. Again, it wasn't the crime itself that drew Huldar's attention but the identity of the officer who had taken the most active role in the raid. The same officer had investigated the burglary at Karl's mother's house: Ríkhardur.

At first Huldar had been puzzled. It was most uncharacteristic of his colleague not to mention that he'd had prior dealings with two parties in a murder case. It went against all their training, so there must have been some mistake.

Without stopping to think, Huldar had phoned Karlotta. She didn't sound particularly pleased to hear from him but seemed to sense that it was serious and soon stopped demanding to know what was going on and started providing succinct answers to his questions.

He asked her if Ríkhardur knew or had any connection to Ástrós, Elísa or Sigvaldi. It emerged that he didn't know any of them. But Karlotta did.

Ástrós had taught her biology in the sixth form.

Sigvaldi had been her gynaecologist.

When Huldar pressed her about whether Sigvaldi had made a mistake or damaged her in a way that meant she might not be able to have children, she had interrupted to ask how important this was; his questions were becoming pretty personal. Then, after a brief silence, she confided that Sigvaldi had been the doctor who examined her, then approved and performed an abortion at her request, without making her specify the reason. So her last pregnancy had not ended in a miscarriage as she and Ríkhardur had claimed.

Karlotta didn't want the child and had aborted the foetus. Ríkhardur hadn't found out until it was too late.

Stunned by the implications, Huldar had been unable to

speak. In the end she had told him the reason, without his having to ask. What she said came as such a bolt from the blue that he began to wonder if he was imagining their conversation. But Karlotta went on to tell him about the letter that had precipitated the whole thing and how Ástrós and Karl's mother were involved.

'Sigvaldi,' Huldar mumbled, his mouth full of gum. 'Say goodbye to Freyja for me and thank her for doing this, but tell her I had to leave.'

The man couldn't hide his relief at being deprived of Huldar's company. 'OK, will do.'

Huldar sat outside in his car for a long time, leaning on the steering wheel and trying to clear his head. It wasn't until he heard the front door slam that he sat up, started the car and drove off. He didn't want to have to acknowledge Sigvaldi and Margrét as they walked past. The man would no doubt be puzzled as to why he hadn't left yet. In his rear-view mirror he saw them walking away from the house, side by side. They weren't holding hands.

He hadn't gone far when his phone rang. It was Freyja. 'I've got something to tell you. You'd gone by the time Margrét and I finished, but I was going to use the opportunity to confess something that may be important.'

'If it's to do with the report or what Margrét said, there's no need. It seems we were barking up the wrong tree, so the case is wide open again.'

'No. It has nothing to do with the report or Margrét.'

He was perplexed. 'OK.' It was all he could say. He realised he simply couldn't face confronting Ríkhardur yet, let alone his boss Egill or the others to whom he would now have to break the unwelcome news. He hadn't a clue what order to approach them in or how he should act. 'I'll turn round.'

'I promise it won't take long. I'd be glad of a chance to make a clean breast of things and I'd prefer not to have to come down to the station.'

Huldar thought. This would give him a reprieve. And you never know, with her psychological training she might be able to advise him on how to confess to his mistakes and incompetence without coming across as a complete idiot. No need to tell her the whole sorry tale; he could set it up as a hypothetical problem. 'I'll be there in two minutes.'

To avoid rousing Ríkhardur's suspicions, Huldar sent him a text to say he'd been held up. His erstwhile friend answered almost immediately, asking if there was any more news. Huldar made himself reply, though every letter stung, saying there was no news and he would be back shortly. His screen went dark and didn't light up again. Apparently Ríkhardur was satisfied. For now.

Chapter 35

'Everyone's gone home. I've switched on the alarm upstairs, so we'll have to make do with this – I won't keep you long.' Freyja showed Huldar into the examination room. For a moment she wondered if she was doing the right thing; the man seemed ill, he was so pale, silent and distracted. She only hoped any germs he might carry in here would die over-night, but perhaps it would be sensible to wipe down everything he touched before she left.

The only chairs were uncomfortable and differed in height; one was an office chair, the other an adjustable stool on wheels for the doctor to use when examining children. Freyja ushered Huldar to the office chair, while she towered over him on the stool, which felt a bit odd, but at least it meant he didn't have to look at the table. It was a grim piece of equipment, a gynaecological examination table designed for children, which violated every instinct. He felt bad enough at this moment without being reminded of the revolting crimes to which some children were subjected.

'What was it you wanted to tell me?'

He must be coming down with some bug, she thought; perhaps he already had a fever. His voice sounded rough and unfriendly. Freyja couldn't help wondering if it had been a mistake to believe she could trust him. Could she invent some other business instead? But what he said next reassured her.

'If I seem a bit strange it's because I've been knocked sideways by something that's happened. Please don't take it personally.'

She gave a short laugh. 'Don't worry. I thought you might have flu.' It was a relief that there would be no need to disinfect everything once he had left. She was eager to go home and Molly was waiting. Freyja hoped the dog hadn't chewed the heels off the pair of new shoes she had forgotten to hide. 'All I wanted to say is that I know who it was in the garden – the man you thought was stalking me. He's not connected to the murder case.'

'Was it your ex?' Huldar seemed completely uninterested.

'No.' Freyja shook her head. 'I've got a brother who's . . . strayed from the straight and narrow, let's say. He hired a man to keep an eye on me because he thought I was in danger. Due to a complete misunderstanding, he was afraid my ex wanted to get even with me. And just to make it clear, it wasn't me who gave him that idea. He thought of it all by himself.'

Huldar exhaled heavily like a man about to expire from stress. 'I know who your brother is.'

'What?'

'I was curious. I didn't think your address fitted your circumstances, so I checked whose name the flat was registered in. Our database showed that you share a mother, so it wasn't difficult to work out.' He lowered his eyes to the floor as he continued: 'I'm familiar with his history. I recognised the name and looked him up in our records. I even had the honour of arresting him myself once. Years ago.'

'I see.' Freyja couldn't bring herself to ask what for.

'Of course, the dog's name should have given the game away.'

432

'What do you mean?'

'Who calls their dog Molly? Not a psychologist from the Children's House, that's for sure.'

'Is there something wrong with the name? What are you on about?'

'You mean you don't know? It's the street name for MDMA – the active ingredient in Ecstasy.' Huldar added wearily: 'Never mind.'

'Oh.' Freyja blushed. Why had it never occurred to her? She hurriedly steered the conversation back to the point. 'Anyway, at least you needn't waste any more time wondering if the man in the garden was the murderer.' She wished she could lean back on the stool; her bag was weighing heavily on her shoulder but she didn't dare put it down for fear Huldar would spot the gun. She had been intending to ask him to dispose of it for her, without revealing where it came from, but obviously that had been a bad idea. He would immediately link the weapon to her brother, and she couldn't trust him. 'That was all.'

Huldar held her gaze and Freyja forced herself not to drop her eyes or betray any other sign of deceit. Sometimes it came in useful to have studied human behaviour. 'I don't quite understand.' He clicked his tongue. 'Couldn't you have told me that over the phone?'

'Yes. I suppose I could.' She smiled in embarrassment. 'I just wanted to talk to you face to face. For all I know your phone calls may be recorded. I have no desire to discuss my brother with the police, as I'm sure you'll understand. I made an exception in your case. In view of the circumstances.' She cut herself off. When lying, it was best to say as little as possible; let him put her down as the excessively cautious type. It irked her that she wasn't quite indifferent to what he thought of her.

'For your information, we don't record all our calls.'

'Thanks, that's good to know.' It was all she could think of to say. She heard the sound of a car pulling into the drive and although she didn't relish the prospect of having to stay on at work, the distraction came as a relief.

'Are you expecting someone?'

'No.' Freyja rolled the stool over to the window and peered through a gap in the blinds. 'It seems to be for you.'

'For me?'

'Well, it's a police car, and they usually give us advance warning. We don't run an emergency reception here.'

Huldar had joined her at the window without her noticing. They watched a man step out of the car. Freyja, who had never seen him before, was surprised to see a figure like that emerge from a police vehicle. He was so sleek and tastefully dressed that he looked more like a banker. Apart from his regulation black police footwear – like the shoes Huldar wore. Before walking up to the house, he paused to run both hands over his neatly coiffured head.

'Shit. Shit. Shit.' Turning away from the window, Huldar glanced around frantically. They heard the front door open, then close quietly. Huldar whispered in Freyja's ear. 'Hide in the cupboard.' In the house's former incarnation this had been a wardrobe but now it was used to store disposable gloves and other medical equipment. 'Don't ask any questions. Just hide. I'll explain later. Everything'll be fine.'

Freyja was about to say she didn't expect any different but read from his expression that it would be wiser to shut up and obey. While she was finding a space for herself among the stacks of small, white cardboard boxes, she was grateful they hadn't recently replenished their stocks. Even so, it was pretty cramped inside the cupboard; she couldn't move without bumping into something, and if she did, she would betray her hiding place. Her main fear was that her bag would slip off her shoulder and knock over one of the stacks of boxes. She pulled the cupboard shut as Huldar opened the door to the passage. Through the thin wood she heard him call 'Ríkhardur!' She made an effort to breathe calmly and noiselessly, then tuned in to what Huldar and the stranger were saying.

'I was wondering if you needed any help. You sounded so worried.'

'There was no need. I was about to head back to the station. Didn't you get my text?'

'Yes.' They were both silent for a beat, then Ríkhardur spoke again: 'I got the idea there might have been a new development since they were interviewing the girl again. I heard a question being put to her while we were talking on the phone and I was so curious I couldn't wait. You should keep me informed if there's something major going on.'

'I was intending to. Why don't we head back to the station and discuss it there? We can't stay here; they're expecting a little boy to be brought in for interview and examination in connection with a suspected assault.'

'Then why's nobody here? Surely you're not going to receive them?'

'No. Freyja, the psychologist in charge here, is on her way. They asked her to fetch the doctor and I offered to wait in case the others turned up in the meantime.'

Freyja gave Huldar credit for quick thinking. Though she ought to have remembered – he was a good liar.

'Couldn't the doctor have taken a cab?'

'I don't know. What's the matter with you? What the hell's it got to do with you?' Huldar sounded angry, much angrier than the situation warranted. Ríkhardur was clearly rather annoying but there was some other reason for Huldar's rage. Something that meant she had to hide in a cupboard.

There was a brief pause before Ríkhardur answered. When he did, his voice was more composed than before; the plaintive note had gone. Freyja's skin prickled at this new, cold tone. 'I went into your office. I saw the report about the items that were missing from the property store. You'd marked the ones that were relevant. Do you think it has a bearing on the murders? It could be a coincidence; so much stuff gets confiscated during house searches.'

'I think it has a bearing, yes. And I don't believe for a moment that Karl's the killer.'

Freyja frowned in the darkness. What was he talking about? She strained her ears so as not to miss anything.

'But, like I said, this isn't the place to discuss it. Come on, let's head back to the station.'

'Don't you have to wait for the woman in charge to get back? In case they turn up with the little boy?'

'I'll leave a note on the door.'

'Why don't you just tell me what's going on? Surely it won't take more than a minute? I don't see what difference it makes whether it's here or at the office.'

'Because I'm tired. I have every intention of telling you, just not here. Can't you just be a little bit patient?'

'I'd rather hear it now. I have no intention of going back to the station.'

'Really? You're going home in a patrol car? It's not like the station's out of your way.'

There was another silence. When they started talking again Freyja thought their voices sounded closer, as though Ríkhardur had entered the examination room. 'You know something, don't you? Karlotta rang. She told me about your conversation.'

Freyja wondered who Karlotta was. She didn't picture her as a policewoman but before she could give her any more thought, Ríkhardur continued: 'I'm no fool, Huldar. I know you've worked it out. But I was hoping you could be persuaded to keep it to yourself.'

Huldar snorted. 'Are you crazy?'

'No. But if you stop and think about it, it's in everyone's interests that this should go no further. It goes without saying that I'd be grateful. And it would spare Karlotta from being held up in public as a freak. You'd keep your promotion. The only loser would be poor Karl, but then he doesn't have anything to lose. So everyone wins.'

'Forget it. This isn't a question of winning or losing. You've committed a crime. The most appalling crime imaginable. Three times. Do you really believe I care so much about a fucking promotion that I'd let you off?'

Freyja gasped, then froze. Had she been heard? What were they talking about? Had Karl not killed Margrét's mother after all? Was the real murderer standing here in this room?

'That's what I was hoping, yes. If it's any help, I didn't find it easy. But they all deserved it.'

'Elísa? What had she ever done to you?'

'Well, nothing. I wasn't after her. I meant to kill Sigvaldi, just like he killed my baby. But since he wasn't home, it seemed appropriate. I didn't like to kill one of the children, though it would have served him right. I'm not a complete monster, you know. In fact, I locked the kids in their rooms before I left, so they wouldn't find their mother's body.'

Freyja felt as though she was suffocating. She concentrated on trying to breathe calmly. There was enough air in the cupboard. More than enough. Slow breaths. There was enough air.

'You could have gone away. Come back when he was home. Elísa had done absolutely nothing to you.'

'That was out of the question. The opportunity fell in my lap – a gift from heaven, if you believe in such things. I was in my car and happened to spot the woman driving into a petrol station. I followed her and took advantage of my good luck. Having the key to the house made the whole thing so much easier. It was out of the question to come back another time when Sigvaldi was home. They would have changed the lock by then and been more on their guard. Since he wasn't home, I had no other choice.'

'He didn't kill your baby, Ríkhardur. He performed an abortion. The only right course of action in the context. Why do you think Karlotta miscarried every time? It was nature's way of dealing with the problem. And what was Karlotta supposed to do once she knew the truth? It was the only way. It wasn't Sigvaldi who made the decision: it was Karlotta. She had no alternative. I don't know if you realise how serious it was.'

'Serious? Of course I realise. How do you think I felt when I found out? How do you think Karlotta felt?' Ríkhardur laughed mirthlessly. 'It's so ironic – if Karl's house hadn't been burgled, none of this would have happened. Karlotta and I would be preparing for our baby's arrival and no one would have had to die. But no. Karl's mother had to go and spoil everything by working it out. She noticed the resemblance between me and her elder son and remembered my name. At first she didn't give the game away, just asked me a load of personal questions and I thought she was some eccentric old bag. I was such an idiot that I told her I was about to become a father and even mentioned the name of my wife. I was so happy and excited. I should have held my tongue.'

Freyja heard a heavy sigh, presumably from Ríkhardur.

'After I'd left, she did some research and became convinced that she was right. That her son Arnar, Karlotta and I were siblings. That Karlotta was my sister.'

'You know it's worse than that, Ríkhardur. Though that relationship alone would have been quite enough to force you to split up.'

Freyja listened in disbelief. Ríkhardur carried on as if Huldar hadn't interrupted: 'Karl's mother wrote to Karlotta. She didn't show me the letter until after it was all over with our baby. The woman told her the whole tragic story of my mother – our mother – and advised her to leave me and abort our baby. We should never have met; we'd been sent to opposite sides of the country in the belief that our paths would never cross. But they didn't take into account how much I loved her. I only had to see her once across the law faculty to know that she was my future wife. It makes no difference that I now know she's my sister. Not the slightest bit of difference.' Ríkhardur's laugh was ugly. 'That business with our parents is all in the past. Our mother's dead and so's our father. Though I don't really know what to call that evil bastard – father, grandfather? Which was he?'

'Both. And you're right, he was a monster, Ríkhardur. He raped your mother, his own daughter. Repeatedly. It's a harrowing story and no wonder she killed him in the end. It's just a tragedy that she felt she had to take her own life as well. She would almost certainly have been treated leniently and given the lightest possible sentence. That's clear from the way the incident was hushed up. It didn't even leak out in the press. She probably did it to protect her children – to prevent people from finding out about your background.'

'She got pregnant. At nineteen,' Ríkhardur choked. 'She'd moved down to Akranes but the man she was involved with refused to acknowledge the child. At least that's what it said in the letter Karlotta received. She had no way of supporting herself, so she went back home. Home to the man who should have helped her find her feet. Home to her father. But instead he took advantage of her situation, of how remote the farm was and how few visitors they had. He had no compunction about breaking her down and abusing her. She bore him two children and was pregnant with a third when she killed him. Shot him with his own rifle. Then shot herself. Arnar was the eldest and witnessed the whole thing – the child who was supposedly the son of the guy from Akranes. Though no one knows if he was really the father or if Arnar was his grandfather's son as well.'

'Ríkhardur, your mother's tragic fate is neither here nor there. You and Karlotta are so closely related that there's no way you can live as man and wife, let alone have a family. Your children would have siblings as parents and share the same grandparents, as well as a grandfather who was also their great-grandfather. The advice Ástrós gave Karlotta was perfectly correct. The chances of the child suffering birth defects were far too high.'

'There was also a chance the baby would have been OK. Ástrós didn't calculate the probability of that for Karlotta. But she did for me.'

'I doubt she'd have calculated anything for Karlotta if she'd known what she was letting herself in for. All Ástrós did was help a favourite old pupil of hers who turned to her in desperation. Where else was Karlotta to go? She didn't dare speak to a doctor; they would have demanded to know who she was talking about. She didn't even tell Sigvaldi the truth; only that she didn't want the child. That was enough. But Ástrós was a retired biology teacher who was flattered that Karlotta remembered her. She tried to advise her but didn't have a clue who was involved.'

'She should still have calculated the probability that everything would have turned out OK.'

'That would be obvious if you actually stopped and used your brain.' Huldar broke off and Freyja didn't dare move in the momentary silence. She held her breath until he began speaking again. 'And what about poor Halli, Karl's friend? And Karl himself?'

Ríkhardur snorted. 'I came across Halli by pure luck. Well, it wasn't only luck, because I recognised Karl's name in his computer when we were going through it in search of pirated content. So I got in touch and promised to pay him if he'd help me play a prank on his friend. That's all it took. He suggested using shortwave radio broadcasts because Karl was obsessed with them. He had all the necessary gear and even came up with the code himself. Said he'd got the idea from a poster that hung over the desk in Karl's basement. He was sure his friend would crack it eventually but he was going to give him a nudge if he didn't. It never came to that, though.'

'What about Karl? What had he ever done to you? Or were you just looking for someone to frame?'

'He suited my purpose. And he stole my brother from me. He had no right to grow up with him. He deserved it.'

'Ríkhardur, you do realise that you're completely insane?'

'I happen to disagree.'

'You killed three people. By the most unbelievably horrific methods.'

'It could have been much worse. I chose those methods precisely because they weren't horrific. For me, anyway. All I had to do was switch on the appliances and they took care of the rest. I could even walk away; I didn't have to watch them die. I'm not a sadist, you know. I've no desire to watch people suffer. It was a question of justice. People can't just destroy my life, destroy my child's life, without facing the consequences.' Ríkhardur sighed. 'You have no idea of the sheer effort that went into this. The lengths I've had to go to. The trouble I've taken to avoid encountering the little girl. The aspects of the investigation I volunteered for so I could keep an eye on what was happening. The phone calls. Did you really believe I wanted to ring all those nutters? And the CCTV at the cashpoint? My car was visible on the footage. I didn't even have to destroy it. You trusted me implicitly and no one had any suspicion. And all the rest of it; pity you didn't tell me straight away where Freyja was living. I injured the wrong dog. But I sorted that out. You must be feeling pretty bad about being made to look such a fool.'

'Ríkhardur, will you do me a favour and turn round, put your hands behind your back and let me cuff you? We'll continue this conversation down at the station as I originally suggested.' Huldar's voice was cold; it was evident that Ríkhardur's taunt had got to him.

'I'd rather not, thanks all the same.'

'You won't get away with it. I'm not the only one who knows. Sooner or later Karlotta's going to put two and two together. And Margrét saw your shoes from under the bed. Regulation police shoes. There's only one way this can end. Best get it over with.'

'No. You need to take a moment to think about it. I'm sorry, I shouldn't have insulted you. I may have made a fool of you but I didn't enjoy it, if that's any comfort.'

'It doesn't matter. I deserve it. I screwed your wife. In the toilets at a bar. At her request.'

Freyja's eyes opened wide. The bloody bastard. He would.

Ríkhardur emitted a blood-curdling howl and a terrible racket of crashing and banging ensued. Freyja heard the sound of the examination table being knocked over. There were loud grunts and the odd cry – she couldn't tell who was making which noises. Then all was suddenly quiet. Freyja didn't dare move a muscle. A long, deep groan echoed round the room, followed by a whimper.

It was Ríkhardur.

Huldar's groans sounded different, as she couldn't forget. He was completely silent, which couldn't be a good sign. In all likelihood he had been knocked out.

There was a scraping of drawers and her heart began to pound. Was the man looking for some weapon to finish Huldar off with? After all she'd heard about the murders she wasn't about to allow another to be committed right under her nose. Unlike Margrét, she was an adult. She wasn't going to be forced to sit by and do nothing. Besides, if the man killed Huldar he was perfectly capable of going straight round to Margrét's house.

With infinite caution she slid her hand into her bag and managed to extract the revolver without making a sound. She knew it was loaded but not whether it worked. But then Ríkhardur wouldn't know that either.

Hastily cocking the trigger, Freyja kicked open the cupboard door, holding the gun in front of her. Huldar was lying curled up in a ball on the floor. To her relief, he was breathing. 'Put the scissors down.' She couldn't stop her voice from shaking.

The man turned, astonished. Then, recovering, he grinned. 'I'm a police officer. Please put the gun down and place your hands behind your head.'

'Drop the scissors.' Freyja could see the gun trembling in her hands. She braced herself, flinging back her hair with a quick movement of her head. 'Drop the scissors or I'll shoot.'

'Oh, I very much doubt that. Put the gun down, dear.'

He took a step towards her.

Freyja fired. He shouldn't have called her 'dear'.

Epilogue

It was such a beautiful shade of red. In the hospital ward that Karl now called home, everything was white or pale yellow. Occasionally this colour scheme was broken up by a drab, institutional green, and although he welcomed the change, the shade brought no pleasure in itself; hospitals had appropriated it for their own use and no one else cared for it. There must be some philosophy behind this choice of palette. It was probably meant to represent health and hygiene – perhaps hope too, though the colours seemed to have been carefully selected so as not to inspire people with unwarranted optimism.

But this blaze of red was different. So bright it was almost luminous. Mesmerising. It was a long time since he had seen anything so beautiful. How long, he had no idea. Time had no meaning here; he no longer had any awareness of hours, minutes or seconds. Even day and night had ceased to be part of his existence, which was now divided into waking, dozing and sleeping. Just now he was dozing.

But the red colour was worth waking up for.

Karl had been laid on his paralysed side to protect his back from bedsores. He tried to open his eyes wider. He couldn't actually tell if they were both open because he could no longer see out of one; had no feeling at all on that side. For all he knew, the eye itself might be all right and it was only the paralysed eyelid that blocked its view.

He didn't know and anyway it didn't really matter. There was so much he didn't know and he couldn't open his mouth and ask. The words emerged distorted or refused to come at all. He was merely grateful for the degree of sight and hearing he still retained.

The worst part was having so little control over what he heard or saw.

He still couldn't make himself properly understood, but the few people who paused by his bed would insist on trying to talk to him. The best times were when two or more members of hospital staff turned up at the same time since they almost invariably started chatting to each other, about him or work or occasionally about their personal lives. Those were the most interesting parts.

His good eye took its time and Karl had to content himself with studying the attractive red colour through a narrow slit. While he was waiting for his eyelid to respond, he tried to guess what the colour represented. It couldn't be blood or roses and certainly not a Ferrari. He was inclining to the opinion that it must be the vertical line of the cross on the Icelandic flag when his eyelid finally lifted all the way and he saw that the staff had not in fact hung a flag on the wall facing him. Instead, a man was sitting in the visitor's chair that up to now had been empty. A man wearing a bright red tie, a dazzling white shirt and a dark blue jacket. Like a personification of the Icelandic flag.

Karl heard the faint sound of a voice and saw the man's lips moving. Rather than trying to pick out the words he concentrated on the face, curious to know the identity of his visitor. He had nobody in the world to visit him now. Not a single soul.

Since he had woken from his coma, a variety of things, both good and bad, had gradually come back to him. Mostly bad, though. One piece of good news stood out, which was when the doctor told him that he had been exonerated of any involvement in the three murders. After that he had expected more visits but no one came. Börkur still hadn't shown his face and his mother's family were apparently hiding behind the excuse of being only tenuously related to him. He guessed Börkur was probably ashamed of having messed up his testimony. Perhaps he had one friend less – which would mean he now had no friends at all. If only Börkur would drop by, Karl could reassure him that he couldn't give a toss about the stupid testimony.

The visitor's words reached him before he could distinguish his face. 'Are you awake? The nurses told me you're conscious sometimes.' Karl knew the voice. He knew it very well, but it took his brain so long to process the information that he had to reconcile himself to waiting a little while longer. From what he could understand, he had suffered a cerebral hæmorrhage and the bleeding had spread over a large part of his brain, which explained why he was so slow. Karl pictured his thoughts being forced to travel further than usual, taking a series of diversions around the damaged area before they could reach their final destination.

The doctors were optimistic but warned that his rehabilitation would be long, drawn out and challenging, and that he was unlikely ever to make a full recovery. Still, anything was better than nothing.

'It looks as if your eye's open. Are you awake?'

Arnar. It was his brother Arnar. Karl struggled to speak but failed. His mouth opened slightly but that was it. No sound emerged – though all he had meant to say was 'hi'. Some days were worse than others.

'I've come to say goodbye, Karl.' Arnar stared at the open eye, apparently searching for a sign that Karl understood.

Karl made another effort to speak, if only to moan slightly to show Arnar that he was listening. But nothing happened. He tried to blink his good eye but the message took so long to travel from his brain that Arnar was looking away when his eyelid finally drooped, then lifted again. This often happened when he had just woken up and was trying to communicate with the nurses; by the time he managed to blink they would have turned away or shifted their attention. No one lingered for long; they always seemed to be in a tearing hurry and as soon as they had done their duty they would dash off to the next ward, the next patient.

'I have to go back to the States. I've been here far too long; I keep postponing my departure but I can't any longer.'

Had Arnar been in the country long? Karl wondered if he'd had the bad luck to be dozing or asleep every time his brother came by. But perhaps he had never been to visit him before. That was the more likely explanation. Why would he have wanted to visit a brother who was believed to be a crazy killer? But the information that Karl was innocent had been available for a while now. Why hadn't he come sooner?'

'I'm going back to the States to pack up my gear. I'm moving home. There's nothing to keep me in America any longer except work and I can easily find a good job in Iceland. Alison and I are getting a divorce.' He fell silent and dropped his gaze.

The fog in Karl's head seemed to lift slightly. Had the awful Alison left Arnar because of him? Was she too much of a snob to have a murderer for a brother-in-law? If so, how come Arnar hadn't corrected the misunderstanding?

'I've been doing a lot of thinking about us – about whether I could have treated you better over the years, but I don't think so. I am what I am, and you are what you are.' He paused again and looked at Karl, his expression empty of regret. Empty of warmth. 'The thing I can't understand . . . just can't understand . . . is why you didn't tell me who my mother was. When the police informed me that they'd found her name on your computer . . . that you'd been searching for information about her . . . my first thought was that you'd discovered the information but hadn't had time to let me know before you were arrested. Then I saw the date. You knew but you didn't tell me.'

Misery had no problem finding its way around Karl's brain. Regret, depression, grief – these painful emotions always managed to get through. It was so unfair. He remembered clearly his intention never to tell Arnar. But he knew that he wouldn't have been capable of keeping his promise to himself once the worst of his anger had worn off. Now, though, he had been robbed of the opportunity. And also of the oppor-tunity to defend himself, to convince his brother that he would have told him her name when the right moment came.

'I got my wish fulfilled in spite of you. I found out who my parents were. Or at least who my mother was.' Arnar fell silent. He turned away from Karl and appeared to be gazing unseeingly out of the window. 'Like so many other things, it didn't live up to my expectations.' Arnar laughed cynically. 'To put it mildly.'

Karl recalled that Arnar's mother and grandfather had died on the same day and he remembered her tersely uninformative obituary. What had happened? Had they been killed? Died in a house-fire? In a mutual suicide pact? Or had one killed the other, then committed suicide? Thinking about it was too much for his poor, maimed brain. The important part was that it might have been Arnar's family who were the crazy killers, not him. Karl's face would have shone if he had been capable of smiling.

'The way I try to look at it is that I had two choices: to know or not to know. Nothing ventured, nothing gained.' Arnar sucked in air between his teeth. 'I lost and I gained. Lost Alison, because she couldn't face living with me after I told her about my family. Americans are more sensitive about that sort of thing than us Icelanders. She wants children. Her own children. With her husband, not a sperm donor. When I suggested that, she said the idea disgusted her. And she used even stronger words about what she thought about bearing my children. She doesn't even want to hear the results of the DNA test. Doesn't trust the science all of a sudden. It makes no difference to her who my father turns out to be. In her eyes my family's too tainted for her to want anything to do with us.'

What was he talking about? Oh, why couldn't Arnar explain properly?

'But I gained too. Gained a sister. Well, maybe only a half-sister. I hope she's only my half-sister. That'll become clear when I get the test results. And I acquired a brother too. Or half-brother. I sincerely hope we're only half-brothers.' Arnar put his hands on his knees, apparently preparing to make a move. 'But I'm not having anything to do with him. Any more than with you.'

Arnar stood up. The beautiful red tie vanished from Karl's view. *Don't go! Don't go!*

'Goodbye, Karl. You'll probably never see me again.' The lean figure disappeared from view and Karl couldn't lower his gaze far enough to watch him walk out. His retreating footsteps sounded uncompromising, but stopped abruptly. 'One more thing: I'm glad you turned out to be innocent.' Arnar stopped speaking but still didn't leave the room. Then he added, in a rush: 'I hope your condition improves.'

Again Karl heard his footsteps, swiftly receding, then dying away.

It took Karl a while to calm down. Fragmentary thoughts wandered through the one-way system of his brain. He kept having to guide them out of dead ends and set them on the right track again. Only then could he digest the visit. His conclusions were:

He would never see Arnar again.

The grim story of his brother's background had come to light.

Karl would get over not seeing Arnar again. But not knowing the story of Arnar's mother would be harder. What could have been so bad about his background?

Then there was the murder case. The doctor hadn't told him any details, only that he himself had been cleared. Naturally he would learn all the information later, when he was well enough to get up and could communicate better. Either that or he would hear via the news, if they ever got round to fixing the radio by his bed or installing a TV in his room.

Until then he would be left to wonder who had killed Halli and the women, and what had happened. How had the case been solved, for example? Why had he been dragged into it in the first place? And who on earth had been behind the shortwave broadcasts?

Or would he spend the rest of his days here, puzzling in vain over the answers?

His eye closed. He was drifting back into a doze. It wasn't all bad – at least he had something to think about now. It wasn't as if he had anything better to look forward to.

When he came to his senses his eye saw red again. A different kind of red. Softer and full of golden lights. Prettier than that other shade of red. Karl waited for his eye to open fully, then saw to his astonishment that the chair vacated by Arnar was now occupied by a little girl. She had red hair and green eyes, he thought, and was wearing an anorak zipped up to her neck. She was gripping the sides of the chair and swinging her skinny legs, which were too short to reach the floor.

'My name's Margrét. My daddy works here. At the hospital. He said I could visit you.' The girl put her head on one side to look him in his good eye. 'He told me no one comes to see you and I thought that was sad.' She righted her head again. 'I can tell you're looking at me. But I know you can't talk much. That's all right. I like talking to people who aren't always asking me questions.'

Karl tried to smile and felt one side of his mouth obeying. He hoped the girl would carry on talking and his wish was granted.

'Freyja says I should try and talk about what happened. Happened to Mummy, I mean. If I bottle it up inside me it could do something bad. I don't know what, though.'

Freyja. Wasn't that the name of the woman who had some connection to the dogs he had been questioned about? Karl pricked up his ears. It was a pity he could only hear out of one, but at least he was lying on his incapacitated side.

'So I'm going to talk to you. About Mummy. About the bad man. Because you can only listen.'

The girl sat back a little in the chair. 'Freyja shot the bad man. You were lucky she didn't shoot you when everyone thought it was you. But I always knew it wasn't.'

Karl felt warm inside. He wished he could have talked to this girl when he had been at rock bottom during the police interrogation. But why had she said she recognised him from a photo? This must be the same Margrét the police had mentioned.

'The police thought that I thought you were the murderer too. But Freyja showed me a bad picture. A picture with your brother in it. He's the murderer's brother. They look quite alike. I wasn't talking about you.' The girl looked sad. 'I'm very sorry. I didn't mean them to think it was you.'

Karl managed to emit a sound that they both interpreted as meaning that he accepted her apology.

'But the murderer didn't die. Freyja shot him in the tummy, not in the heart. I don't know if that's good or not. I haven't decided. If he was dead I'd never have to think about him again.' The girl's account wasn't very coherent, but he understood her well enough. 'But perhaps I would anyway. I often think about Mummy and she's dead.'

Karl managed to nod slightly, if a bit crookedly, and the girl smiled at him.

'You're going to get better. Daddy says so. Not quite like you were before but better than now.' She made a face. 'There's blood on your brain.'

She fell silent and seemed to be casting around for something else to say. 'One of the policemen got into trouble because he thought you were the bad man. He didn't know it was his friend. He was a cop. The bad man was a cop!' The girl's face radiated astonishment and disbelief. 'I didn't know cops could be bad men. But Freyja shot him. And he can't be a cop any more because he's going to prison. The other policeman might have to stop being a cop too. Because he didn't work it out. Policemen need to be able to work things out.'

The girl turned to look out of the window. 'Freyja went on holiday. She's not allowed to work for a long time because she shot a man at her office. At the Children's House. That's not allowed. But I was glad she shot him. And she must be happy to be on holiday. Everyone's happy on holiday.'

Her white fingers pulled up the sleeve of her anorak to reveal a large, colourful watch on her wrist. 'I've got to go. I can only stay a little while. Daddy's waiting outside.' She stood up, her red hair vanishing from view, and Karl found himself staring at the light blue anorak instead. Again he felt an overwhelming sense of loss and wished the girl would sit down beside him again.

'I'll come back. Daddy said I can come as often as I like.' She fell silent and seemed about to walk to the door. 'Bye for now. I'll come back tomorrow. I wanted to bring Molly with me. You'd like to see her. But I wasn't allowed. Oh well, maybe later. When you get out of here.'

The girl disappeared and Karl listened to the sound of her footsteps receding. He couldn't remember the last time he'd felt so happy. Now he had visits to look forward to; the girl had managed to rekindle the sense of hope that he had been so desperately lacking.

Karl concentrated on clenching his fingers as the physio-therapist had shown him. Clench. Release. Clench. Release.

He could swear he was doing better than last time. Clench. Release. Clench. Release.

Finally he dropped off to sleep. From tiredness this time, not lethargy. Her parting words were the last thing to wander through the blind alleys in his brain.

Maybe later. When you get out of here.

Turn the page for a sneak peek at
Yrsa Sigurdardóttir's next novel

"THE QUEEN OF
ICELANDIC THRILLER
WRITERS"
—*THE GUARDIAN*

THE
RECKONING

#1 INTERNATIONAL BESTSELLING AUTHOR OF *THE LEGACY*

YRSA SIGURDARDÓTTIR

Available February 2019

September 2004

Prologue

The school building cast a chill shadow over the empty playground. Beyond it, the sun was shining. As they entered the shadow the few passers-by clutched their coats around them and quickened their pace until they emerged into the warm sunlight again. Over there the day was still, but here in the school grounds an icy wind was blowing, stirring the swings in the corner into life. They rocked slowly back and forth as if occupied by invisible children. Bored children, like Vaka. Worse than the boredom, though, was the cold. It stung her cheeks, and made her toes ache. Every last bit of her was frozen. Sitting on the stone steps only made matters worse because her new padded jacket wasn't long enough to cover her bottom. She wished she had listened to her mother and chosen the longer one, but that had only been available in dark blue; the waist-length one came in red.

Vaka shifted the school bag on her back and wondered if she should move into the sunlight. Then at least she would be warm while she waited – though still lonely, of course, and bored of having nothing to look at. But the shadow cast by the school extended so far that if she moved out of its gloom, she was afraid her dad would fail to see her and drive away again. No, better put up with the cold than risk that.

A car the same colour as her father's drove past, but Vaka saw that it was the wrong make, the wrong man, and her spirits fell again. Could he have forgotten her? It was her first day at the new school, so perhaps he would assume she'd be walking home as usual.

For the hundredth time she felt a stab of longing for her old home. The only thing that was better about the new place was her room, which was larger and way cooler than the one she'd had in their old flat. Everything else had changed for the worse, including school. The other kids, especially. She didn't know anyone. In her old class she had known everyone, had even known what the other girls' pets were called. Now a crowd of new names and faces were jostling in her head and she couldn't begin to put them together. It was like the memory game that she never won unless her mother deliberately played to lose.

Vaka sniffed. How long would it take her dad to realise that he should have come to collect her? She looked up at the main building in the hope of spotting someone, but the windows were dark and there was no sign of movement. Another gust of wind stung her cheeks and she shivered. Getting to her feet, she walked up the steps to the entrance. There must be a grown-up inside, someone who would let her use the phone. But the door was locked. Knocking did no good; the thick wood muffled the sound. Lowering her fist, she gazed up at the big door in the faint hope that it would open anyway. Nothing happened. She might as well sit down again. Hopefully the steps wouldn't feel as icy as before.

All thoughts of the cold were banished from her mind when she turned. At the bottom of the steps stood a girl Vaka recognised from her new class. She hadn't heard her approach. Perhaps she had been tiptoeing, though Vaka couldn't for the life of her imagine why. It wasn't as though she was likely to bite, or they were enemies. They didn't know each other at all, though Vaka remembered her clearly. It was impossible not to. She had two fingers missing: the little finger and ring finger of one hand. The girl had sat alone in the front row and seemed very quiet. At first Vaka had thought it must be her first day too, but the teacher hadn't introduced her like she had Vaka, so that couldn't be right. When the pupils were allowed to talk to each other in the lessons, the girl hadn't said a word. During break she had sat on the sidelines, staring into space, like Vaka on the steps just now. Her expression had remained blank even when two boys started chanting a nursery rhyme that Vaka remembered her granny reciting: 'Little finger, little finger, where are you? Ring finger, ring finger, where are you?' Vaka thought this was unbelievably mean but none of the other kids turned a hair. In the end she had looked away, not daring to interfere. She was new, after all.

'It's shut.' The girl gave a shy smile that vanished as quickly as it had appeared – perhaps it had only been a trick of the light – but Vaka was left with the impression of a pretty face. 'They always lock up when school's finished for the day.'

'Oh.' Vaka shuffled her feet, not knowing what to say. She had never been very good at making friends or talking to strangers, and it was the first time that day that anyone had tried to draw her out of her shell. 'I wanted to use the phone.'

'Maybe you could use the one at the shop. It's not far away.' The girl pointed down the street. She was wearing mittens to hide her maimed hand.

Vaka swallowed and answered awkwardly: 'I haven't got any money.' Her mother was supposed to give her pocket money on Fridays but she always forgot. Usually it didn't matter but there were times, like now, when it was a pain. As bad as Dad forgetting to pick her up. Grown-ups were useless at remembering things.

'Oh.' The girl looked sad. 'Me neither.' She opened her mouth, then changed her mind and closed it again. Unlike Vaka's jacket, which had been bought with room for her to grow into, the girl's anorak was far too small; the sleeves were too short and she couldn't even zip it up properly. She wasn't wearing a hat either and her tangled hair whipped around in the wind. In spite of the dry weather, she was wearing a pair of old, faded wellingtons. In contrast, her brightly coloured mittens looked clean and new.

'It's all right. I'll wait.' Vaka tried but failed to smile. It was hard having to wait in uncertainty like this. She was cold and hungry. If Dad had come at the right time she would have been sitting in their new kitchen by now, enjoying a slice of toast. She could taste the melted butter and jam, and this only made her hungrier.

The girl shifted from foot to foot. 'Would you like me to wait with you?' She didn't look at Vaka as she asked this but off to one side, at the empty playground. 'I can if you like.'

Vaka had no answer ready. Would it make things better or worse? The choice was between sitting alone and getting cold or trying to find something to talk about with this girl whose name she didn't even know. Yet despite being only eight, Vaka knew that there was only one right answer to some questions. 'Yes, please. If you feel like it.' When the girl turned towards her with a beaming smile, she added: 'But I'll have to go as soon as Dad comes to pick me up.'

The smile faded and the empty expression returned. 'Yes, of course.'

Mindful of how the boys had teased the girl and how lonely she seemed, Vaka tried to make amends. 'Perhaps he could drive you home too?' The moment she had blurted this out, she regretted it; she'd often heard her parents moaning about the price of petrol. She didn't want to ask her father to drive miles out of their way, especially when they had so little money left after buying their new flat. 'Is your house far away?'

'No. I live just back there.' The girl pointed at the school, presumably referring to the row of houses that Vaka had noticed when she had wandered around the back of the building during break. They were separated from the school by a high fence, on the other side of which all kinds of rubbish had collected: disintegrating, faded packaging; bits of paper; plastic bags and withered leaves. Vaka didn't like litter; it was disgusting, but as this was one of the few places in the playground where the boys' cruel chanting couldn't be heard, she had gone over to the fence and stared through it, ignoring the mess.

She had studied the houses, feeling thankful that her parents hadn't bought one of them. They looked as rundown and shabby as the fence; their paint peeling, their gardens like jungles. She glimpsed a rusty old barbecue standing in a patch of tall weeds; it looked as if plants were growing out of the little grating in the lid. Grubby curtains hung crookedly at the dirty windows. In some places a blanket had been used instead; in others, old newspapers or sheets of cardboard. Unsettled by the sight, Vaka had turned away and gone back to the other children, who behaved as if she didn't exist.

The street did have one advantage, though: it was close to the school. Perhaps she could use the girl's telephone? It would only take a few minutes to walk there and her dad wouldn't have time to go far if he arrived while she was gone. Plucking up her courage, Vaka asked: 'Hey, could I maybe use the phone at your house?'

She was disconcerted by the frightened look that greeted this request. 'At my house?' The girl gulped and dropped her eyes. Staring down at her mittens, she fiddled with her maimed hand. 'Shouldn't we just wait here? Your dad must be coming soon.'

'Yes, maybe.' Vaka shifted her school bag again. It seemed to grow heavier and heavier on her shoulders, as if weighed down by all the minutes she had been waiting. 'If I can use your phone, you can come round and play at my place afterwards.' Vaka guessed the girl would be grateful for an excuse to go out if she lived in one of those horrible houses. Perhaps that's why she had reacted so badly to Vaka's request. Perhaps she didn't want anyone to see her room.

The girl seemed to be having trouble deciding how to answer. 'OK.

But you'll have to be really quick. And only if we can go round and play at yours afterwards. You mustn't make any noise, though. Dad's probably asleep.'

Vaka nodded, highly satisfied with this outcome and also with having made friends with someone from her class. Of course she would rather have got to know one of the other girls, especially the fun, popular ones, but they had cold-shouldered her, obviously having no need of more friends. Perhaps this girl would turn out to be all right, in spite of her missing fingers. At least she wasn't mean.

But as they set off, Vaka began to have her doubts. Remembering the shabby houses, she suddenly felt a powerful reluctance to enter any of them. It would have been better to wait on the freezing steps. It was too late, though. They had left the school grounds and were approaching the houses, walking in the sunshine now.

Yet instead of growing warmer, Vaka felt colder with every step.

Vainly she sought for an excuse to turn back without hurting the girl's feelings. Her new friend was also silent, apparently just as conscious that every step brought them closer to their destination. They didn't exchange a word until they found themselves standing on the cracked pavement outside one of the houses. Vaka ran her eyes over the front, careful not to move her head so the girl wouldn't notice what she was doing. It looked like the most rundown place in the whole street.

It had two floors and was clad in rusty corrugated iron that hadn't seen a lick of paint in years. The front garden was as scruffy as the ones Vaka had seen that morning. A tricycle lay on its side among the dandelions, chickweed and scrubby bushes, as rusty as the house itself. Almost all the windows were cracked and no attempt had been made to hang better curtains on the side facing the road. As if that wasn't bad enough, the front door was hanging crooked on its hinges. This was a bad place.

Vaka racked her brain to think of a reason why they should turn back but it was too late. The girl looked at her sadly and said: 'Come on. This is my house. Don't make any noise and be quick. Then we can go round to yours and play. Can't we?' Anticipation shone from her colourless eyes and Vaka had no choice but to nod.

She followed the girl, feeling as if her school bag were full of rocks, her heart heavy in her chest. Every step was an ordeal. She felt as she always did when she was doing something she knew would end badly. Like the time her parents had held a party and she had tried to carry too many plates in one go when laying the table. The instant she lifted the pile she had known it was too heavy but she had done it anyway. And every single plate had smashed. That was exactly how she felt now.

The girl paused with her hand on the doorknob. 'Come on. Remember, you've got to be quick.' It came out almost in a whisper, as if there were a monster lurking inside who mustn't know they were there.

Vaka nodded apprehensively and took the final step to the door. Next moment she was inside. Out of the sunlight into the dark. She was met by a reek of cigarettes and a sour smell that made her wrinkle her nose. The girl closed the door behind them and the darkness became even blacker. Perhaps that was just as well. It would hide the mess inside, and the girl wouldn't be able to see Vaka's look of disgust.

'The phone's upstairs. Come on,' the girl whispered, almost too quietly to be heard. As Vaka's eyes adjusted to the gloom, she noticed that the girl kept glancing from side to side. She beckoned impatiently when Vaka didn't immediately react. She had taken off her coat but only one of her mittens.

Vaka tore her gaze from the mitten that hid the missing fingers and stepped warily into the hall. As she did so the floorboards creaked overhead. The girl's head jerked upwards. Her face was twisted with terror.

Vaka went rigid and felt her eyes growing hot, as if she were about to burst into tears. What was she doing here? She gave a little moan but it hardly made any sound, in spite of the silence in the house. This was a terrible mistake. Worse than the plates. Gripped by panic, she couldn't think properly. The only thought in her head was that she didn't even know the girl's name.

Hafnarfjördur Police are appealing for help in finding a missing girl. Vaka Orradóttir, 8, was last seen at 3 p.m. this afternoon, leaving her school in Hafnarfjördur to go home. She is described as small and slim, with shoulder-length light brown hair, and wearing a red, waist-length padded jacket, a red woollen hat, jeans and pink trainers. Vaka is believed to be still in the area. Anyone who has information on her where-abouts is asked to contact Hafnarfjördur Police on 525 3300.